Spindrift

Spindrift

A NOVEL

STUART SHEPPARD

CREATIVE ARTS BOOK COMPANY
Berkeley ✪ California

For information contact:
Creative Arts Book Company
833 Bancroft Way
Berkeley, California 94710
(800) 848-7789

Author website:
www.stuartsheppard.com

No character in this book is based on or intended to depict any real
person, living or dead. While the general locale of Nantucket is real,
the specific restaurant where much of the action takes place—the
Lobster Trap—exists only on these pages and in the author's
imagination, and is not modeled on any restaurant of that name on
Nantucket or elsewhere.

Cover illustration, *Voyager*, from *N by E* by Rockwell Kent. Courtesy of
Plattsburgh State Art Museum, Rockwell Kent Gallery and Collection,
Plattsburgh, NY.

"Scotch and Soda" Words and Music by Dave Guard. © 1959, 1961
(Renewed 1987, 1989) BEECHWOOD MUSIC CORP. All Rights Reserved.
International Copyright Secured. Used by Permission.

Map illustration reprinted by kind permission of Yesterday's Island, Inc.

ISBN 0-88739-463-9
Library of Congress Catalog Number 2003106006
Printed in the United States of America

To My Mother

With deep appreciation to Mark Bell, David Conrad, and Nathaniel Griggs for their help in unique ways, and to Mrs. Wilhelmina Shaw, who taught me more about the spirit of Nantucket than anyone. I am grateful to the staff of the Nantucket Atheneum for their kind assistance with research. And I am especially indebted to my agent, Alice Tasman, for her faith in this novel, and to Jebb Curelop, who first brought me to the island—without either of whom this book would not have been possible.

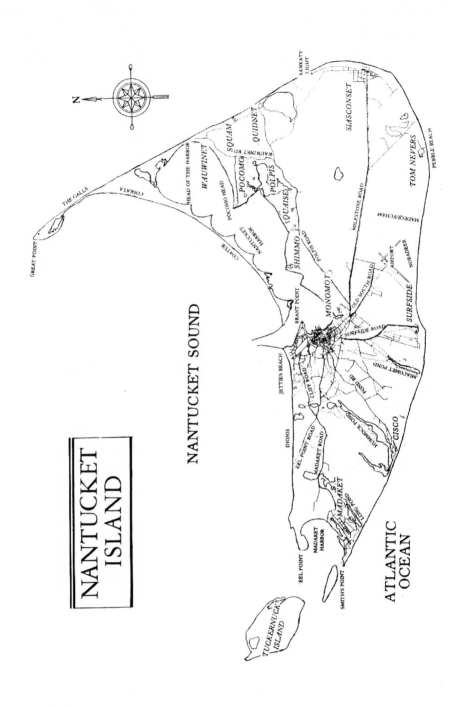

NANTUCKET ISLAND

NANTUCKET SOUND

ATLANTIC OCEAN

GREAT POINT

THE GALLS

COSKATA

COATUE

HEAD OF THE HARBOR

WAUWINET

SQUAM

QUIDNET

POCOMO HEAD

POCOMO

WAUWINET RD

POLPIS

SQUAISE

SANKATY LIGHT

SIASCONSET

TOM NEVERS

PEBBLE BEACH

MADEQUECHAM

MILESTONE ROAD

POLPIS ROAD

NANTUCKET HARBOR

SHIMMO

MONOMOY

BRANT POINT

OLD SOUTH ROAD

AIRPORT

NOBADEER

SURFSIDE

JETTIES BEACH

SURFSIDE ROAD

MIACOMET POND

CLIFF ROAD

POND RD

DIONIS

EEL POINT ROAD

MADAKET ROAD

HUMMOCK POND

CISCO

MADAKET

LONG POND

EEL POINT

MADAKET HARBOR

SMITHS POINT

TUCKERNUCK ISLAND

Spindrift

Nantucket! Take out your map and look at it. See what a real corner of the world it occupies; how it stands there, away off shore, more lonely than the Eddystone lighthouse.

—Melville, *Moby Dick*

I too have bubbled up, floated the measureless float, and
  been wash'd on your shores,
I too am but a trail of drift and debris.

—Whitman, *Sea-Drift*

A man may stand there and put all of America behind him.

—Thoreau, *Cape Cod*

Part 1

Go west, young man.

—John Soule (1851)

1

The crush of a breaking sunrise. Below, the ticking ocean. Waves roll in and wash out, back and forth, a frothy pendulum swinging on an invisible chain. I am comforted by this rhythm, as an infant is by his mother's heartbeat. The sun up and down, the days in and out. Every morning I wake and conduct this undulating symphony, arms outstretched, face flattened by sunlight. I watch the sun arrive on a Spanish galleon, my back to America. My bedroom lies on the tip of an island detached from the rest of the country, a sea anchor dragging behind America on its inexorable journey west. "Always moving west" is the definition of America. I have swum east against the tide. Living here on the edge of Nantucket, thirty miles east of the contiguous United States, I am standing on the lip of my existence, casting a long dark shadow that sweeps over the land and sea every day: I am a human metronome.

I came to this island three weeks ago, out of work and alone, parched of human connections and commitments.

I'm standing on the deck drinking coffee, staring into an incomprehensible wall of sunlight. No one else up yet. Thoughts of the long day ahead, the long weeks behind, the winter that will never come.

The ocean churns crisply this time of day. No tourists or cars to deaden its sound. At night it lulls me to sleep. I can almost throw a stone into the water from the deck.

But in the morning it calls me. This is the secret of my early rising. No matter whom I might have spent the night with, I always rise to greet the ocean first—the great, serene, monstrous, petulant, unpredictable, irresistible Atlantic Ocean—wading toward the shore in her skirts.

Surveying the horizon, my eyes move left to the house on the bluff. Cinzano umbrellas flapping on the gray wooden deck. Children's toys littering the yard. To the right, the bare bluff, and a high hedgerow, shielding magnificent homes.

We live in a house that sits on a divide in the bluff, cut by a road leading to the beach. Our deck is really a bridge which stretches over the road. Anyone can cross it. Those who do usually ask us about the giant sundial affixed to the south wall of our house. Even the tour buses point it out. We feel like we live in a landmark. Below us on the road is an official-looking sign with an arrow pointing seaward which reads, "3000 MILES TO SPAIN." We tell the more egregious tourists that the house is an old station for the ferry to Spain, and that the sundial was the station's clock before the island had been wired for electricity.

A yellow jeep rounds the bend. The blond girl waves. I don't know her name but I've noticed her turning past the little rotary in the village here onto Sconset Road, toward the big Rotary about seven miles away.

The Rotary, the gateway to Sconset Road. How many times have I waited there with my thumb out? I usually get a ride fairly quickly, unless it's late. Then it can take hours. Once I nearly walked halfway home before a faggot in a Porsche—tipsy and horny—picked me up. I had to sweet-talk the guy for four miles so he wouldn't dump me out. When we made town I jumped out and said thanks—quickly. The guy blew me a kiss.

The Rotary is the wheel that holds the island together. Keeps it spinning. All roads lead to the Rotary, like spokes. From it you can go anywhere by taking a few steps in any direction and sticking out your thumb. Hitchhiking is a profession on Nantucket, a craft, a practiced form of Americana.

Spindrift

I walk back into the house for more coffee. My roommate is still sleeping, so I catch the kettle before it whistles. Sun streams through the kitchen window, illuminating the steam rising from the mug and kettle. I slowly stir the grounds, savoring the cerulean clang of the spoon. The wind carries a dull sifting of waves. . . .

I shower and dress for work. My uniform consists of jeans, Top-Siders, and any old T-shirt. I'm a dishwasher in one of the island's more popular seafood restaurants. Not a hard job, but a physically demanding one. They started me out as a pot scrubber but soon promoted me to head dishwasher because of my promptness and reliability—traits rarely seen in summer help. I guess that coming from Ohio I didn't know any other way of operating.

I'm not sure why I chose to live on Nantucket. Now, after barely a month, I can think of no other way of life. All the things I love are here: undeveloped beaches, fog-covered moors, shingled sea cottages—not to mention beautiful women, friendly bars, and a joie de vivre I haven't experienced since college. All soaking in a rustic marinade of history centuries old.

The house I live in offers a sweeping view of Sconset Beach. Sconset, short for Siasconset, occupies the eastern edge of the island, and is the only village here with a zip code independent of Nantucket's. It had been a summer retreat for the wives of the whaling captains in previous centuries, and still retains the flavor of escapism from the hordes invading the center of Nantucket proper. No one calls it Siasconset anymore, although the full name might appear on rental agreements.

I walk up to the little village market and enter through the back door, since it hasn't officially opened yet. As I stand in front of the dairy section contemplating the selection a hand shoots through the cartons holding a pint of milk.

"Have you had your milk today?" a voice asks. I peer through the back of the compartment and see my friend Grant standing in the freezer behind it, stocking the display.

"Hey thanks, buddy," I reply, taking the carton. I place it on the shelf and grab a bottle of orange juice. "How's the dairy business?"

"Oh, chilly, you know. Gotta milk those cows early." Grant,

like me, had come to the island early in the season to find a job. But unlike me, he had no desire to work in town, among the tourists. His father had just died of cancer and he didn't really like to be around a lot of people.

Grant and several close friends that graduated with him from college live in the apartment above the store in a communal fashion. They always travel, eat, and play together. It is fascinating to me, someone who has basically always been a loner, to observe this pan-symbiotic relationship. The way they share clothes, space, money, even lovers; the way they depend on each other emotionally: their separate egos merged into one identity in a near-utopian style of existence. There are six of them—three of each sex. I'm not sure who is attached to whom, but it doesn't seem to matter to them. Nor does the issue of money. They all appear to be from wealthy New England families. Once, when I joined them for a drink, one of the girls went to buy a beer. She came back carrying what looked like a cord of glass bottles. No one blinked. She put the bottles in the middle of the table and the empties were pushed to the edge like poker chips. When there were no more beers left, someone got up and brought back another armload.

I head to the little rotary in the center of Sconset. The silence is unearthly this time of morning. The flagpole stands like a stiff drunk that never made it home last night, weaving against the bright serge of sky. I put on my sunglasses and wait, sanguine that the first car will pick me up and take me to town.

Hearing the sound of a jeep from behind the tennis courts, I think of the blond girl, whom I know lives in that direction. But it isn't her. A middle-aged guy in a VW stops to pick me up. This seems like a good omen: the first car of the day giving me a ride, and the sky so bright. I'm still smiling with amusement at Grant's humor.

We drive down Sconset Road not talking much. The ancient stone mile-markers tick by, reminding me that this stretch is officially known as Milestone Road—but none of us who live here call it that. I feel content with my existence, the simple routine, the lack of pressure from my former life in New York, working as a stockbroker. Tufts of fog still cling to the moors. No other cars appear on the road. I lean into the chanting hum of the motor and close my eyes.

Suddenly we're in town. I thank the driver through the dissolving mist of my nap and walk toward Main Street. I still have a few minutes to kill before the restaurant opens.

The plants are dripping in front of the Club Car—one of the fancy restaurants. Inside, the tables have been set for lunch, a ludicrous picture this early. I amble toward Straight Wharf, crossing the bulbous cobblestones like an old man. On a bench by the water sits the town drunk whom everyone calls Cappy, a scant glance of sobriety still clinging to his eyes. I sit next to him, neither one of us speaking.

The sun is bearing down violently on the water. Most of the town is asleep; hungover. Morning is the only time one can enjoy the beauty of town these days; soon the crowded masses will seep between the buildings, the au pair girls with lovely tanned legs will push strollers, the jeeps will roar in, the merchants will begin dumping their garbage, the children will scream in many directions; a cacophony of buying—selling—eating—crapping—renting—shuttersnapping—and screeching will rise in a tornado of desire, and all we on the sidelines can do is watch and avoid being dented by the detritus.

Ah, Monday in Nantucket. Perhaps the wind will blow away the tourists. Perhaps the shops will close and people will run rejoicing into the street: naked, laughing, clasping. Perhaps the boats will form a flotilla and sail for the golden horizon. Perhaps the shutters will fly off the houses and all the great literature in the library will fly through the windows. Perhaps the rats and the cockroaches will jump off the pier in holy suicide, chanting, "Our work is done here." Perhaps the breeze will carry all the garbage into the barrels, then lift them into the sky to float like star buoys. Perhaps the traffic will stop and people will carry each other on their backs. Perhaps the sun will not rise any higher than right now, and it will remain morning. . . .

"Every once in a while you get one like this. I've been sittin' here for an hour tryin' to get this damned thing open. D'ya think you could help me a bit?"

Cappy looked at me appealingly, and handed me the miniature vodka bottle he had been struggling with. I opened it with an easy twist. "No problem. Here you go."

"Chris' sakes." He downed the bottle and tossed it in the bush next to him. The sound of breaking glass rang out—a well-practiced throw.

After working many such early shifts I grew fond of these moments with Cappy. I knew that he arose every morning at sunrise to look for coins dropped by tourists in restaurant doorways. Then he'd sit on one of the benches along the wharf or Main Street for the rest of the day, drinking his "nips" and flirting with the summer girls on their way to work.

Cappy was nothing but a drunken old bum, but since he was a native of the island and descended from one of its historic families, there was nothing the town could do with him but tolerate his existence, until one day several years ago, someone ingeniously thought to dress him up like an old sea captain. They gave him a captain's hat and seaman's clothes, and the bum turned into an old salt for the tourists to photograph. He even grew a snow-white beard. Overnight, he went from eyesore to tourist attraction. Watching him I had to laugh because I, too, had traded in my normal clothes, stopped shaving, found a comfortable line of work, and spent a good amount of time flirting. I could only hope that I might change my destiny so utterly, if not so easily.

2

After work I went to the Atlantic Cafe, the central nervous system of the island: a meeting place for tourists, amateur sailors, college kids staying with their parents and, at mealtimes, families. In essence, the AC is not the favorite meeting place for the working people of the island, but I go there because I know John the bartender, and John has a loose wrist. I should be honest and admit that I know all the bartenders in town, but the AC is close, and sometimes you just follow the breezes where they blow you.

As usual, the music—radiating with warm effervescence from the high tech stereo system—is by the Police, the group that the bar played to the exclusion of all other bands that summer. It is a music that drives you without conveying the sense of being driven, answering the tonal mutterings of the young adult mind after a few drinks in an affectatious way. I settle into the chair on the empty side of the bar and smile at the cute bartender.

"What'll it be?"

"Well, I was hoping John could make me one of his famous PCs, but it looks like I may have to place my trust in you."

"Well, I think I can help you out if you can trust me. Myers's okay?"

"Ah—actually, John always makes it with that dark stuff. You know, I wouldn't want to deplete your tourist stock." She smiles and, in a flurry of wrists, ice, and bottles, produces a succulent piña colada. "That looks great. What's your name?"

"Jeanie. What's yours?"

"Guy. I'll make sure to ask for you next time. I've already forgotten the name of that other bartender."

"What other bartender?"

I take a sip and survey the room. Stand-up tables across from me; booths behind me. It's a slow time, this lull between lunch and dinner. Families just returning from the beach; workers like me just going to the beach. Shoppers buying. Drinkers imbibing. Waiters waiting. Two attractive blonds sit to my right. I decide not to engage them, but rather, to sway with the conviviality of the room, the beating music, variegated smiles, and bibulous air passing from one mouth to the next, exchanged in breaths like a cloud of gas.

I could have sat there for weeks: sated, humble in my existence, an absorbent beacon sucking in all that I saw, but sending out no signal. The warm hands of contentment massaged my shoulders as the drink sank to my shoes. The stool wooden and supportive, gently rocking back and forth. The calm trees of Ohio came to mind, so beautiful yet seldom seen by America. Ohio, the unsung state of the Union, where nothing important ever happened: no famous battles, heroes, schools, or landmarks—but what glorious trees! And sumptuous fields, passels of cornstalks, swaying to the earth's rotation without even needing wind, so finely balanced are they. Shipwrecked in thought, trammeled by the flotsam of day-trippers, I stared blankly ahead. . . .

"Another one?"

"No thanks. I gotta book." I paid the check and left a healthy tip for Jeanie, in case I might need her services again.

I went to the right down Water Street. A crowd of rushing people emerged from Steamship Wharf. The ferry must have come in, for these people were moving too fast for the pace of the island. Off the steamship they came: barbarians from New York, bohemians from Vermont, motorheads from Boston—

sharp-edged people trying to fit into the round parts of Nantucket. The old leading the young, traveling in over-packed station wagons. Peroxide women unmasked by the island winds, unable to hide the dark roots of their urban existences. Doe-legged ladies who find the irregular cobblestones disturbing. Tomorrow they would be biking unhappily behind their families on the way to Madaket Beach, worried that they might be stranded without a bathroom. So passed this cavalcade of city-dwellers.

I could hear reggae music coming from the white shack by the alley—Ted's ice cream store. Ted and I had gone to the same college several years ago, but he dropped out and I hadn't heard from him until he popped up on the island. It's strange whom you run into in out-of-the-way places. Ted is someone I probably would have never thought of again, and now we are good buddies. I decided to drop in.

"Jah mon," Ted said as I entered. A Bob Marley song blared through his portable cassette player. Marley, the father of reggae music, and Ted's hero. "Would you be likin' some cold-assed chips o'flavor?" he asked.

"How 'bout the Marley Mocha, mon."

Ted scooped the ice cream with his skinny torso. He is a scarecrow man. The string bean ectomorph of Nantucket. A shaven Afghan dog, overcompensating in his jerky movements: even his hair is curly from nervousness. But one of the most interesting guys on the island. A fringe person, a hugger of edges. A new Patagonian, drawn to the brink of America, and still gazing eastward.

He had one of the best jobs on the island. Somehow he had met the old woman who owned the store, and convinced her to let him manage it. Ted kept his own hours, hired and fired on whim, and made as much money as he wanted, or rather, needed, for Ted was one of those rare people not driven by avarice.

We chatted for a while about Rasta bands and happenings on the island, then I decided I had had enough ice cream and reggae music. I left Ted bopping behind the counter, his hands in the air. I don't know why, but he never set them down, as if they were sharks that had to constantly move or sink. Ted is a catatonic snapshot in my memory, a man surprised by the flash-bulb: caught in a movement between two points, but never reaching either one.

3

The nights are inexplicably wonderful on the island, the moon turning on a barstool, breezes sifting with the texture of chamois. Images glow with a neon vibrancy; it must be the water's reflection. Sounds are crisper here. When the wind is still you can hear the old, shingled houses shifting, bracing for storms gleaming in the ocean's eye.

What a feeling, to walk along the breathing streets, haunted by the memories locked in the gray cottages: the Indian settlements, the British blockade, deaths at sea, famine, cast iron kettles, harpoons, rope burn, hearth fires, and the stink of long winters. In town the streets are packed with tourists; just a few steps away they are deserted. What a gift—this peace. How beautiful—this desolate tranquility. Occasionally a passing moped or jeep may stir the agate night air, but a crushing serenity eventually snuffs the sound. All is smothered between the walls of water surrounding the island.

Eventually I surface on Orange Street, the main road leading to the Rotary. I decide to hitchhike, but so few cars pass I feel silly walking down the center of the narrow street. It is strange that no sounds come out of the houses. They are old and, this being a summertime community, many are not insulated. Could everyone be asleep this early? Finally a car comes down the street. I stick out my thumb but the car rides by without hesitating. This constant dependence on hitchhiking is becoming irritating, not because people aren't generally friendly on the island—many do pick me up—but because there is so little traffic during my bar-belled schedule, my success ratio is abnormally low. It really would make sense to get a motorcycle or moped.

By the time I reach the Nantucket Bakery I still haven't been picked up, so I look through the back door for Benny. He, as a baker, has the unenviable task of starting work when everyone else is going to bed. For if the muffins and rolls are to be fresh in the morning, they must be made at dawn. I imagine the thousands of bakers throughout the country rising at this hour with Benny. But in our small circle on the island, Benny is the man who lives in the Twilight Zone. Amazingly, he has acquired a good tan for someone keeping vampiric hours; he brags that he doesn't miss his sun-time because he can sleep on the beach.

No one appears to be in back so I rap on the window, forcefully. After a few minutes Benny comes to the door rubbing his eyes. His apron hangs untied over his neck. "How's it going?"

"Okay. I'm still a little sleepy. Just got up. Want some coffee? I got a fresh pot going."

I walk inside with him. It's early in Benny's routine; he hasn't started anything yet. A good time to visit. He hands me a paper cup of coffee and asks if I want milk, pointing to the cooler. I walk into the front part of the store where the baked goods are displayed. The glass cases are mournfully empty. Stores are lonely places without customers.

"Hey Benny. Got anything fresh?" I ask, not too sanguine.

"Not really. But try one of these apricot tarts. They last pretty well."

Good old Benny. Never charges me anything, but I always buy him a drink when I see him at the Chicken Box, the most exciting bar on the island.

His partner in the back starts the motor of one of the mixing machines. A hum runs through the store. I notice that everything is coated with flour. These men work inside a confectionery snowdome.

"All right, bud. Gotta let you do your job. Stop by the Lobster Trap some night; I'll slip you a nice bug out the back door—anytime."

"Sounds good. . . ." Another motor starts. I head out the door with a wave.

I could see a jeep coming up the road. Hoping it was the blond girl I ran toward the street, spilling some of my coffee. The jeep wasn't yellow, but it stopped. It was our housemate, Ken, who worked as a bartender at the Rose and Crown. It must be later than I thought: Ken doesn't drive home until long after the place closes. I often looked upon him as my savior on those occasions when the streets had swallowed all the cars; when the cold, damp wind would rise, and my thoughts turned to the packs of wild dogs allegedly roaming the desolate roads at night. Pete the fry cook had told me these stories, which I always laughed off in his presence.

"Hop in."

"Thanks."

"How'd it go tonight?"

"The usual."

That about covered the main topics of conversation between Ken and me. He never spoke much, especially late at night. We had an eerie relationship. Here was a man who lived in the same house, one floor above me, yet we rarely saw each other there— only meeting by chance late at night like this, or during his shift at the R&C.

Ken drove fast, rounding the Rotary without braking—the wind washing through the doorless torso of the jeep—and accelerated into the darkness.

This is a good ride, the seven miles between the Rotary and Sconset. Scudding along through the euphonic gusts; the motor climbs, reaches a plateau, then reacclimates to the road's gradation. Ken stares somberly ahead, unblinking, a chiaroscuro of silence, or concentration, or melancholy—I don't know which— hurtling forward beside me.

By the time we reached Sconset Ken's red hair and beard had declared anarchy. I felt totally invigorated by the ride; he looked ashen. "Thanks a lot. Really appreciate it."

"No problem."

He parked the jeep around the side of the house and I went up the stairs. My roommate Larry was already asleep; he must have started drinking early. A bunch of records lay disheveled on the living room floor among several empty beer bottles. I killed the power on the stereo. The kitchen looked much worse. Dirty dishes and food everywhere, and a happy swarm of flies having a feast. I made some coffee and went on the deck.

The wind came in hard off the ocean. I thought back to where the tracks of my former existence stopped, on the shore of the mainland, only thirty miles away—but as the spirit travels more like a camel-ride through the desert. I had left no trail across the water.

So many friends back there driving forward in careers. Climbing ladders, painting white picket fences, mowing lawns, pushing strollers, feeding dogs, inviting mothers-in-law to dinner. Harvesting fallow ground.

I had been on that track. But I left because I couldn't stand paying the price for that definition of success. It all boiled down to kissing someone's ass. Big, wet, puckering smacks, continually raining down: as soon as one set of cheeks moved aside another pair lined up in its place. First it's the guy who hires you, then your boss, then your boss's boss, then the president of the company every time he reads a management book that tells him to "wander around" and chat with the employees; then, if you work with a woman you have to kiss her ass too, because of equality in the workplace. And it doesn't stop there. You've got to kiss your landlord's ass, and his bookkeeper, and the building superintendent's (in case you ever need your toilet fixed)—and he's foreign but it doesn't matter because ass can be kissed in any language: it's the universal means of communication. Then there's the bank officer; he's holding your money and you have to convince him how creditworthy you are! Great lines of ass forming in the cities of America. The gas company. The maître d' at the restaurant. The traffic cop. Even the priests, the bartenders, and the plumbers. And the line keeps growing longer. . . .

So I walked away, not feeling cowardly but rebellious. I did it to save my flat, anemic lips, I tell myself, but the coffee has soured in its mug, and the wind makes me blink.

Something kicked the door open. I turned to see Larry staggering toward me. He clutched the railing as if he was standing on the deck of a tossing boat. "Fuck. What a dream." I handed him my coffee. He stared at it as if he didn't recognize the object. I took the mug out of his hands, afraid he might drop it over the side.

"How're you feeling?"

"Egh. I had the worst dream."

"I thought you were drunk."

"No. I went running after I got home. Something I ate. Felt awful. I shouldn't've run."

"Who drank the beers?"

"Ah, they're from this morning."

Larry's hair looked like it came from a carousel horse. He stood bare-chested in his running shorts, shivering. "Tell me your dream. You'll forget it if you wait too long." He thought for a few seconds; I couldn't discern if he was trying to remember it, or deciding whether or not he wanted to tell it to me.

"I was at my father's house, back when I was in college. He told me I had to pick all the tomatoes in the garden or my mother would die. For some reason I had to pull them out by the stalks. But they wouldn't budge. All my friends stood on the porch, laughing at me. I got really mad, then scared. My father was in the house, smoking a cigar, yelling, 'What's taking you so long!' I called for him to help me but he couldn't hear me, because everyone was laughing so hard. And that's it. I woke up."

I handed him the coffee and he drank it this time. Larry had been a high school teacher for a few years and had just quit to finish his masters in the fall. We had met in the dishroom of the Lobster Trap and he invited me to share his apartment. He was about two years younger than me.

"Pretty gruesome."

"No shit." He looked down. I gotta get some new running shoes." He set the coffee on the railing and looked toward the door. "I never took psychology in school."

"Probably a good thing."

"I dunno. It might've been helpful."

"Look, only fucked-up people become psychologists, and only the fucked-up people who aren't smart enough to become them go to them. Just be thankful your parents never did anything kinky to you as a child, like dress you up in a tutu, or paint your pee-pee green and make you dance on the kitchen table. You don't have to know all the answers in life, you just have to like asking questions."

Larry mumbled something and trudged inside, like a man with too many bones in his body. I felt incredibly tired, and wasn't looking forward to the early shift in the morning.

4

The good thing about going over to Steve and Alex's place is the
chance to see Steve's books. He reads voraciously like a man
infested with literary tapeworms, gnawing on books until he's
sucked out their sustenance, then tosses away the bones. Piles
of literature lie everywhere: Melville, Tolstoy, Bukowski,
Bowles, Algren, Homer, Lowry, Broch, García Márquez,
Rabelais, Cervantes, Nabokov, Joyce, Hemingway, Unamuno,
Yeats, Agee, Conrad, Durrell, Beckett, Dostoyevsky, Brautigan,
Proust. He is an arsonist of reading. On his bedstand would be
what Alex called the "book of the week," because it never took
him longer than that to read anything. I often stopped by their
garage apartment in the late afternoons when I got home from
an early shift; Alex would be painting in the open maw of the
garage, and Steve would be reading or out riding his bike somewhere. They lived right off the Sconset rotary behind a high row
of hedges. Although their apartment had only one tiny window,
they only needed to swing open the huge door to be flooded
with light and air.

I had just come from the market with some muffins, and
decided to stop by and offer them some. "How's the island's
best painter today?" I said to Alex as I approached. She stood
painting behind her French easel.

"Well, I don't think Cezanne's trembling in his grave."

"How about the gallery rats on the docks?"

"They get scared when they see a four-year-old finger painting." The popular galleries in town were located in quaint, gray-shingled boathouses on the wharves. Many were owned by the artists, who tended to favor allegorically commercial styles. One specialized in misty Nantucket seascapes; another in bright flowers; others in ersatz depictions of what tourists expected Nantucket to look like. I offered Alex a muffin and watched her work for a few minutes. The muscles in her back lapped up and down as her arm moved; her loose tank top revealed peeks of her breast. I soon realized I was watching her more than the painting, staring as I have many times with an unfocused gaze into the rhythmic eyes of a fire, or the sea.

She turned, smiling, but I lingered on her body a moment too long. A warm flush enveloped me, seeped down my chest, over my groin, down the legs, spreading into a large puddle, and I felt myself sinking into it. She said nothing but continued to regard me, her arms still in the painting position, shocked I am sure at the depth of my gaze. Her smile widened. "Do you like it?"

I looked at the painting, purposefully. I told her I liked it a lot, but I wanted to express something more profound. However, I didn't. I turned away from the alluring scent emanating from her and walked into the garage toward the bedstand.

I am profoundly influenced by the olfactory sense; it acts as my sexual Geiger counter. It didn't take me long to fall in love with the fragrance of Alex, the tangible evidence of her aura that could be inhaled but not seen—a mélange of womanly sweat, paint, and perfume. She followed inside and offered me a drink. I responded by asking where Steve was, revealing the thought highest in my mind.

"He's working a double-shift today. Someone was sick." I looked at the books stacked on the floor. *Walden* sat on the top of the pile. "Ever read this?" I asked, picking it up.

"No. I don't think so. Is it any good?"

"Yeah. It's a classic."

"Does the boy get the girl in the end?"

"No, but the guy gets his pond, so to speak."

"Now that sounds interesting. Kind of kinky. Love in the water." Alex started putting the paints away, piercing the air with her long, brown limbs. "Would you like to go to the beach? I could use a swim." I looked at her and nodded yes, picturing sand stuck to her skin. I was becoming increasingly aroused and afraid I might develop a hard-on, so I stood up abruptly.

We stopped by the package store at her suggestion to pick up a bottle of wine. Walking by the ancient fishing cottages-turned-summer-homes, I thought about the hidden beauty of Sconset, the part never seen by the tourists. We walked across a slender street ironically named Broadway, went between two cottages built in the 1700s, and emerged on the shell-lined path overlooking the bluff. The sea churned softly below. To get down the hill we took a little hidden lane called Bank Street, still lined with cobblestones after hundreds of years, and seldom used. We moved through the wounded silence of huts and shacks before the beach. No life, no sound, no wind. I looked at Alex's brown shoulders, the gray walls of the dwellings, the fading sky.

It was the time of day when the intensity of the sun softens, but the color of its light hardens toward yellowness. Edge-time. Shadows melt into pools. Alex kicked off her sandals as we reached the sand and she ran ahead. I picked them up and followed. "Let's go this way!" she shouted over her shoulder.

Few people were left on the beach, now mottled by the low sun. Alex ran into the dunes. I finally found her, spread luxuriously over her tapestry blanket, eyes closed. Sitting, I surveyed her long, tawny body cupping the dimming sun with the soft tremor of mink. I tried to gauge my position in terms of her intentions. She had never acted so invitingly to me before. Alex had always been friendly, but I never sensed this degree of sexual proclivity in her. I decided to start the ball rolling, gently.

"Great sunset." Her eyes slit open.

"Yeah. I love it here this time of day." A dog ran down the beach, seemingly unattached to a master.

"How about some wine?"

"Great idea," she said, and sat up. I pulled the bottle out of the bag and suddenly realized that we forgot to get a corkscrew.

21

"Shit. I don't have a corkscrew." This upset me more than I let her know.

"No problem. I got one in my backpack. Never leave home without one, just like the commercial says." We took turns drinking from the bottle. The air started to chill, and the moist wind rolled in. After a fair amount of chatting and drinking Alex took off her shirt, revealing her bra. The sudden disparity of white cloth against brown skin struck me like a slap. "How 'bout a swim," she cooed.

I was not thinking. The lower, motor functions of my brain took over. I noticed a spot of blue paint on her arm and wanted to lick it off. She rose and slipped off her jeans, leaving on her white panties. Alex ran to the water, not as women normally do in that clumsy side-to-side swinging motion, but with the graceful strides of a cat. The churning triangle covering part of her ass darkened with water as she ran toward Spain, high-stepped the first wave, then dove in. Following closely in my boxer shorts, I dove for the spot she last occupied. Emboldened by the wine, I felt for her under the surface, unable to see through the brown murkiness. I brushed against something like a leg and swam toward it, feeling the gleam of her sex as a blind man senses the draft of a doorway. Her feet churned in front of me. I grabbed an ankle and pulled. Then I had a thigh, and a hand on her ass. She stopped swimming and uprighted her body. We surfaced. For the first time I looked at her without my mask of civility. We wanted each other desperately; no words spoken. To have spoken would have ruined everything. To have spoken would have been an acknowledgment of society, its mores, and our respective positions: pointing inexorably to the fact that she belonged to someone else. We were without facts now, alone in the ocean with only the buoyancy of our flesh to support us.

I started kissing her slowly, but soon became a starved man eating a peach. She almost drowned as she clung to my neck, her lips clawing my face. I bit her hair and shoulder, grinding into her. She freed herself to release her bra by sliding under the water and twisting. Suddenly my shorts were yanked off. I felt her grabbing my cock briefly: it is a ritual with women, the first time they encounter a new lover's nakedness, to instinctively grab his genitalia. What atavistic reason accounts for this I don't know; it could be an act of insatiable lust, or merely a way of checking the quality of the goods.

Alex rose, calmed by her submersion. The outer crust of urgency had shed itself; we were now one object floating together rather than separate entities crashing into each other. I hugged her brutally hard, sucking the warmth through her skin. Her legs wrapped around me. The dark mass of land bobbed unobtrusively in the distance. Water smacked between us. I slowly slid my cock into her, barely able to keep our chins above the water. My feet scratched the sandy bottom. She started to cry out but her mouth filled with water before the sound could escape. I kissed her and also got a mouthful of water.

Eventually we made our way to the beach, having lost all our underwear. The greyhound sky made us difficult to see, but we didn't really care in our invigorated state. A postprandial glow illuminated us as we slipped into our clothes among the dunes. Before Alex lowered her shirt I kissed each of her breasts, then I kissed her, cupping her buttocks firmly with both hands. She drew toward me as I inhaled, her breath flushed, then she softly pushed against my chest with her forearms and said, "I want to, but Steve will be back soon." I had wondered if she'd be matter-of-fact about him.

"What will he say?"

"Nothing if he doesn't find out. And he won't, but don't worry. It's not as if I ever signed a chastity agreement with him." Somewhere in the distance a dog barked. We walked toward the road—my arm around her, our hair wet, eyes stinging from the saltwater—very relaxed.

Delivered from the hands of the sea.

All of the houses on the lane were dark. "Is everyone dead on this street?" I asked. "God, what do people do for fun here, attend funerals?"

She smiled and replied, "At least it's quiet out here. Don't look a gift horse in the mouth. If you lived in town the drunk preppies would keep you up half the night."

"I guess you're right." I could see that the light in the kitchen was on, indicating Larry's presence. "Do you want to come up for something to drink or eat? It looks like Larry's making one of his famous beach dinners."

"No, I better get back. But bring some muffins by again."

"Don't worry, I will." We kissed in the dark under the deck, licking the salt off each other's skin, lingering in the redolence of our act.

"Okay," she whispered. "I'll see you soon."

"Okay," I whispered back, not sure if I should say thanks; but she slipped away quickly, dissolving into a shadow among the patches of blackness up the hill. Her kiss seemed more like a souvenir than a good-bye.

I entered the kitchen to find Larry cooking. The room smelled wonderfully of spices and coffee. Finally he noticed me in the doorway.

"I think I'm in love."

"Great. How 'bout some beans?"

5

My work arrangement had been improving over the past two weeks as Buff, the manager of the restaurant, gave me an increasing amount of responsibility. Although the morning shift for dishwashers began at ten, Buff asked me to come in at eight-thirty to do the inventory. I appreciated the assignment and the boost in my hourly wage. I think he figured that having a college education, I could handle more sophisticated duties than the average transient summer dishwasher. On the other hand, Buff didn't want to give me too much responsibility, because I sensed that at base level he felt threatened by my background, probably because he had graduated from a cooking school. But we coexisted peacefully. I adapted to my routine easily, working three morning shifts and three late ones. The late shifts were more enjoyable of course, the kitchen being more exuberant in the evening; the staff had more fun and the food we served was better.

We had two head cooks: Al and Jason. Everyone liked Al—or "Easy Al" as he was known—better, except Jason's buddies from cooking school: Buff, Tony the broiler cook, and big Tim, a curly-haired palooka from Brooklyn. Easy Al and Jason were diametrically opposed emotionally: the former calm and unflappable, the latter nervous and short-tempered. The disparity of

25

their personalities reminded me of the classic conflict between the Athenians and Spartans which I had studied in college.

Kitchens are very hot. Tempers flare easily, and character flaws are exacerbated. Easy Al never lost his cool all summer; his keel remained even through grease fires, waitress tantrums, evil practical jokes, and even the time a careless deliveryman bumped Al's arm as he was filleting a fish, causing him to slice off a fingertip. Al calmly stopped the bleeding, bandaged his hand and, as the deliveryman passed him on the way out, asked him to be more careful next time. When the deliveryman asked why, Al held up the bloody knife and smiled, dementedly.

Jason, on the other hand, yelled at the staff constantly and obsessed over every detail. No one's efforts were good enough for him; he never admitted his own mistakes, and he managed to bring one of the waitresses to tears almost every shift. When in good humor he loved to direct dirty jokes at the female staff, or make sick sexual innuendos. Whenever a new waitress started he performed his favorite trick by ripping a claw off a live lobster and shoving the jerking body in her face as it raged in pain. Then he'd throw it into the boiling water and give voice to the lobster's silent screaming.

The staff tolerated Jason only because he was Buff's buddy, but Al stood above everyone in stature, even Buff. Although both Jason and Buff would scream at any staff member without provocation, they never reproached Al, because they knew Al could out-cook them with his eyes closed, and that he could easily get a job at any of the better restaurants on the island. Although relatively young, Al was a career chef with an impressive résumé. He had worked in many well-known kitchens, and also had passed the Master Chef exam, which we heard Jason had failed on his first attempt. Al migrated like many resort chefs, working the winter season in Lake Tahoe, and the summer in Nantucket. No one knew why he came to the Lobster Trap every year when he could have gone anywhere. But we heard he got an enormous salary.

As I started my duties that morning, an image of Alex, head thrown back in the water, resonated in my mind. I couldn't shake the powerful feeling of our connection at that moment, the overwhelming clench of desire, of two colliding objects imploding within each other. Then, in an hour, complete separation.

The image of Alex in the water slowly dissolved as another concern grew in my mind. Something about our parting left me uneasy. I think I was bothered by the valence of her last kiss. It lacked the passion of our time in the water. But after a minute of consideration I shrugged it off to her hurry to return before Steve came home. At least for now that explanation would suffice.

A stack of boxes confronted me. I looked over the dates, arranging them chronologically in my mind before moving them. All bore the proud S.S. Pierce label: a deep maroon and white crest of three rampant lions and an eagle, whose wings enveloped the motto "PURITAS ET CURIA." And on the scroll underneath, "ESTABLISHED 1831 BOSTON, MASS." I marveled at the grandness of the S.S. Pierce name instilled by this image, the hubris it invoked. The logo would have been appropriate as a coat of arms for a European sovereignty, or the back of an American coin. You found it everywhere in New England, on every type of canned or bottled food product. You couldn't escape that maroon logo. They even had a line of liquors, which the bars stocked on the bottom shelf. Sailors often asked for it, especially the vodka. The S.S. Pierce name was invoked with reverence on the Cape.

The logo would make a fitting banner for this country east of America, founded on tourism and focused on the consumption of food and drink, I thought, stacking three cases of S.S. Pierce tomato sauce gallon cans.

The rest of the shift passed uneventfully, except for the occasional interference of Tim, who over the past week had asked me to help him with his prep work with increasing frequency. This involved chopping parsley, cutting garnishes, and stocking his part of the line. I didn't mind helping him, and in fact enjoyed being one step closer to cooking, but it slowed down the inexorable train of dirty dishes and pots that needed to be cleaned before each shift. I sensed that if his interference got any worse, I would have to confront him, not an easy task being in the subordinate position of dishwasher to cook.

The ragged edges of my experience with Alex framed my thoughts for the rest of the shift. Finally, Larry came in through the back door to relieve me on the dish line.

"How was the beach today?"

"Not bad. We were body-surfing out by Nobadeer. Caught some decent waves."

I climbed up the steps to the changing room, smelling of fish, grease, and saliva from the throats of the 137 tourists who had eaten lunch that day. After stripping and washing, I rubbed lemon on my hands and arms to get rid of the seafood smell. Fish stink wasn't a bad odor to have on the island—just as the aroma of cow shit is acceptable in farm country—but it reminded me of work and I was happy to mitigate it as much as possible.

As I got ready to leave Tim came bounding up the steps. "Hey, Guy, can you chop some vegetables for me?"

"Not a chance, pardner."

"Look, I'm really behind and we're gonna have a rush. . . ."

"Sorry Tim." I ended the conversation by leaving through the employee exit next to the changing room, which led down a flight of steps to the alley behind the restaurant.

"Howdy, Captain!"

I looked up and saw my friend the carpenter on the roof of the structure across the alley. "Yo Kendall! Nice lookin' roof."

"Thanks, buddy. Here—" A handful of licorice sticks whizzed by me. I managed to catch one.

"Thanks, man." Kendall the carpenter had a genuine, good soul. I had learned from talking to him that he had grown up in the 1960s, served in Vietnam, and lost two fingers in the war. You could not meet Kendall without liking him, and you could not pass him without receiving a piece of red licorice. His great gift was the ability to cheer people up who were down. I sensed there had been some catalyst for this in his past; he projected the vibrancy of one who had met the bottom of his own despair and now lived to ward it off, day by day, like a recovering alcoholic.

I turned the corner around the restaurant and ran into Mark locking up his moped. "So you're doing the late shift with Larry?"

"Yeah. I'm bummed. Would have been a nice night to ride around."

"Hey, would you mind if I borrowed your bike? I'll gas it up and have it back before you get off."

"Sure. Make sure you lock it up. Here's the key."

Mark was a young, good-natured kid, still in college. He kind of looked up to me because I had trained him on the dish line, and I treated him like a peer, which he appreciated.

I took the bike down the cobblestone alley and turned right, past the Easy Street basin where the low tide had pulled back its skirts, revealing its gnarly old legs covered with seaweed. Gulls swooped through the dusk, alighting on pier posts. A launch headed into the muffling embrace of the harbor, bound for some yacht. I looped around the town, parked the moped, and walked down Straight Wharf.

Off-duty shiphands passed me, walking to town in their uniforms. Footsteps resonated between the dock and the water, percussively. Underneath, the ebb and flow of the harbor rubbing the planks. The truckle of water over flat stones: notes from a distant piano. As I went further out, the voices of the shore lost meaning: bar laughter, gallery shoppers, boat owners—all converged into a witless hum strangled by the wind. I sat on the edge of the dock facing the ocean, suppressing a primitive urge to yell toward the mainland, as if anyone would care to hear me, a lunatic sitting on a dark shore who had walked out on a great job on Wall Street to work as a dishwasher in the middle of the ocean.

How silly, this retreat from the evolution of my life. How stupid, this job washing dishes in a restaurant run by cretins. But that's the price of freedom from responsibility I thought, and I guess it's worth it.

My gaze dissolved into the grain of the piling before me. Foghorns traded tones as if an organ were being tuned. Over the sea, gulls threaded the horizon like burnt stars. The wind rose and the boats bumped uneasily against the docks. I listened to their sounds all at once and then in groups; first those nearest me, making loud slapping noises, their steel lines pinging against metal masts; then those further away, their tones muted but still distinct, the incessant clanging of one unfettered line; and finally those in the distance, a dull trill of constant noise, setting a low base rhythm to which the entire harbor kept time.

Twenty minutes passed. A light flicked on in the cabin of a motor yacht to my right. I walked over. A woman came onto its deck searching for something. Seeing me she jerked abruptly.

"I'm sorry if I frightened you. I was just taking a walk along the dock here. I'm sorry."

"No. I just wasn't expecting someone way out here. People rarely come this far." She was elegant, tanned, and just on the final cusp of her beauty. The type of woman leading a comfortable, kept life, I figured. No big worries. The kids away in school. Rich husband with a paunch, and probably off on a lot of business trips. I could picture the whole damn stereotype. She continued looking for the object of her intent. I decided to continue engaging her if I could.

"Whad you lose, a contact?"

"No, my watch. I left it out here this afternoon and I'm afraid it might've been stolen."

"Where did you leave it?"

"On that table, I think. It's gold, and very thin." I looked from my vantage point above her.

"Could that be it, beside the chair?" She walked over. "No, over there." She moved the chair and saw it.

"That's it! Thank you so much."

"I could see it from this angle. It's just a matter of perspective." My eyes trailed her lithe figure as she bent over. Not a bad looking broad, I thought. A huge diamond pulsed on her ring finger, next to a gold band. She looked up at me slowly. "Nice boat. What is she, about fifty feet?"

"Fifty-five."

"That's a lot of teak to polish." She didn't know which way to steer our conversation. Night sifted between us as our exchange paused. She wrapped her arms around her upper torso. All she had on was a sun dress.

"It's chilly out here. I'm going to go in. By the way, what's your name?"

"Guy."

Spindrift

"Thanks for finding my watch, Guy. I'm Marsha. We're going to have a little party here on the boat Saturday. Why don't you stop by."

"What time?"

"Oh, around eight. Come as you are."

"Well thanks, that's nice of you."

"I owe you the thanks. So you'll come?"

"Sure."

"Okay. Well, have a nice night."

"You too." She went inside and I walked down the dock with the tingling of a nascent hard-on. There's something about older women that you don't find in the younger ones. The way they put themselves together. Their smell. It's as if they try harder, but don't show it. And an affair with one is usually much more satisfying, sexually. Less bullshit. Less beating around the bush. And they aren't afraid to pick up the tab, either.

6

Anxiety divides the minutes of cities.
Time is a matter of stoplights.
Dogs strangle themselves with anger.
Bums dissolve into the cement.
Thousands of windows gasp for sunlight.

Each shuddering dawn bears gulls.
Dogs bark at the surf.
The days have no order.
The hours stretch like growing shadows.
Each wave swallows its own memory.
There are no answers on the beach.
The island drifts too slowly to be reached.

1

The fabric of light lay heavily upon me as I dozed on the beach. Every so often I awoke to the face of a bright lamp, but could not turn away from it. Dreams would start but never materialize, like a television with poor reception. I rolled over to escape the heat from above but regained consciousness, sputtering sand.

I had decided to spend my free morning at Surfside Beach. There were not many people this far down. Behind me a dozen or so houses lay spread in the distance. Houses seemingly abandoned but not neglected, probably used only sporadically. A few kids tried to surf in the lugubrious waves. One actually managed to get a short run, but for most of the time they sat on their boards, backs to the shore, like hopeful wives waiting for sailors. Thirty yards to my right lay two well-tanned young women. They looked vaguely European—something about their mannerisms: the way one girl held her head to the side as she sat up. The other smoked too quickly to be American. I watched them and the surfers, but neither held my interest.

I had brought a book—borrowed from Steve a few weeks ago—which turned out to be dull. Sweat oozed out of me. Sand gnarled my hair. The sun struck a dissonant chord. It had turned into one of those insipid days only experienced by those who live on the beach; tourists will make the best out of any situation. Even an overcast beach can be exciting to the day-tripper.

I walked to the dunes to urinate. When I returned the two girls were packing up to leave. I lay down on my towel and the thin one walked over to me. She had skinny legs, and breasts large for her body. I watched her curiously, having no idea what she wanted.

"Pardon me. Do you have the time?"

"Sure," I said, opening my backpack for my watch. She loomed over me, dark in the face of the sun; the shadow over her features made her look stern and older. Her curt accent sounded northern European. Perhaps Dutch. "Yeah. It's about one twenty-seven."

"Thanks. Would you like a beer?"

"I'd love one."

"Here," she said, handing me the three-quarters full bottle in her hand.

"Ah, thanks. But this is pretty warm."

"That's okay. It's dark beer. Very good when warm. We always drink it that way."

"Where are you from?"

"Amsterdam." I tried the beer.

"Not bad. You're right."

"Goot." She moved to leave.

"What's your name?"

"Lena."

"Lena, I'm Guy."

"Nice to meet you. Well. See you." She trotted back to her friend. The beer tasted a bit strange at first, but by the time I finished the bottle, I wished that I had another one.

The surfers looked so pitiful bobbing up and down. After a while I got restless and decided to leave.

A plane flew in at a low angle to the beach, sounding like a tin box full of bees. Why would anyone want to fly onto the island? The ferry ride is an integral part of the transition to island existence, as pressurization is to the ascent of the scuba diver. Perhaps that is the problem with many of the tourists who come here. They treat Nantucket like a gentrified Caribbean island, like a whore they land on, use, and leave the quickest way possible. They exist on a plane of consciousness opaque to environmental and aesthetic sensitivity. I have seen men in thick, gray suits walk down Main Street beside women in pumps and formal dresses, as if they were on Park Avenue. What pleasure do they derive carrying the sooty encumbrances of cities on their backs? Would you wear glass slippers in a cow pasture? How uncomfortable they must be with the idea of acclimating to a foreign environment. Like the Japanese who visit America and stay in Japanese hotels, eating their native meals, as if they hadn't left home. How vapid, not to grapple with the strange and new. Think of the uncharted excitement in the discovery that another country's toilet paper is thinner, thicker, or coarser than your own. Or even better, that there is no toilet paper!

I walked up the sandy path leading to the parking area above the beach. The sun shone, scathing, as if the air consisted of sand. A white truck sat on the ridge of the lot. Two guys stood inside the back, waiting to sell ice cream. I could see them through the counter window: both bare-chested, one with curly, sandy hair, and the other in a faded Boston Red Sox cap. Seeing no other shade, I walked over.

"Nice truck."

"Thanks."

"What're you guys selling?"

"All kinds of ice cream. We got fudge bars, Nutty Buddies, Popsicles. Ah—sodas, candy bars, that kinda stuff."

"Great. Glad I didn't eat breakfast." We chatted for a while, trading backgrounds. They were on a break from school, and shared a big house on Orange Street with several of their buddies.

"Looks like you guys are makin' a killing out here."

"Yeah," said the one in the cap. "We're gettin' killed. But this is a good job. We get to use this truck, which is pretty cool since we don't have a car."

The other guy added, "We just come out here to relax. We'll probably go to Nobadeer later and make some money."

"Hey Bart, we better head back to town now and pick up that stuff."

"Yup." Turning to me he explained, "We've got some ice cream bars coming in on the ferry."

"Great," I said. "Can I hitch a ride with you into town?"

"Ah, I guess so, but keep your head down. We're not supposed to give rides to anyone. If the owner catches us, we'll get fired."

"And there goes our wheels."

"No problem. I'll sit down here."

"Cool." They secured the coolers, folded up the counter, and we were off on a buggy ride down the rutted sand road. As I sat on the vibrating bum of the truck, erotic thoughts of Alex rose in my mind. I realized I hadn't seen her all week and wondered if she was avoiding me. Our next meeting would be crucial.

A candy bar dropped on the floor next to me. They didn't seem to care, so I picked it up and ate it. This triggered my hunger; I realized I hadn't eaten anything all day. As the truck approached the Rotary I asked them to let me out, and thanked them for the ride. I told them to stop by the back door of the Lobster Trap and I'd return the favor.

Traffic blew around the Rotary in a wind of coming and going. Crossing the road I walked toward the Turning Point, a little shack of an eatery with picnic tables out front. A week ago I had met a girl who told me she worked there. I think her name was Jill; she had long brown hair, large breasts, and a beautifully angular face, probably the result of some Spanish blood in her ancestry. It wasn't just sexual attraction that made me want to see Jill; the island, unlike most cities on the mainland, nurtured a camaraderie among its inhabitants—the waiters, cooks, shop assistants, and boathands—casting us in a strata between the tourists and wealthy business owners, which defied the traditional male-female dialectic. Entering through the screen door I approached the young blond girl behind the counter.

"Hi. Is Jill working today?"

"Ah, no. I think this is her day off." The girl spoke with a teenager's accent, overpronouncing her words and adding unnatural stresses.

"Oh, too bad." I quickly read the menu: sandwiches, sodas, chips, and a smattering of vegetarian items. I ordered a ham sandwich and a coffee. The girl fingered the leather bracelet on her wrist. When she went to get the coffee I checked her ankle and sure enough, around it was the ubiquitous string anklet, a de rigueur item for the island's teenagers.

"Is Jill like, a friend of yours? I can tell her you stopped."

"That's okay. I'll catch her later. Thanks." As I walked out to the picnic tables I thought I saw a familiar blue car coming toward the Rotary. It was Easy Al. Waving, I yelled his name and he pulled over. "How 'bout a ride buddy?"

"No problem. Hop in. Looks like you got a little food there. What's wrong, you don't like my cooking?"

"No, I'm starved. What're you making the staff tonight?"

"Oh, I figured something fancy for a change, probably chicken cordon bleu. That's if you guys behave. If you don't it'll be fishhead soup!"

Al dropped me off in town and said, "I'll see you at four."

"Great. Thanks for the ride." As he pulled away I felt silly, standing on Main Street with a half-eaten sandwich, mustard on my face, barefoot, wearing nothing but a pair of shorts and a red bandanna. I sat on a bench and finished my sandwich, feeling slightly guilty, like the first person through the buffet line, eating while everyone else is watching you. A little boy walking by pointed at my bandanna and exclaimed, "Look mommy, it's a pirate!" She smiled at me and I imagined what I looked like: sunburnt, unshaven, and unruly.

An hour later I walked inside the restaurant, still smoking from the sun. Al was already dressed and on the line, doing his prep work. I could hear Tony singing in the changing room.

"Yo, Tony, you shoulda been on stage. Whada you doin' here slingin' hash?"

"Hey, I am on stage every night. A thing of beauty to watch. I'm the artist of the broiler station."

It was true that Tony did his job well. He made all of the meat dishes, as well as the broiled seafood dishes. Sometimes half his body would be inside the inferno-like broiler racks as he checked the progress of the fifteen or twenty orders he might have going at any one time.

The line was a ballet of timing, a dance performed by the caller; the two line cooks at the broiler and fry stations; the waitresses, who nagged from the wings like nasty swans until they could leap off with their trays; and the dishwashers, who kept a constant stream of plates and cooking ingredients flowing to the line. During rushes the kitchen would swell into a crescendo of motion, the staff communicating in grunts and gestures, well-oiled and omniscient, a clockwork of seemingly disparate mechanisms meshing smoothly through each other. Every so often the system would crash, tempers shooting out like grease fires, the shouting and clanging of pots growing so loud that old Joy the hostess would have to come back and hush us. Caught like schoolboys in the middle of a scuffle, we would freeze in our positions, suddenly realizing the absurdity of our passions, and return muttering to our stations. All could be forgotten almost immediately in the kitchen, washed away by the next flow of orders, although the burns and cuts on our hands served as stigmata of the nature of our work.

I had been on the dish station only a short while when Buff stalked into the kitchen and asked if anyone had seen Pete, the fry cook. Pete had been showing up later and later for work over the past few weeks. Al said he hadn't, and Buff gnarled out the words, "That bastard." A few minutes later I went outside to dump some garbage, and saw Pete tying his dog to a post. It was a big, black animal, a mixture of Labrador and something else; it always had a bandanna around its neck and a feverish look of wonder on its face—a thyroid-eyed, wild dog of the moors.

"Hey Pete, you better hustle, Buff is pissed you're late."

"Ah, fuck him, that asshole." He dropped his cigarette as the dog pranced against his shins. Pete went up the outside stairs to the changing room, to avoid Buff. I looked at the dog who had settled down but was still panting.

"Hey buddy," I said, and he ran over to me, wagging in that bumpy-lovey way universal to dogs. "Don't worry, Petey will feed you in a little while." The cobblestones of the alley glowed gray-blue as the sun moved behind the restaurant next door. I looked over to see the work Kendall had done that day; virgin beams of wood lay across the old tar roof like fingers on the body of a violin. Someone inside yelled my name. I dropped the bag of trash in the dumpster and went back in.

8

Larry and I both had the day off, so we decided to get up early and catch some of the festivities in town during the big regatta, called the Figawi. He offered to make breakfast, but I had tired of his cooking—burnt toast being his pièce de résistance—so I suggested that we eat in the village. We walked into the market, where our buddy stood behind the counter in a white apron.

"Hey Grant, how's it going? I'll have the usual."

"So that's a six-pack and a Snickers Bar?"

"Kind of early for *that* usual. How 'bout a coffee and a bagel."

"Okay, and you?" he said to Larry.

"Same for me."

We carried our food to the town pump, a historic landmark that sits in a little square off Center Street, just hidden from the main part of the village. The inscription on its plaque read, simply, "Dug 1776." No one ever came to look at this desultory little monument, but I found it a comforting symbol of Sconset: ancient, out-of-the-way, and unpretentious. To the right sat a little public house with a bathroom, hardly marked, and a pay phone hanging over a couple of park benches. Down the road you'll find the Casino—home of the local tennis club—and across the street is the Chanticleer, probably the fanciest restaurant on the island. Waiters' jobs were coveted there because the tips were extraordinary, but positions were hard to get—you had to speak French, have had formal training in similar establishments, and it helped if you were gay, or so the rumors went.

A yellow jeep shot through the square.

"There she goes."

"Who?" Larry asked.

"That blond chick. She gave me a ride once. I don't remember her name. Kelly or Stacy or something."

"She's cute."

"No kidding. You musta had a little hair of the dog, you're normally not so astute in the mornings."

"All right, that's enough. And I was gonna be nice to you today."

"Wouldn't want to break two habits at once."

"Let's go." We picked up our litter and walked to the little rotary. The yellow jeep sat in front of the market. We waited for a car to pass, but none came. A few minutes went by, and then the blond girl drove up.

"Want a ride?"

"Tha'd be great," I said, hopping in the front seat, leaving Larry to take the back. "My name's Guy. This is Larry."

"Hi. I'm Tammy. Where do you guys live?"

"We live down in the Sundial House."

"Oh, that's a great place. I live out by Sankaty."

"By the lighthouse?" She nodded. "Great. Whada you do?"

"Um, I work at a store called the Clotheshorse."

"I would have guessed you were a waitress."

"No, I hate wearing uniforms." As the jeep picked up speed the sound of the motor and wind coalesced into a numb roar, causing us to shout. Larry could no longer participate in the conversation.

I looked at Tammy's legs when she shifted gears, sculpted, brown calves—hard enough to crack an egg; the muscles of her thigh clenching, the hair blond on her thighs and arms; I saw her naked by following the tone of her musculature under her clothes, imagining the tensile quality of her skin as she lay supine. She saw me watching her as she tried to harvest the hair out of her face.

"Here," I said, holding out my bandanna, "Let me put this on you." She smiled and I tied the bandanna over her head, pushing her thick hair out of the way.

"Thanks. I should get one of those. My mom always wore one when she drove my father's convertible."

"Thank God for the older generation. I stole that bandanna from my immigrant grandmother." We passed a shirtless man running on the bike path. I had seen him almost every day running this seven-mile stretch to town.

"That's what I should be doing," Tammy said.

"No. He's always late for work. You're better off driving." She smiled. The hum of the motor slid between us for a while.

"Where are you guys going?"

"We're just going to hang out in town, hit some of the parties, that sort of stuff."

"Bummer. I gotta work. Is there anything exciting I'm gonna miss?"

"A clambake, live music, all the food you could want and all the booze you could drink, dock parties, that sort of stuff. No, not much."

"Wow."

"What time do you get off?"

"I work till six-thirty."

"Great. No problem. Why don't you meet us at the Boarding House then. I'll be the good-looking guy sitting at the bar, and he'll just be cross-eyed." I smiled at Larry who was swallowing a face-full of wind. "Then we can hit another party I know of that starts at eight."

"Okay. I could do that. Sounds good. The Boarding House."

When we got to the outskirts of town I told Tammy to let us off. I pointed to the bandanna on her head. "And you can keep that. . . ."

"So you can remember what he smells like," Larry said, finishing my sentence.

"Gee thanks," she replied, and roared off.

"Man, what a woman," Larry said. "What's the deal? Did you get her number?"

"Don't worry, we'll see her later. I got it all worked out."

Larry mentioned that he had a friend on Orange Street that had invited him to stop by. We entered the hush of the historic district, stepping, it seemed, on eggshells made of brick, so quiet were the streets, the houses, the sky and trees—calcified under the nodding beard of an old man frozen to his porch. We tended to talk less in the historic district, I don't know why, but the need to speak weakened in this ambience. Passing rows of gray houses, medieval in their stillness, I marveled at their age with the respect that flows toward old people who are well-preserved. As always, Larry claimed to be sure of where we were going, but couldn't locate the house we wanted.

"I remember it was right around here. A gray house with a porch."

"Great, you've just described every house on the island." Finally Larry found his friend's place. We knocked on the door, but no one answered.

"This is it, I'm sure."

"How do you know?"

"I recognize this door." Larry knocked again, waited, then pushed the door open. "He's probably still asleep." We entered the house trepidatiously, and asked timidly if anyone was home. No answer came.

It was an elegant old house, with a formal entry way, off of which ran a parlor or sitting room. We heard music coming from there, so we went in. The room had antique furniture, bow-back chairs, a beautiful old braided rug, and a stereo, which was playing a record. It sounded like Indian sitar music. Dull light filtered through the panes; behind us a clock ticked. The emptiness of the house swelled with sullenness. The sitar music sounded strangely appropriate, playing to an empty room in gray light, through the palpable dust.

Larry suggested we go upstairs. I followed, assuming that he knew where he was going. We looked in each room on the second floor but didn't find anyone. There were three bedrooms filled with old-fashioned furnishings, and two had the clothes of young people, burning brightly against the dark wood surfaces. Larry inspected these belongings. I began to feel uneasy, afraid that someone would walk in and take us for burglars.

"You know, none of this is Mike's stuff. I don't recognize anything. I think these are all girls' things," he said, holding up a purple bra.

"Then let's get the fuck out of here!"

As we walked down the stairs I heard the sitar music and realized that it was from a Beatles album, one of their Maharishi-inspired songs. The sun shone coldly through the window, the record spinning, the furniture waiting to be dusted. I noticed a bowl of oranges on the dining room table and had an overwhelming urge to take one, but refrained.

We hurried down the porch stairs and walked quickly away from the house. Something made me look back at the place. An old moon-faced woman peered at us from the attic window. I tapped Larry's shoulder. When he looked up the shade had been drawn.

9

There are only two or three places that serve a proper breakfast in the town of Nantucket, and those that do specialize in it, meaning they don't serve lunch or dinner. Breakfast is a tough business on the island; the market for it is smaller than the other meals, probably because vacationers don't rise very early, and many of the boarding houses serve their own breakfasts. Ironically, breakfast is the one meal at which a tourist might encounter a native, such as a carpenter, house painter, or a similar land worker; the fishermen are all out at sea by then.

Larry suggested we eat at the Dory, a little place on India Street in the north part of town. Instead of waiting for a table, we were able to sit immediately at the counter, something the tourists don't like to do, this being one of the small keys to existence on the island, like the Straight Wharf dock rest room, the unlocked door of the Sankaty lighthouse, the shortcut to Nobadeer beach, and the abandoned boat by the Town Pier—all of which no one knew about, or bothered to care about, but served to heighten the quality of my life. Sitting at the counter behind a good short order cook can be an inspiring experience. Nowhere else can you find the economy of movement, the spatial exactitude, the ergonomic perfection, or, to be truly honest, the poetic sublimity of simple human effort. I ordered eggs and coffee.

Spindrift

As the morning passed, the restaurant filled with the ranks of tourists: cute couples in matching sweatshirts ready to bicycle to the end of the world together; young balding fathers looking tragically victimized by their screaming kids; groups of middle-aged women wearing heavy make-up and designer labels trying to outdo each other with plastic surgery stories; and the occasional loner clutching his newspaper for companionship.

We ate until filled as you can only do at an unpretentious restaurant, ordering more and more coffee, while two or three generations of customers came and left. The waitress, a woman in her mid-thirties and certainly a native, treated us nicely, relieved that we were not demanding and unreasonable like the tourists. We left her a big tip, thanked the cook, and departed with the woozy feeling of too-full stomachs: a food-drunkenness—which impeded our perambulation. Larry burped and said, exhaling, "God that was a great meal. I'm stuffed." Feeling a mutual call to answer the demands of the coffee, we both headed straight for the public rest room next to the police station in the center of town. The public john had saved me many times that year, not just from the need to relieve myself, but also on a more spiritual level. You could always go to the public john to decompress during a night of excessive drinking; it was a cool, quiet place amidst the overpopulated streets of the town center. You could escape there for a sobering splash of water on the face, or take a sink bath after a roasting day on the beach before you went for a drink. For when the bars closed at night, the john would welcome you. If you crashed with someone in town, the john would be open for business to take care of you before the eight mile trek home. Luckily for Larry and me that morning, the public john had two stalls.

Larry and I walked from place to place as we always did, but we never really got anywhere: no matter where we went we ended up on the same spot of sand and dirt that we had started out on. We were dispossessed from America, not in a political or religious sense, not because of discrimination or poverty; no, we represented a new kind of disenfranchisement: we had defaulted on our careers and lives, the hopes and dreams of our colleagues and parents; we had stopped in mid-race when everyone else assumed we were just catching our breaths; we had left the course and headed for the tavern. We represented a new breed of the alienated—not that we were truly new, for history has a way of recurring, according to Vico, hence at best we were some sort of strange *ricorso*—but instead of walking out of step, or to a different drummer, we just stopped trying to move forward.

The 1980s had turned into a decade of excess; we wanted no part of it. Personally, I felt safe on the island, as if I were living in a natural fallout shelter, except that there were no yellow signs with triangles, and all the provisions came from S.S. Pierce. Every time I stacked another can of beans or tomatoes I thought to myself, they'll be plenty to eat if the bottom falls out.

Haven't we always had periods of excess, such as the 1920s, the 1870s? Sure. But there was something especially virulent about this decade. The number of people fired from their jobs due to the excesses of Wall Street: the buying, selling, merging, and splitting of companies in a pyromaniacal lust for revenues. The number of mentally ill people our president had turned out of treatment programs, now wandering the streets homeless and dangerous. The new class of poverty our legislation fostered. The farm bust. The senseless skyrocketing of real estate values, and the dire lack of affordable housing. It was not like our parents' time: work hard and your life will fall into place. The social and cultural excesses of the 1960s were not the celebration of a new order, but the last hurrah of a nation whose foundation was falling away. And instead of standing on solid ground, we were now treading water, scraping for the sand with our toes. Before I left for the island, I remember my landlady saying to me, "Money was never a problem in the sixties. What happened?"

I sat on a bench outside the Hub, the newsstand and central gathering place for information on the island. Larry leafed through a week-old *Boston Globe* inside. On the sidewalk, across from the entrance, stood a large vertical billboard—about three feet wide by seven feet tall—which the entire island used for communicating: listings for apartments, jobs, rides, flights, ferry tickets, concerts, and plays were all displayed here, as well as messages for missing friends, descriptions of lost-and-found items, and the work of anonymous poets, artists, and photographers. The island bared its soul on this placard, turning it into a battleground littered with rusty staples, thumbtacks, and the torn corpses of unanswered flyers. I read a few listings, the most interesting one being, "Would like to have lunch in the nude. Call Darby. . . ." Bored, I wandered inside the Hub. While all the adults clamored around the newspaper and magazine racks, a lone kid stood reading in front of the comics carousel. Fascinated by the intensity of his concentration, I looked over his shoulder at the comic, called the *Silver Surfer*. The hero looked like a chrome submarine fashioned into the shape of a man, but without toes or a lump in his crotch, a smooth metallic figure bulging with muscular undulations like you find on sea rocks.

"S'that a good book?"

He turned and looked at me. "Yup."

"What's it about?"

"Saving the universe from disaster."

"Pretty big stuff. So the Silver Surfer, he's a good guy?" The kid looked up at me, slowly.

"Don't you read comics?"

"Not as much as I should."

"You should read this one." He looked disparagingly at another kid who had walked over and started reading *Archie*.

"All right, my friend, thanks for the advice." I picked up a copy and took it to the counter. The man in front of me had bought the *Economist* and the *Wine Advocate*. I slapped the *Silver Surfer* on the counter next to them. The checkout woman asked me if that'll be all.

"Isn't that enough? Unless you have some Tolstoy. I'm here all year."

"Bag?"

"Save the tree."

Larry was waiting outside. "Whad you get?"

"The *Silver Surfer*. You?"

"The *Globe*."

"Any news?"

"America blew up."

"I sure hope the S.S. Pierce truck made the last ferry." But we'll be okay anyway, I thought to myself. We have plenty of inventory at the Lobster Trap.

I opened the comic book to the middle. The Silver Surfer floated above a beautiful woman on his surfboard. Apparently it worked like a magic carpet. The dialogue balloon above his head read, "I have come to save the universe. I am . . . the Silver Surfer." The woman looked relieved. I wondered what she thought of this metallic, muscular hunk floating above her. Would they fall in love? Of course, I thought, until I realized: how long till she notices that he doesn't have a penis?

10

We spent the next few hours walking around town, meeting people, stopping in shops we never bothered to visit, seeking the unusual, tacking with the wind on the streets, killing time before the Figawi festivities were to begin. At one point we entered an art gallery on Water Street because some attractive women were inside; they left almost immediately, so we were stranded. I feigned interest in the drippy oil paintings depicting marzipan seascapes. Behind me I heard Larry ask, "How much is this one?" I turned, surprised he would ask such a question, and saw him pointing to the "Store Hours" sign on the door. I ushered him out, smiling at the saleswoman, who didn't see the humor in his question.

Outside, Larry said, "Fuck this shit. Let's get a drink."

"Now you're talkin'."

Cappy sat on a bench near the liquor store, a little sloshed but not too far gone yet, a gaggle of tourists snapping his hoary visage and handing him dollar bills. He smiled through boozy eyes cast in slits, trying valiantly to keep his head floating above his shoulders. Eventually he would fall asleep on the bench and the tourists would drift away; then, awakening in the early dusk, dry and coughing, unable to focus, he would manage to find the way to his house by identifying the colors and shapes he knew well—the blue-gray cobblestones of Main Street, the three crosswalk stripes at the corner of Orange Street, the burnt-red bricks of the sidewalk, and the black lampposts which looked like tree trunks, leading up the hill toward his house—an old cart drifting through the fog.

A church bell sounded; it must be something-o'clock, but it hardly matters. Time has a way of creeping past you on the island, then spreading out to fill the space needed for whatever you happen to be doing. It's different from the cities, which are run by deadlines. We have turned Parkinson's Law on its head. The ferries may come and go on schedule, but they pass Brant Point like dreams, like sounds heard through the walls of sleep, resonant but diffused, moving without acceding to the physical laws of the universe.

Larry and I cast violescent shadows over the sidewalk, the sun breaking through the trees, charging the air.

He asked, "Where do you want to go?"

"Ah, is Ken on at the Rose and Crown?"

"No, I don't think so. He usually doesn't start till six."

"Okay. How 'bout the AC?"

"Sounds good."

We rounded the corner from Main to Water Street, passing the old Pacific Club, an always-deserted building filled with dust and old furniture, looking like the designated reunion place on judgment day for the crews of all the whaling ships ever lost at sea. "What's that place?" Larry asked.

"I dunno. Some sort of private club for old sea captains or something. I don't think the place has been used in a hundred years."

"Well then the beer is probably flat."

The din of tourists and music buzzed through the windows of the Atlantic Cafe. We stood at the bar where some islanders were drinking. I saw Benny and a few other people I knew.

"Hey, thanks for helping me out the other night," I sang out to Benny. "Get this vampire a beer. No, make it a Bloody Mary!" The group at the bar turned and looked at me. I spread my arms, "Beers for the house on me, and I'll take a Courvoisier . . . just kidding. I always wanted to say that."

An hour or so went by quickly. I started to feel the effects of the alcohol that I had consumed, entering that giddily acute state when the sense of hearing sharpens but the brain's reaction time slows, imbuing one's motor skills with a thickness that causes drinks to be set down too hard, and words to be blurted out too loudly. Larry had been getting friendly with a young woman that worked as a waitress in one of the fancy restaurants. A warm glow spread from the base of my spine.

Everything was lovely: Larry and his girl; the bartender; the Police, playing on the stereo; the French family eating through Gallic faces across from us were especially lovely; the sunlight mashed against the dark haze of the bar; my coaster with its beautiful circle of sweat, three-quarters full like the moon; all of Nantucket drinking in loveliness; the boats nudging the docks with their soft bumpers; Cappy asleep on his bench, holding up the island with the weight of his beard; the chrome dish station shining as it waited for me tomorrow; the surf breaking in Sconset, wrapping around the island; and a lovely sunset gliding toward Wauwinet. The face of my watch grew before me—time to meet Tammy. I nudged Larry to go.

"What about her?"

"Bring her! The more the merrier."

Soon we were sitting on the patio of the Boarding House—a middle-priced restaurant with a bar that had become popular with the hip kids and gays—watching passersby clack through the dusk. Larry had brought his new friend, Laura, and Benny had come with his buddy Cooper. I was afraid of becoming sloppy drunk in front of Tammy, so I switched from drinking vodka-rich Cape Codders to beer.

The white picket fence surrounding the patio swelled with the influx of patrons over the next hour; we were a rollicking swarm of drinkers passing pitchers of beer, sharing tables, turning to strangers and embarking on convivial conversations; laughing, singing, and dancing to the music from the bar.

I noticed an attractive blond through the fuzz of my vision, and in a delayed epiphany, realized who it was. "Hey Tammy, over here," I blurted out, much too loud for the short distance separating us. But the force of my voice seemed necessary to pierce the consuming darkness, and my tongue had become a difficult rudder to steer. "Glad you could make it."

"So am I. I'm sorry I'm late, but we had to do inventory today, and it took longer than we thought."

"Don't worry, I know the feeling. What're you drinking?" We sank into the crush of tables and bottles, with me less nervous than I normally would be, and Tammy feeling slightly ill at ease as anyone does upon entering a party in progress. After a couple of rounds, I suggested we take a walk.

"Where to?" Tammy asked.

"I thought we might check out the clam bake. I'm kind of hungry; how about you?"

"I'm starved. Tha'd be great."

The air glistened with humidity as we walked toward the wharves. Benny had left with his friend to get ready for work at the bakery. Larry and Laura strolled several paces ahead of us. "How do you like living on the island?" I asked Tammy.

"It sure beats summer school."

"Why, was that your plan this summer?"

"Yes. I needed some extra credits for my degree since I spent a year in France. But I eventually managed to get credit for my coursework over there, so I didn't have to go."

"Lucky you. So this was your last year?"

"Yeah."

"Where'd you go?"

"Wellesley."

"Great. I've been there. The only thing I can remember is that the bathrooms in the dorms are unisex. You just flip the sign to the appropriate gender when you go in. Very democratic."

We passed the docks—boatlines drooling into the water—through to the beach where we could hear the clambake. Emerging in a sea of sailors and would-be sailors, Tammy and I pressed together, as if to comfort each other but really to avoid being separated by the roisterous crowd. Larry announced, "We'll scout for liquid sustenance, you two set up base camp."

A woman covered in green and pink madras bumped into me and asked, "Did you race?"

"No, we just got here."

"Well you're still early. A lot of the boats haven't even landed yet. Knowing some of those captains, they're probably half-way to Spain by now. No wonder they call it the Fugawi. As in, where the fug are we?" She went off laughing and spilling her drink.

Through the crowd Larry waved and shouted, "The beer's over here!" Standing in line for the keg made me feel like I was back in college. Here I stood once again among a bunch of wide-eyed people clamoring for beer and food, all in that swaggering state of disregard for social decorum—spilling, jostling, bumping—an amusement park landscape of gratification, of intrepid revelry, of indulgence to the lower urges. People drank plastic cup after plastic cup of beer for no reason, it seemed, other than to piss it out later. I found the shift in tone from the Boarding House to this party rudely disturbing; centered in the kegs, enmity radiated through the crowd, weaving like sea grass among the coral of white cups.

I grabbed our beers and took Tammy away from the crowd.

"I have something for you," she said.

"A present already? You shouldn't have. We hardly know each other."

"Well, it's not really a present." She handed me my bandanna.

"No, that's for you. You might need it again."

"No, it's yours."

"Look, I wouldn't want you to get in an accident because your hair flew in your face."

"Okay, thanks. I'll treasure it always."

"You might want to wash it first."

As we walked, her face floated beside me like smoke, the sea churning its incessant laundry-like motor rendering us aphasic, or else it could have been the motor in my head churning, fueled by dusk and alcohol. I reached for Tammy's hand and we drew together, without looking. The wind rose and the sky darkened. I felt the humidity swilling through the air and feared that it would rain. A soft rumbling in the distance confirmed my suspicion.

"We better head to town, it might rain. We wouldn't want to get caught out here."

"Okay."

Instead of moving we both stopped. I put my arms around her and squeezed tightly, the extruding press of trying to pass someone's body through your own, down to the pulp, to the essence.

I squeezed Tammy to steady myself, to steady my unstable life reeling eastward from all that I had known. Perhaps I was really clutching for an anchor, as if an anchor could tie me down. Perhaps, like Tammy, the anchor I searched for was not tied down itself, perhaps it would move like a sea anchor attached to a ship, and I could follow it wherever the wind blew us.

A sparge of rain covered us with spots. We kissed, and for the first time I felt I had made the right decision in coming to the island. The rain did not thicken; rather, it coated us like spindrift, made us lighter. Her nose nuzzled my neck and cheek; I inhaled her scent, sharpening in the humidity. There is nothing more beautiful than a blond woman in the fading light. My fingers moved through her hair. She looked at me, glistening, raw, the surrender of two shucked oysters.

The rumbling started again, and with it the possibility of lightning. "Let's go. We don't want to get caught out in the open."

We came upon a pier, and behind it a dry dock. Boats sat in various states of repair. In the center a thirty-odd foot motorboat stood on supports. Sizing up our options as the rain sheared down, I led her over and suggested we go in. She hesitated for a few seconds and said, "We can't go in someone's boat," but a sharp wave of rain changed her mind. She squealed as I pushed her up the side and shoved her bottom over the gunwale.

The boat smelled of mildew but was welcome relief from the rain, now driving hard against the hull. We both quickly warmed to the idea of being in the vessel; the harshness of the conditions outside justified our trespass. I led Tammy to the sleeping compartment in the bow to escape the water splattering us.

"Who do you think this boat belongs to?"

"Certainly not a native. It's no good for lobster fishing. I think it's just abandoned."

An oil-stained cap lay on the worn seat cushions. I noticed several places where crumbs of foam padding poked through. We stood close to each other since there wasn't enough headroom to stand anywhere else in the cabin. I touched Tammy's face the way a blind man would, wanting to feel the veracity of her features. Her eyes closed as my hand climbed her cheek, smoothing the fine hair around her ear.

"This is going so fast. . . ."

"That's okay."

"But, I'm worried," she said, rolling her head back. A pumpkin light filtered through the cabin windows.

The boat drifting, emulsified in the rain and burnt light along the thrum of the storm. A melting release of our physical boundaries, and with it, the need of separation. Her clothes slid off and she lay back on the rough cushions, the deliquescence of her eyes more compelling than any invitation through words. I could not move watching her; I felt the warmth of her vision on me; closing my eyes I could feel her gaze travel down my body, trickling warm water; a man in a well consumed by its silence, air moving with each breath, a metronome of inhaling, exhaling; the wind pregnant with humidity.

Crushing into her I realized that everything would be all right: the boat might rock but it wouldn't capsize; the storm would eventually subside; tomorrow would glow of morning; in the distance the sun would rise to warm the island, spinning at sea as it always has, allowing the gulls to land and the ferries to dock; a thousand summers might come and go but none would end, because summers never really end, the way some people never really get old.

//

Somewhere in the warm awareness of dawn I realized that I had forgotten to stop by Marsha's party. This bothered me inexplicably, like a Zen koan. There is an affirming quality inherent in older women, a feeling of reassurance I had come to savor, something no doubt related to the separation a male feels from his mother upon adulthood. Maybe it is the idea that to a younger man, an older woman has no need to take anything—such as his money, or his freedom—she is interested in him for another reason; her motivation is usually more pure, and more salient. Younger women have so many currents, running deep and shifting, of many temperatures; you may dive into the stream and find yourself carried away by turbulent water that appeared calm on the surface.

I once had an affair with a woman twenty years my senior. It was a very positive experience sexually and, as there were no ulterior emotional issues, I found it spiritually rewarding as well. We enjoyed each other in many ways other than the purely physical, simply because the issues of commitment and dependence were moot. It is amazing how much space in the soul these two words occupy—the amount of time couples spend analyzing, discussing, and fighting over them. However, they are the crux of any relationship that is to be permanent. Take away the issue of permanence and they disappear; take away commitment and dependence and the permanence vanishes.

Rolling away from the sun I felt the crust of my union with Tammy from last night. We drove home in the chittering aftermath of the storm, somewhat scared, or perhaps fearful of the consequences of our acts. The issues of commitment and dependence obviously at the fore of our minds but unspoken. An exciting trepidation had infused us as we stepped past the shadow's edge of emotional susceptibility.

Still, I could not eviscerate the murky image of Marsha from my thoughts. I heard her like a siren across the island, floating in her boat upon the harbor while I rolled between the sheets of my bed on the antipodal lip of Sconset. The compelling eyes of the older woman! The carnal twist of the smile, the ardent wave of the hair—tangled sheets and smoldering ashtrays. I drifted back to sleep, watching Marsha smoking on her deck, looking directly at me, the warm thigh of the sun against my back. . . .

Entering the dining room I found Larry already working on a beer. "It's not even noon yet. How can you drink so early?"

"A little hair of the dog. Does wonders. Try one, you'll feel better." The suggestion seemed repugnant at first, but the throbbing in my head made me feel that I had nothing to lose.

"Not bad." After a few more sips I did indeed begin to feel better. "How was your night with . . . what's her name?"

"Laura."

"Right. Laura. How'd it go?"

"Pretty well. We hung out at the clambake for a while, but we lost you guys. Where'd you go?"

"For a walk."

"A walk. Right. Did you gut her?"

"You're sick."

"Single-minded. And honest."

"So what about you, Casanova?"

"I don't remember much. Things got a little dark after about the tenth beer. But she was nice enough to drive me home, so I couldn't have been too bad."

"I'm heading up to the store. Do you want anything?"

"No, I'm fine. Liquid breakfast."

"Okay. I'll see you later. Gonna head into town before work. I hope Al's on tonight."

"Nope. It's Jason. Welcome to hell."

"Great."

Inside the market I ran into Steve, whom I hadn't seen since before my affair with Alex. His sudden appearance caught me off guard, and I felt my face flush. I tried to act as nonchalant as possible.

"Hey Guy, how's it going?"

"Pretty good, Steve; what's up?"

"Not much. Grabbing a little chow. Hey, how'd you like that book?" I tried to remember the title I had borrowed from him, but couldn't. "Invitation to a Beheading. Nabokov." I had read only the first twenty pages.

"Not bad. A little too Kafkaesque for my liking—did he copy him?"

"No, I don't think so. Just a crazy book. Did you like the ending, when the character just walks out of the story?"

"Yeah—" I was saved by the cashier, who asked what I wanted.

"Gimme a coffee and a roll. You want anything, Steve?"

"No thanks. Gotta shop for Alex. A lot of girl stuff: plumbing and that sort of shit. She's really flowing this week. Never needed this many tampons before." I didn't know what to make of that remark, but the topic made me nervous.

"Listen, I gotta run. I'll drop the book by later. Talk to ya."

I walked down the road to get away from Steve, instead of trying to hitch a ride at the rotary. Landscaping trucks lined the lawns in front of the big homes. Gardeners—mostly shirtless young summer kids wearing ripped jeans and Top-Siders—scampered over the grounds. Once I had gotten out of sight of the market I sat on the road and ate the roll. Shit, I thought, I forgot to get orange juice. These affairs are draining me nutritionally.

A landscaper bounded around my side of the truck and hoisted a big lawn mower over the side. He looked at me and said, "What's up?" A typical good-looking college kid from the east coast, probably attending a prestigious, small liberal arts college; preppy, a bit cocky, but friendly. The island was full of them: working, eating, drinking, and sleeping together; for every guy like this there was a pretty Connecticut girl like Tammy, or an artsy Rhode Island School of Design-type like Alex, all looking for such a mate and finding him effortlessly, naturally, like a falling leaf finds the ground; we covered the island in this manner—twirling, floating, cascading onto each other and laying, imbricated, waiting for the next landscaping truck to cart us off.

Once on the island these young summer people become citizens of another culture, one in which the normal rules of civilized America do not apply. A lone woman will pick up a man hitchhiking late at night. Strangers speak on the cobblestone streets. Anyone dances with anyone who asks; I hadn't been turned down once. The waiters and waitresses make good tips, rarely getting stiffed. People trust one another, for we are banded by the diaphanous ethos of Nantucket, rooted in the history of its survival against many outside forces over the centuries: war, disease, economic devastation; but most of all the cold shoulder of America, shaking its fist on the arm of Cape Cod.

After finishing my simple breakfast I began hitching, or waiting to be more precise, as no cars passed for a long time.

Eventually a car came down the road, driven by a woman with wet brunette hair. She stopped and I got in.

"Headed to town. Going all the way in?"

"Yup."

"Great."

"My name's Guy."

"I'm Patty."

"Thanks for picking me up. I was ready to walk into town. There just isn't anybody on the road."

"Yeh, it can be slow. Don't have a car?"

"Nope. Don't even have a skateboard. I'd like to get a bike or a moped or something."

"How 'bout a motorcycle?"

"Sure."

"I know where there's one for sale."

"What kind?"

"A Honda."

"Who's selling it?"

"I am."

"Really? You ride a motorcycle?"

"It used to belong to my boyfriend, but he got a jeep and gave it to me. I never use it cause I got this. It's just sitting in my backyard."

"Wow. I'd like to see it." As we rode Patty told me about the cycle. I could tell she wasn't very mechanical, but she seemed sincere about selling it.

She looked at herself in the rearview mirror. "I look like a mess. I just came from the beach and didn't have time to dry my hair; I'm late for work. Do you mind if I drop you off on Union Street? That's where I park my car."

"No problem. Where do you work?"

"The Opera House. I'm the pastry chef."

"Tasty job. Must be a lotta fun."

"If you like sweets, which I don't. It helps to keep your objectivity."

She gave me her address before we parted and I told her I'd stop by tomorrow to look at the bike.

Main Street on a Sunday morning. A cacophony of tourists, ice cream, and credit cards. A flatbed truck selling fruits and vegetables. Two little girls hawking painted stones with pictures of sunsets and the word "Nantucket" misspelled. A menagerie of human beings floating between store entrances. The excited clip of shopping parlance, "Daddy, I want it!—Is it too much?—Does this look good on me?—Brett would love this." The chatter of children infused with too much sugar and sea air, idling furiously like overheated cars. People lined-up to enter Runo's restaurant, thrilled to be paying New York prices for brunch, and happy to be waiting in a long line for a table. Grown men dressed like kids, looking awkward in garishly colored, tight-fitting outfits, bellies sloshing over stiff, white, hairless legs.

Quietly on the side of this scene sat a man playing the guitar; he was dressed differently than the colorful procession of tourists: wearing dirty jeans and a brown Hawaiian shirt—a tall, thin twang of a man with droopy eyes and a soggy mustache. Between his feet sat a turned-up straw hat, and beside him lay a sleepy dog. I sat on the far side of his bench. He sang an old blues song I had never heard before. In fact it wasn't really a blues song except for his delivery. As few people stopped to listen a camaraderie of proximity grew between us. After he finished the song I clapped politely.

"Thanks, pardner."

"Thank you. What else do you know?"

"Oh, a coupla chords, nothin' fancy. Got any requests?"

"Well, another one like that would be just fine."

"That's my specialty: 'How about another one.' Sounds like I'm talkin' to a bartender." He held the guitar on his right thigh like a construction worker might hold a baby. His foot began tapping, causing the dog to look up; then the animal lowered its head back on its paws. Staring straight ahead, toward an imaginary stage, the guy sang:

Scotch and soda
Mud in your eye
Baby do I feel high
Oh me oh my
Do I feel high

He turned to me with a mock-serious expression and continued:

Dry martini
Jigger of gin
Oh what a spell
You've got me in
Oh my
Do I feel high

A teenage girl passed, looking askance at us. He smiled at her.

After the song I shook his hand, which completely enveloped mine, and wondered how such thick fingers could form such delicate chords.

"What's your name?"

"Dave."

"I'm Guy."

"Pleased to meet you."

"Welcome to Nantucket."

"Why thank you. Seems I missed the reception."

"Well, we all lined up in front of the Steamship landing, but you must have come in on the Hy-Line."

"Damn. Sorry to disappoint everyone."

"That's okay. We can try it again tomorrow if you don't mind comin' in again. So where are you from?"

"Somewhere that way," he said, pointing westward.

"Oh yeah, me too."

"Small world."

"Yup."

Dave looked to be in his late thirties: rough-edged, a drifter, a contemporary troubadour in the true spirit of the word. The sense of emancipation that infused him was a bit unsettling even to me. I'm sure to the tourists he looked like a bum.

"How long you here for?"

"As long as the change keeps droppin'."

"Where are you stayin'?"

"Where ever I set this down," he said, indicating his sleeping bag.

"I gotta run. You gonna be here tomorrow?"

"I'll be here. Or somewhere."

I dropped a dollar in his hat. "See you tomorrow."

"Thanks."

"What's your dog's name?"

"Dog."

"Not very original."

"Neither is he."

As I left he started to smoke a corncob pipe. Walking down Main Street I listened to the clatter of tires hitting cobblestones, the horns of vacation cars fighting for the right of way, the shrill laughter of affluent shoppers, the radios of kids—all clamoring in a wave of commerce and gratification. The island needed a good rain to dull this pink tenor. Dave sat strumming on his green bench, oblivious to the stores and sales and bargains, an unwitting first citizen of Nantucket: stationary in the hub of a wheel spinning away from itself.

Part II

Sharp knives, of course, are *the* secret
of a successful restaurant.

—George Orwell

12

The harbor at rest, boats spinning above yawning lobster traps. An absence of light across the island; gulls stabbing moors of darkness. The tide pulls away from the sinking boats; sleepers dream below the water, warm in the womb of their hulls. The island rocks itself asleep. Somewhere beyond the clangor of buoys a continent rumbles.

"Hey Larry."
"Yeah."
"What the fuck am I doing here?"
"Where?"
"This fucking island."
"How 'bout another one?"
"Another what?"
"Cold-boy."
"Sure. So am I wasting my life?"
"You tell me."
"Come on."
"Where?"
"That was the last question."
"Who's on first?"
"How many have you had tonight?"
"One too few. Pass me the bag."

Glass shattered below us. "Don't throw the bottles off the side."

"Why not?"

"Cause you might hit one of those little plastic kids that look so nice running around the houses."

"Oh." A minute passed.

"When are you going?"

"To bed?"

"Back to America."

"Oh Christ, I dunno. I gotta figure out if I'm going back to school. How 'bout you?"

"I guess when my life starts. But I don't know if that'll be in the fall."

"What were you doin' before you came here?" Larry laid flat on the deck, placing his head on the rolled-up paper bag.

"I had a job in New York."

"Oh yeah—doing what?"

"Sales. I was a stockbroker, or at least tried to be."

"Make any money?"

"Some. But you never make enough once you don't have a ceiling. That's why sales stinks: you're never happy, no matter how much you make. Cause there's always someone making more, and that's the standard they set for you. Even when you make your bogey, they ask you for one more sale. It's an existential crisis. When I realized that, I bailed out."

"And became a dishwasher."

"At least I don't have to wear a suit everyday."

"Just an apron and those silly whites."

"Well, I always thought I looked good in white. Except I stunk in science, so an MD was out of the question."

"You do look cute in white."

"Go to hell."

"You're welcome."

Larry closed his eyes. I opened the last beer and sailed the cap over the deck toward the sea. To my disappointment, it made no sound. The wounded sky had bled itself to death. I looked at our house. The sundial's gnomon—because of the streetlamp beside the deck—absurdly signaled four o'clock, off by about six hours. I thought of making a joke about how we could rig the sundial to work at night, but Larry looked half-asleep, and the beer had washed all the animation out of me.

I heard someone walking on the street below us. A woman sashayed through the shadows. Footsteps hit the wooden stairs. Alex appeared, walking toward us, most of her hair pulled back except for a swatch which spilled beside her eye. She wore ripped jeans and a loose-fitting white shirt, probably Steve's. The sleeves had been cut off. She stood over me, expressionless.

"You've been avoiding me."

"I was just telling him that," commented Larry, whom she hadn't noticed in the darkness behind me.

"Alex, do you know Larry, my roommate?"

"Hi," she said. Larry waved his foot at her.

"You wanna beer?" he asked her.

"None left," I answered.

"Oh well. How 'bout a beer bottle? They make nice flower vases."

"You threw them all over the side."

"Sorry. Try us tomorrow. We're bound to be restocked by noon."

"That's okay," she said.

I rolled my eyes toward Larry. Alex smiled. He hadn't moved. "Here, you can have mine. Hey buddy, why don't I help you into bed?"

"Okay. I can take a hint. I can tell when I'm not wanted." Larry struggled to rise, but a wave of inebriation knocked him back each time he tried to get up. Finally, after laughing with Alex, I helped him onto his feet. "You shouldn't make me drink so much Guy. It's not good for my self-image. I'm starting to feel that people think I'm a drunk."

"No way—where'd you ever get that idea? Everyone I know says you can hold your liquor as well as any thirteen-year-old Italian girl."

"Thanks."

"Hey, have you ever been to an Italian wedding? Those little girls can drink. Right Alex?"

"*Si.*"

I led Larry to the door. He pointed at the sundial. "The little hand is moving, Guy."

"You think so?"

"Yup. I can see it."

"There is no little hand."

"Then what's that moving?"

"You're imagination."

"I knew it was something. 'Night Alex. By the way, she's cute." I took Larry in and set him on his bed.

I could see Alex through the window standing with her arms folded over her chest, so I grabbed a cotton blanket. Her back pressed against the white railing, her behind a smooth, firm ball wrapped in denim. I had an atavistic urge to squeeze her ass, to wrap my arms around her and grind her against the railing, but instead I calmly walked beside her and asked if she was chilly.

"A little."

"Here. I brought this for you." I placed the blanket around her shoulders. "How have you been?"

"Miserable."

"Why?"

"I can't stand living with Steve."

"But I thought you guys were doing great together."

"We were. But it's tough living with someone. It's not like going out. There's so much more to it. You see everything. The way they do things. Their personal habits. Their emotional shit. I dunno. It seemed like such a good idea living here this summer on the island. It sounded romantic and free. But it's not."

"Well, it could have been worse."

"How?"

"You could have roomed with Larry."

"Fuck you, I'm serious."

"I'm sorry. Do you want some coffee or something?"

"No. I want to take a walk. I was just on my way down to the beach, but something made me come up here."

Obviously not my famous java, I thought to myself.

We sat on the swing set that stood at the entrance to the beach. The sea wallowed in purple heaves below the crest of sand. Clouds covered part of the sky, but the moon shone clearly. I pushed Alex's swing. The beach glowed with silver luminescence; waves churned in the distance like the static of a radio in an abandoned room. Alex's hair flew behind her with each swing; she swung out, taut legs pointing seaward; then returned, legs tucked under her, triceps contracting with the metallic squeal of chains.

When she came back this time I held her and didn't let her go. She let her head fall back and looked at me. We eased forward slowly to release the energy of the swing. I held her face in my hands as if peering into a deep well. As her arms circled my body her neck arched upwards, the chin an arrow aimed right at me. The blanket fell off her shoulder. I placed my tongue on the exposed skin. Salt and the taste of her sex; kindling. Her body undulated against the stationary force of the swing. I lost myself in her hair.

"It's so beautiful out here. So quiet. I'm glad we lived here before Sconset gets overrun by tourists."

"We are blessed," I breathed into her ear. I paused a while before asking, "So what are you going to do about Steve?"

"Nothing for now, I guess. What can I do? The lease is in his name."

"Sounds like a typical New York City relationship."

"He took the last ferry to Hyannis—he'll be there for a few days. Come over tonight. I can't stand sleeping alone in that place with all those cold books. They look like bricks; I feel like I'm living in a bomb shelter."

"We all are, here."

Alex is painting when I awaken. The room is seasoned with the odor of watercolors and musk of sex. Music is barely discernible through the dust glowing in the sunlight: a chorus of birds singing in all directions. I hesitate to move, not wanting to disturb the current of particles above me. Someone once told me that dust is composed of epidermal cells, a fact I find hard to believe ontologically, having always thought of dust as a self-propagating moral affliction suffered by those guilty of untidiness.

She is unaware that I am watching her. I relish the opportunity to observe Alex in this way. Before her are a set of paints, brushes, and thick sheets of paper. I want to tell her to stop as she applies a few smears of water to the paper—that she is finished, that the beauty of those translucent stains is insuperable —but I don't; I watch. She dabs soft tones of yellow, green, and blue, building them up; they meld like hot wax into a soft riot, then begin to evaporate into the air, the dust.

"I like that."

"I didn't know you were awake."

"Are watercolors hard to do?"

"They are for me. It depends if you're the kind of person who likes to plan things. I prefer oils."

She sits on the floor in that uniquely feminine manner, with one leg drawn under her, and the other straight out. I reach forward and rub her back. She leans toward my hand; her hair brushes my fingers.

"How do you feel?"

"A little stiff . . . but wonderful." I massage her shoulders. "That feels great. You have soft hands."

"Hands of experience. The hands of a dishwasher. The filthy tales they could tell."

The room is bursting with sunlight and contentment. Morning on the island. If only it lasted all day! How invigorating not to wake up with the alcoholic rhythm of Larry's breathing and the concurrent sense of regression. There is progress in Alex's brushstrokes, a feeling of creation—evolution. An aesthetic of existence: crushing the fear of looking back from old age and regretting the past. That should be one's challenge. To hell with the old way of life! To hell with the futility of self-actualization through employment.

I pull Alex through the dust into bed.

13

A week after my encounter with Patty I bought her motorcycle, a tough little Honda 300—not a powerful bike but fast enough to pass the cars that race down Sconset Road, the fastest strip on the island (and the most dangerous). The bike could do seventy easily, and the feeling of letting the engine open wide—the great throbbing wind smashing your face—engendered a sort of mad serenity, for at the center of this roaring constellation of gas, oil, and steel was a quiet sense of agility and control. "Control is the mother of speed," Dr. Wu, my old Tai Chi teacher used to tell us. "Speed is not blind fury. Without control it is useless, futile."

Larry and I had had a tough night on the dish line. Joy, the senile hostess, kept seating customers for a half hour after the close before Buff realized what she was doing and stopped her. I could hear him reprimanding her softly near the kitchen door. She responded, "But they looked so hungry."

"Then send them to the Sea Shanty and let them get a greasy hamburger. We have to close!"

We were an hour late breaking down the line and scrubbing the rubber mats. By the time we had finished we were sloshing through four inches of water—a flotsam of mussel shells and lettuce leaves, lobster claws and fish bones. Larry's pants were wet up to his thighs; mine were just as bad. He looked down at his dark, soggy sneakers, "We gotta get some rubber boots. Hell, fishing waders."

"Yeah, then we gotta get decent jobs. This is the pits."

"That old bitch seating people after closing. I had half the fuckin' pots scrubbed."

"Why doesn't the old man fire her? She probably scares away more business than she seats."

"No shit. But she's worked here forever. She probably drove the Indians off the island."

We ascended to the upstairs bathroom for what we called the "Purification Ritual," the almost futile attempt to wash off the grease and smells of the kitchen, and look presentable. Basically, we stripped to our underwear and bathed in the little sink. Once in a while a late patron from the bar would enter and take us for homosexuals. Larry liked to play-up these instances as much as possible. "Oh baby, it itches and I can't reach it," he would say, "You know what to do." Then he would smile at our new friend.

After doing our best to clean up we went over to the Easy Street Cafe for a drink. The Lobster Trap staff usually gathered for a post-shift drink at our own bar, but Larry and I preferred to get away from them as soon as possible. It's no fun having a drink with a group of people that smell just as bad as you do.

The amber glow through Easy Street's windows beckoned like a warm fire. A good crowd had gathered around the bar: workers like ourselves, just off their shifts and ready to unwind. The joint is all wood inside; beams crisscross the high ceiling giving the place the cozy feeling of a ski lodge. Maybe that's why I always feel that it's chilly outside when I'm in Easy Street. The wind is stiff where it sits on the edge of Steamship Wharf, and there's nothing beyond the place but an empty parking lot, and then the black water. A parking lot for the abyss: leave your car and take the plunge. But before you go, have your last drink at Easy Street. Jim the bartender will make it a stiff one, and if you say nice things about the Red Sox, he'll lay down a dark rum floater for free. Come to Easy Street, it's not hard to find—at the end of the road that ends in the water. . . .

We surveyed the room as we entered. All the tables were

empty except for one which held a somber young couple: tourists, though not New Englanders, judging from their clothes. Someone was playing darts to the left of the door. A bunch of attractive women were at the far end of the bar, so we headed over. One was the cute hostess from the White Dog Cafe, named Millie. Jim greeted us.

"All right boys, what'll it be?"

"The usual for me." I looked at Larry. "What'a you want?"

"Beer."

"A beer for the chief pot scrubber."

"Thanks. Let's not try to impress these women too much."

"Yeah. But wait till they see your yacht."

"As soon as I get two oars."

After a few minutes I managed to catch Millie's eye and I said hello. She remembered me vaguely; I had made a habit of stopping by every week to chat about whatever movie was playing at the White Dog—it was a restaurant with a movie theatre —but we had never really exchanged any personal information.

"What's playing next week?"

"Something, The Wrath of God. It's by that German director, Werner what's-his-name. Supposed to be real artsy."

"Well, I'll have to catch that." I noticed that her glass was empty. "Jimbo, why don't you fix up young Millie here. What're you drinking?"

"Sea Breeze."

"Very appropriate, very sensible." Larry walked over with his drink. "Do you know this guy?"

"No."

"You should."

"Oh yeah, why?"

"Do you send a lot of mail?"

"Sometimes."

"Well, his picture is hanging in the post office."

"Very funny."

"My name's Larry."

"Millie."

"Thanks Larry, that'll be all. You can finish buffing the Porsche. . . ."

"Are you always this friendly to your friend?"

"No, I'm even nicer on his day off."

A bunch of people entered the restaurant. "Hey Lar, look who's here. It's Derrick."

"Haven't seen him in a while." The group approached the bar, a mix of summer guys and gals.

"Hey Derrick, what's up?"

"Not much man; with you?"

Derrick was an ersatz eccentric: he wore mod shirts with what looked like his grandpa's trousers, and clunky old wingtip shoes. He usually sported a bright purple bandanna and kept his long brown hair in a ponytail. His features were unusually triangular: the nose and chin looked like two pyramids on top of each other joined at their bases. For some reason, his olive complexion muted the severity of his features, making him oddly attractive, or at least singular—until he spoke: the droll affectation of his accent destroyed the believability of his facade.

I inhaled several gulps of my drink. Millie's face glowed incandescently. I realized how young and pure she was, and how she symbolized all the young people on the island. What a perfect colony this place would make, what an excellent model of tranquility for the world. You never thought about war here, or other such tragedies. For Nantucketers have a way of withdrawing from the world's problems rather than being washed away by them. The Nantucketer has his job and his house, and between them lies a bar and a church at which he can stop. But most of all he has the sea surrounding him at all times, punctuating his movements, casting his horizons, spinning him back to the center like the wind through a pinwheel, like the cries of the gulls circling the shores. So many pure faces, so many perfect triangles, unmarked by the creeping debauch of age, of experience, and the winds of societal rhetoric. The worst thing we do to ourselves is to abandon the one act we perform perfectly: being young.

Several drinks later Millie's brown knees are clutching my sides as I drive her home to Shimmo on the motorcycle. She is light and feels more like a pillow behind me than a human being; she holds my waist tentatively at first, but after a few jolts from the cobblestones her arms encircle me firmly. I have only one helmet and make her wear it. Looking back at her head encased in white plastic, I feel like I'm giving a ride to a spacegirl.

I take the rotary curve at a lean angle, compressing the distance between the cycle and the concrete. We flow toward our destination as if on water. Millie lives in the lap of the island, a relatively uncongested area between Wauwinet and town. Many of the houses we pass are new, their shiny oak beams gawking over the cup of the harbor like well-dressed arrivistes. We are unable to speak through the river of wind and the roar of the engine, so Millie guides me by pointing: left, right, right; the beam slicing through a primeval darkness. No streetlights, no reflectors—save for the occasional mailbox—no signs; here among the high hedges and woods we could be reeling through the fog of any age.

After dropping Millie off I take the Polpis Road home, wanting to enjoy the sweeping curves along that route, instead of the hurtling forward pitch of Sconset Road. Banking into bend after bend, massaged by the forces of counter-inertia, feeling the ponds pass by in chill pockets of dank air, the metallic hum of the marshes, an occasional set of glowing eyes at ground level—the air so dark that the road could fall away and it would still support me—I course through this artery of darkness: an unheard scream of light, gas, and metal, fading into the misty blanket of crickets, cicadas, and whatever else is left in the wake of our passing. . . .

14

In my dreams I stack monkey dishes. I stand in a white room with white shelves surrounded by the little monsters. I dream of monkey dishes the way bricklayers dream of bricks, or firemen —fires. They are my livelihood. Washing them is what I do every day, every week. The line cooks do not call me by name; they scream out "monkey dishes!" and I find myself moving toward them like Willie Mays hearing the crack of a bat. I can scoop a stack of them off the shelf—a good forty or fifty—and have them on the line in a couple of seconds. That is a long time in the restaurant business, time enough for an entrée to burn, a customer to walk out, or a cook to throw a knife at you. For we are regulated by the most sensitive clock of all: the stomach. And nothing hates to be kept waiting more than a stomach.

Tonight was a typical night at the Lobster Trap, or the "Tourist Trap" as we lovingly referred to it. Jason, Tony, and Tim were on the line above me doing their prep work. I was trying to finish the overload of lunch dishes; one of the morning dish guys had called in sick, and we had served an inordinately large number of meals—over 170 according to Buff. I broke down the bus trays with practical efficiency: silverware in the stand-up bins; plates, cups, and glasses in their respective racks; food and trash in the garbage can; and anything that didn't sail into one of these receptacles ended up on the floor. I moved in a coordinated flurry, hands grasping, directing, and releasing objects; utilizing inertia: pick up plate turn shovel trash in can while tossing knife in bin spin toward rack aiming plate letting go other hand on next plate one two three four wipe tray next one. Soon I become an automaton without thought, a man-made machine existing only to clean that which is placed before me. The lower orders of the brain take over. Reaching in eight directions at once, I am an octopus.

One must trick himself not to be repulsed by the dullness of such routines. One must believe he is working toward a greater end. My greatest end is a beer at one A.M. I therefore decided to exploit the aesthetics of dishwashing, to find and revel in its poetry. Otherwise I would be doomed by the absurdity of my situation. A college-educated, Wall Street dropout plate scrubber. I could try to fool myself and others with such euphemisms as kitchen assistant, or I could use the French term *plongeur*, as Orwell did, but I would still just be an ordinary dishwasher; in other words, a failure. A soft voice inside me recalled the words of Martin Luther King, Jr.: "If a man is called to be a streetsweeper, he should sweep streets even as Michelangelo painted, or Beethoven composed music, or Shakespeare wrote poetry. He should sweep streets so well that all the hosts of heaven and earth will pause to say, here lived a great streetsweeper who did his job well."

But no one on the island cared about such posturing. I would only have to rationalize my situation to those on the continent. Because those on Nantucket were in the same boat: none of us had jobs that made sense to the rest of America. Why would anyone come to this godforsaken place and work in a menial position? No one else would understand the sense of community we have, the unspoken level of support, or the fact that all the backdoors of our restaurants connected through one great tunnel of understanding like the Maginot Line; we could duck into any one any time and get a free meal or drink; no one was down on their luck here because you couldn't fall any further: in essence, we were walking on the safety net every day of our lives here, while above us gulls flew in the trapeze breeze.

"Hey Guy, I need you to cut some lemons."

"Sorry Tim."

"Guy! Here. Cut these lemons."

"I can't Tim, I'm backed up." The lemons sat on the edge of the dish station, still tingling with Tim's anxiety. I continued loading plate racks and feeding them through the dishwasher. Mark stood at the end of the machine, catching, or unloading, the racks as they came out, and stacking the clean dishes. Three minutes later Tim looked down from his position on the line.

"Guy! What's the problem? I thought I asked you to cut those lemons."

"Look Tim. These dishes are backed up for miles. I gotta get them washed for dinner, or we won't have any dishes to serve on. You do your job and I'll do mine. Otherwise the whole process breaks down." Tim stomped down the three steps from the platform and stood right in front of me on the other side of the counter.

"Listen! You're a dishwasher and I'm a cook. You do what I say!"

I looked at him with the seriousness of an unsheathed knife. "I can't do your job; my job comes first." Just then Nat the busboy brought in a tray bursting with dishes and glasses. Tim had to dance out of the way. He grabbed the lemons and grumbled back to his station, not talking to me for the rest of the shift. I worried that he might try to get Buff to fire me. Instead, he never bothered me again with his prep work and, in fact, treated me with a higher level of respect thereafter.

I had noticed over the past week or two that Larry had been disappearing for short spells during our shifts. Usually I was too busy to think much about it. I figured he was in the bathroom, or sneaking a phone call to some girl to make a date later in the evening. We were very busy this particular night and the cooks had us running to the walk-in cooler to bring supplies to the line—heads of lettuce, vegetables, lobsters, butter, and so forth. Jason called for some milk, and I looked behind me for Larry but he wasn't at the pot scrubber's station. Perturbed, I went to the walk-in myself, opened the door, and there was Larry, sitting on a white bucket of coleslaw, frozen in mid-bite of what looked to be an entire lobster claw, dripping with blue cheese dressing.

"What the fuck are you doing?"

"Shh, close the door."

"They need milk."

"Here," he said, handing me a carton.

We always kept a large container of lobster claw and tail meat in the walk-in for lobster salad, and evidently it was too much for Larry, a native New Englander, to ignore. He looked like a cat found devouring a mouse, ready to fight to protect his catch.

"So this is where you've been hiding out."

"I like to have a little snack from time to time." He picked out a big chunk of lobster tail and, with practiced ease, swabbed it in the open tub of blue cheese dressing, then popped it in his mouth. "Keeps my strength up."

"If Buff caught you he'd fire you on the spot."

"Ah, what's a little lobster meat? Here, try one."

I ate the small claw he handed me. "Not bad."

"It's really good with this stuff," he said, pointing to the dressing. Through the door I heard Jason yell for the milk.

"All right—let's go. We're really getting backed up."

The main reason we were happy to fetch things for the cooks was the chance it gave us to grab a handful of the french fries that sat in a large baking tray by the fry station. The cooks kept a batch of those fat juicy fries at the ready so they'd never have to hold up an order if the fry cook screwed up. We considered it a point of honor, actually our duty, to nab as many fries as we could each time we passed, as if we were assessing a toll in retribution for our menial chores. The cooks begrudgingly let us have our way, but occasionally Jason, and only Jason, would yell at us if the supply of fries got too low. We just ignored him, clutching our fries with hands covered in soap, grease, or whatever mucilaginous substance we had been touching. We didn't care. After seeing the filthy state of the kitchen and the dishes we served food on, we figured human beings could eat anything.

Spindrift

Larry and I worked very well together. We didn't take our jobs seriously like the other employees. After the first few weeks, having mastered the efficiency of our tasks, our chief aim became to do whatever we could to make each other laugh. We invented nicknames for all the staff, made up songs about the kitchen to the pop tunes on the radio, and flirted with the waitresses, but most of all we enjoyed making fun of Joy, the senile hostess, who made our lives miserable by her inept handling of the guest seating. She inevitably seated customers before we opened and after we closed, and would often load up one waitress's section to the exclusion of another. All of this caused havoc in the kitchen: order overloads, mistakes, unnecessary rushes, stress, and flaring tempers. Of course, everything in the end flowed down to the dish station, like the vomit gutters in Roman arenas. After the cooks had gone, after the waitresses had added up their checks, we would still be slogging through the backlog of dishes: two convicts trying to dig out of an inexorable tunnel of mud in a rainstorm; each rack of dishes run through the machine seemed only to make room for another dirty tray.

And of course, there was the inexplicable irony of her name which appeared too unkind for God to have predetermined. This must be some cruel hoax, we thought, having to suffer the constant reminder that the cause of our misfortune was an old coot named Joy.

But that was a small price to pay for all the fun we had on the job. Looking back I remember the problems less and less. Plus, we were able to get even with her on occasion, although the fact that she probably wasn't aware of it dampened the exhilaration of our revenge somewhat. For instance, one time during a particularly heavy shift Larry snuck out the back and called her from a payphone, pretending to be the leader of a large tour group, and reserved an entire section of tables. When the fictitious party never showed up Joy was perplexed, but Larry had saved us an extra hour's work that night. I later bought him a beer and bragged of his genius to our friends in Easy Street.

The night dragged on like a band that only knows one tune. Nat kept bringing in loaded trays, teasing us that Joy had just seated another table of eight. The cooks had already broken down their line and left. We were one dishwasher short. Undisturbed, Larry and I sped up the process. I went to the pot station with the water gun, and he set up the racks of dirty dishes, pushed them through the dish machine, then caught them at the other end. Normally that job took two people, one at each end of the machine. But we were fast. As soon as he pushed one rack into the machine he would run to the back and unload the one that popped out, like a tennis player playing both sides of the net against himself. Meanwhile, I furiously scrubbed the burnt pots with steel wool and the powerful water gun. The gun was attached to a hose that stretched across the kitchen. Normally, it stayed by the dishwasher, to blast the crap off the racked dishes before they went into the machine. Since I had it on the other side of the kitchen, Larry would yell "grease" every time he had set up a rack and I would turn like the Sundance Kid and spray from across the room. Naturally, the gun's accuracy wasn't good at that distance, so water went everywhere. But we saved the precious time it would have taken to walk the gun over repeatedly.

We worked intensely. Pots flew. Dishes sailed. Silverware shot through the air like arrows. By midnight we weren't talking; we couldn't waste the energy. Our movements vibrated in synch with the dishwasher. Larry would yell "grease," I would turn without looking and shoot the gun at the rack, which was always in the same place. We were going so fast this happened every two minutes. "Grease!" Turn. Fire. Sometimes a particularly bad plate would need special attention. Larry would hold it at arm's length and I would zap it. Water splashed all over him until he was completely soaked.

Finally around twelve-thirty Larry announced that we were on our last tray. I whooped ecstatically. He yelled "grease." I turned and fired. There was no rack, just Joy standing stunned behind the counter, looking like she had been in a rainstorm. Larry was crouched under the dishwasher, laughing hysterically.

Later, after Buff left the dishroom having just balled us out, I looked at Larry.

"You're crazy."

"I just couldn't resist."

"It was pretty good. The look on her face: I'll never forget that." The back door opened, and a guy wearing a Nantucket Red cap walked in.

"How's it going?" he asked.

"Not bad," I replied.

"Thought you could use these." He handed us each a cold beer.

"Hey, thanks. What's your name?"

"Brook."

And as suddenly as he appeared, he left. Larry looked at me, smiling. "What a night, man."

"Heaven."

15

An overcast Tuesday. A perfect day for riding. Whenever the dull pain of my mortality would rub through my body, I'd visit the old Quaker graveyard and watch the tombstones settling on the grass. I did not walk among the graves because I felt it would be a violation.

Not many people ever came here; those who stopped were usually on their way somewhere else. It is comforting to visit graveyards: they are monuments to life; only by looking at the markers of so many finished lives can one feel the full pulse and pull of his own.

A field of frail shoulders, deckled by centuries of wind, honed bone-white against the noonday sun.

It is amazing that so many horizons, the enormity of their overlapping skies, could be stuffed into these tight boxes of damp earth, crushed under wooden lids, and patted smooth by the dark faces of iron shovels. I listened to the silence like a haunting prelude to the somber music beneath the ground: the distant timbal of a finale, buried under the brass sky in a scherzo of sunlight.

Not wanting to disturb those at rest I walked the motorcycle to the end of the graveyard before starting the engine. A car slowed and the driver asked if I had mechanical trouble. I thanked him and waved him on. Then I drove into town and stopped for a coffee at Ted's ice cream shop.

"What's with the black armband?" I asked him. He pointed to a newspaper clipping taped to the refrigerator. A full-page headline declared: "Bob Marley, Reggae Music Legend, Is Dead." He had the stereo playing louder than usual, and I heard the words:

Rise up, rise up, rise and take your stance again

Ted swayed behind the counter, eyes closed. I reached over and poured a cup of coffee. The somber song ended, followed by a happy, upbeat number. Ted opened his eyes.

"We're playing nothing but Marley from now on this summer."

"Good. How's business?" I yelled over the music.

"Fine. I got a coupla young girls running the place on afternoons. Allows me to catch the prime beach time."

"Wouldn't want your work to get in the way."

"Nope."

Tourists drifted by the window: serious folks, intent on renting mopeds, or buying T-shirts, or eating a vacation meal. A young family walked in. Immediately the two kids began clamoring for attention. They looked up at their parents with the faces of starving Third-World children, straining for eye contact—necks locked into this position like hung men.

Ted served them but did not turn down the music. The young couple noticed this, and spoke in loud voices to indicate their annoyance, but Ted was not moved. He rocked with the beat behind the counter, a kinetic assemblage of colors—red and white striped shirt, green bandanna rolled into a headband around his kinky brown hair (which he was trying to turn into dreadlocks), Union Jack shorts, and purple tennis shoes. The ice cream had placated the children, so the family left. Ted changed the tape to a live recording. Through the sound of clapping he intoned, "I hate tourists."

"Well, the Nantucket Merchant's Association appreciates your warm service." He smiled.

"No, not all tourists. Just the parents and their spoiled tots. The kids who come to work here for the summer, they're cool. They own the island."

Two grandmothers walked by examining the Nantucket T-shirts they had just purchased, which portrayed lobsters doing silly things, like cooking people for dinner.

"We have become a giant T-shirt factory."

"Yup," I replied. "They just put up another T-shop on Water Street. So fuckin' ugly."

"It kills me. They come for an afternoon, buy a T-shirt to prove they were here, then leave. And they don't see a god-damn thing but the inside of a coupla stores. . . ."

"And the Lobster Trap."

"Exactly. These day-trippers will be the death of this place." Marley sang, "Lively up yourself" in a knotty tenor, but with a child's exuberance.

"So Guy, are you ready to take the big plunge?"

"What plunge?"

"Off the top deck of the Steamship."

"The Steamship? Why?"

"Haven't you heard about this yet? We've been planning it all week."

"No one told me about jumping off the ferry. That'd be suicide."

"No it wouldn't. I've dove off higher places when I was a kid."

"So why are you jumping?"

"To make a statement."

"What statement?"

"The statement of the year. The island's statement. It's time we did something here to leave our mark. I'm not much of a writer, or a painter, so I've been trying to think what I could do. Besides, all the novels written here suck, and the little pink beach paintings make me puke. I mean, can you stand looking at another lighthouse or a sea gull pastel? Ugh. 'Nantucket, the Faraway Island!' Who cares. That's for people who think buying a Renoir poster shows their appreciation of art. I'm talking about an artistic *act*, something tied to the core of the island, that no one's ever done, or dreamed of doing. Something that will shock people a little bit." Ted's hands shaped the air as he spoke.

"So what does that prove."

"Exactly. It proves nothing, which is the point. There's no commercial gain, no warning, just a splash. Think about it. All those stupid tourists on the top deck, feeding the gulls, snapping pictures. Then we all walk over to the railing, climb up, genuflect, then leap. They'll flip out. It'll be a blast."

"Who all's in on this?"

"Besides me, Penman from the AC, and Breland—a buddy of mine. Benny's thinking about it. Depends what time we jump. You in?"

"I dunno. I'll have to think about it.

"We're jumping Saturday, so think fast."

Later in the afternoon I'm peeping through the window of Tammy's store, trying to catch her eye. She's dressed in a short skirt and a loose tank top, and although I can't see her breasts, the gap between her shirt and skin—which is visible every time she raises her arms—accelerates my pulse. I wait until her boss goes into the back before I enter quietly and stand behind her as she folds a sweater. I try not to make a sound, but scream "I want you!" psychically to see if she feels my presence. Her movements slow and she turns.

"So it's you," she sighs with a slanted glance. I give her a quick, deep kiss, causing her eyes to widen.

"Don't worry, the coast is clear."

"What are you doing here?"

"I need a sweater for my horse."

"Your horse. Very funny."

"Yeah, he's parked out front. I think he'd look good in something heather, like this."

"That's teal."

"Oh. Well, he's color-blind. He won't care."

"I see."

"Hey, how about lunch? Do they let you out of this place ever?"

We grabbed a couple of sandwiches at the Natural Food Store and went to the park behind the library. Although set in the absolute center of town, few tourists used the park because it was hidden behind tall hedges. But the bums and summer kids knew about it. The bricks below the benches were stained from the thousands of lunches that had been eaten here before. A bee flew around us as we chewed on our sandwiches.

I heard the gate swing open. Dave the street musician came toward us. I said, "Hey buddy."

"You know him?"

"I know all the important people." Dave sat on the bench across from us. He carried all his belongings—backpack, sleeping bag, and guitar. His dog walked lugubriously behind him. After Dave sat down the dog immediately curled around his feet and slept.

"What a nice day for lunch alfresco."

"Dave, this is my friend, Tammy."

"You're a very beautiful woman, Tammy."

Tammy laughed.

"How 'bout a little 'Scotch and Soda' for Tammy?"

"I think my voice is in tune. If not, I'll have to get some new underwear. These feel a little tight," he said, squirming in his seat.

We spent the rest of Tammy's lunch-hour with Dave, calling out requests and singing along. The wind filtered through the trees surrounding us as he played old songs. I slipped my arm around Tammy while Dave held both of us with his voice, his somber eyes suggesting that all of his unhappiness could be forgotten as long as we kept listening.

16

It is always saddest to awaken on the guillotine of evening, that awful hour separating night from dawn, when birds sing to the black sky in mad anticipation of sunlight, and the wind rises to reinforce the night's chill; I find this the most depressing hour because it seems unholy to wake during this creeping darkness, rather than in the warm embrace of first light, falling like the hair of God across the world.

I walk onto the deck. The sky is blacker than I have ever seen it. Vainly I search for traces of blue. The treble of the wind is horrifyingly sharp. No cars, no human sounds. Just the abyss of the ocean. I wonder what people are doing across the sea in Spain right now. They would be basking in sunlight. Somewhere out there the water is changing color. The warm winds must be on their way. At least I will see the sun before everyone I know in Ohio, I console myself, as I make my way back to bed.

Dawn arrives in its own good time, reluctant—the sensual awakening of a woman. The sun rises like a man once it appears: hard, fast, cocky.

The days are embossed with the sheen of peppermint light, sailing one into another, a flurry of white wings beating stroke by stroke, wave by wave, until one can no longer be distinguished from the next.

Tammy and I saw more of each other as June faded into the long days of July. I fell in love with her as I had with Nantucket, with the wind, with coffee on the deck, and with my motorcycle. But she italicized my existence in a way the other things I loved did not.

I saw in her a kind of purity that I never had, a background different from mine; she came from a big loving family with many brothers and sisters and pets. The children came and went from home like birds to a nest, but there was always that warm nucleus ready to embrace them, a net to catch them, a wide base of support which any member of the family could plug into as if they were working an old telephone switchboard.

I had been raised an only child by an aunt after my parents died in a car crash; I was nine at the time. My aunt had been loving but I knew growing up that I was different from all the other children. I stood back and watched them because I felt I was above their adolescent march toward adulthood. My grief at the time of my parent's death had advanced me beyond the stage of their emotional evolution, I thought. True, the pain of death had made me more mature in many ways. But my loathing of adolescent rites of passage was really based in fear, not maturity. I did not want to face the painful emotional consequences of asking girls out, of being in popular groups, of competing in the social games common to every secondary school. So I grew up independent, introspective, a loner. It wasn't until my senior year of high school that these became admirable qualities. Many of my intellectual and artistic peers respected my individuality and non-conformity. But that had been a long bridge to cross, exacting a heavy psychological toll. I didn't cry for ten years after my parents died.

One day in college I was watching the summer Olympics alone in the dorm TV room. The women's marathon had just ended, the first four runners having crossed the finish line in the huge Olympic stadium, which looked bigger than any arena I had ever seen. Hundreds of thousands of people cheered in the stands, and millions were viewing from around the world. I felt like one small electric socket plugged into an immense wall of eyes, the size of a planet, watching the event. Then, as if an afterthought, the camera caught sight of a lone runner entering the stadium to complete her last lap and finish fifth. As the camera closed in it appeared that something was terribly wrong with this runner. She wasn't running straight but in wild zigzags, and her arms flailed about her contorting body. She bent so far forward as she ran that she almost hit the ground several times. The final lap that the other runners had completed in a quick dash of long-limbed strides was lengthening into what seemed like a torturous mountain climb for her. Her teammates rushed to the edge of the track to coach her on, but they were not allowed to help her physically in any way—the commentator pointed out—or she would be disqualified. He speculated that she was suffering from heat stroke, and that judging from the severity of her condition, she could damage her brain if her body temperature remained so perilously high. But the runner would not quit. Her teammates could not help her. Her lap dragged on in an agony of minutes. Several runners entered the stadium and passed her. Still she ran, disoriented, toward the finish line. Then it happened: a well had been unearthed inside me. I felt the crank turning in my head, and up very fast came an outpouring of tears that I could not stop or control.

In Tammy I had found my warm embrace. The vicarious acceptance of a large, loving family. But underlying all of this, she was meltingly beautiful: she had struck that archetypal chord in me which waits to resonate in all of us. I looked at her and saw the best moments of my youth magnified: the game winning Little League homerun, the thrill of a first crush, the first glimpse of a girl's naked body. The sun glowed through her blond hair.

Alex had grown more bitter with Steve and with me. And as I became more attached to Tammy I lost my physical attraction to Alex. Eventually I became her unenthusiastic confessor. The last time we made love we ended up banging our bodies together more out of animosity than pleasure. It was a wild fuck, but empty. We went from the bed onto the floor to the other end of the room, scattering Steve's books in all directions, like a demolition crew. I think that gave her the greatest satisfaction that day.

I see Alex painting on the beach now and then, but I keep my distance. I just don't have any desire to watch her pave the sky with dark bricks.

17

After an especially hard day on the dish line I went to the public rest room to clean up. There were too many customers in the restaurant for me to do much more than wash my hands. The late afternoon sun had died behind a gray sheath of clouds, and it looked like it might rain any minute. I had nothing to do: Tammy was off the island on a buying trip with her boss, and Larry was working the late shift. I wandered up Main Street looking for someone to pass the time with; I didn't want to ride the bike and get caught in a storm.

The shops were doing good business; bad weather drives the tourists off the beaches and into town, and all of those credit cards get itchy in their pockets. I walked to the north part of Main Street where Dave usually played, but his favorite bench sat empty. Having nothing better to do I went into Congdon's Pharmacy.

Congdon's is the best deal in town. For two bucks you can have anything on the menu, and it will fill you up, too. You can sit on an old-fashioned swivel stool and watch the kids behind the counter make sandwiches and mix shakes on the chrome soda fountain. The sunlight that filters through the storefront is always mellow, the kind of light a lazy dog would love to wallow in.

The people sitting at the counter are invariably friendly. They talk to each other in a way you'd never see at most of the island's regular restaurants. Someone asks me what type of film they should use on the beach and I tell them. Others compare suntan lotions. The counter workers talk about their college plans. I advise them to make the most of their time on the island. "You'll never have another chance like this. There's nothing more interesting at Princeton than here. A Nantucket diploma is priceless." The kids—a guy and a girl—look at me and nod, not sure what to make of my advice. I order a coffee and watch the counter empty.

"Are you on vacation?" the guy asks me.

"No."

"What are you doing?"

"I'm working here. I quit my job early this spring and moved to the island."

"What were you doing?"

"I was a stockbroker. On Wall Street. Not a fun job." The guy looked at me with blank eyes across the counter, his forehead feigned interest, but I could tell he really couldn't identify with my experience.

The sun had given up its attempt to punch holes in the sky. The air darkened to the hue of a crowded bar. I looked outside at the cobblestones, puckered like warts along the ancient street. Hard as I might try, I couldn't suppress the twinge of anguish caused by Tammy's absence. I had prided myself over the past couple of years at being noncommittal, but somehow she had burrowed under my skin while I slept. The flash of her hair when she laughed, the movement of her back muscles when I entered her from behind, the way her calf clenched when shifting gears—all these images rushed to the surface of my mind like an unsinkable object, a buoy clanging away in the darkness. But these were merely symbols of deeper feelings which I did not feel comfortable admitting to myself. Yet.

I started to worry about events in the future, which I had promised myself I would not do until I left the island. Tammy entered my life like the symptom of a disease one cannot ignore once it appears. "A lesion of love," I thought, and laughed. To contemplate Tammy was to contemplate my future and all that I was hiding from.

Spindrift

Rain hit the pavement. A flurry of girls shrieked past the window. I paid the bill and left. Standing in the doorway I watched the drops coagulate and eventually coat the entire sidewalk. People ran for cover. Across the street stood one of the island's two bookstores, the door invitingly open. I walked over, relieved that I had found a place where I could pass the time without having to talk to anyone.

A depression in the brick sidewalk had filled with water. I stopped and bent over it, seeing my face in the metal lid of the puddle. My features were distorted. I hurried into the store.

The shelves are pregnant with books, stuffed together like hymnals, each one its own psalm, each with its own voice, ready to sing if opened. I am always drawn to the lonely titles in bookstores, those in the back or on the high shelves. I never bother with the best-selling hardbacks out front, preening the feathers of their bright covers and fancy artwork. They are for people who care more for the title than the content, like my friend Arnold in New York, who brags of his signed first editions. I have never heard him extol a book's literary beauty or express his love for an author's writing. Arnold's ebullience is that which drives best-sellers to the top of the list. It's funny that there's never a list for "best read," or "best written." Even more revealing might be a "most stolen" list.

I sat on a stool and pulled out volumes of poetry. Editions of Hardy, Tennyson, Robinson. There is nothing more ironic than a dead poet. A poet celebrates life. What are we to make of his observations after he's dead? Was he right? Is he laughing at us now? I looked for something more modern, tired of the old rhyme schemes and meters, the academic subjects—drooping like a tired model for a Greek statue. I picked out Jarrell, Lowell, and Wright. Less dust on the covers. Poems about war, graveyards, hangovers. Two of the three subjects I knew something about.

In the back room of the store is a chair. I grabbed a copy of Tolstoy and settled into it. After a few pages I felt that I could have lived in another time and have been happy. A time of no electricity and woolen underwear. The epoch constantly being celebrated on Nantucket, in the boarding houses and restaurants run by the nouveau riche owners, many of them transplanted from New York. I try to recall that famous exchange between Fitzgerald and Hemingway, about the rich being different. Yes, replied Hemingway, they are different. They have more money. And that's it. I ponder the term nouveau riche. Every age thinks it is the first to suffer them. But there's nothing "new" about them, they've always been with us. The whaling families who built the mansions on upper Main Street were probably considered *arriviste* in their day. Now we look at them as the symbols of "old" money.

Outside, the puppetry of wind continues as I walk down an alley: the play of branches, dancing clotheslines. Trees nod in agreement like obsequious executives, rows of shivering men chanting affirmative choruses. I think of my friends back home getting richer, becoming fatter, shifting more in-line. I could say they are losing their nerves but that wouldn't be fair nor accurate. They are simply losing themselves, stepping aside into their shadows, gray and cool like their suits, indistinguishable from one another. The color has drained out of them, the vibrancy of original expression. They have not lost their ideals but the will to express them. And that is the saddest thing for me.

I had visited my friend Conrad before I left my job. He had been a promising writer in school, then a professor of English at a prestigious little liberal arts college. During the summers he had done some free-lance writing to help a friend of his in public relations, and ended up writing an annual report for a corporation, an oil or chemical company. At the end of the summer they offered him a job in their communications department at almost double his teaching salary. With a baby on the way, he couldn't turn it down. Or so he told me as I sat in his office three years later. And he had undergone all the predictable evolutions people in his position are prone to. Once a staunch Democrat, he had voted Republican in the last two elections. "I'm a fiscal conservative . . . but still a social liberal," he rationalized with weak eyes. He and his wife don't do any more volunteer work, but they decide upon two "causes" a year and write a "substantial" check to each. I asked Conrad if he still wrote and he said "sure" with a smile, and flipped an annual report at me. "Buy the stock," he advised me with a wink. "It's all up from here."

I have no quarrel with Conrad or any of my friends. I just didn't want that to happen to me.

Later I went to the Rose and Crown. Ken was behind the bar. His eyes looked bloodshot.

"Hey Ken."

"How's it going?"

"Great. How 'bout a beer. Draft."

"Sure kid."

Music played to the sparse crowd. A few tourists were finishing meals, wiping the ketchup-stained chins of their children. Two or three locals stood on the other side of the horseshoe bar. I waved at one of the guys I knew, a cook from the restaurant next to the Lobster Trap.

On the far wall hung a curious, antique sign I had noticed several times, but never when sober. It read,

THE GREASING OF A CAR

Very important is the fact that,
When your car is greased here, it
is done thoroughly.

S.E. Gifford

After a few beers the sign started to read like poetry. Dark and massive, with gold lettering beautifully rendered on the black wood, it hung like a great tombstone over the dining room. But no one ever commented on the sign or seemed to notice it. People walked by it as they did so many headstones. It was, in its stilted way, the best possible expression of Mr. Gifford's feelings about customer satisfaction, and now hung in smoky disregard over a bar of tourists, still customers to another proprietor, of another time. Ken set another beer in front of me, I being his customer, but I knew I would only have to pay for one of the several beers I would consume, just so his boss would see him going to the cash register. For in that distorted worldview, we make customers of our bosses, our friends, our lovers even. The flesh we insert in each other is a form of credit for which future payments are exacted. It should all balance out in the end.

Again I confronted the street. The rain had cleared. A shot bottle of gulls scattered over the rooftops. I turned left toward the Atlantic Cafe. Pretty girls everywhere, lining the sidewalks. I swayed with the rhythm of the island, feeling tall, blond, and tan. Wearing comfortable old jeans, a corduroy shirt, loafers, and a red bandanna, I thought, I am an Island Man. A pack of girls passed, and I stared at them. They looked me over like a piece of raw meat. The lead girl's gaze traveled up and down my body. I smiled and turned to look at her. They turned too, and she whistled at me, smiling. One said, "Baby, baby!" I walked like I had my cock pinned to my chest. I felt like an officer in uniform.

The AC was packed. At the bar I struck up a conversation with some tourists on the island for the first time. John and Jeanie kept the drinks flowing toward me. Soon I was floating on a sea of dark rum. My voice thickened under the encumbrance of alcohol. The conversations across the room sounded more and more like percussion; I heard beats, not words. The woman next to me spoke in triplets. I caught only every third word. She seemed intent on finding the exact location of some famous landmark, but I couldn't make out what she was saying. So I nodded and smiled and said "That's great," antiphonally. There were enough nouns and verbs floating around to make sentences, but they didn't belong to the same people. I heard surreal snatches of conversation which connected in the distilled swamp of my brain.

Then I started to see things in slow motion. A guy took what seemed like minutes to set his drink down. A woman's head turned incrementally in clock-like ticks. The path of her hair defied gravity, hovering in the air. I swallowed the last gulp of my drink and went outside to breathe.

An avalanche of dark horses clouded the sky. My feet slid effortlessly below me as I glided up the street. I sat on the steps of the library, twinging just on the level side of drunkenness, a plane scraping the cloudline, one drink short of stupefaction.

Thoughts of past loves swirled in my head. I kept seeing Alex's face, thrown back in orgasm as we floated within each other on the ocean. I saw the girl from the Bible college I had seduced in my dorm room many years ago in a sweaty flash of bra straps and safety pins. A dark-haired farmer's daughter with the body of an angel, who had held me so tenderly, and gave me crabs. I had never come so hard in my life: she drained me like a stomach pump. Thoughts of her gave way to a moist night at summer camp, lying on the jetties with the prettiest girl on staff, listening to the cluck of water against the rocks as I caressed her huge breasts, gasping at their fullness. Finally I remembered the most important object of my desire, the little girl with the page-boy hair that I had chased down the hall every day in nursery school. I realized, at that moment, that I was still chasing her, that my entire life had been devoted to finding her. To sleep with every incarnation of her image until one day, finally, a pair of eyes would look up at me from the sheets and say, "Yes, you've finally caught me."

18

I stopped in the public john on the way to the White Dog Cafe to dip my face in a sink of water, and hopefully wash away some of the fog sticking to my eyes. The room hummed with porcelain florescence. Exceedingly quiet. I washed my face and beheld the reflection in the mirror. Two wild eyes that couldn't focus avoided my gaze. They were drawn to the wall. I followed their path and saw, scrawled in capital letters:

THERE ONCE WAS A MAN FROM NANTUCKET . . .
(YOU KNOW THE REST)

I relieved myself in the urinal with the slow unwinding of a fisherman's cast, a long string of urine spinning out of me until I felt my midsection arch forward, involuntarily, with great relief. I realized that I hadn't gone to the bathroom all night, and that my bladder, once emptied, would now fill up more quickly if I kept drinking—which I intended to keep doing.

The cobblestones vibrated in the luminous dusk; a paucity of tone had bled the air gray.

On the corner an old woman in a light blue gingham dress walked a little white poodle. "Come on Corky," she said. "It's time to go eat your suppah." Her ruddy face looked like it had been chipped off the brick wall of the nearby post office. I knew the woman, Mrs. Walsh; she ran a boarding house where a couple of my friends lived. She was a true native, born on the island in the house she still lived in, which had been built by her father. She pretended that she didn't like outsiders, or "invaders" as she called them, yet she depended entirely upon tourists for her income. Every time she spoke she looked like she had just been sucking a lemon.

"Hello, Mrs. Walsh."

"Well how are you?"

"Great." I tried to hide my drunkenness, but I knew she could see through the contrived mask of my face.

"You look a bit flushed. Been gettin' around I suppose?"

"Yeah." I waited for her famous "invaders" speech, which she liked to give to all the young summer people.

"All you invaduhs have been muckin' things up somethin' awful this summer. I've never seen so much garbage on the streets than this year. You'd think people could put their trash in the cans where it belongs."

"Well, those are the tourists, Mrs. Walsh. Those of us that work here aren't so careless." She gave me a sour look. Corky tugged on her leash, saving me from having to hear the old lady's retort.

"Now what do you think you're doing?" she said to the dog, who had probably enjoyed the moment's respite from her master's constant banter.

"I'll be seein' you, Mrs. Walsh. Nice talkin' to you."

"Tell your friends not to throw their pizza plates on the ground."

"Don't worry, they're good people," I said, sliding away. And I'm sure she muttered all the way home about the litter problem.

I went into the White Dog and sat at the bar. I ordered a beer and looked around for Millie. After a while she walked in from the restaurant side of the cafe with a piece of chalk in her hand.

"Suddenly get the urge to draw?"

"No, I had to list the specials on the blackboard. How're you?"

"Fine," I said, raising my beer. "Care to join me?"

"Sure." She sat with the spunky bounce common to young, athletic women. "So you're here to see the movie?"

"I suppose. I mean, where else can you have a beer and watch a film at the same time? I figure I'll kill two birds with one stone." A group of people came in. Millie ran over to seat them and returned. I remarked, "Man, this job sure can get in the way of your social life."

"Such is life."

"At least these tourists could all come at once, or in shifts, so they wouldn't waste your time. How're you supposed to talk to any of your friends?" She went over to seat another party. I leered at the pretty blond waitress who looked like she had just walked out of an Iowa cornfield. At best I could secrete a hazy ebullience toward her. God, she epitomized physical purity. Perfect face, body, skin, hair. Even her damn smile. She could have won any beauty contest in the world, unanimously. The thought of her standing naked before me terrified me too much to contemplate. She was Miss Nantucket wielding her scepter, and I was the corny MC, singing her glory, albeit off-key. What a ludicrous image. Crazy, but palpable. For on Nantucket anything is possible. You can be walking down the street and a girl you've never seen before can grab your heart with the thrill of a plunge into an icy lake. In a matter of seconds you can say "Hi," start talking, and see your whole life together spread before you in a beautiful Connecticut home. With three kids, station wagon, and a golden retriever named Tripper. Or a girl that smiles at you in a bar might ask you to dance and twenty minutes later ask you to bed. I've seen it happen. If you are one with the spirit of the island you can breathe in the air and walk on water if you like. People will call out your name as they whiz by in a jeep; a hand will smack you on the back and a voice will offer you a drink. You can turn on a dime, drive in the winning run, set the record, win the lottery, and find the pot at the end of the rainbow on Nantucket. Your ship will come in, six times a day, and ferry you back to the mainland if you wish. It's always your birthday here, every day an anniversary marking the decision you made to come to this place. The church bells ring for us in celebration. The liquor flows. The bands play to packed dance floors. The dogs bark. Children waving. Women kissing men in the streets, while we wade knee-high through ticker tape beaches to the applause of the wind, ringing in our ears, with the cheers of gulls, buoys, and foghorns. . . .

Millie is back by my side and talking to me before I realize it. I watch her mouth move, and think of leaning forward and filling it with my tongue. I consider easing her back onto the bar and making love to her in slow motion through the brown folds of her hair. Standing back from this image I see her taut muscles working, grinding against me, neck twisted in begrunting admission. Slowly I let a jar of honey drain over her flat stomach, then lick it off with tantric restraint. But as I step further back from this double image of me watching myself I realize that I am immune from this lust for her; that I am fulfilled by my Tammy, and that this sensual transgression is due solely to her absence, an irrational and drunken reaction to my loneliness, panging through my body to the throbbing beat in my temples. It would be wise, I tell myself, to talk to Millie and stop these prurient fantasies. Ask her about the movie: simple facts easy to communicate and concentrate on.

"What's the name of this flick?"

"*Aguirre, The Wrath of God*. It's in German."

"How soon till it starts?"

"About five minutes."

"Great, just enough time for another beer." She goes to get me a ticket and I watch the waitress, trying not to catch her attention because I am afraid to talk to her and reveal my drunkenness. I may have many faults, but one thing I will not do is play the drunken fool for a pretty girl, no matter how much she baits me. Ha! Baits me. I'm lucky if a girl like that would even want to talk to me looking the way I feel now.

The air staggered in front of me in shifts of white light. People's lips moved before emitting sound, like a man hammering in the distance. Millie returned with the ticket.

"Enjoy the show."

"Thanks," I said, watching for any reaction to my inebriation.

But she smiled and placed the ticket into my hand warmly, making me wonder if I had exaggerated my inability to hold liquor. "I'll see you after the show," I ventured, and received no ill reaction.

The entrance to the little theatre is right off the bar, and after parting the red velvet curtains and stepping inside, you begin to think that you have made a mistake, that you have entered a children's theatre instead. I took a seat in the last row and still had rarely sat as close to a screen in my life. Only about six or seven people sat down by the time the movie started. I stretched my legs over the seat and struck a languid pose, sucking on my beer the way Greta Garbo imbibed cigarettes.

Images perambulated with the staggering pace of old men; fast, then slow for a while, then all the colors rushing toward me. I tried to keep up with the subtitles but couldn't; the native German of the actors set a pleasing, guttural rhythm which I eased into, and the titles were too much of a distraction, nagging at the bottom of the lush cinematography—filmed on location in some rain forest in South America. Every so often I would read a phrase and turn it around in my mind until I felt like agglutinating another few scraps of dialogue, but the meaning of the plot was so obvious that the subtitles weren't necessary. Essentially, a bunch of conquistadors were rafting down a river in search of El Dorado. Led by a mutinous madman, they flowed toward their doom. Drifting on the wash of beer and rum, watching stoically, I cared nothing for the fate of the characters, being seduced instead by the sedulous rain forest, a panoramic green abyss of vegetation, sonorous birds, and rushing water; a fat whore of fear, beauty, and enticement.

A numb pain grew in my groin shortly after the film began, an urge to urinate, exacerbated by the sibilance of the river. I had to relieve myself, but to leave the vision of that screen was impossible. The pain seared my midsection, yet I remained transfixed. A bleary idea crept into my mind which, when sober, would have immediately been rejected. But suddenly I felt for the empty bottle below my seat and, in the mist of the green light, filled it with twelve warm ounces, then, checking my surroundings, delivered the rest of my burden to the floor. I made sure no one sat in the line of fire, maintaining some standard of decorum in my wet dignity. I had never felt so relieved.

The conquistadors continued down the river. Their princess escaped the madman by walking into the jungle to her certain death. None of the party would ever return, so lost were they in this uncharted world. One by one they died or were killed, until only the madman remained. The camera spun around his solitary figure several times. He did not mind his fate; in fact he appeared to enjoy the push of the water, the ebb of his existence, as he sat on his raft, drifting toward nothing.

19

Everyone loved my bike. And of course, all my guy friends wanted to borrow it. There is something about a motorcycle that incites a sense of freedom in men. Even the little runt that just had sand kicked in his face will rise up, brush himself off, and drive away on a motorcycle like a knight on a charger. It's tough to turn down those who request a quick spin because you can tell how much it means to them: their eyes widen, they run a hand through their hair, and they start talking out of the sides of their mouths. And if you say no, they become crestfallen and sulk (and will always remember the incident if you ever ask them for a favor in the distant future). Let's face it, a motorcycle is a big pulsating cock between any guy's legs, and the minute he straddles the seat he starts looking for a sexy blond hitchhiker (who of course will be French) to pick up. The only problem is, you can't ride your cycle into a bar, so you carry in your helmet, like a cowboy strutting through swinging doors with his saddlebags. It is true that I have mildly fallen prey to some of these fantasies; but then, I paid for the damn cycle.

Larry's inane trick was to ask for the use of the bike after showering, for the purpose of "drying his hair." Ironically, the frequency of his showering increased significantly after I acquired the "machine," as we called it. There is a helmet law on Nantucket, but we found out the first time he tried mine on that it would not fit over his megacephalic proportions. He could not get the chin bar over his nose, a problem he blamed on his eastern European heritage. Unfortunately, the helmet was the only one of my belongings which he could not physically borrow; my underwear, socks, shirts, jackets, and toiletries were all magnetically attracted to his skinny body. I soon discovered that any items I valued or hoped to wear the next day could be preserved only if they were locked in my trunk.

But Larry was lovable, the kind of guy you couldn't hate for more than a few minutes no matter how badly he let you down or hurt you. He'd throw his arm over your shoulder and with his big stupid grin framing his Mount Rushmore teeth, the anger in you would chill and subside—the way you can't hate a little kid for long. And that's why I loved Larry; he was the playmate I never had in my youth, my little rogue brother.

On this particular day Larry had borrowed my bike very early in the morning, for he had not been drinking the night before. In fact he hadn't had a drink for about two weeks, a record he was proud of. Larry's softer nature surfaced when he stayed sober: he liked to rise early, fix things, and do chores around the house. He also exercised and read; "a sound mind in a barely sound body" he liked to say. From these sober respites Larry emerged a new man, but unfortunately for him, they never lasted too long.

I had been awaiting his return for about an hour. As usual, he said he just wanted to dry his hair, but he could be anywhere between Sconset and Barcelona by now. I lolled in the depurating sun on the deck. The town rose to life slowly; the first people trickled under me to the beach—the usual early-morning types: joggers, dog walkers, and an occasional lonely soul.

Every so often I could hear the caesura of the waves: rising . . . falling . . . silence. Two or three flocculent clouds drifted harmlessly. I went inside for more coffee. When I returned, I saw a familiar black dog running around the road below the deck. Then I noticed Pete coming up behind him. He held a green rubber ball which he bounced on the ground every few steps. The dog heard the ball and jangled excitedly about

Pete's legs. He threw the ball toward the sand and the dog scattered, sixty pounds of barking hair hell-bent on recovering that slobbery piece of rubber.

"Hey Pete."

"Guy! Didn't see you up there. How's it goin'?"

"Fine. Just hangin' out catchin' some sun. What're you up to?"

"Takin' my dog for a walk. Here boy. Good dog. Thata boy, King."

Pete's relationship with his dog came right out of the movies—the archetypal two souls against the world, both wild, unleashed, undisciplined. Pete didn't walk King as much as tromp along with him. He never used a leash, which sometimes got him in trouble with the law. Pete without his dog was a sad, incomplete boy. Strangely, for a kid of seventeen, he never talked about girls, his family, or any other personal interests. King defined his blond, uncombed, ragged life. Like the two characters in *Lord of the Flies* whose names became one, no one spoke of Pete without mentioning his dog.

Pete walked up the stairs with King—a nervous skittle of nails on wood. The dog took an intestinal path around his master's legs, eyes glued to the green ball. If Pete had thrown it off the deck the dog would have gleefully jumped off after it and broken all his legs.

"So this is your place. Not bad. I like the sundial."

"Thanks. It's entirely self-winding."

"King! Sit. Sit!" Pete said in a mock-authoritative voice. But it was no use, the rasping dog had no intention of lowering his bum. He looked at Pete with a stupid, gaping grin, thinking, "Ask me something I can do well, like chase something, then I'll show you." His tongue hung limply out the side of his mouth; he wouldn't let Pete alone, nudging him with his panting snoot. Finally Pete took the ball into our yard and closed the gate so we could have some peace. King appeared to be assuaged with his prize and the cool grass.

Pete bitched about the restaurant and how much he hated Buff. I told him how lucky he was to have a cooking job, especially at such a young age.

"Yeah, but I've been doin' this for years. My family used to live on the island. Then my dad got a job on the mainland, and I stayed behind to finish high school here."

"Well that was smart. What does your dad do?"

"He's a carpenter. He's workin' for some big construction company now. They live in an apartment outside Boston. I just couldn't hack it there."

"So what are your plans?"

"I dunno. Maybe I'll go to cooking school. Or build boats."

"You could cook on boats. Kill two birds with one stone."

"Right," he said, smiling.

Pete surveyed the shoreline as if looking for a long-overdue ship. A cloud seemed to pass over him. He looked toward the yard but King wasn't making a sound. Then he faced me. "Want a snort?"

"A what?"

"You know—some coke."

"Um, I dunno."

He produced a little vial, twisted it, held it to his nose, and inhaled violently. Sniffing in that dramatic way all cokeheads do, he handed me the vial and said, "Here. Just turn it like this, and it refills. See?" There was a little chamber to collect the powder from the well at the bottom. I turned it in my hand, not sure what to do. Should I? What if it's bad? I looked at Pete, who was still breathing, and smiling luxuriously, in fact. Fuck it, I thought. Go for it. I held the vial to my nose and inhaled while pinching shut the other nostril.

A warm flood of powder entered me—like snow falling upwards on a dry night when the air is glazed with silver—a sweet sensation of tin crawling down my throat.

"Here. Try another hit."

I rotated the vial until the white eye opened, unblinking.

"Go ahead, take a couple hits. I owe ya for savin' my ass with Buff enough times."

A warm wave of sunlight washed over me. The air coming through my nostrils thickened. In the distance a barking dog, acrid coughs . . .

"Gotta go get King."

Pete brushing past me. The sun blocked, then full force. The deck swinging, melodious; the sky ablaze, Saturnian.

The brool of a seductive breath, craquelure air, metallic crashing of waves—far off, far off—numbly laying an easy jazz beat . . . undulating with the rhythm of sex, swaying as I lay back into the railing, fingers sinking into the warm grain: wrapped in the sibilant embrace of the island.

King must have taken off the other way because I heard Pete sing his farewell in the distance. I moved a hand through the warm light toward him.

Beholding the entire horizon spanning thousands of miles through quarter-inch slits, I marveled at the power of the drug Pete had given me, and how seductively it trilled, in a siren's voice, the call for more. For a minute—it could have been ten—I polished this thought like a marble ball, seeking the vein of decision in it, then a deeper voice rose inside me and said, No! No! . . . Don't be deceived by the superficial luster of it. The rush of the high sunk leadenly, the sunlight congealed into a saturnine cloud, and I felt the raw withdrawal of pleasure that had been artificially induced. Immediately I realized it had been the same demon I had run from, call it plastic intoxication, green joy, the salacious smile of money—of spending—of earning—of counting, yes counting, for that is what it boils down to: that quantifiable measure of wealth that dictates how good you can feel, and more important, indicates what you must do to balance the equation. So much of this for so much of that. Quid pro quo. Three snorts to be high equals X amount of dollars. And to get the dollars you need to . . . fill in the blank. Here I am dancing to the same music as some sorry kid who doesn't even know the name of the song. But somehow he can sing it. And somehow he had found me.

I went inside, still tingling, drank a glass of water and lay on the bed. The sea quilted the horizon. No matter how hard I looked I couldn't see it move.

Sometime later I awoke to the sound of a ringing phone. As I rushed through the hallway I called Larry's name but heard no response. By the sixth or seventh ring I got to the phone, knocking it over in my haste to pick it up. The light coming through the window had thickened and yellowed; how long had I been sleeping?

"Hello."

"Guy?"

"Yup."

"Guy, this is Buff. Pete didn't show up for his shift. We need a new fry cook. You're it. Do you want the job?"

"Uh—uh—yeah, sure. . . ."

"How soon can you be here?"

"I'll come right now."

"Good. Hurry up."

I ambled into the bathroom and splashed water on my face. My features looked disjointed; Picassoesque. One eye hung lower than the other and all the hair had been pressed to one side of my head. I grabbed my keys and wallet, then got my helmet and bounded down the stairs. Halfway down a horrible thought entered my head. Fuck! That bastard still has my bike! I rounded the house ready to scream but there it sat, innocent as a puppy. Larry had left a dandelion on the seat. That beautiful skinny bastard! I laughed out loud as I started the bike and flew down Sconset Road on the way to my new career.

20

Some of my favorite times on the island were spent alone. I looked forward to those nights when Larry worked the late shift without me, and I could cook a big beach dinner and have the house to myself. It's a tough feeling to understand—the intoxicating joy of solipsism—unless you were raised as an only child.

Usually on those nights I would take a long ride along the bluff, helmetless into the Beethoven wind, watching the sea settle like a sleepy animal, so vast and undisturbed, so powerful and humbling. Often the tourists would be clicking along the road to the Summer House, fresh clothes and tans painted on, smiling with the scent of air fresheners, blazing smears of color against the gauze of dusk, oblivious to the enchantment laying just beyond them.

I would ride until the wind had raked me clean. Then I'd park the bike and get food from the market. I'd buy spaghetti and clam sauce, French bread, garlic, a bottle of wine, fruit and cheese, and I'd scurry back to my house, throw open all the windows to let in the blue sea air, and cook. Cutting no corners I would set the table, light candles, and put some Bach on the phonograph. Of course, I would eat facing the sea, my true companion—a rutilant portrait framed by the window, always changing and engrossing.

One night Tammy stopped by unexpectedly and, seeing my elaborate preparations, thought I must be doing this for another woman behind her back.

On other occasions we'd invite all of our friends and throw the house open for a big dinner party. Larry and I would cook pots of steamers and lobsters (smothered in seaweed—I don't know why, it just seemed appropriate); we'd also serve corn-on-the-cob and baked potatoes, and our friends would bring jugs of wine and beer. After dinner we'd gravitate to the deck to lean against the shoulder of the ocean. I'd play the guitar and Larry would sing through the wide tips of his nostrils; he knew all the great songs from the fifties and sixties; everyone would join in, culminating in a great wall of sound, or so we imagined, a vagabond troupe of jetsam, crumbs from America, trying not to slip through the slats of the deck.

We never knew who would show up at our parties, nor exactly when they would occur; sometimes they'd combust spontaneously on a Friday night when people tired of the same old bar bands. I'm sure one or two marriages resulted from those affairs, with all the strange people meeting and mixing in odd combinations, so many chemicals with attractive valences.

The days rotate, driven by the kiss of something mad. Days with Tammy, days without Tammy. Casting into the stream of bars for old friends, new friends. Warm days, cool nights. Working. Playing. Sunning. Running. Riding. Drinking. Spinning. Each morning's Eucharist from the chalice of the sun. Twelve hours later pouring a drop's libation into the sea for good weather the next day. For the spirit of the ocean. For the thighs of the sky to part, to let the sun conceive again. Rising, lying— a cycle of renewal; a phantasmagoric *ricorso*; the report of sun striking sand; the orgasm of a lit jewel; the clap of a cool puddle; the scratch of water over shore—all spinning in that mad kiss, the one that sucks your mouth off and leaves you reeling, arching your belly for more until you are exhausted and have nothing left to give.

And yet, you wake up again not thinking of the future but the day upon you. When the day is so large that it eclipses the future, and the future is so tremendous, even though you have nothing planned. When the creeping moments compose a sort of spontaneous, antic painting: a torch drawing held for a blink in the darkness. The lie of your lover's hair on a pillow. A shock of paper writhing on the road. The lucent cilia of dusk, burnishing the gulls settled on the beach into white embers. Then darkening into coals.

Laying with Tammy in the early adagio of evening. She is wrapped in my blanket, napping. I have cleared away the dinner dishes. She faces the window, wearing my cotton sweater and socks, a lithe pile of straw in the corner of my room. I have been watching her for a long time. Her face slowly turns toward me, eyes fixed upon mine, as if she knew exactly where to look. She smiles in the most honest way possible; there is not a mote of contrivance in it, so that I am totally exposed to her; I realize she has exhumed any emotion I might have been trying to withhold. Her face casts a calm iridescence, a turquoise sobriety of understanding. We lie in the embrace of our eyes until we both fall asleep. . . .

"Forgive me if I take a minute to strike a few matches in the dark interior of these pages. Perhaps if we move quickly now they won't catch fire."
"Who are you talking to, Guy?"
"Nobody Tammy. Just thinking out loud. Go back to sleep."

Because of my promotion on that fateful Saturday I missed Ted's ferry jump. A growing number of people talked about it for the next few days, and someone said it had even made the Cape newspapers. On Monday I stopped by Ted's store to hear his account of it, but he wasn't in. The story around town was that the "mystery jumpers" weren't caught. In fact, no one was sure if they were hurt or not. Stern signs were posted around the offices of the Steamship Authority warning of the severe penalties for such an act, as well as the inherent danger.

I walked around town wishing I could get more information, and hence, vicarious pleasure, from Ted's act. I looked in the

Rose and Crown and the Atlantic Cafe but didn't see anyone from our crowd. The police station loomed across the street, but asking them about the event would be tantamount to a confession of my prior knowledge of the so-called crime. So I walked along the docks, my usual harbor of solace, to see what boats the wind had blown in. An idea struck me and I picked up my pace. But upon rounding the bend I saw that the slip formerly occupied by Marsha's boat was empty. I walked over to it as if there might be a psychic clue to her whereabouts shimmering in an oil slick. A bald guy in the adjacent slip was washing down his boat, named Cash Flow.

"When did these guys pull out?"

"Who, the Hatteras? A couple days ago I think. They'll be back. They keep the slip all season."

"Thanks." I tried to see my reflection in the water but the shadow of the dock eclipsed it.

I had some time to kill before my shift. Music from the waterfront bar beckoned; I sat at a table facing the water in the sunlight. A deafeningly beautiful chestnut-haired waitress walked over to me, her gaze so direct that for a second I forgot she was waiting on me.

"Hi."

"Hi."

"What're you having?"

"What's your name?"

"Debbie."

"Hi Debbie. Guy."

"Hi Guy." We laughed. I could tell she wasn't in any hurry, and that she didn't mind flirting with me; she was probably sick of all the demanding vacationers and their snotty kids. We talked for several minutes before I thought to order a drink.

"Look, why don't you sit down and join me. There's no one else to wait on."

"I wish I could. But my boss would kill me."

"I doubt it. He can be put in jail for that."

"I wouldn't put it past him."

The rhythm of our banter was comforting, like steering a boat over the open sea. I quickly found out a lot about this beautiful stranger: her age, place of birth, family structure, where she lived on the island, went to school, and so forth. The amazing openness of Nantucket, the conviviality. I felt, in a giddy wave of ecstasy, that I could have asked her to marry me on the spot, and that I'd at least get a fair shot of meeting her father.

Some of the tables around me filled up and we had less time to chat. As I started to leave after my second drink, Debbie said, "See you at Wopatoola."

"Oh that's right. This weekend."

"Yup."

"Maybe even before then." She gleamed, and I imagined sitting before a fire with her, adjusting logs with a long brass poker. She had big-sweater eyes; bundle-me-up-and-hold-me-on-a-cold-night eyes. If only another time, I thought, the image of Tammy growing stronger within me. Passing her, in a voice of afterthought, I asked, "Do you ski?"

The day I came into work to start as the new fry cook, Buff took me to the raw bar gazebo across the way, made me a formal job offer, and told me what he expected of me. I was to go off hourly pay and onto a salary. Apparently, this was the first time a dishwasher had been promoted to cook in the same season. Pete had started out well, he recounted, but his performance deteriorated sharply over time. My responsibilities were very important, he told me, using the grave tones of my grade school principal, the man whose face always jumped to the forefront of my mind from the crowd of authority figures milling in the hallways of my past.

To the outsider—the restaurant layman—a line cook's job may not appear to be hard. But as the precision of movement is crucial to the art—and the life—of a trapeze artist, the precision of time is essential to a line cook. Especially in a big tourist restaurant like the Lobster Trap, known in the trade as a "turnover" place. Since such restaurants have thin margins and must keep their prices in line with the competition, they can only make money by squeezing as many dollars out of a table as they can over the course of a day. We might serve four, or if we were lucky (depending on your perspective), five parties per table per shift. That's a lot of lobsters, fried clams, raw oysters, and chowder. But it requires even more sweat, yelling, and skin burns than an outsider would ever imagine.

In most restaurants on the island, a good cook was a fast cook. Fast, not in the simple sense of speed, but in the ability to execute, simultaneously, a wide array of dishes with incongruous cooking times. Steaming a lobster takes a third of the time needed to broil a steak. An oyster in the calloused hands of an expert can be opened in a second; in the tender hands of a novice it might take half-an-hour.

We worked on an "L"-shaped line. At the far end stood the broiler man with his ovens for steaks and broiled seafood entrées. Next to him, the sous-chef, who prepared sauces and performed other stovetop work; to his left, the "caller." He pivoted in three directions where the arms of the L met, calling out the orders, conducting the symphony of dishes, supervising the waitresses, and making sure that my fast dishes meshed in readiness with the longer-cooking oven entrées.

I stood on the short arm of the L. Besides cooking the fried dishes, which ranged from clams to onion rings, I also prepared the steamed items, such as lobsters, mussels in wine and garlic, and little necks, as well as the raw offerings like oysters on the half shell. And on certain mornings I prepared the salad bar and made the desserts.

I cooked in a red and gray blur: a tornado of scalding lobster claws and sharp oyster shells flew from my hands night after night. After a week my palms looked like the unshod feet of a desert soldier. My mind carries no memory of any individual action in my routine; I only see myself in motion, running hundreds of miles over a landscape the length of my arm.

At night I dream of the lobsters I have killed. We swim together off Sconset Beach. They are so trusting, so gentle. As they crawl toward the beach I try to stop them, but they cannot hear me. So I steal the sign pointing to Spain and pound it into the sand under the water, where they can see it pointing away from the awful maw of the America that wants to consume them.

21

A stick of licorice hit my shoulder as I walked down the steps from the restaurant.

"Hey Captain Lobster Trap!"

"Yo Kendall!"

"Here's another one."

"Thanks. The roof looks great. When's it gonna be finished?"

"A work of art is never finished. But I'll be done with it in about ten days."

"I'll be sorry to see you go."

"Oh, I'll still be around. There's enough leaky roofs on this island to last me a lifetime."

I walked down the rest of the steps and crossed the alley toward him. "Yeah, I guess all these ancient houses have a lot of problems."

"Hell, they're in the best shape. It's these new ones that're falling apart." Kendall gave me his big Cherokee smile and a woodsy wave. "Say, did you enjoy those beers I sent in the other night?"

"That was you? I didn't know that. Yeah, they really helped."

"Looked like you were havin' a long night."

"Sure was. Thanks buddy. I owe you one."

The late afternoon air filled me with hunger for some type of aesthetic stimulation. I thought about hitting the galleries, not that I expected to see any great art, but I just wanted a few breaths of painted air, and to talk to someone about anything other than lobster roux and steamed mussels. Cutting through the shortcut next to the restaurant, I surfaced on lower Main Street and entered a gallery in a little white building, holding what looked like an opening reception. At least I might get a nice glass of wine.

The paintings on display were all derivatively cubist: discombobulated beach imagery splashed with fluorescent colors. Pepto-pink nightmares of a sexually depraved actuary. But the artist turned out to be a woman who looked like a Connecticut housewife. I glanced at her biography and saw that she was previously an interior designer, which made sense in some lewd way. Behind me, a woman with a metallic voice said, "She's so LeRoy Neiman, isn't she?" to her nodding friend. I left, wondering if she meant it as a compliment or an insult.

I wandered up the street to a gallery housed in an old brick building. I liked this one better because it had less lighting, more space, and fewer critics. It breathed freely compared to the oppressive fluorescence of the other place. A bald guy with a goatee banged raggy jazz on the gallery's baby grand piano, set in the middle of the artwork. I surveyed the paintings and watercolors, which were relatively original and engaging.

"He's pretty good," I said to the woman behind the desk, indicating the pianist.

"Gregory? Oh yes. Brilliant. Julliard. Played with the Boston Symphony." A tone of finality underscored the word "played," as if something had happened to him. I didn't inquire any further, feeling it wasn't appropriate. But if this is where he chose to play, instead of the Boston Symphony, good for him. I admired his evolution.

Outside, the marrow of the brick sidewalk coursed with hundreds of hungry feet. The great dinner procession had begun; diners gazed with oppressive earnestness at posted menus; husbands conferred with wives in hushed tones; children tugged at extended limbs; and the occasional tethered animal sulked at the base of its pole. I fought back the urge to sing out, "It's not worth it! I'm a cook, and I really do know! The plastic red bibs and half-price for kids, it's all just a farcical show." But instead I only stared, redolent in fish ether, sucking the latest wound on my hand: Jason had slapped me on the back when I was shucking oysters, causing me to slice open my palm. Tonight I had a party to look forward to, and Wopatoola tomorrow. My spirits lifted. Better stop by Tammy's and make sure she's on track.

Her store was crowded with ancient ladies tossing wool sweaters around. It looked like a Turkish trading post. I caught her attention from the doorway and yelled, "See you at eight."

Driving home on the Payne's gray road: scatter of birds, thrush of crickets, criblé of insects engraved in the air; Sconset, a distant magnet pulling the bike over the easy dips and bends, my dank kitchen shadow gusting away and, at the end of the road, of all the roads on the island, the susurrus of the ocean, playing the soundtrack for 60,000 spiraling lives.

A bunch of teenagers lounge around the rotary flagpole in languid poses, the girls pretty and tan with slim legs, the boys bedraggled in their nascent manhood. They eye me as I drive past, then drift back to the contemplation of their cigarettes.

Larry asleep on my bed, an empty six-pack scattered around him. Breeze swilling through the curtains, heaving asthmatically to the cellophane din of the shore.

A face ready for Modigliani to paint.

After showering I threw my towel over his head. "Wake up buddy. We gotta big evening in store."

"Wha—"

Lifting the towel I burped in his face. "Let's go Lar. I'll make you some of my special java."

"Not that crap."

"Come on. You love it."

"It always makes me shit my guts out."

"The beer makes you shit your guts out. Why don't you take a shower?"

"I don't need a shower," he said, sitting up, trying to find his balance.

"You smell like camel piss and besides, it'll make you feel better." A cannon ball of mucus roared through his throat. "There's the old Larry we all know and love."

"Ughhh."

"Okay Pavarotti. Here's a towel."

After eating, Larry and I sat on the deck in the exhausted light.

"What ever happened to that girl you met at the AC? Did ya gut her?"

"Laura? No. I lost her number. Just haven't seen her."

"It's pretty tough to lose someone here. I mean, my college campus was bigger than this island."

"So many women. So little time."

"You mean, so many beers, so little time."

"Not a bad idea." Larry started toward the door.

"You mean you're gonna have another one, after you passed out this afternoon?"

"I was just getting warmed up."

I saw Grant walking up the beach with one of the girls he lived with, and wondered if it was the same one he had been going out with before. I leaned over the railing and called to him.

"Guy. What's up?"

"Just waitin' for the moon. How 'bout you?"

"Takin' a little walk on the beach. You remember Katie."

"Sure. Hi."

"Hi."

"Come on up. Have a cold-boy."

We brought out more beers and chairs. Katie preferred to sit at Grant's feet, snuggling between his legs. She was barefoot and wore blue jeans. Grant took a swig of his beer, wiped his lips, and pushed back his curly brown hair. "You guys going to Wopatoola tomorrow?"

"Wouldn't miss it."

"I hear you're supposed to bring a bottle of any kinda booze, and they mix it all in a big bathtub or something. Like a giant cocktail."

"Sounds like heaven," Larry said.

"People coming from as far away as Boston, and New York."

"Must be some party."

"Where's it gonna be?" Larry asked.

"Surfside."

"That's good a place as any. Who throws this thing?"

"Dunno."

Tammy drove us to the party in her jeep. I'd consumed a few beers, not enough to be drunk, but I could feel a buzzing numbness all around me, polarizing the acuity of my senses. Sights and sounds were less discernible far away but sharper than normal at close range. We droned through the darkness, splitting the roads with our headlights. Few cars crossed our path.

Tammy's friend Jennifer was having the party. Her parents had just built a large house overlooking the harbor in Quaise. They were out of town, so Jennifer and her brother had the house to themselves for the week. They invited several friends down for Wopatoola weekend, and their party would be a kind of kick-off for our crowd.

Larry's marble teeth were chattering as we pulled into the crowded cul-de-sac.

"A little nippy back there, buddy?"

"I coulda froze to death."

"The wind's good for you. Great way to dry your hair. Hey— now you look windblown. Chicks love that."

"Right."

He patted down his Einstein hairdo and we went inside. The party had started, but people were still fairly restrained in their spatial relationships. It appeared that everyone was on their first round.

Larry went straight for the refrigerator. A cute girl came up, kissed Tammy, and introduced herself as Jennifer. She pointed across the room at a clean-cut kid in chinos and loafers. "That's my brother, Jack." They looked like a pair of siblings that got along all their lives and now had a mature relationship. The type that act like husband and wife. Too well-groomed, affable, and pert. Jack came over to greet us and Jennifer politely offered a selection of drinks. Larry smiled at her awkwardly as he closed the refrigerator door, open beer in hand, and introduced himself. "Well, I see you found the beverages, Larry."

I looked around. The house was too orderly; not a dirty dish in the sink, not an open magazine anywhere. Coasters on all the tables. "What can I serve you, Guy?" Even her enunciation was pitch perfect. I couldn't believe people our age lived like this. Hell, they were even younger than me. They must indulge in torrid incest, I thought, watching Jack hand his sister a glass.

We all went out onto the deck where clusters of people were engaged in earnest conversations about wind surfing and tennis. At least the breeze swept the sterile ambience away periodically. I noticed a pretty blond girl wearing a pink cotton sweater with a green collar, and yellow shorts. She had huge breasts. What a waste, I thought, looking at the inane preppy kid who had charmed her with his dry conversation and vacuous eyes. I walked over to Larry as Jennifer and Tammy immersed themselves in girl talk, giggling occasionally.

"So what do you think?" I asked.

"This place must be worth a fortune."

"No. About the party."

"What party?"

"That's what I mean. At least there's plenty of beer."

"That's true. There's always a bright side to any situation, as long as there's a cold one left."

"So you've been reading Marcus Aurelius."

"Plato. Boy could he sweet talk women."

"That so?"

"Yup. It's all logic. Just watch me and learn tonight."

The party crawled on, until mercifully a throng of exuberant people streamed in. Soon voices rose, music played—as if someone had turned on the electricity; a rim-shot vibrancy charged the air. People swayed to an unconscious beat, felt but not heard, conducted through the oak beams of the two-story living room. Couples lounged on the second floor balcony, out on the deck, in the rooms, and on the porch. Several rounds were imbibed, conversations loosened, the topics swung away from water sports to a trapeze of subjects; people mingled from cluster to cluster.

Several attractive women caught my attention but Tammy outshone them all. She was the prettiest girl at the party and everyone knew it. Every so often I went over and placed my arm around her, just to stake my territory and let her know I wasn't drifting away. I've learned it's especially important to do this just after you've been talking to a pretty girl.

By midnight the room got really loose. More people came after their work shifts. I saw Benny's friend Cooper, Jim from Easy Street, and Jill, the girl I had been trying to find who worked at the Turning Point. Derrick appeared in his de rigueur purple bandanna, with his hippy girlfriend. It appeared that news of Jennifer's party had got around. Everyone seemed to be high on Wopatoola excitement.

I went to the kitchen for a beer and found Cooper cooking hot dogs on the stove.

"Where'd you get those?"

"Found them in the ice box. Thought it'd be a good idea to cook some dogs." As I reached for the refrigerator door, Cooper said, "Ah, you don't want one of those. Go for the bag on the table. They're cold, don't worry."

"Hey, Pilsner Urquell. Shit, who brought these?"

"I did. Figure they're worth a coupla these—y'think?" He danced around prodding the dogs, which jumped in the boiling water as if they were alive. Then Cooper bent over the stove, tending the two silver pots with the concentration of a drummer.

"What are you going to do for buns?"

"Improvise," he said, this Gene Krupa in a stranger's kitchen, tapping drunkenly on the bursting skins.

Gradually the party moved from the house to the beach. I went upstairs to take a leak before following the crowd. Jill stood outside the bathroom door.

"I haven't seen you for a long time. Still working at the same place?"

"Yeah. Why haven't I seen you?"

"Well, I got a motorcycle, so I don't hitchhike anymore."

"That's too bad, but good for you. Are you still washing dishes at the Tourist Trap?"

"No, I'm cooking now."

"Great." Just then the occupant came out of the bathroom. I sat on the railing of the balcony and Jill went in. She was prettier than I remembered. She now had a deep tan, her hair had lightened from the sun, and an intrepid glow lit her blue eyes. Only a few people were left in the living room below me, and a couple stood necking on the deck. I watched the guy slide his hands over the girl's back, smooth her hair, then frame her face with his cupped fingers. He gently brought her face to his and held it there, aloft in the air. Her body hung below. A silent wind chime.

The door opened and Jill came out, smiling.

"I left the seat up!"

"Thanks."

I could smell her scent as I let the water flow from my body. A warm, womanly smell, the soft drift of perfume with the lambent tang of her vaginal essence. I stroked myself, growing hard, closed my eyes and pictured her, walking across the Rotary in shorts.

It wasn't easy stuffing my cock back in but I figured by the time I got outside my erection would disappear. I opened the door. Directly across the hall the bedroom door was wide open, and I could see straight through to the balcony, on which Jill stood, her back to me. I walked toward her.

At first I noticed the wind blowing her hair. The lights below cast a warm nimbus around her. Then, a sfumato of hair and smoke. The smell of sour flowers wafted into the bedroom. Her hand rested on the railing, a loosely-rolled joint between the fingers. I paused by the sliding door, one foot violating the plane of the balcony. The hand returned to her face. Smoke scattered hysterically. I found this disappointing; it would have been more satisfying to watch it drift away, sculpting itself into oblivion. The air hardened beneath my feet as I stepped further.

Beside her at the railing.

The joint in my hand.

A rush of smoke.

Smiles.

White stream.

Eyes.

The joint in her hand.

Her hand on mine.

We finished the joint together. The air bled itself to an anemic gray. The walls began to hum. My arms found themselves around Jill's waist. We hugged without kissing for a long time. I licked her cheek, her ear; tangled in her scent, breathing in her hair—a child exploring darkness, reluctant to turn on the light and lose the thrill of his fear.

Laughter sifted up from the beach. The sea grass shimmered in the glow of a fire. Jill walked inside and closed the bedroom door. Her silhouette shed its clothes. I entered the room, disoriented, until the warmth of her skin brushed against me and took me by the arm to bed.

My clothes slid off. I splayed open her legs with my upper arms and fucked her in torrents of that thing we always try to deny in ourselves. Her thighs hooked around my shoulders and she thrust back, surprising me with her strength.

I heard someone coming up the stairs to use the bathroom. The voices of two people talking. For some reason they got louder as the room filled with light.

"This is my parent's bedroom, which you have to see. . . ."

In the open doorway stood Jennifer with the one person I did not want to see.

Part III

These sands might be the end or
the beginning of a world.

—Henry Beston

22

No end to the swill of clouds in the septic sky . . . spiraling higher, tails dangling . . . mercurochrome seeping into the darkness over the blue calm . . . the deserted harbor . . . distant clangor. . . .

During the first weeks of our relationship, Tammy and I loved to take off and explore together. We shared exhilaration in the pursuit of the unknown. Whereas our friends gravitated toward prosaic activities such as lying in the sun on a public beach, we exulted in intrepid excursions, especially in exploring off-limits areas. Climbing fences. Vaulting parameters. Going around the hard way. Eschewing the mundane, the tried. We found in each other the partner to forge new paths and, ultimately, to raise the level of our existence on the island to the height we had been seeking all along, but could not reach separately.

One evening she brought me a beer through the back door when I was still on the dish line. My buddy Mark was catching behind me, and talking about his parents' motorboat.

"Do you have water skis?" Tammy cut in.

"Sure. We could go out anytime."

"When's your next late shift?" she asked me.

"Tomorrow."

"Is that good for you Mark?"

"Yup."

And the deal was done. Larry had the day off, so he came with us.

Mark suggested that we ski along Coatue, a long strip of beach delimiting the harbor, shaped like a steak knife: serrated on the inside but sleek along the ocean where we would ski— and only reachable by boat. Tammy and I readily agreed, as none of us had been there before. Larry, however, expressed concern, pointing out that we would be cut off from all forms of alcohol, but we won him over by packing two coolers full of beer. When we began loading the boat, Mark questioned the amount of space the coolers occupied. Larry countered, "It's only fair. I'm not bringing a girlfriend."

Mark eased the motorboat through the array of yachts anchored in the harbor. We were one of the smallest vessels on the water, but Larry adopted the simulacrum of a regal yachtsman. He wore a child's captain's hat that he had bought in one of the souvenir shops, and tied his bandanna around his neck like an ascot. Then he proceeded to bark corny sailing commands. "About face there matey. Hard alee! We're about to come out, er, about. Hoist that anchor, sailor."

I grabbed a beer and sat beside Tammy. Wind ruffled my hair. The pressure of the sun eased. As always, the sea air made the beer taste better. When we reached the jetties guarding the mouth of the harbor Mark opened the engine, and we began hammering across the water. I could feel the throb of the motor through my scrotum. My legs rested against Tammy's, which were now covered with goose bumps. The little blond hairs on her thighs stood up. Birds settled on the jetty rocks which were partially covered by the rising tide. We droned by as they stood, insouciant, feathers flayed by the gusting currents. Mark steered us through the funneling rock walls until we broke free and landed in the open sea. "That was the long way," he said. "I wanted you to see the whole jetty. On the way back we'll take a shortcut." He turned right and we sped toward the sloping coast of Coatue.

Mark anchored the boat close to the shoreline. There were no discernible waves, just the lugubrious tug of the water over the glistening back of the sand. The shore sloped upward on an incline well-suited to sunbathing. We all stripped to our bathing suits and waded to the beach. "Aye, don't forget our treasure," Larry called out from behind us. Then came a splash and a plopping sound. He had jumped in the water with a cooler and lost his balance. "Damn, lost it," he bemoaned, watching his can sink. A trace of suds lingered on the surface, then became part of the sea.

We spread our towels and lay in the sun. Larry and Mark made furtive glances at Tammy's long, sleek legs. It was a hot day; all of our hormones were boiling. Tammy asked me to rub oil on her body. Larry offered to help.

"Thanks, buddy. I think I can handle it. You could open a few coldboys, though." I felt proud of Tammy, gorgeous and glowing next to me. She moaned softly as I smoothed the first strokes of oil into her skin. Larry handed me a beer. It looked like he was getting a hard-on. Sure enough, he lay down on his stomach after scooping a little "nut-hole"—as we called them—in the sand. He gave me a wry smile.

Tammy's flesh melted in my hands as I massaged her. The sun bore down, dulling my vision into dark hues of brown and gold. I wanted to roll over on Tammy and enter her from behind. Beads of sweat formed around the vitreous hairs on her temples. I bent over and licked them, then brushed my tongue over her lips. Her exposed eye squinted open. My hand slid down her back, kneading her warm ass cheeks. "What are you doing?" she said through flushed breaths.

"I can't do anything," I answered, pressing my hand between her upper thighs.

We lay in the salacious press of the sun for almost an hour. Tammy sat up and asked if I wanted to take a walk. I assented in a sleepy daze. We grabbed a couple of beers and walked over the ridge of sand into a cluster of dunes. There were no other boats or people within sight. Sun, sand, a few shells; the desolate hum of a plane. The buzz of saliferous light. Tammy's incandescent skin. Another surge of lust in my groin. I could feel the sperm multiplying frantically. Tammy turned.

"All right, you tease." She yanked down my swimsuit. My cock sprang straight out as she dropped to her knees. "This is

what you get." She impaled her face, sucking with the abandon
of some crazy Greek god trying to vacuum the stars out of the
heavens. She didn't bother with any foreplay; just anchored her
hands on my ass and pulled me back and forth. I looked up into
the blinding light, the sun broiling my face, swinging with her,
sliding—pelvis contra tempo to head. Then I surged into her as
if dousing a fire, the light in my eyes liquefying, my knees filling with water, sinking. I fell to my left and she rolled on top of
me, thrusting me inside her. "That's what you get!" she snarled.

When we returned I suggested to Mark that it might be a good
time to start skiing. I couldn't handle lying in the sun anymore.

Larry volunteered to ski first, which was fine with me.
Tammy glared at me with sated cat's eyes. I sat in the spotter's
seat while Mark drove.

My roommate turned out to be quite a skier. Mark took off a
little too slowly, prohibiting Larry from getting on top of the
water, but he hung on, bisected by the dull blade of the boat's
wake: a tenacious sea anchor. "Speed up!" I yelled at Mark over
the roar of the engine.

"Right-o!"

As he pushed the throttle forward Larry's body rose from the
water like a Ziegfield Follies girl. We traced the smooth crescent of Coatue, Larry flying in a warm glissade behind us. Mark
turned sharply away from the curve of the beach. Larry handled
the divergent thrust of momentum gracefully, cutting through a
shroud of spray, echoing the shore with his arc. "He's pretty
good," Tammy said.

Let's give him a little more fun then," Mark answered. He
steered the boat through a series of turns. Larry gave the
thumbs up sign, grinning. In turn after turn he continued to
impress us, skiing on one leg and doing tricks with the rope.
Finally, as Mark swept by the beach, Larry released the cord
and glided right to the shore, landing on his feet in knee-deep
water. We all clapped as he turned, bowed, then ran up the
pitch of sand for a beer.

"Not bad for a white guy of uncertain parentage," I yelled.

"We'll see how well you do, Captain America."

Of course, I didn't do nearly so well; it took me four starts just to get up, and I wiped-out in less than a minute.

"Do you think you'll have time to give me some lessons?" Larry asked, handing me the rope.

"I still haven't finished teaching you how to wash dishes."

By the time the sun had crossed the sky we were all water-logged and drunk. Larry wanted one more turn, and I offered to drive. I lurched the boat forward accidentally but Larry still managed to get up. I took a few turns along the placid shore as we had done all afternoon, then decided to break the invisible groove we had cut in the water. I pointed the boat straight out to sea.

At first Larry enjoyed the challenge. The waves rose higher as we skidded across their corrugation. "It's getting rough out here," Mark warned me. I took a swig of beer and looked back at Larry's blur. He was doing fine. I kept going. The shore receded. A huge motor yacht crossed us in the distance. I knew the wake would be devastating. Mark said, "You better not take him through that."

"Don't worry, he's a big boy."

We climbed the large, rolling wave, flew through the air, then smacked down hard. Larry plowed through the parapet of water, holding on tightly with both hands and grimacing. Still I didn't turn back. I pictured us going all the way across fucking Nantucket Sound. Right into the triceps of the Cape. Tammy sat behind me with her arms around my waist. I had a beer in my left hand, the wheel in my right. The throttle full out. If it weren't for the reality of our gas supply, we might have spent the night in Spain.

Wave after wave pounded him. Larry began to look haggard. Compassion finally overcame me. I slowed the boat and turned back toward the harbor. It felt like the wind had torn a whole through my chest. The space between my ears was shot-through clean. My hearing had sharpened to the point that I could discern the turns of the engine. I gave Larry the thumbs up sign. He gave me the finger.

We rounded the bend into the harbor drunk, giddy, burnt; a platform of bronzed young people cutting the waves, except for Larry, who wanted to ride all the way in. He held on laughing but the exhaustion of his arms was apparent. We had given him a can of beer which he drank from triumphantly, toasting the yachts as they passed, this skinny, cross-eyed water rat, mottled with salt and bruises. Larry continued bravely until we reached the break in the jetty wall that Mark had pointed out earlier.

"It's too dangerous here," Mark said, giving him the cut sign. Larry released the rope. Tammy tightened her grip around my waist and told me to turn around and pick him up. He held his posture stiffly, sinking like a flooded statue with his right hand skyward, and that loony Cheshire grin. The water rose over his knees, climbed to his waist, swallowed his stomach, neck, and finally, for one tumescent second, only his face and arm remained. He looked like a demented Statue of Liberty. A wave devoured his head. His forearm cut the water like a shark fin then, with a silent plop, the hand and beer can disappeared. I cut the engine and waited for his return under the molten horizon.

23

Tammy and I also shared a love of dancing. Not ballroom dancing, or cute jitterbug twisting, but ring-out-your-shirt sweaty dancing: full tilt boogie. She was the first girl who had ever pushed me to the lip of exhaustion. Her energy level was boundless, her exuberance—unquenchable.

The best place to dance on the island is the Chicken Box, a rundown shack of a bar not far from the Rotary. The atmosphere whirls in a zydeco of sweat, bandannas, pool cues, loafers, sticky tables, working class beers, and worn denim—against a wall of live music and punctuated by a brass bell rung every time one of the bartenders gets a dollar tip. You might see the cutest preppy girl on the island doing the tango with a crusty fisherman in there. If Nantucket attracts mostly a homogeneous brand of vacationer, then the Chicken Box is the place where the oddballs end up. When archaeologists uncover the lid of this midden someday, the bones excavated from the Chicken Box won't match those found on the rest of the island. The bacteria alive in the marrow will still be dancing.

There were other places to dance and hear music—Thirty Acres, the Muse, the Rose and Crown—but none of them compared to the Box. They were, respectively, too sedate, conformist, and sterile. For instance, one night Larry and I were dancing at the Muse. He left the floor to go to the bathroom, and when he returned his arm was totally wrapped in toilet paper, which made a reasonably convincing faux-cast in the dim light.

His partner started unwinding the stream of paper and threading it through the dancers. Everyone loved it. Larry exclaimed, "I'm cured, I can move my arm!" The beefy bouncer kicked him out. No sense of humor.

Humor is the essence of dancing. Look at a dance floor and you will find everyone on it smiling. If they're not smiling then they probably need to urinate. If they're frowning then they most likely have to move their bowels.

This isn't to imply that bar dancing shouldn't be taken seriously. It's an art. Not everyone can dance well in a bar. Even professional dancers have trouble. Watch ballerinas—they're often the worst. Usually they are too rigid, moving like technicians, unable to escape the parameters of their training. To be good you have to forget about style, form, impression. To dance well in a bar you have to not worry about looking good. It's like falling from a height; go to the edge of your balance and the arms will flail, the legs will stretch, the body will twist. Take that step into space and fall. You can't help it or direct it, you're moving involuntarily. Now you're truly dancing.

Good dancers like Tammy move with their eyes closed. It may seem tougher to dance this way but actually it's easier. For whatever reason, the body flows better through darkness than the distracting vision of spinning lights and enjambed limbs. Perhaps it's less intimidating in the dark. One could dance along the edge of the abyss and not be afraid.

Many believe that alcohol enables them to dance better. These people belong to one category of what should be known as the "Dancing Fools." They are the worst offenders of the dance aesthetic, worse than "Inexperienced Dancers," or "Dancers Without Rhythm." Dancing Fools have no comprehension of the negative space shaped by their contortions. Better to be a timid dancer or a poor dancer and do your best than to be a Fool. The drunken variety is the worst, not simply because they are the ugliest to behold, but because they are offensive to other dancers and often hurt people with their sloppy gyrations.

There are other varieties, such as the "I-Think-I'm-Great-But-Really-Stink Dancers." They jump and contort maniacally, like idiots on pogo sticks. Some look like they are trying to screw themselves into the ground. Their crowning offense is the smug look on their faces. I'll mention just one other type of Dancing Fool: the "Women With Antigravity Arms." For some reason they think dancing with their arms over their heads looks sexy. These women also love to mouth the song lyrics. With *feeling*. Those arms never come down. Those lips are held in an ersatz pout. Every so often they shout, "Woooo!" These women make a career of shaving their armpits.

I am dancing with Tammy directly in front of the band. If I stick my arm out I can strike a chord on the guitar. Tammy's eyes are closed; she is pulsating outward from the center of her body, pullulating with vibrations. The room is shrouded in sweat. We have reached the reactive level of locomotion that occurs when the brain surrenders control of movement to the environment. Synapses flood with sound. Nerves jerk responsively. I have never heard this song before but I can predict the pattern of every beat, the occurrence of each caesura, like a metered line of verse.

Her pelvis is grinding against an invisible object. I move closer, spin, brush her, then sail away in the wake of her smile. We are geniuses of rhythm, breathing in time with the instruments. Moving without thinking. We could be flying, or swimming. It wouldn't matter. The air or water would be our music.

The sound is crisp by the speakers. Pure. We are encased in crystals. Every note felt as well as heard. To think is to pause. Our movement is *a priori*. Each action is historical. By the time it occurs another chord has been struck. To dance is to forget the present as it happens. We are denying time, moment by moment, movement by movement.

The band breaks into a fast song without pausing. A jolt suspends the crowd in the air. Suddenly, people rush to the dance floor as the guitarist cranks out the familiar opening of a Rolling Stones song. Everyone is thinking back to a special time when this song made him or her happy. A college dance. The high school prom. A night he or she got laid. The crowd swells with the ether of fantasy. For the duration of this song everyone is beautiful, perfectly coordinated, holy. There is not an atom of animosity in the room. Moving shoulder to shoulder, a hundred beating pistons in the same machine powered by the words everyone knows and sings out loud or to themselves:

I was born, in a crossfire hurricane

Tammy and I are serried. We are dancing laterally, and fast. Energy surges through the floor into the feet of the pressing crowd. I am moving without thought through the landscape behind my eyelids, guided by the forces of gravity like a planet, careening off the auras of the other dancers. Hundreds of arms, legs and torsos meshing together without colliding. A microcosmic Grand Central Terminal sped up to a blur.

A space opens to my left. I am spinning into it. When full-circle I catch the beat, pause, then jump into the air on the downbeat of the chorus-to-refrain switch:

Jumpin' Jack Flash it's a gas gas gas

The space closes. I'm back in front of Tammy. She sways in time with me. Another space opens. I start to spin into it, even faster. My body winds and arms spread for torque power. I thrust to the left with all my might, right knee raised. Suddenly a chubby girl moves directly in my path. Time slows to a crawl. The crowd moves in slow motion. I watch my body prepare to cream the girl. There is no chance of stopping. I am spinning too fast. It's impossible to change my direction. She doesn't see me coming. My shoulder is a foot from her face. Now inches. My only chance is to accelerate. Lift the knee higher. Push the turn harder. Incorporate the avoidance of her into my motion: make it the essence of my spin. I am a driver approaching a chasm who knows that it is too late to brake.

I contort inward, a giant held-breath, arms constricting as if in a straight jacket, that knee driving toward my left shoulder . . . until I clear her. But I have so altered my center of gravity that I am no longer balanced. At three hundred sixty degrees I must continue the spin to stabilize and avoid plowing into the wall of dancers surrounding me. My right foot is seeking the ground, the ball of the left foot turning, supporting me wonderfully, magically through this perdurable moment. As my body clicks around the second time I am able to lower my airborne leg and land safely. Only a blink of time has passed. Nothing has happened. Except that I've just completed a fancy double turn, and Tammy smiles approvingly. But I know that the beauty of the spin was entirely due to the chance interference of the chubby girl. I turn my head to get a better look at her, but she has vanished into the crowd.

The pool tables are busy. Earnest faces hover over the balls, shining with the radiance of fresh fruit on the uliginous surfaces. One player sharpens his eye to a knife-thin slit, taking aim through the miasmic waves of smoke and music. He makes his shot—nine-ball in the corner pocket—then returns to a sinewy girl in a tight T-shirt, who offers him a bottle and a drag of her cigarette. A game of pool is a serious affair in the Chicken Box. There are so many onlookers and people lined-up to play. The proper chalking of a cue stick requires an artful blend of élan and insouciance.

Tammy and I watch from the serrated periphery of darkness. The low fluorescent lamps cast a funereal tone over the players' faces. They move belatedly, like afterthoughts, as they calculate shot angles.

"Let's get a beer," Tammy suggests.

"Good idea."

We edge into the shapes surrounding the bar. I catch the bartender's eye. "Two Buds," I yell, loud enough to be heard across a lake, but barely discernible through the present din. He sets down two longnecks. I hand him a five. "Keep it." The cowbell clangs.

"Big tipper."

"You bet baby. With me you're on the top shelf all the way."

"Right next to the Budweiser."

"Why don't we get some air."

We stand in the humid darkness of the parking lot, a pocked minefield of sandy ruts and muddy puddles. Tammy rubs my back languidly. I feel very open in the phatic breeze.

"You know, I fell in love with you the first time you drove by me."

"When was that?"

"Early one morning. You never saw me. I was walking toward

Sconset Road to hitchhike, and you blew by me before I had a chance to get my thumb out."

"You gotta get up early to catch the worm."

"So I learned. There was another day—in the market. I was behind you in line. I wanted to say something to you but I couldn't think of anything. You were buying a six-pack; I figured it was for your boyfriend."

"It was for me! Why didn't you?"

"You seemed so cold. Distant."

"I thought you were cute."

"You did?"

"I'd seen you around town. Running around in those little shorts. But you acted like you weren't interested. For all I knew, you and your roommate could have been gay boys."

"Larry? Ugh. He stinks. No self-respecting fag would smell that bad. I'm just shy."

"Sure. I've seen you with other girls. I figured you were just one of those guys with bad taste."

"Oh, I was just lonely. They were my buddies."

"Uh-huh."

"Good thing you finally picked us up that day."

"Yeah. I might've grown old before you ever said hello."

"Women."

"Men."

"Fuck."

"Don't push your luck," she said, smiling.

A car entered the parking lot and rumbled past us. The headlights illuminated the intaglio of Tammy's face. A drunken couple stumbled out of the bar. Sound flooded through the doorway, then ceased suddenly. Tammy moved in front of me.

"So. Are we 'buddies'?" she asked.

"Nope. We're good buddies."

"Fuck you!" she said, laughing.

"Don't push your luck!"

"Oh yeah. You're the lucky one."

I looked at her, afraid that she was right.

24

The morning of Wopatoola broke, reluctantly, through an ice gray sky. No gulls were visible. I had slept little, running from the edge of a dream that I didn't want to see: staked to a shore, the frothy wash of an acid wave coming again and again, bringing its recreant nausea.

A broken memory lying in shards around me.

I lay in bed looking through the doorway, reminded of the shattering image from last night.

Larry is a corpse sprawled over the bed, great winds funneling through his nostrils, the historic stench of 10,000 beers rising from his skin and barbed wire hair. My groin is a sack of mercury. I urinate and shower, rubbing my body in an attempt to activate feeling, but I am moving through a leaden mist. The steam is comforting, womblike. It would be easy to stay in here all day. It would be even easier to stay in here forever.

Coffee helps to break the crust of my hangover. So would a little hair of the dog. I crack a beer and take a sip. It goes down warm, like medicine.

Larry will need some hair of the mammoth.

It's chillier than usual out on the deck. Planks float below me like stale strips of air. Across the ravine, Cinzano umbrellas flap anemically on the neighbor's porch. Fog obscures most of the water.

Scenes from last night flicker by in a sickening shadow play against the encompassing whiteness. The look on Tammy's face—a crushing, horrific epiphany, crumpling into a dark rage. Her eyes leaving a burning streak of light in the dark room as her head turned and the door slammed. The ruptured orgasm shooting painfully out of me into a void of numbness, a plug ripped from my body. The taste of bark under my tongue.

I see in a blinding moment of comprehension the absurdity of my life on the island, of my professed feelings for Tammy, of my job, and this journey toward spiritual fulfillment. I have been fooling myself on all these counts; there has been no greater purpose to my life than my own selfish desires and the pursuit of immediate gratification. Although I'm not chasing a dollar bill, I've been seeking the same end as the greedy crowd I supposedly left behind in New York.

We all have the same absinthe flowing through our veins passing for blood, the same malefic breath of avarice cut into words, which we salt with empty promises and devious actions.

Normally the intensity of the sun would be blinding at this time of morning. I now craved that unfiltered exposure to light magnified by water, thrashing its ignescent tail, attacking all vision. I sat, comminated by the horizon, like a weak shadow trying to fight its absorption into oblivion.

A gull freed itself from the grainy wall of fog, swooping in a roller coaster dive to the ground, then upward in a tremendous surge through the frayed mist. I leaned back into the railing, dozing with the sour taste of coffee at the tip of my consciousness, preventing any dreams from taking contrived turns of happiness. . . .

Larry found me on the deck sometime later. I heard his voice squeezing through concussional blocks of wind: hollow whales pushing the clouds.

"Guy. Time to wake up. Come on."

"What time is it?"

"Eleven o'clock. A little after. What the fuck. You were drinking already this morning?"

"Yeah. A little hair. . . ." He picked up the empty bottle. I picked my head off the floor of an empty parking garage. Every minute, a little boy had been dropping a glass bottle from ten floors up. In my dream I had chased the boy, but could not catch him. "I'm either going to need some aspirin, or another one of those. Something for the pain. I wish I could take something for the depression."

"Have an aspirin for the pain and a beer for the depression. Works for me."

"Sounds good." We went into the house and I downed the pills with the beer. Absentmindedly I scratched my chest, and my fingers tripped over a bead necklace Tammy had given me as a humorous gift. For an instant I had the guilty urge to remove it, but I let the feeling pass.

"So, she didn't say anything to you last night?"

"Nope. Just slammed the door. That's what hurt. The silence."

Tammy had driven off immediately. Larry and I managed to get a ride as far as Sconset Road, and then hitched the rest of the way home. A couple of high school kids picked us up after we had waited for almost an hour. I had left Jill at the party, and didn't say goodbye to anyone.

I drove Larry to the beach party on my cycle. I didn't much feel like going, but anything would be better than staying home alone, wrapped in the gray cloth of my thoughts. We pressed against a dishwater rainbow of desolate tones. I found this pleasing, this moaning etiolation, spread across the undulating moors and faint violet trees, the gray gulls white against the sky, the silver glissando of our engine, the plaintive groan of the roads, all wrapped in a mussitation of bleakness that could not be pierced no matter how fast we rode. So I drove into the sibilant arms of the island, glad that it was not sunny, clear, and bright. . . .

We joined the tail of the procession to Surfside Beach, a long row of jeeps, cars, bikes, and pedestrians—people our age and younger, moving dutifully ahead with their bottles and coolers, as if toward some great offering or sacrifice, but not a party. The river of cars broke into tributaries for parking. We pushed the bike ahead, half walking it over the now sandy road.

A drunken guy stumbled along the road several cars ahead of us, coming away from the beach. I could see that his clothes were covered with puke; he had the ravaging eyes of a wild dog. He approached a car, demanding something in sputs of phlegm and expletives. The car accelerated past him. He dove for the hood of the next car and bounced off into the ditch, unconscious. As we passed him we saw that he was barefoot, which disturbed me more than the sight of his vomit.

"Some fuckin' party this is," I said to Larry.

"I just hope there's enough booze."

"Why don't you ask his opinion?"

We locked the bike a safe distance from the entrance to the beach. The crowd appeared mellower the closer we got; the antagonism we sensed and the shouts we heard seemed mostly a parking matter. As we stood on the hill overlooking the beach we saw crowds of people moving slowly back and forth, some in groups and others just wandering lazily along the sand. Most people were drinking; a few smoked joints.

"That looks like one of the tubs," Larry said, motioning. "Let's check it out."

Larry led the way, threading through the milling drinkers and sand dancers, a happy crowd sombered by the overcast weather. Thank God that freak on the road was the exception, I thought. We stood in line around a huge trash barrel filled with a muddy, sweet-smelling liquid, into which people dipped their cups. Larry fetched two drinks. "Here, try this. Not much ice but it should knock any bad thoughts out of your head." I sipped the concoction and grimaced.

"Tastes like your cooking, Lar."

"Tangy."

I scanned the crowds for the only person on my mind.

"Don't worry. She's not here. She's probably upset as hell and a party like this would be the last place she'd be."

I knew he was right, but my eyes still sought her, involuntarily. People passed in dull blurs of color. "Let's move down this way," I suggested. I kicked off my Top-Siders, tied the laces together, and slung them over my shoulder. The coolness of the sand felt reassuring and made my sense of touch especially acute.

Down the beach we ran into a bunch of waitresses from the Lobster Trap. Kelly, the most gregarious person on the staff, called out our names.

"C'mon and join us."

"What's up?" Larry answered.

"Great day for a beach party, huh?"

"Yeah."

"Have you guys tasted that crap in the barrels?"

"I think it sucks, but Larry seems to like it."

"Yeah," he responded. "Got a bit of a kick to it. Not too bad."

"Just like my old man," I said, smiling. "He used to say, 'Lock me in a room with it for half-an-hour, and I'll learn to like anything.' He was referring exclusively to booze, of course."

"I wish I could've met him," Larry said.

Kelly pointed to the cooler by her feet. "Here, try one of these. We came prepared."

"Now you're talkin'." I grabbed a cold bottle of Rolling Rock. "I knew you'd have bottles. Why is it that girls never drink from cans?"

"They like the shape," Larry said.

"You're hopeless," Kelly replied.

We chatted with the girls for a while, but I wasn't interested in hearing work gossip. Again I found myself looking about the beach for Tammy's ghost. Larry stepped behind me and said under his breath, "There's bigger game on the beach. Lots of gut-victims. Let's go hunting."

"This from a guy who once put his arm around me and said, 'Guy, if you want to get laid, just do what I do. Lower your standards.'"

"Sound advice. Come on."

I followed Larry, not really caring where we went, just happy to have a cold beer in my hand and the cool sand between my toes. After a while a voice called out to us, "Hey, where'd you get those beers?" We turned and saw two teenage girls sitting on the sand. One had brown hair and wore a halter-top under an unbuttoned white shirt. The other wore a loose sweatshirt. They were fairly cute, but definitely too young for us. Larry walked right over. "You guys wouldn't want to trade one, would you?" the girl in the sweatshirt asked.

"For what?" Larry asked.

"A joint."

"Sure," I said, suddenly liking the idea of getting stoned. I handed the girl my beer, and took Larry's.

"Hey," he said.

"You don't mind drinking that rotgut." We sat next to the girls and shared a joint. By the end of it the brown-haired girl didn't look too bad. I watched her heavy breasts move inside her halter, but felt nothing move inside me.

Larry had begun one of his inane conversations about the Kennedys, his favorite "new acquaintance" topic. But it all went over the heads of these two teenagers. They weren't interested in stories of JFK, the Camelot years at the White House, or the jeep accident one of the kids had on Polpis Road, a short drive from where we lived. The sweatshirt girl stood and said she had to pee. I winked at Larry and we said good-bye, thanking them for the joint. The brown-haired girl gave me one for the road.

"Thanks. I owe you one."

"Don't worry. You can buy me a beer at the Box sometime."

"You got it."

We continued down the beach, seeing a few friends, chatting briefly, but for whatever reason, everyone seemed to be drifting —unable to connect at any level other than the most superficial. We met like unanchored boats on a calm sea, slowly driven apart by unseen currents. I tired of this routine and finally said to Larry, "I'm going over by that dune. You go ahead. We'll catch up later."

"What's wrong?"

"I just need to mellow out by myself for a while."

"All right, man. See you in a bit."

I settled in a sparse bed of sea grass against a gray beach fence. The thickening clouds made the day grow colder.

Waves ran over the shore in an irregular yet comforting cadence. The sky murmuring. Clangor of blades around me. I fished the joint out of my jean jacket and lit it. Smoke wound through the corrugated light. For a moment brightness swelled within the lactic skin of the sky, but then sank behind a dark bank of clouds. I held the smoke in my lungs for as long as I could, until my organs dissolved, until my blood became like the blue-gray sea air: just a layer of skin separating the mist inside me from the mist around me.

Silently, a girl with vivid olive skin sat beside me. I offered her the joint. She took a hit, passed it back, and then took one more. Rising, she smiled, then walked over the bank of sand.

I finished the joint, buried it in the sand, and lay back, like a little boy nestled in a huge canopied bed. Grains of sand scratched over my clothes. The light dimmed. My breath slowed to the pace of the ocean's.

25

I remember starting out on a walk along the beach. A light rain had fallen. Tammy sat in the pocked sand way beyond me. The sand became thicker, making it difficult to walk. Like water, it rose above my knees, over my waist. I tried to run. The current flowed against me. Something below the surface held me by the back of my pants. She stood, looking at me. I waved my arms and called her name. She turned away and walked to a white sailboat resting at the water's edge. I could barely move forward. A rope floated on top of the sand, which I hoped was tied to the boat. I picked it up and pulled it. The boat didn't move toward me, but still I hauled the rope in. An anchor burst through the sand. The boat moved away from the shore. I started to run toward the water, but someone was calling my name from the deck of the house.

"Guy. Guy. Guy!"

Something grabbed my shoulder.

"Wake up." Larry stood above me. I felt disoriented and wet. "You were sleeping in the rain. Man, are you out of it."

"Fuck. How long was I out?"

"About an hour. Hey listen. I got someone who wants to meet you."

"Ah no. I don't want to meet anyone. I just need some coffee." I rubbed my head. Sand had lodged everywhere—in my hair, ears, crotch. I walked around the dune and took a leak. A group of people could see me but I didn't care. Piss streamed out of my body in a holy arc.

"I met these two beautiful chicks. I hit it off with one and the other is dying to meet you. Her name's Helen. I told her all about you. She loves motorcycles."

"Fuck man, after last night, I feel guilty just touching my dick to pee."

"You need to cheer up buddy. You know the old saying. Women are like buses. There's another one along every fifteen minutes."

"I really don't want to meet anyone right now."

"Just hang tight."

Larry trotted down the beach and came walking back with two young women—both teenagers. That's just great, I thought. Teenagers. And they were cute. He introduced the blond first, who was a little chubby. "This is Clare." And then he indicated the one with chestnut hair, "And this is Helen."

"Ellie," she said, as she slowly held out her hand.

The four of us exchanged greetings, then entered that awkward silence common to all meetings of sexual proclivity. I made a weak joke about pulling up a chair as I saw that I was condemned to talk to these girls. Larry said, "Clare and I are going to run over for some drinks. You guys hang out. We'll be right back."

"Get me a beer," I yelled after him. "And what do you want?" I asked Ellie.

"Whatever."

"And a whatever for Ellie."

She had a perfect face and body, perfect like so many young people on the island—who all must have been raised in genetic laboratories: no blemishes or body fat, thick full hair, aerodynamic features—an island of preppy mannequins dressed in white cotton and blue denim. I had seen the parents who bore such children and was amazed that they did not possess corresponding beauty; it was as if their offspring blossomed magically from flawed cocoons, rising into the air from bald paunchy fathers and wrinkled peroxide mothers like the respiration of butterflies. I wondered if the parents knew how miraculous their children were. I also wondered if these children of the island saw the halos floating above them.

How could they! As if there were any mirrors that could reveal to them their futures: how they would grow old like their parents, have children, and relinquish this ephemeral luminosity to the next generation. But as long as they stayed cradled in the lap of the island they would remain eternally young and beautiful, like Ellie. Their heads would turn with the delicate rapture of Picasso's harlequins, painted against the blue canvas of air. . . .

She leaned back on her hands, legs bent before her, head turned toward me, contraposto, an innocently lascivious sculptor's model. Soft blond hairs showed on the exposed skin between her moccasins and pant legs. A macramé bracelet hung from her wrist, dirty-white against deep copper skin.

"Do you work?" I asked.

"I'm an au pair for a family on Union Street."

"What's that like?"

"It's not too bad, but it makes me not want to have kids for a long time."

"I can see that. How many are you taking care of?"

"Two little brats. One's five and the other's seven."

"At least you don't have to change any diapers."

"There's no way I'd do that."

She had a handsome face, most likely her father's, but it gave her a sense of strong character, laying a special angle to her beauty. Like the old Hollywood starlets who didn't hide behind the overstuffed lips and exploding hair of today's movie idols, hers was a black-and-white loveliness, brought to the surface of her face in calm shimmers, not hydraulic embellishment.

As we spoke, her eyes cleared like heated water. The wind blew through us, constantly unpinning the hooks our words hung upon. Music grew behind us, dogs chased a Frisbee, couples necked on the sand. A girl ran screaming after a guy who had untied her bikini top, which he swung over his head, out of her reach.

"I'm not used to all the fighting. I'm an only child," she said.

"No kidding, so am I. Are you glad?"

"Sure, but it might've been nice to have an older brother."

"Yeah, so you could steal his sweaters."

I felt warmer toward this young woman the more we talked.

149

She was just about to enter her first year of college in Boston, and accepted it complacently as the next step in her life, unlike most kids her age—rabidly worried about clothes and other superficial matters. I thought back to my anticipation of college, and how awkwardly I had dealt with it. This young woman had arrived at the security of her emotional breakwall years before I had. Seeing life as a day-by-day process instead of worrying about the future. Not being swayed by peer group judgment. Setting one's goals in a realistic manner. Give me a call when you graduate, I kept thinking to myself.

We caught up to Larry and Clare who were drinking and wanted to stay. Ellie said she wanted to leave, so I offered her a ride home on the motorcycle. She said she would enjoy that.

"Go for it, buddy," Larry said with a wino's sagacity.

"How close are you and Clare?" I asked Ellie as we walked up the sand bank.

"Not very. She lives on our street. We only met this summer. She runs with the party-hearty crowd."

"Sounds perfect for Larry."

"Yes, they drink well together."

As we rode Ellie put her arms around me with a sweet gentleness that made me think of Tammy. The sweetness mixed with my guilt and I felt my back grow cold and rigid.

Ellie got off the bike in front of her house, reluctantly. "Do you want to come up? The family's gone till tomorrow."

I looked at her, flooded with nausea and compassion, until the image of the wind lifting the hair off her face drove me to say sharply, "No. I can't." I got on the cycle and started it violently, as if I was trying to stamp out something small and ugly under my foot, something hairy and sticky that could crawl in your throat and choke you if you didn't drive away from everything very fast and end up somewhere cold so you could feel the breath passing through your lungs and forget about what had been dogging you until you could sleep and then nothing mattered because you couldn't stop whatever the dreams brought.

26

Dusk.
Shadows rust along the ponds.
I float on the dross of a dark marsh.
Reeds scratch the enveloping vellum with
Soft jots of wind.
The skin of the water tightens.
Gulls dive through the decaying gouache of sky
Like desperate timpani.
Marooned in aluminum.

21

Several days passed and I had been unable to speak with Tammy. She would not return my calls, answer my notes, or see me at the store. I had become a nomad with nowhere to roam. The four walls of the sea redounded my sense of guilt and anguish.

Larry and I strolled up Main Street after work. Lamps burned through the salty darkness. Dave sat on his bench, calmly smoking a pipe. His guitar lay beside him. I sensed something out of kilter, but didn't know what.

"Hey Dave. How's it goin'?" He looked at me solemnly, expressing an emotion I'd never seen on his face.

"My dawg's gone."

My eyes shot to the missing piece of the picture at his feet. He turned his head away. A moist intensity saturated his eyes and filled the space around him.

I didn't know how to react. Part of me felt like laughing at the twangy way he had just spoken. But the sincerity of his sadness overpowered the corniness of his expression.

"Where did he go?"

"I don't know. He didn't tell me."

"When did this happen?"

"Yesterday."

"Maybe he's just lost. This is a busy place. He'll probably turn up soon."

"Nope. He left me. It's my fault."

"Your fault?"

"Yup. I told him I was gonna go in the bar and get some food for us. I parked him by a tree outside and told him to stay. After about ten minutes he came inside and found me havin' a drink. I could tell he was pissed. I hadn't fed him since the day before and he musta been hungry. Well, I had to take him back out. When I came out with some food a few minutes later, he was gone."

Dave relit his pipe. "Yeah," he said, exhaling smoke, "I ain't been a good friend. He's been ticked at me. I don't think he likes it here. Probably figures he can do better on his own."

"No, I'm sure he'll come back. Have you checked with the police?"

"No. They'd just make me fill out some forms and waste my time. Besides, he's not that stupid. He's probably off with some rich poodle."

Dave took out his guitar and started to sing:

After you've gone
And left me cryin'
After you've gone
There's no denyin'
You'll be blue
You'll be sad
You'll miss the best pal
You've ever had

He sang through the moon in his throat, his voice filling the void of his loss.

We sat for a while, not talking, steeped in the exilic tranquility of the island's motor—turning incessantly, humming, drowning out extraneous sounds and magnifying the immediate—listening to the mewling whine of the wheels below, the teeth of ancient gears, enjoying our gentle ride like old folks on the carousel benches. . . .

The air grew thin, inviting. The thrill of the bars beckoned; excited voices carried up the street.

"Dave, why don't you have a drink with us?"

"No. I think I better stay here. No tellin' what'll happen."

"Okay, buddy." I turned his hat over and stuck a bill in it. "That's for one later."

"Thanks. I appreciate it."

We drank for a couple of hours at the Atlantic Cafe. Nothing exciting broke the dull thudding rhythm of our glasses. Around midnight I suggested to Larry that we visit Benny at the bakery.

"Why not," he replied. "There's nothing happening here."

"I could go for a good cup of java. Something to perk me up."

"Something or someone."

We went up Orange Street as we had so many times, pacing between the four walls of Nantucket; the idea of walls calls up the image of walking: put a man in a cell and watch him go. It points to the fallacy of the "grass is always greener on the other side" maxim: even when a man is chained to one side he'll still move around behind it. This is the myth of America, the myth of the diaspora west. We traveled past the frontier not to seek the unexplored, but simply because we needed to walk and kept going until the Pacific Ocean stopped us. We walk like robots powered by solar batteries. Up and down, back and forth, until the walls crush us or we fall off the edge.

I traveled to this sandy vortex, this epigamic paradise, for reasons that were different from those of the annual shipment of college kids on summer break. I am on a life break. The longer I live here and seep into the fabric of the island the more I realize how transitory my existence is in any place. Hordes of tourists may flock here every summer but I am standing on the edge of the sand, ready to take the next wet step. This was the escape hatch for America during its first days—the place where the early settlers came to flee from the reactionary Puritans who ruled the Massachusetts Bay Colony in the seventeenth century. I have all the requisite means for a life of departure—an ethos of isolation—at my disposal. Nantucket overflows with the raw materials for the spiritually deracinated. The water. The moors. The wind. . . .

Strolling up the lifeless street with Larry, I realized that the one thing I was not ready to cope with here was attachment; not the friendly persiflage of social acquaintance, but the nascent roots of love and commitment which I had ripped out of Tammy: painfully; carelessly; foolishly.

I had not anticipated Nantucket as a garden. It was to be my tree house, a place of refuge. A childhood friend had told me about it, the wild summers he had spent here as a teenager; the lonely winter after he finished college. He had come then to map out his future and write a book. Instead he discovered his latent alcoholism and languored in a cold depression.

I began to wonder how long I should stay, if I should continue through the winter. Nantucket, an Indian word meaning faraway island. Also known as the Gray Lady. Ironic, how all of the island's nicknames are desolately poetic.

It was now the middle of August. The summer kids were already starting to leave. I enjoyed watching the ranks of the vulgus thinning. The days growing shorter, reminding one of the long winter nights to come. Larry would leave in two weeks, and I would have the house to myself, except for Ken on the floor above me. This both elated and saddened me. I rolled like a coin along the sidewalk, just as happy to land on heads or tails.

We came to the bakery but found it dark. I knocked. No one answered.

"Let's wait. Benny should be here any minute."

"Fine with me," Larry answered, then wandered back to the corner.

I stood by the door, peering inside, fascinated by the huge, crude machinery used to make such delicate edibles. A car came down the alley next to the bakery. I moved toward the door to get out of the way. As the car paused at the corner before turning onto Orange Street, two brawny guys, natives, happened to be walking up the sidewalk. They looked inside the car and said something to the occupants, which I couldn't hear. Then one wearing a tight green T-shirt started drumming violently on the roof of the car with his fists. The car peeled out and they crossed the alley haughtily—stomachs drawn in and chests puffed out like faux soldiers. This all occurred in the periphery of my awareness; my eyes returned to the luminous interior of the bakery, the mixing machines waiting with the hibernating patience of frozen dinosaurs.

Something unnatural in Larry's movements caught my attention. He stood further down the sidewalk, almost out of my sight, staring provocatively at something. His gaze projected a seductive intensity—the false challenge of an emboldened terrier. He began moving away like a body falling through water, then shouted, "Fuck you." I took an inquisitive step toward him. At the sound of footsteps he ran down the street without any explanation. Suddenly, the two brawny guys rounded the corner and came at me. A blind punch glanced off the side of my head as Greenshirt careened me into the side of the bakery. I bounced off the wall but still managed to stay standing. Enraged, I dove at the one who pushed me, swung my fists at his head, and sent him reeling. His friend grabbed me from behind and held me tightly so Greenshirt could punch me out. Without thinking I backpedaled with great force and drove him into the wall. In the momentary lapse of his movement after impact I smashed his face into the wall with my elbow—so quickly that I hadn't turned yet. He fell to the ground. As Greenshirt stood up, an immense anger rose from the base of my being—I saw myself tearing through ferns in a dark forest, hacking at foliage with a crude machete—and I bellowed, "Fuckin' come on!" The yell was so loud and overpowering it even surprised me. Greenshirt looked at me, sneered, helped his friend up, and they ambled away. I was glad, for the yell had drained me. I leaned against the wall, a cored-out shell. The sore spot on my face throbbed.

Benny came up a minute later. "What happened to you? Your shirt's ripped, there's blood on it."

I rubbed the lump on my head. "A coupla local boys got a little rough."

"Why?"

"Fuckin' Larry taunted them, then ran. Typical Larry. When the going gets tough, Larry goes."

"Let me get you some ice. C'mon in."

"Thanks, man. A cup of your coffee, I'll be good as new."

28

Benny fixed me up pretty well. He gave me ice and a bandage for my cut. I sat in the front of the store among the empty glass cases—away from the throbbing mixers—to relax. My right elbow started to feel sore from being slammed into the wall or hitting the kid; maybe both.

I was pissed at Larry, that skinny little megacephalic runt, not just because he ran, but because he provoked those kids with his fake-macho, epicene manner. So many times that summer I dragged him away from little scuffles and near-fights that he had no business being in. Like the time he bad-mouthed the bouncer at Thirty Acres and would have been stomped if I hadn't interceded. I don't think Larry had ever been in a real fight because if he had ever felt a solid punch he wouldn't dance with so many hairy fists.

When I felt better I thanked Benny and walked back toward town. The streets were very quiet, morgue-like, making me confront an even deeper bitterness I harbored from the attack. Something within me, something intimate had been violated, beyond my trust in Larry. The sacred seal of the island's tranquility had been shattered by that punch. I thought I had escaped the ugly, faceless face of violence endemic to cities. Nantucket had been my outpost—what I thought of as the last vestige of America's spiritual frontier. A place where a man could light his pipe and watch the smoke rise without being shredded by a cacophony of fouled winds.

I could feel the bruises in my body conspiring to blossom tomorrow. My steps became angry. For the first time in months I hurried with the stilted cadence of a city-dweller. As if I had somewhere to go! As if I needed to risk my life to cross a busy intersection. As if money was at stake—the great calibrator of time. As if the seconds saved by my accelerated pace could profit me. Boy did I move down that street: like a lawyer to his meeting or a shopper to his sale.

I slowed down when I hit Main Street. The anger eased out of me as I looked in the window of Congdons, at the ancient steps of the Pacific National Bank, and then noticed the apartment of the first woman I had made love to on the island. The dark little window on the second floor next to the artist's studio—closed, unlike that night we had spent together, when our sounds tumbled down to the street and must have raised the eyes of a few passersby. I tried to remember her name . . . Carol. She had left immediately afterward because of a family illness and never returned or wrote. Larry had kidded me that I scared her away, and I wondered how different things would have been if she had stayed.

Probably not much different.

I remember lumbering down those wooden steps to the muddy alley beside her house and walking to the public john— the same path I now took—down India Street, then left on Federal, drunk with sexual fulfillment. Wanting to shout through the dark windows of the little boarding houses and share my elation. The air was so crisp that night. . . .

There is more graffiti on the john walls now—a wave of summer kids had left their marks: the drawings, poetry, philosophy, and advertising of a transient civilization. The stuff on these walls was no more clever than the writing in other rest rooms, but I held a sense of pride for it, the way one does watching the Olympics when a countryman wins some obscure event like the luge or hammer throw. I drank, ate, and worked with these people and, if nothing else was written about this summer, this splice of existence, then this was our signature, for whatever it's worth.

But it's not important, because you can't capture the experience of a place in such ways—whether through graffiti or hieroglyphics—you can just carry the memory of it for the rest of your life. You can try to relate your experiences to others but it's tough to pull off, because the caducity inherent in human nature kills belief. When the young hear the stories of the old they can't fully comprehend them because they aren't able to imagine the old being young. I could spend my grandparenthood trying to convince my descendents what a sexually exuberant experience I had here and they would just chuckle to themselves, the way I laughed at my grandpa's stories. Which is fine. Because any story that ends in laughter is fine.

I waited for a middle-aged couple to pass before leaving the dark entrance of the john. The lateness of the hour made me feel subversive. As if there was anything to subvert here. Maybe a few sea gulls. No, even they fed off the litter of the tourists.

A couple of laughing kids squandered the dripping serenity of Easy Street by the basin. I had hoped to sit on my favorite bench facing the water but they forced me to search further for solitude. The musk of exposed seaweed hit me abruptly. It's funny how smells spring at you on the island without warning. Must be the whim of the winds.

The wharf bar was closed, the docks silent. No boat parties. I ambled along, tired, sore, but happy to be alone, walking over the water into the arms of the sea's darkness, surrounded by the chimes of the sail lines. I walked to the end of the last pier. Something sat in the stern of a big boat. Slowly the brown outlines of a human form dissolved into clear features.

"Marsha."

"You're—"

"Guy."

"That's right. The young man who found my watch."

"That's me. I see you're back in port."

"Yes we are. Fabulous Nantucket."

"We're so happy to have you back. I know I speak for the entire island in welcoming you—"

"Thanks." She lifted her legs off the couch and set them on the floor.

"Tough time sleeping?"

"Yes. I hate it in the cabin. It's so stuffy. I'd stay out here all night if we weren't on this dock where anyone could walk by."

"Anyone?"

"My husband's away. He flew to Boston on business and left me here . . . as 'captain.'"

"You look very commanding."

"You're just full of compliments tonight."

"Well, that's my quota. Don't expect any more." I leaned against a stanchion.

"Would you like to come aboard?"

"I've never been on a boat this big before. Well, I was on the QE-Two once. But that doesn't really count. It was a tour."

White sandals lay scattered on the floor. On the table sat a thick fashion magazine with a French name something like *Haute Vapid*, next to a bottle of fingernail polish. She had on a white cotton sweater and pressed blue jeans that look like they hadn't been worn much. Her hair was pulled back in a ponytail, accentuating the deep tan glazed across her face. Pearls jangled against her collarbone when she moved.

"This is really nice," I said, sitting gently. She looked at me studiously.

"What happened to your face? Did you bump your head?"

"No. I got into a little fight tonight."

"Fight? Where?"

"By the bakery on Orange Street. Seems somebody wanted the last cranberry cupcake, but I got to it first."

"Here, let me get you some ice."

"No need. What's done is done."

"There is a need. Look at that bump. The ice bucket's right here." She popped the lid off of a container that looked like a futuristic cookie jar and put a cube into a napkin for me. "Here. And how about a drink."

"Ah—that's very nice of you. What do you have?"

"Everything. What do you like?"

"Uh—" hundreds of drink names flashed in my mind, but none appealed to me.

"How about Scotch? Do you drink Scotch?"

"Sure," I said, trying to appear sophisticated. She went into the cabin.

"Would you like to look around?" she yelled up.

I walked down the steps. Everything teak and brass—humming with chestnut dignity. "This is really nice. Did you decorate it?"

"Decorate. Ha! It came this way. I just picked the flotation pillows." She worked at the sink making our drinks.

"How many does this sleep?"

"Ten, almost comfortably. Two in the master bedroom. Two in the guest cabin. Two back there. And those turn into beds."

"Wow. It must be great for entertaining."

"I hate entertaining. Here. Let's go back up." She brushed past me as she handed me the drink. I could smell the germ of her sex—the essence of a middle-aged woman: burnt-out ovaries, stress-free sweat, Chanel No. 5. The thought of my mother hung before me momentarily.

"Now tell me what really happened to you," she said, stretching out on the sofa.

"I'm not really sure. It happened so quickly and irrationally."

"Violence always does."

"I was standing outside the bakery with my friend Larry. A couple of townies walked by, two husky kids—younger than me. I didn't really notice them, but Larry said something to them and they came back toward us. Then Larry ran away, and as they rounded the corner they just saw me standin' there and jumped me. One hit me, I slammed him in the wall pretty hard, I guess they sobered up, and then they went away. The strangest thing is, they didn't say a word. Nothing. I mean, it was fucking surreal."

"Two on one, that's hardly fair."

"Yeah. Thanks to good old Larry."

"Sounds like a fair-weather friend."

The Scotch went down warm and wrapped around me like a blanket. I leaned back into the creaking wicker chair as my eyes followed the line of Marsha's body from toes to face. "You want to know the strangest thing? I don't know if I can explain this, but there was a weird sexual aspect to this whole thing. I mean, you should have seen Larry leering at these guys as they passed, the way his lower jaw swung forward, like a little animal looking to mate with a bigger one, as if he was imploring these young guys to smother him with their muscular bodies. And when they came at me—no taunts, no insults, just insidious grins, like they wanted to rape me. I dunno, there was something lascivious about the whole thing which disturbs me."

"That is strange. Hmmm." Marsha looked at the sky. I took a big swig of my drink, not sure if I had made any sense. But I didn't care. It felt good to get the feeling off my chest. We sat for a while without talking, then she refilled my glass.

"How long are you here for?" I asked.

"Till the end of the week. Then my husband flies back and we sail for Newport."

"Is that where you live?"

"Yes. Yes. Newport." She sighed. I didn't feel like getting into the details of her life, and she didn't look like she wanted to either.

Water sloshed against the boat. I felt the pull of the sky above and the suction of the sea below. This is all that is left to us, a narrow landscape of existence between two dark planes. Marsha's eyes were closed. We sat inches apart. Shortly we would slip away from each other, never to meet again. Now we were squeezed together, unable to fit anywhere else on the face of the earth. I put my feet on the table and settled into the chair. The Scotch had wrapped another blanket around me.

"It's not working," Marsha said with distaste. "Can you tell?"

I let the words hang in the air, then said, "What?"

"My husband. My life. The whole thing."

"It doesn't look that bad to me."

"That's it. That's just it. Here I am, married, with three kids, two houses, and a boat. Doing well by any relative standard. And all I can think is: is that all there is? Is this *it* for my life? I'm not going to get any younger or happier or healthier. And I couldn't be any richer."

I closed my eyes. I had no answers for her. Then I said, "This is pretty ironic. I end up on Nantucket trying to escape my life before I've even lived it. And here you are, living a great life, and hating it. What kind of hope does that leave me! Doesn't anyone come here just to have fun?" She laughed.

"Here, have another. This will let you sleep well." By now I didn't know whether I liked the taste of Scotch or not, but I craved its warmth. I thought of my father's expression and chuckled.

"What's so funny?"

"Oh, nothing. My dad had this expression about booze. 'Lock me in a room with it for half an hour and I'll learn to like anything.'"

"That's good," she said. "I was just thinking about my own parents. I'm more amazed, the older I get, how people can stay together that long. My mother always looked so happy. So satisfied with her life. And she adored my father—to the end."

"That wasn't uncommon with their generation."

"One day, many years after I was married and having my first crisis with Jim, my husband, I asked her about that. How she kept that . . . I don't know . . . cheery facade. And I'll never forget what she said."

"What?"

"Your tears will bleed through other organs."

Marsha lay quietly, folding into herself, her mind revolving in the foil eddies of a pool of gin. I let the darkness flood into my mouth, through my nostrils, between my fingers. There in the lines of my palm lay the crushed dirt of my aspirations—different from hers. Not tilled and irrigated, but fallow; unplanted. Her disillusionment was with the life she had led, mine with the life I did not want to lead. Perhaps we were on the same road but I had taken this exit marked by a sign that read "3000 Miles To Spain." I had thrown away the map. There must be other roads, I mused, as I sat wrapped in warm arms I couldn't see or feel or . . .

29

I awoke under a bright sun, under a blanket, on the deck of the boat. The sofa Marsha had been lying on was empty. Before me sat an empty glass and the open ice bucket, partly filled with water and dead bugs. I tried to get up, but a dull pain shot through my lower back and thighs. I crunched around on the wicker chair trying to loosen my joints. A painful urge to urinate propelled me out of the chair and down the steps of the cabin to find the head. My pants bulged with an erection, pointing like a divining rod to the place of my relief.

I passed the partly open door of the master bedroom. Marsha lay naked on the bed, a Neapolitan mélange: white ass, brown torso, pink sheets. I paused to admire her tan form, voluptuously entwined in the sheets, but a higher calling pushed me forward. I flipped up the lid of the head and let an orgasmic rush of white urine pour out of my body.

An aberration in the mirror made me look up. A note was taped to the glass. It read:

> *Guy,*
> *Join me?*
> *M.*

Her words made my cock grow hard again.

I pumped the head out and took the note into the cabin. Folding it, I wrote on the outside:

164

Spindrift

Marsha,
Thanks for talking. Right now that's all I can do . . .
Guy

I put the note on the counter and left.

Stepping into the held breath of daybreak, I felt like an astronaut moving through a lunar landscape shrouded in lonely white light. Boat hulls sparkled with diamond reflections. Everywhere the bleating lap of water. The clack and plop of shifting tides. No human voices or motors.

As I went toward town, I noticed the huge cruise ship that had just come in, tethered like a brontosaurus to the pier. How incongruous it seemed, next to the ancient wooden dock. What an ugly way to visit Nantucket—motoring through the water inside thick metal walls. Of course, there will be more of these ships as the years pass, and more T-shirt shops to serve them.

Cappy sat on his favorite bench by the mouth of Straight Wharf. His eyes were glazed with the yellow mucus of alcohol and insomnia. He didn't look well. I gave him a dollar and he smiled in imitation of a human being; distorted, like the refracted image of a fish in murky water.

Down on Water Street an old woman stooped over and picked up a piece of litter.

"Good morning, Mrs. Walsh."

"Can you believe this? Have you ever seen so much guck on the streets in your life?"

The wind blew a pizza plate against her leg, which stuck to her knee. She didn't notice it.

"Yeah, it's pretty bad. Inconsiderate tourists."

"Well they can all stay home if you ask me. We don't need 'em."

We stood surrounded by an economy entirely fueled by tourism. "Well, maybe they need to be told—"

"Told smould! What are they, three-year-olds?" She bent over, grabbed the pizza plate, and carried it to the trash barrel. I noticed the doughnut-shaped sign hanging over the Downy Flake restaurant and my head filled with the thought of warm

165

baked goods waiting to be consumed.

"Good talkin' to you, Mrs. Walsh." She didn't seem to hear me. "Invaduhs."

The Downy Flake is the first restaurant to open in the morning, hence it attracts a lot of native workers, as well as a few tourists queuing up for the early ferry. The place is famous for its fresh-baked doughnuts. It's a nice joint for breakfast if you can get in early, but after 7:30 it becomes clogged with the bed-and-no-breakfast crowd. I judged that it must be a little after six. The doughnut line hadn't formed at the door yet and few people were inside.

As I looked around for a table I noticed a familiar figure in the back booth.

"Ted, is that you?"

"Yeah, man."

"Fuck, what happened to you; I haven't seen you since before the ferry thing."

"I've been laying pretty low."

"No kidding. What happened? Did they catch you?"

"Well, yes and no. I mean at first everything was cool. . . ." The waitress came and took our orders.

"Wait, start at the beginning."

"Okay. There were four of us. We got on the noon Steamship heading to Woods Hole. Our plan was to jump off when we rounded Brant Point and swim to shore. Me and Breland, a friend of mine, were going to jump off the top deck, but the other two guys were scared of the height so they were gonna jump off the lower one. The plan was to jump on the island side of the boat because it's closer to shore and less dangerous. We set our watches so we'd all go at the same time. Well, the time comes and Breland and I are just about to go when this siren goes off and we hear 'man overboard!' We look down and don't see anything; then I realize that those two jumped on the wrong side of the boat. They're caught out in the middle of the sea-lane tryin' not to get munched up by motorboats. So I look at Breland and say, 'now or never,' and we go over the side beautifully. It was an incredible rush, flying through the air, then, splash!—we're under water in a world of bubbles and foam. I can hear the Steamship's engines churning and my stomach's in my mouth. We break through the surface gasping for air and there's the ferry a couple hundred feet away. Then this Coast Guard boat speeds out to pick up the other two guys and we got scared, so we see a sailboat coming by, stick out our thumbs like hitchhikers and they picked us up."

"Wow."

"Yeah, it was incredible. These guys were really cool—a bunch of college kids down from Boston renting this big sailboat. We told them what we did and they thought it was cool so they took us sailing all day."

"Did the police ever find out?"

"Well, when we got back that afternoon I called the station and said that we were the other two guys that jumped and we were okay and everything. So the cop says, that's great, and why don't we stop in for a minute to chat? I told him that it was okay and we'd rather not—we were hungry and wanted to get a bite. Then he said if we were smart we'd stop in the station or else."

"Did you go in?"

"They found Breland the next day, so I had to. They really chewed us out; they were pissed. We're gonna get fined and we have to perform some community service."

"At least they didn't charge you."

"That was the alternative. But it pisses me off—everything would have been cool if those jerks didn't go over the wrong side. They also jumped right in front of one of the ferry hands. Really stupid."

The food came and we started eating.

"So, are you working at the store?"

"No, I got this kid running it for a while. I want this thing to blow over before I show up there. If the old lady found out she might fire me. See, the cops don't know that I work there. Anyway, this community service kind of screws up my schedule."

"Oh yeah? What do they got you doing?"

"Garbage detail. In fact I gotta report to work now. Here—"

"Hey, let me catch this."

"Thanks. Hey by the way, I got a great new scam for making money."

"I'm not sure I want to hear this."

"No, it's great; can't fail. What's the one thing you can't get here on the island?"

"A date with a Jewish American princess."

"True, but no: Big Macs."

"You mean McDonald's?"

"That's right. We're gonna take the ferry to Hyannis, buy a whole bunch, and then bring 'em back and sell 'em here at a big markup."

"You're crazy."

"Think about it. Catch you later."

"Later."

I had the early shift that morning. Looking at my watch, I saw that I had just enough time to ride home and shower.

The roads were clear as I swung around Washington Street, past the churning power station on the way to the Rotary. The bike catapulted around the empty circle and shot between the white lines converging in the distance. Nickel-laced drafts coated my mouth and throat. Helmetless, I wore only my shades for protection. Cold blasts of air showered through me. I rose out of the seat, invigorated by the speed, the hum of the motor, the grainy lucidity of the cement rushing at me. Standing in a scream of wind, I felt like a pilot flying naked without the metal clothes of his airplane.

A car approached from the distance. It appeared to be a jeep. My heart thudded deeply. Both lungs swelled with air. As it passed in an orange flash of sunlight, I yelled out, "Tammy Barrett!" as if it was her.

As if I might get her back.

And then, suddenly, I believed that I could.

I started laughing with gulps of joy so hard that I had to sit down.

30

When I arrived at work old man Fisk had already started making the day's batch of chowder. Part of the first wave of modern tourism that came to Nantucket in the 1950s, Fisk had built the Lobster Trap into a profitable business after much hardship. Competitors had turned his advantage of being the first big restaurant on the wharf into a disadvantage by building in front of him, blocking his customers' view of the water. Fancier restaurants lured customers away with gourmet appeal as the island ascended in affluence, but still Fisk persevered, catering to the mass of unsophisticated tourists drawn to his cartoonish sea shanty decor. The place was actually seedy compared to the elegant establishments around the harbor, but to most undiscerning day-trippers, lobster is a lobster is a lobster, so his business thrived.

The Old Man—as we referred to him behind his back—never said more than a clutch of words to me during any one week. Usually he just grunted to signal the negative, and nodded to indicate the affirmative. His words fell like stones out of loose mortar.

He stooped over the huge chowder pot as he did every day, stirring in the ingredients of his personal recipe with a wooden, oar-like device, cigarette in mouth—off to one side—like a man stirring the contents of his soul. He had delegated every task of his business to managers, cooks, and accountants except this one, and as I watched him I tried to fathom why.

On one hand, the answer was obvious: it probably gave him pleasure to keep one finger in the kitchen, but seeing him throw in the ingredients with nothing more than the most quotidian level of enjoyment—no, engagement is the best word— this didn't make sense. In went the salt pork, the onions, potatoes, quahogs, and cream, tossed with the stoicity of a Balthus subject. He stirred and grunted and watched the pot simmer.

Ashes fell from the old man's cigarette into the chowder. I had noticed this several times and concluded that it was his secret ingredient. Maybe this is why he never wrote down his recipe, nor let anyone else make it. I once asked Easy Al what happened if Fisk didn't show up to make the day's batch. He told me he always kept a pot frozen just in case.

This well illustrates the ethos of the Lobster Trap. Not only did we stock frozen chowder, but frozen lobsters as well. Serving frozen lobsters in Nantucket is like putting Russian-grown apples in the pie served at a state dinner in the White House. People travel hundreds, even thousands of miles to this island to eat an authentic fisherman's meal in the seafaring birthplace of America, and they get something that could just have easily been served in Indiana. And, as if to magnify this insult, this injustice, we microwaved the frozen lobsters, too.

If people only knew what we did to their food, what every restaurant does. . . .

Tony the broiler man had devised a fail-safe system to protect food that fell on the floor during preparation. I discovered it one day as he handed Jason a filet mignon. It slid off the sizzler plate used for broiling, and smacked the floor like a dead fish. "Don't worry," Tony yelled, "it fell on a napkin."

I had to see this so I turned and looked.

"Where?" I asked.

"Right there." He pointed. I still looked nonplussed. "Don't you see it? It's right there on the ground. I got napkins everywhere. On the floor, behind the stove, the broiler. It's a simple rule. Every time somethin' falls, it lands on a napkin. Saves time." He picked up the steak, wiped off the wet debris sticking to it, then put the refurbished filet next to its garnish on the serving plate. "A little dust-off, and wa-la. Good as new. No one can tell the difference and, in fact, I sprinkle a little oregano on the floor every night before my shift. Adds flavor!"

Around four Larry came in to change for his shift. He saw me on the line platform.

"Guy! Man am I glad you're all right. I was worried when you didn't come home last night. . . ."

He paused, as if to let me cut in with an explanation, but I didn't, standing above him, simmering in a duet with my lobster pot. I have discovered that there is nothing you can say to cause a person more stress than saying nothing. The guilt poured out of his mouth, and I enjoyed it.

"I'm really sorry I ran . . . I'm glad you're okay. You're okay, right?"

"I almost got pounded, because of you."

"I went and got the police. We expected to find you in some ditch."

"Thanks. For nothing."

Larry could think of nothing to say. He looked around but all walls pointed back to my gaze. Having no other physical outlet he worked his big New Hampshire jaw back and forth under his skull; the pockmarks on his face glowed like burning craters. I let a long beat pass, and then said, soberly, "You ran Larry. You got me in trouble, then left me." He looked at me with repugnance, which confused me at first. Then I realized it was directed at the unfiltered picture of himself I had shown him. "I thought you were a friend, but you're just a fucking coward."

"Look I—"

"I pulled your drunk ass out of a lot of fights this year, and stood up for you, too. So just forget about it and don't give me any of your horseshit rationalization." He huffed and went upstairs.

Tim came on the line to replace me. "Hey, how'd you get that cut on your face?"

"Got into a little fight last night. Nothin' serious."

I hope you kicked his ass."

"I stood my ground, that's all."

"That's what counts."

"Ah, everything's stocked. You got two dozen oysters left and I pulled some cans for you. Plenty of bugs in the walk-in. Lots of bread crumbs left—slow lunch."

"Thanks."

I threw my apron in the bin and left through the back door, not wanting to see Larry. Kendall gave a big wave.

"When's it done?" I hollered.

"Tomorrow," he said, chewing on a licorice stick.

"That's great. We'll have to celebrate."

"Don't worry. We'll have the beer."

"I'll be here."

"How 'bout one for the road?"

I caught the red projectile before I had even finished the sentence.

Following my thoughts up the road. A quick wash-up in the public john. Barnacle-like corrosion gnawing the chrome fixtures. Back up the street, past the Boarding House. A voice shouts, "Guy, how 'bout a beer?"

"Who's buyin'?" I call back.

"I am!" the voice answers.

Rounding the corner, I find Grant and his entourage around two tables pushed together. They're rollicking on uneven keels, the table full of smiles and empty bottles. As I sit down, his girlfriend Katie returns with an armful of beers.

"Just in time," someone says.

"Just born lucky," I explain. Grant hands me a beer.

"So. How's work?"

"Pretty good. I'm cooking some dinner shifts now. Big game dishes. You know—bugs, mussels, steamers."

"Not bad. And how's your lady?"

"Ah—we haven't been too close lately. Kinda takin' it easy for a while."

"Sorry to hear it. She's somethin'."

"Yeah. She sure is." The words hung before me, stinging my eyes with their smoke. I lost my appetite for conversation and welcomed the oncoming wall of alcohol building around my senses. Bottles piled up like bricks. The level of sound grew as people flooded the terrace, conversations mixing, slapping in crosscurrents, washing through the ashtrays, chairs, and hair in lush waves. After three or four beers I ambled into the bar to buy a round for the table.

"Give me some beers."

"How many?"

"As many as this will buy," I said, slapping a wad of bills on the bar.

While setting the beers on the table something caught my attention. With a blur of recognition a familiar form passed through the periphery of my sight. My blood pulsed. Tammy walked by on the other side of the street.

I knew she hadn't seen me. "Here you go," I said, sloppily placing the last beer on the table. "Gotta book." Grant looked at me. "Internal affairs. Very important."

I ran down the street after Tammy, not knowing what I wanted to say. Jogging up next to her, a riff playing beside the melody, she gradually became aware of a presence, realized the footsteps were moving toward her, then turned—and saw me. She hesitated for a second and then swung back.

"Hi."

"I don't want to see you." She kept walking.

"Tammy look I—"

"I *really* don't want to hear it." She walked away stridently. I stood in her churning wake, stunned by the darkness of her furrowed eyes.

The horizon ripened, swollen with pre-dusk color. Clouds hung in the sky's maw like bloody rabbits after the kill. Looking back up the street, having another beer with Grant appeared to be my most promising option.

31

A man with a six-pack is a friend to the world. He has no ene-
mies. Leaving Hutch's package store the next day at dusk, a
warm hand landed on my back.

"Help you lighten your load?"

"Hey Steve."

"Haven't seen you in a while."

"Crazy schedule."

"Yeah? We're slacking off now. Just finished a job."

"How's Alex?"

"Alex? She's takin' a little vacation over on the Vineyard visiting a friend. We've been kind of hot and cold the past month.
More cold than hot."

"Here." I flipped him a beer. "I'm headin' over to Brant
Point. Wanna come?"

"Sure. Got nothin' better to do."

We got on my bike and drove toward the beach. On the road
out of town a hairy guy pushing a cart sang out, "Sharpen your
knives, scissors, blades," repeatedly. He rang an old cowbell as
he clanked down the street, one of the last blunt edges of an
increasingly sharp world.

Sights like this barely seem ironic on Nantucket, a place
where poor people still fish for a living, and rich people come to
eat their catch. An island that tried to secede from the United
States, but depends entirely upon it for its livelihood.

Rounding the bend onto Easton Street, Steve pointed to a

couple of expensively dressed girls. "Check it out."

I yelled over the motor, "I'm sure they're heading to the White Elephant. Probably just flew in from New York. They'll rent a jeep, buy some sweaters at the Loom Shop, have dinner at The Chanticleer, and send postcards of the shops on Main Street telling everyone what a wonderful experience Nantucket is."

"You're pretty cynical, Guy."

"Just realistic."

Later, six empties lie at our feet. Star rays rend the sea grass. The sky to the east is dark blue. To the west, a deep red. Overhead, it looks like two oceans making love.

Steve picked at his sandal. "So, what do you think?" he asked, floating with the driftage of beer. "I'm in a relationship, but not part of it. What does she want? I don't understand."

"Well, here we are, supposedly in America, but I don't feel part of it either."

"Women."

"Nantucket."

"A world apart."

"Which?"

"Take your pick."

We listened to the Pentecostal surf, as though it had any answers.

"You know, there's one thing you have to say about this place, it moves at its own speed."

"Is that good or bad?" I asked.

"I think it's good. I mean, I've been here for five months, and it feels like a year. Time is so full. You could live three or four lives here. Raise a couple of families. Get married a few times. Like Picasso, a new wife every ten years. Trade her in when you get tired. Never grow old."

"A kind of 'Mormon aesthetic' if that's not an oxymoron."

"Sorta. Think of what you could accomplish. Write ten *Moby Dicks*. Sculpt a hundred *Pietàs*. Paint a thousand *Mona Lisas*."

A brightly lit ferry rounded the point. It reminded me of Ted's ludicrous "creative" act, and I chuckled to myself. I felt sad for all the people going home, but happy that I wasn't leaving.

"When's Alex coming back?" I asked without forethought.

"Who knows, next week maybe. We had a big fight before she left."

The subject of Alex made me uncomfortable. I quickly asked, "Is that the last ferry?"

"Think so." We sat in the darkness.

"There's something about boats that I like."

"Maybe because it's easy to pull anchor and get the hell out of wherever you are?"

"That may be it."

We stared into the long, silent tunnel of darkness. Here, even at the aphelion of my life, I could feel the pull of the continent before us, and the compunction to reenter an imperfect life rather than live on the fault line of a supposedly idyllic one.

"So are you gonna stay, Steve?"

"For a while."

"The winter?"

"I don't know about that. Depends if I have something to keep me warm."

"You've got your books."

"That's not what I mean."

"I know."

"Whada you say we get a drink?"

"Hell. I was just getting up the nerve to give you a kiss."

"Gotta move faster than that. No time for indecision."

Steve suggested we try the White Elephant first.

"Don't get your hopes up. Those girls are fast asleep by now."

"No way. They're at the bar having bloodies."

"What. To stimulate their shopping hormones?"

As I thought, the bar was almost empty. A few bored waiters stood around polishing surfaces that didn't need to be polished. "Not much atmosphere."

"What do you mean? Out here under the stars, the moon reflected in the pool, how much atmosphere do you want?"

"Alex's been gone too long. Let's head into town."

After parking the bike we walked up Broad Street.

"You know where I haven't been for a while?" I said.

"Where?"

"The Brotherhood."

"Sounds good."

Rain broke in glass shards upon the pavement. Nothing stood out against the dark canvass of this night—even the lamp-posts were painted black.

Usually, a line of tourists would be outside the Brotherhood waiting to get in, but we were now past the prime dinner rush.

"Just in time," Steve said wiping the drops from his face.

Walking into the Brotherhood is like entering the basement of your grandparent's house. Dimly lit and low-ceilinged, the restaurant's brick walls and dark wooden furniture exude a feeling of intimacy. Customers sit on benches and share long, common tables, spilling conversation on each other in a glazed euphoria. The atmosphere is woven in brown cloth. A fireplace warmth infuses the room.

We were seated next to two girls at the end of a table. The waitress dropped off menus: two-foot long, corn-yellow sheets, crammed with delicate brown handwriting.

"Have you ever seen so many drink choices?" Steve asked. "Christ, there's enough words on this thing to fill a novel."

"You're not kidding. Listen to this," I said, reading from the menu:

"'Brotherhood of Thieves'—the name of this bar and ordinary is taken from a pamphlet written on Nantucket in eighteen forty-three by Stephen S. Foster who fanatically attacked those forces of his time that supported and perpetuated the then American system of slavery. Nantucket with its shores far from the intrigues of the mainland maintained a rugged sense of its own individualism and its distinct identity that carried forth through its people's individual character and its inherent eccentricity and a sense of uncompromising independence. This sense of personal freedom could not only permit the development of ideas and ideals of self-definition but, by design created a definitive 'Island Heritage.'

"Heavy stuff for a menu. What do you think?"

"I remember the fries are great. They're called shoestrings, and come in baskets like—over there. Pardon me miss." Steve pointed at the fries in front of the girls next to us. "Do you mind if I show this to my friend?"

"Here, do you want the rest of our food?" one of the girls asked in mock annoyance.

"No thanks. Just a little graphic illustration."

"You see, I've never seen a shoestring fry before. I'm from Ohio. They're banned there. I wasn't allowed to read *Catcher in the Rye* in high school either."

"His was a deprived childhood. Thank you ladies for making his day special."

"Our pleasure."

We won the girl's friendship quickly. Not a hard task on the island. An easy peace exists between the sexes. An atmosphere of trust. Potential partners float past like barges on a canal: slow, steady vessels—easy to board but hard to steer. So why all this worry over Tammy? Surely I could find another mate. I looked at the girls, mouths open in laughter, wrapped in fresh sweaters, long brown hair. I saw them growing older, thickening; becoming grayer and wrinkled. I saw them heavy with children, thin with age. Moving along a track of unvarying speed toward an inexorable end. Two attractive cutouts with cardboard skin. One of them—either one—panting below me, legs held in stirrups of darkness. The dolphin light of television painting our lives. A soundtrack of lawnmowers and doorbells. Litanies of delivery trucks and children's complaints. Quotidian sex, clipped from coupon circulars. Abandoned exercise regimens. Saucy glances in checkout lines. Intoxicating fantasies at the gas pump. Lingering neighbors. A lifetime family history recorded in burnt pots, hand-me-downs, outmoded appliances, neglected neckties, and pet graves. I saw the luminosity of memory rise like a wave of nausea and dissolve in wistful puddles of rain. I saw lives fattening like the moon. The saga of accumulation, replayed in thirty-second spots on TV and radio for the rest of our days. A swimming pool of coffee that had passed through my throat over sixty years. A man I had created, shaking my hand in a cold room, the screams of new children echoing off bare walls. Soft hands arranging things, touching me briefly, propping my head on pillows. A hand turning a knob, the flicker of light, and an image appearing before me, smiling beguilingly. All collapsing in the horror of this final vision.

With Tammy none of this seemed possible. A crushing sunrise lit the future I envisioned with her. The evening of our years settled into a warm adagio. I felt marriage could be the graveyard of love, or just as easily its salvation.

Reluctantly we left the warm cocoon of the Brotherhood when it closed. The patina of the hot rums I had consumed encrusted my body as we stepped through the chill air. We had listened to a good folk singer, a black woman from Boston with thick braided hair. She sang about love and pain—I think her songs were original compositions—in a way that hurt but felt good, cathartically. Like the soreness that comes after exercise. Her songs were about the female perspective of love, about broken women, abandoned, lying wide-eyed in the darkness. As she sang something opened in me. For the first time I thought about the other side of the commitment issue—the female side. For years I had believed that women held the power in relationships, but listening to this woman and hearing her describe the vulnerability of her experience, I could see that men might cause the most hurt. There's nothing specific I can point to, but something happened when the lights dimmed, enabling me to see through the glass of the singer's eyes, to a darker stairway descending behind them.

For some reason I thought I could reach Tammy now, although I didn't know exactly how. I felt I could at least begin to communicate with her, instead of just insulting her with excuses. There's no visible starting point when you've hurt someone; the end, the resolution, is all that matters.

I remembered looking at New York the night I first arrived there, staring at all the moving lights. Standing across the Hudson River, they all seemed to blend together into a horrific galaxy. Like the stars, which to the untrained eye all look the same. Then, as I grew to know the city, I could associate each one of them with the job they had to do—direct a lane, sell a product, stop a thief, mark a subway stop. Street lamps, traffic signals, construction blinkers, office windows, taxi globes, Broadway marquees—all pulsed with their own voice. I would figure out how to talk to Tammy. I would figure out the language that needed to be spoken.

32

The sun hit the window with the force of a wrecking ball. I had overslept; in a gray nightmare Tammy had inflicted the worst form of rejection upon me: indifference. She was living in a city I had moved to to be near her. I tried to visit her. She opened the door and looked through me. Behind her on the couch sat another man. This scene replayed itself, ending with her closing the door on me each time, not saying a word. Finally, the third time I entered the apartment. All she said was, "You can stay if you want, I don't care," then she slipped off her clothes and positioned herself on all fours so the man could enter her from behind. Suddenly she was on her back and I stood outside the door of the frame of a house, looking up through the scaffolding as Jennifer, the host of that fateful party, knelt in front of me, saying, "See, she's done with you, she's gone to the next level," while loosening my fly and then sucking my cock. The dream ended when I couldn't get a hard-on.

I made coffee and watched the cursorial waves chase the shore. Larry was already up and gone. His absence instilled the house with an eerie ambience. He had put the mail on the table. I found a letter addressed to me in strange handwriting; the envelope had been forwarded from my Manhattan address. It was from a friend in New York who wanted to let me know about a job that was opening up. One of the medium-sized brokerage firms he dealt with was starting a new family of mutual funds and they needed a salesman. He mentioned my name to the managing director and the guy had heard of me through a mutual acquaintance, an old client of mine for whom I had made a lot of money. He wanted me to call him if I was interested in the job. I put the letter back into the envelope and took it to my room.

I got to town a couple of hours before my shift started. The population of tourists had thinned considerably since its peak in July. It wasn't hard getting a seat at Congdon's counter. I had coffee and a hot dog, watching the current of people pass, making short little trips to shops or restaurants before they made the ultimate trip home.

Then I noticed a very strange sight, a man in a heavy charcoal suit walking down the street. And not just any man; as he neared I realized that he was a vice president at one of the firms I used to work with. I laughed out loud. "Look at that stiff, clueless bastard," I said to the kid behind the counter. "He doesn't know how out of place he is. Look at that, a fucking suit on Nantucket. Eighty-six degrees! And my God, wingtips to boot!" I looked back at the kid. "Have you seen any suits since you've been here?"

"No, I don't think so."

My first impulse was to go out and say hello to the suited-man, but looking at him simply disgusted me. Besides, what would he say to my ripped jeans, three-day growth, and bandanna? What would be the point of communicating? It would be like trying to feel the wind through glass. I wondered what he hoped to experience here that he couldn't do in New York. Buy a few expensive dinners? Walk on the beach in sandals, black socks, and a short-sleeved dress shirt? Purchase scrimshaw earrings for his wife? He was probably staying in the Harbor House, the most affluent and sterile of the island's hotels, driving a rented sedan, and chartering a motorboat.

Images of my former life flooded up from memory: I saw the reptilian face of my boss, gills rippling, yelling at me about some inconsequential matter as she drowned in her insecurity, waves of captious invective washing over me with her daily tsunami. I saw her scratching her arms and legs from anxiety to the point of bleeding. What a sour nadir of existence: a life consumed by tedious work and self-inflicted stress, a life that served to make other lives suffer, as though she wanted to drag as many souls as possible down to her unique hell. A woman, a human being, so infused with animosity that she moved with the crippled jerks of an unoiled car, grinding its gears to death. An appropriate symbol for the cankerous side of New York City, a place where people grind by each other without words in a rush to board subways that will carry them to a job for a few hours every day until the oil runs out of their lives. Go to work there a few thousand times and watch the humanity evaporate from your soul.

Amy Stein! How can you justify sacrificing that which makes you human for your job? What satisfaction do you derive from your arid life as your panting face hits the pillow every night? How many years will pass before you lose *all* human semblance? When will you finally wake up as a lizard, unblinking, alone on a blighted landscape, a plane of existence with no perspective, no shadows, no feeling, except your quick tongue lashing through the empty wind?

Smiling girls walked by. I thought of the intellectually constipated women of Manhattan, the ones who speak as they inhale, wearing the fractured-porcelain smiles of affluence or attitude, depending on their station. How brittle, compared to the easy smiles of the island girls. The au pairs without cares. How could anybody leave this life to join the doxology of accumulation? Isn't it enough to accumulate experience? To collect the honest touches of innocent summer girls? To feel the naked mouth of the sun on your groin, on an empty beach, singing in its reflected glory? To ride along the bluff at dusk against the wind and feel the world lighten its grip on your shoulders? To smile at a woman you don't know and will never see again, exchanging a thrill tremor that can be carried the rest of one's life? Are these not the pillows we wish to have on our deathbeds? Who can rest on cushions of money? How comfortable are the sharp edges of tin dollars? Which lays heavier on the scales, our experiences or our bank accounts?

Of course there are no answers to these questions. There is only a cup of coffee on the counter, a bookstore across the street, and the ocean surrounding it all. There are only a few weeks till

183

the pace of the island slows to a crawl, till all my friends will be gone, and then I will be left on the true island. Time to shop for a sweater and a winter job. Time to think. Time to savor the last viscous drops of sunlight, before the clouds roll in and the sand freezes. Even the birds are packing their bags.

Walking up the back stairs to work I notice the completed roof across the alley. Kendall and his crew are gone. I can still feel the warmth of his work radiating from the fresh wood.

Easy Al is on the line and I am glad. Mark is at the dish station. We'll have a good night. Joy will seat the tourists and we will cook for them, giving our best effort. The lobsters will stand on the plates, balancing lemon wedges on their noses like seals. It will be a goddamn beautiful night on this little outpost of America. In a way, I think, shucking my stock of oysters, the order of the country starts here. If the sun rises over this spit of land and everything is going right, then it can roll right over the edge of the country and continue west, undisturbed and smooth. We give birth to the waves of resonance that wash over the United States. And if something isn't right, ordered, settled here, if the island burps or hiccups, then it sets the whole country off-balance. It doesn't take much: a car could crash, a house could burn, or we might not have enough oysters for tonight's meal. That could do it. Then Buff would have to write "86 oysters" on the chalkboard over the call station and the signal would go out. It would sweep across the country like a barometric reading: Mr. Smith didn't get his oysters-on-the-half-shell, the island lurches, the continent tips, and the whole country feels the aftershock. Thoughts of grandeur on a humid Tuesday night in the kitchen of the humblest restaurant in the universe.

The back wall of the restaurant is white, and each night I watch movies of my life play across it. I'm never lonely when I work here, except when the radio is on when I'm cleaning up and I hear that song they've been playing all summer:

I cried when I wrote this song
Sue me if I play too long

Spindrift

I'm never lonely because I don't have to think about what I'm doing; I move in the brush-strokes of a jazz drummer, so used to my routine that I watch my hands perform as if they belong to someone else. I've got the timing down so tight that I usually have my orders up before Al calls for them. With Jason it's different; he's busy insulting the old waitresses and flirting with the new ones, so he often screws up the timing. But I really don't care anymore. I've proven myself and mastered the job. No matter what, it affords me a lot of time to think—to think in the delicious mode of rhythm which is very different from the type of thinking one does in an empty room, or on a park bench. There is a meditative quality that infuses rhythmic thought. The repetition of motion frees one somehow to enter a more rarified plane; perhaps the brainwaves deepen to the alpha state, where phenomena such as rapid eye movement occur? I feel like a Platonic automaton.

I have no inclination to jar the easy routine of my life, but something about the irenic pace of it disturbs me. Perhaps it is the Puritanical spirit inherent in Americans, prodding, cajoling, warning that one should never accept an undemanding routine in life—one should strive for that which is beyond reach. Looking down at my feet, I wonder if they have dug too deep a groove where they are. I feel like I'm standing in the surf: the longer you wait the harder it is to pull yourself out of the suck of the sand.

We have a good night, serving two hundred fourteen dinners and running out of only one item: baked potatoes. The lobsters sell well to this late-season crowd, but the raw shellfish aren't as popular. These are mostly non-New England tourists and they like their seafood cooked. Occasionally one of the waitresses will relate that a customer asked for a lobster to be prepared "well-done"!

The only event that manages to spoil this otherwise idyllic night is the sight of Nat the busboy gobbling up the half-chewed leftovers from the plates he has cleared off the tables. Nat is the goat of the kitchen; he will eat anything left on a dish: stray kernels of corn stuck to the cob, bits of meat on a lobster's mangled ribs, even the last sip of a beer. He's proud of his indulgence, and we learned long ago that his behavior couldn't be modified through embarrassment. Buff doesn't seem to mind Nat's habits. He probably figures it saves money on garbage bags.

At the end of the shift Larry came through the back door with a six-pack. Ever since the bakery altercation he has been trying to solicit my goodwill. I can no longer remain angry at him; I was hardly hurt during the incident and I realize that he acted within the boundaries of his character, and without conscious malevolence. Who am I to judge someone else, I thought as I washed my hands, watching the six-pack swing under his arm, a glass and cardboard pendulum swaying with the rhythm of anticipation we had shared so many times that summer.

33

Storm prelude. Pressure of dark keys. Ivory clouds. Humid tones. . . .

A rainy mid-week morning and I am up early after a full,
refreshing sleep. The night's moist air held me with cool arms.
Larry must have spent the night in town with a new girlfriend,
as his bed is undisturbed.

While the coffee is brewing I discover we're out of milk so
I'm forced to go to the market. Going out the backdoor I nearly
bump into Ken, who is walking down the steps in his bathrobe,
unshaven and seemingly disoriented.

"Morning Ken."

"Yeah."

"How's it going?" He doesn't answer as he paces around the
foot of the stairs. "Are you okay?" He looks increasingly agitated.

"If the cops come, just tell them I'm not around. That you
haven't seen me. No, don't tell them anything . . . just say I'm
not here. That's good. That's the truth."

"What's wrong?" He looks at me, able to focus for the first
time.

"Wha—well . . . it's a long story. I don't have any time. Hey,
could you do me a favor?"

"Sure."

"Here." He takes a set of keys out of his robe pocket and
throws them to me. I notice he's only wearing boxer shorts
underneath, and he has on sandals. "Would you park my jeep

down the road somewhere—anywhere. I'll find it. Just park it there and leave the keys in the glove compartment. I owe you one. Thanks." He walks off toward the beach, hands in pockets, head looking down. I watch the back of his legs move away; they are whiter than the rest of his body. He looks very old and weak in this undressed and unkempt state. The gray light has bleached his normally ruddy features: his reddish hair looks like the burnt end of a cigarette.

After moving the jeep I went to the market. When I returned I found a police car and two unmarked automobiles parked in front of the house under the sundial. Four men stood together, two in uniform and two in plain clothes. A third uniformed man led a dog around the yard. I slowed down as I neared the group, which stood between me and the steps.

"You live here?" one of the plain-clothes cops asked.

"Yes. On the first floor."

"With Ken Robinson?"

"No, he lives in a separate apartment, on the second floor." One of the cops started to jot things in a small notebook.

"What's your name, son?"

"Guy Sherborne."

"You live alone?"

"No, a guy named Larry Gillman lives with me." They asked a few more personal questions, then the cop taking notes asked, "Do you know Ken Robinson?"

"A little. I see him occasionally. But we're not good friends, if that's what you mean."

"Now, we have a warrant to search these premises. Do you mind if we look around?"

"No, go right ahead. Is it okay if I make my breakfast? I got some coffee on the stove if you'd like some. . . ."

"No problem," he said ignoring the second part of my statement.

I followed one of the plain-clothes men up the steps, wondering if I had any illegal paraphernalia they might discover. I knew there were no joints in the house and couldn't think of anything else. The detective walked through the door of our apartment with me, gave a cursory look around, and said he'd be back. I waited in the kitchen until he left, then looked around the rest of the apartment quickly just to make sure there wasn't anything incriminating about. I realized that my fears were unjustified, but there's something about the glare of a policeman that can make the most lawful citizen feel guilty. As I returned to the kitchen I thought, shit, my only crime has been the way I've treated Tammy. And I've already been busted for that.

I left the house as soon as I finished eating and checked with the cop leaning against the patrol car. The other ones were still in Ken's apartment.

"It's okay," he said, "we're only concerned with the guy upstairs. We know you're not involved with this."

I didn't want to appear overly inquisitive, but I was too curious not to inquire about the nature of Ken's crime. "Whad he do?"

"This Robinson fella's a dealer. Brought a lot of cocaine onto the island. God knows what else."

I then realized why Pete was out here the day he gave me the coke.

"Good luck," I said, wanting to get as far away from the house and the stern-faced cops as possible.

I'm terrified of policemen because you can't joke with them; they rarely have a sense of humor. Their world view is so dark that they usually jump on the negative side of any situation. They are prone to overreact and misinterpret. Not because they are inherently negative people: they are trained to be that way. Bred from thousands of years of violence. Weaned on sour milk.

Once in high school, a friend and I were walking down the street with a few unopened cans of beer. A patrol car saw us and stopped. Two cops jumped out. I froze in a position of surrender, but my friend tried to throw his beer cans in the bushes. The cops threw him to the ground and put him in handcuffs. They made me out to be a good guy. It was black and white. We were held at the station house until our parents came to get us. They never returned our beers. We had committed no crime, but the perception of our potential to do so—to drink in public —got us in trouble. And my friend's reaction ignited the tender

189

fuse of violence in them. To this day I'm convinced the cops just wanted a free six-pack.

On a deeper level, I am disturbed merely by the sight of the police, who are rarely seen on the island. Their presence is a reminder of the laws of a more violent society, thirty miles across the water. As each day passes, I feel America moving closer. Somewhere a wench is turning, sucking the chain of the continent over its teeth. I can hear it clanging through the salty lips of the surf at night.

I rode to the Steamship dock. Sunlight hit the water in hard, caramel strains. Few people were around as the first ferry pulled out with the dark lurch of organ music, sad as a skating rink melody. A man pushed an empty loading cart back to its resting place; it clanked in loud metal reports without the burden of luggage. A young boy on a bicycle stood as he pedaled over the ocean of asphalt toward the fast food establishments not yet open.

Gulls swooped over the lip of the dock like factory workers starting a shift. A squabble followed the ferry out to sea. Tourists and students looked solemnly over the Steamship railings at the island they were leaving. People seldom smile on ferries bound for the mainland. More pictures are taken on the way out than in. It is as if all at once, the departee realizes what he is abandoning. It's not like stepping into a plane: ferry departure is a mournfully slow process, one sees what he is leaving diminish by degrees; the island recedes with the speed of a funeral procession.

The passengers step backwards into the sea. I turn and follow the path of my shadow back to town.

On one of the streets in town I find a sparsely attended garage sale, hosted by a very content couple in their sixties. Perhaps self-satisfied would be a better term to describe their demeanor. There is nothing contrived about them; their faces are calm and the wrinkles turn upwards, making them appear happy. The items they are selling are simple and useful; you can tell they have lived utilitarian lives without ostentation.

The phone rings in the adjacent house; the husband moves slowly to answer it. "It's probably Anne," the wife says. "Tell her we'll call after supper." She turns back to a young woman who is asking about a blender. The wife shows her how it works and explains what it is good for. She offers to sell it for an inordinately low price.

I flip through old records. On the table before me are the husband's clothes. Old wing-tip shoes he obviously has no need for; sweaters too small for his now-stout frame. Nothing interests me. No; it all interests me, but I have no use for any of it. The wife comes over and asks if I need any help.

"No. I'm just looking. You never know what you might find."

"That's right," she beams, lighting a cigarette. "Christ, we've had all this stuff for so long, and we figured, we're not using it. Someone else could."

"Sure."

"Our kids are all grown. We've been living in this house for twenty five years—we're not going to have any more children!" she says laughing. Picking up a set of dishes she continues, "These would be real nice for some young family."

"Were you born on the island or did you come here?"

"Oh, we came in the late fifties, before the whole tourist thing took off. This was a different place in those days."

"What did you do?"

"Just about everything. We ran a couple of shops. Tom, my husband, worked as a carpenter. We rented out rooms in this place until we had all the children. There were a lot of young couples that came and settled here then."

"Did you know the Fisks?"

"Sure, Barbara and Joe; they started their restaurant and did very well in the end. But it was very tough for them. Lots of problems with money in the beginning, and the place next door that awful man put up."

"I work there—at the Lobster Trap."

"Oh that's nice. What do you do?"

"I'm a cook."

"A young man that cooks, that's rare these days. Are you married?"

"No. Not even close."

"Where are you from?"

"Originally from Ohio, but I came from New York. I was

working as a stockbroker and just got sick of everything. So I came here in April. Just looking for a simpler life."

"I see. Well, we came here to start out and raise a family. We bought this house for peanuts back then. Now, my God, we get offers to buy it every week."

"Are you gonna sell it?"

"No! Tom's just getting around to fixing it up the way he wants it, now that we're retired and the kids are gone. He just lined all the closets with cedar and I'm having a new kitchen put in."

The husband comes out and says, "She wants to talk to you now. The baby's sick."

"Oh well," the wife says. "Children never really leave, they just phone in their problems."

I look over the tables covered with tired objects, listening to their dusty breathing. It's scary to think that a person's life can be spread out on folding tables, scarier still to realize that any item a person acquires can outlive him. A simple spoon can feed you every day for a lifetime, never show its age, and then as you die it can look forward to numerous subsequent lifetimes, serving others without the slightest memory of your time spent together.

I imagined the wife's daughter setting down the phone, growing old, and moving into this house, on the phone with her daughter one day. I saw each generation rolling their eyes as each daughter called, and a shudder passed through me as I followed the tracks of this evolutionary train and realized my sons could be standing here, watching. I walked out of the yard to escape my fate, or at least the thought of it. And as the images dissolved behind me in the yard, I found myself back where I had started, turning slowly in a circle—facing all directions but moving toward none of them.

34

The dreaded day has come to do laundry. Our apartment is a jungle of rotting cloth. I have gone three weeks without doing the wash; Larry has managed to survive seven. The day of dread only occurs when you can avoid it no longer. It waits in the distance like death: dark, ugly, inevitable. Larry is a master of recycling clothes. Our friends call him the clothes ecologist because he wears the same items day after day. Larry claims he is simply conserving soap and helping the pollution problem, but everyone knows he likes being a little stinky.

Larry had borrowed a moped from a neighbor and we met at the only laundry on the island, located near the Rotary. The place does good business as any monopoly is bound to do. We find machines and start the washing ritual. I throw the whites in one washer and darks into another. Larry calls me "anal" and stuffs the entire contents of his bag into one washer. He has too much for one load, but he forces the clothing through the throat of the machine like an evil baby-sitter feeding a baby. He has no soap, so he happily finishes off my bottle. "Boy, you had just enough. Let's go outside and sit in the sunshine."

"Great," I reply. I take out my book.

"Hey, did you see my book?" he asks.

"No."

"Fuck!" he shouts, jumping up. He runs to his washing machine and opens the lid. Below him is his copy of *The Naked and the Dead* churning in soapy water. "Fuck! I lost my page. It was just getting to a good part."

"Sex?"

"Exactly."

"Put it out in the sun. It'll dry out, eventually. In the meantime you can use it as a pillow." He took the bloated paperback outside, then found an old copy of the *Boston Globe* to read.

Machines hummed behind us in a factory of sputters and rattling metal. It's tough to keep track of time in a Laundromat. You feel so helpless waiting while the machines churn, each cycle bringing a new tide of waves, back and forth with unvarying intensity, unlike the ocean. The ocean makes a good clock because no two waves are the same in magnitude or speed. That's the problem with uniformity; it's liquid, invisible. Time passes without notice in such an environment.

This is why people have such a different perception of time on the West Coast. The seasons pass with little variation. Once, during a vacation in Santa Barbara, I explained this theory to a bank teller as she cashed a check for me. We continued talking for several minutes after she finished the transaction. A long line had formed behind me and it was a busy lunch-hour, but not one person complained or asked me to hurry. The teller was skeptical of my theory, until I pointed out that what we were doing proved my point.

To my surprise Dave walked up to the Laundromat. It struck me as strange that a transient person needed to do laundry, but then I thought, why not? Just because he's a drifter doesn't mean he's without basic human needs. Even the troubadours must have needed to wash their stockings between villages.

He came over with his dog, guitar, and a small sack of clothes. Sitting next to me he said, "Damn, it's a long walk in the sun."

"Where's your hat?"

"Back in town. I didn't think to bring it 'cause I didn't plan on performin'."

"You ought to wear it on days like this."

"I suppose so. Hell, I woulda had a beer if I knew how tough this'd be." He sat facing the light, eyes closed, sweating. The dog moved into the shade.

"I see your friend came back."

"Yeah, found life on the road wasn't all he imagined without me."

"That's good. See, I told you he'd come back."

"Gave me a good piece of his mind, though. We came to a sort of an agreement, about feeding and drinking and such. Got our priorities straight, now." Suddenly Dave looked at me. "Hey, got any soap I might borrow?"

"Nope, Larry here cleaned me out. He was ready to scrape that stuff off the ground," I said, pointing to a lump of soap powder spilled on the parking lot. Dave didn't move. We sat silently, until it came time to put the clothes in the dryers.

When I came out, Dave was on his knees scraping the powder off the asphalt. He looked up at me with a smile, "Damn good idea."

I laughed incredulously. "That stuff's full of dirt."

"Well, that's true, but you can't get soap dirty, and you can't get dirt clean without soap, so I'm gonna use it."

Dave put his laundry in then joined us back on the bench. "What's that?" he asked, looking at Larry.

"My book fell in the wash."

"Looks knocked up. Like it's gonna have little books."

We listened to the labors of machines and watched people walk in and out.

"It's almost September, Dave. What're your plans?" I asked.

"Florida. Goin' south for the winter."

"Where abouts?"

"Key West. What they call 'Mile Zero'."

"Wow. That's all the way down, right? How're you gonna get there?"

"Hitchhike. Walk. Whatever."

"Ever catch any trains?"

"Sometimes. Whatever it takes."

"Why Key West?"

"Good audiences, climate. Gotta keep those pluckin' fingers warm. Besides, the dog has a girlfriend there."

"Poodle?"

"How'd you guess! He goes for the fancy ones."

"So you really just drift all year?"

"It's a job like any other. You gotta attend to its rules. You gotta let go, and to let go, you gotta lose everything. Count all your belongings on the fingers of one hand. I got my dog, this guitar, a pack of clothes, and a sleeping bag. Then your job is to follow the sun. Find a good gig, make some moola, and every day you wake up, you're a millionaire." We sat for a while. "It just happens. But you gotta want it to happen. And don't believe me. There's lots of days I don't feel like a millionaire."

"Ever get married?"

"Once. A long time ago. But it doesn't fit in well with my profession. I like sleeping on the grass and leaves. But my wife didn't like havin' that stuff in the bed. How 'bout you?"

"Never. Couldn't even imagine it. I came here to get away from all that."

"What's your hurry?"

"Hurry?"

"To get away from everything, at your age. You get away from everything when you're my age—that is if you don't got a lot of money. If you do, you don't need to run off; you can just mail out the alimony checks."

His long limbs skewered the sunlight awkwardly. I tried to imagine his existence. Walking down roads, thumb out. Struggling into a ratty sleeping bag under bridge abutments. Talking to the dog, and hearing replies. He looked liked he enjoyed it. His features told me that, resting on his face with the armchair-peace of a satisfied man. It made me realize, seeing the serenity in Dave's face, how often affluent people grimace —actually grimace. You won't notice it at the time, unless you're looking for it. My first boss used to do it. His eyes would narrow, the corners of the mouth would draw back, furrows squashing his brow, and then a look of intense pain would flash across his face. And no one thought anything of it, probably because everyone does it. For such an aberrant expression to be normal, we must really be in pain. We must be unconscious of our feelings of pain. What imaginations we have, to create such a false world. We're living in a new Ptolemaic universe, warped and centerless, where stars are pebbles under our feet, and gravity repels what it should attract. The goals we create for ourselves should be the eventualities we fear, but we continue drifting along with everyone, unaware of what we are doing, how we look, how we perceive. Dave rose to get his laundry. The dirty soap had worked beautifully. He would continue on his way a clean man, whether anyone would ever realize it, or care.

35

With most of our friends leaving on Labor Day weekend, Larry and I planned to throw a party on our beach the Saturday before. We made invitations that read "CLOSE TO THE EDGE PARTY," under which we drew a picture of Nantucket with an "X" marking our house on the eastern shore.

I spent my entire day-off handing them out. It wasn't easy tracking down people like Dave, Benny, and Ted, but eventually I reached everyone important to our lives that summer. Most important, I slid an invitation under Tammy's door, with a note that read:

> *Tammy,*
> *I was wrong and stupid and sincerely apologize. Can't we please talk? At least let me say good-bye.*
> *Love,*
> *Guy*

There was nothing else I could do. She had walked away from me every time I approached her so I knew it all depended on her coming to me. Tammy was stubborn—a typical Aries. You can't call an Aries that to his or her face, instead you have to use an euphemism such as "single-minded." But I admired that quality in her, the way it augmented her beauty—the riding defiance of her face as she coasted over the road in her jeep: a luscious clutch of blond hair and golden skin.

The pain of her absence still gnawed at me. Of course I tried to shake her out of my mind, but every time I came across one of our old hangouts, fibers of nausea spread through my stomach. The only thing that provided any relief was to stay away from those places. It didn't suppress the pain but made it bearable, the way an injured person will cocoon himself in the fetal position.

Many times after her initial rejection I had wanted to just barge in on her and say "I still love you," but I now felt, after the time I approached her on the street, that I would have to penetrate her vulnerability slowly, like those force fields in science fiction stories which repel sharp blows, but not gradual thrusts.

I walked through rooms bruised with her scent, breathing a megrimish fog of burnt flowers.

Time passed in painful clicks. The little prick of each hour spread into a numb throbbing that worked its way through my extremities to settle in my guts. The image of Man Ray's metronome sculpture kept returning to me: when his lover left him in Paris he cut out her eye from a photograph and glued it to the swaying stick. I now could see why he called the piece "Object of Destruction."

There have been a lot of fires on the beach at night. Every morning I go down and throw the charred driftwood into the sea. I can't stand the sight of empty wine bottles on the sand.

A week after the cops came a voice called to me from the bushes as I walked down the beach early in the morning. Looking up, I saw Ken coming toward me, unshaven and slightly maniacal.

"Ken, where have you been?"

"Staying out of sight with a friend."

"Are you okay?"

"So far, so good. Did the police give you any hassles?"

"No, they just asked me some questions and let me go. They said they knew I wasn't involved in anything."

"Good. The less you know the better. Can you do one more favor for me?"

"It depends—"

"This won't be any problem. Oh, and thanks for taking care of the car."

"What happened to it? I noticed it's gone."

"I sold it to someone. They painted it and changed the license plate. I'm gonna jump the island. I just need one more thing from the house."

"I don't think it'd be cool for me to go into your apartment. There's a lot of unmarked cops driving by every day. And the police have sealed your door."

"Don't worry. What I need is in the basement. Go in the back way, it's not being watched, I just checked. Behind the fuse box—you know where that is. . . ."

I nodded.

"There's a chink in the wall. Reach back in there and you'll feel a box. Pull it out, don't open it, and throw it at that tree out back in the ravine. I'll take it from there."

"I can probably do that."

"All my important shit is in that box."

"Okay." A chill wind blew between us. The sun lay buried behind dark, torn clouds. "Send me a postcard from wherever you end up."

"Sure." He looked mentally haggard. His hand came forward with a forced smile. "Thanks for everything, man."

"Hey, thanks for all those drinks."

"That was nothing. Here." As we shook I felt something scratch my hand. He pressed a folded bill into my palm. "Don't say anything. Don't have much time." I shrugged and stuffed the bill in my pocket. Protesting would only have drawn attention to it if anyone was watching. "Later."

"Good luck, man."

I followed his instructions, then went in the house and looked out the windows for Ken and the cops. Nothing happened, and I never saw Ken again. Later in the day when I took my pants off I checked the pockets and found Ken's money, which I had forgotten about. He had folded it into a crisp green square, so precisely, so out of character with his ragged appearance. It took me a while to unfold it and discover that it was a hundred dollar bill.

Spindrift

A few days later, Grant invited me to a boat party on the Old South Wharf. A friend of his had sailed down from New Caanen. I had made the mistake of mentioning the party to Kelly, who always grilled me about my social plans between orders. I was really tired at the end of the shift and didn't feel like going, but Kelly insisted that I take her.

Kelly looks as striking as she acts; her hair streams in red directions from her head; she's tall, thin, and quite beautiful— when she wants to be. But she usually downplays her beauty, realizing that it would be overkill to be so vivacious *and* made-up. She had gone through several boyfriends over the summer —both younger and older, but none were quite up to her speed. She'd wear them out, and for that reason many of the guys I knew regarded her as out-of-reach. Kinetic women like Kelly make good friends but can be scorching as lovers. You have to be well lubricated to run with them.

We found the boat easily; it was one of the bigger ones on the private dock. About twenty people appeared to be situated in and around the cabin and deck areas. Grant was sitting with a couple of his housemates on the gunwale. He saluted us with his beer and invited us aboard. I introduced Kelly to everyone I knew.

"Beers are in the cabin, Guy."

"Cool." I squeezed through a small crowd of people below deck and found the cooler. It doesn't take many people to make a boat crowded. I couldn't help but remember the cabin in which Tammy and I first made love that night during the storm.

I didn't like being down there, so I got topside quickly. Dank air, dank thoughts. Too many people crushing the eerie light cast from the brass cabin lanterns.

My head climbed into the vibrating darkness. A stray spotlight lit the halo of Kelly's hair. "Here. You look like an angel."

"What does that make you?" she said, taking the beer.

"I dunno, but I've noticed that I've been awful horny lately."

"We have ways of dealing with that. Why didn't you say so sooner. I didn't get these wings for nothing." Kelly smiled. With each beer the joking got more lascivious.

Her eyes narrowed as I watched her head bob in and out of the light, propelled by her laughter. Swatches of mist parted to

201

reveal the stars, casting a docile glow. It is hard to reconcile the stars with anything but the quietest landscapes; we usually never notice them unless we happen to be reclining. I settled down against the rope railing in the penumbra of the group, looking up, then back at Kelly as she spoke.

Kelly told the story of the day Jason bought a huge bluefish from a door-to-door fish merchant, and how when he tried to filet it it jumped off the table and flipped around on the floor, infuriating him as it kept evading his grasp. Kelly talked and everyone laughed, than Grant told his market stories, about the senile lady who thought she was in the post office, about the girl who accidentally locked herself in the cooler naked—wanting to surprise her boyfriend on his birthday—and so forth. The boat rolled with laughter, and as a chill current of air sailed in from the Atlantic, I thought how in a mere week or two these people would all be gone, along with the boats; and then in a month or two most of the shops would close as would the boarding houses, and the island would again become the province of the natives, floating under the long skirts of winter.

A grayness infused these thoughts, obscuring the inevitable decision I would have to make about leaving, about Tammy, and about getting on with my life. When we drift we often discover new lands, but we lose the satisfaction of navigation, the sense of teleological achievement. Columbus probably felt this as deeply as anyone. I had no desire to return home, to America, but I was tired of drifting. It felt comforting to sit on a boat tied to the shore. Listening to the stars' obbligato, I felt myself folded into a vortex of tessellating options, the days of my life scattered into rough pieces, not fitting together, not making up a coherent existence, but inchoate: an abandoned mosaic. Time spent here, spent there, not adding up. Relationships that never mesh. A truncated career.

Grabbing a beer I walked to the end of the dock. Standing on the last plank of the pier, I raised my arms as if I stood on a huge diving board overlooking the ocean. The air hummed with the paucity of light.

"Don't do it, amigo." A voice came from behind me, "It's pretty cold in there. The water is slick with oil, and besides, the sharks like to feed here at night." Turning, I saw a middle-aged man with long hair reclining on the deck of a boat.

"Don't worry. I was just seeing how close to the edge I could get."

"Well you got there. How does it feel?"

"Not a feeling. Just an urge. The urge to jump. I usually get that when I'm standing on the top of a building. You know that sick, electric urge, that dangerous thought: why not do it! It's like, sometimes when I'm watching a play, I get the urge to jump on the stage and make a fool of myself. You know. Crazy thoughts. But I never act on them."

"Yeah. Had a lot of those over the years."

"This your boat?"

"Yup."

"Nice. Sail it yourself?"

"If I have to I can. Usually I'll take a companion along for the ride. Nice way to pass the time—having someone to talk to."

"You go far?"

"Anywhere I want to."

"That's pretty far." I liked this guy—his easy manner, tequila voice coated with salt, long brown hair softening a serious face; the way he reclined along the sloping deck which held him like a chaise lounge. I liked the honest amber light of his eyes and the melodious pulse of his speech.

"You been here all summer?" he asked.

"Since April."

"'Swhat I thought. A summer rat. You've got the look. Bet you've had a good time here."

"Right again."

"Gonna stay the winter?"

"Not sure."

"That's when you really get to know the island. Shake its hand."

"I've heard it's rough. Cold and lonely. Nothing to do but drink."

"I've been to worse places in winter."

"So what do you do, if you don't mind my askin'. By the way, my name's Guy."

"Guy. I'm Mike. Pleased." We shook hands. "No, I don't

mind you asking. This is what I do."

"Just sail around?"

"Couldn't have said it better myself."

"Sounds like a nice job."

"Has its ups and downs."

"You sail charters, or just for pleasure?"

"I do charters when I feel like having some company, or when a nice, well-off divorcée feels like taking some intense sailing lessons." He smiled. "No, I retired early. Came up with a mechanical device a few years back and I still got the patent. Keeps me in sailcloth and sandals."

"That's great. What kind of device?"

"Christ. It'd take me an hour to explain. Basically it's a self-lubricating mechanism for generators. It's not a famous invention that you'd ever see. Strictly for industry."

"I see. . . ."

"Hey—how about a snort of something good? Take a break from that cowpiss." He brought a bottle of dark liquor from the cabin. "Now. This is Barbados Rum. One-fifty-one. Try a taste of this." He held it up to the sky, then poured a thin twill of brown liquid over the side of the boat. "Always got to start with Old Man Sea. It's where we all come from. Can't forget that, if you don't want bad sailing the next day. Here you go. Bottoms up!" I coughed and he smiled.

"Nice."

"Bet the hairs on your balls are standing on end, eh?"

"Just about."

"So. What do you do? In school?"

"No. Outta school. Worked in New York for a coupla years. Actually, I came here to try to sort things out, if that doesn't sound like a cliché. You know, take a big time out."

"The only answer is living, and you gotta do that day by day."

"Yeah. I was sick of the day-to-day in my old job. It all seemed so pointless. No one ever got anywhere. Or anywhere I'd want to go."

"I remember when I was your age. It all seemed real complicated then. Now, the older I get, the simpler it is. How's that for a cliché."

"Better than mine."

"What did you do in New York?"

"Stockbroker."

"Well, no wonder. You didn't like being somebody's whore. Very understandable."

"I hated the people I worked for. Or maybe they hated me. I don't know. It got to the point where I couldn't do what they wanted me to do to the clients, so I quit. I just couldn't condone it ethically. I got sick to my stomach every time I listened to those pedagogic reptiles lecture me about working hard. Work harder! What, so I could rape more old ladies? So the partners could stuff more jewelry down their wives throats in Scarsdale? Fuck."

"Here's another one, amigo. Relax. You got nothing but your whole future ahead of you. Can't grapple with the past, it's oblivion. You don't know how lucky you are."

I took the shot and liked what I swallowed. "You ever feel cramped livin' on the boat?"

"Not when the ocean's your living room."

"No TV, though. No phone. Must be nice. What do you do for entertainment?"

"The sea is a symphony. A different film every night. And sometimes, an opera. I just sit back, listen, and watch."

Laughter spurted from our boat and ricocheted around the basin. "Those are my friends. Better get back."

"Here. This is for you." He handed me the bottle. "Bet this'll water their eyes."

"Thanks, man. Hope to see you again, Mike. Where you headin' next?"

"Whichever way the wind blows is fine with me."

Boats bristled against their lines as I made my way back to the party.

36

Some guy I didn't know was sitting close to Kelly on a dark part of the forward deck. I felt an irrational twinge of possession, but then I looked away. Why should I care?

Grant's girlfriend Katie walked over and we chatted about Wopatoola. She said she didn't like the event; too many drunks and crazy people.

"I just found a quiet corner of the beach and smoked a joint."

"Sounds like you were smart."

"Yeah. That kind of sums up my philosophy of life. Find a seat and let everyone else dance into the abyss. Problem is, I haven't found a conclusion yet. What do you do after you finish the joint?"

"Two options. No three."

"Okay."

"One: smoke another joint. . . ."

"No, still no conclusion."

"Two: Have a beer."

"Same result, different means. What's three?"

"Make love."

"I like that. Good resolution. Just one problem."

"What?"

"What do you do if you're alone?"

"Find someone."

In the periphery of my vision I saw the guy make a move on Kelly. I offered Katie some rum.

"No thanks. I just like beer."

"I like everything." The mouth of the bottle moved toward my lips.

I slid down the curve of the bottle, into its dark water, and began swimming away from the glass, past the island on the label, till the sounds of conversation dissolved to murmurs, my vision ebbing with every stroke, plucking the water with the lassitude of a Spanish guitarist. I swam nearly to the bottom of the bottle—no one else caring to share it—when Kelly came over to me and said, "It's time to go."

For one seraphic moment I saw Tammy's face.

"Yes," I said, and she led me down the dock, holding my arm, her other hand around my waist. "I gotta go home."

"You're too drunk to drive," she said in a motherly tone. And I knew it was true, watching my feet move miles below me, the mists of Barbados swirling about my head. "You can stay with me," I think she said.

The little streets were utterly desolate, calcified in somnolence. A shout would have shattered the air.

"Here we go," she said. "Here goes the big chef."

"You're talking to me like I'm a child," I said, chopping the consonants of my words into big sloppy chunks.

"You sound like a child."

"All right. But a well-educated child. . . ."

"Sure. Why don't we put the bottle down. You might drop it and hurt yourself, or me."

"No," I blurted out, "I need it."

"You don't want to give up your bottle?"

"No."

"Come on, big boys don't need their bottles."

"Be nice or I'll make the lobsters scream."

"That's Jason's trick. You don't do mean things like that."

"I will."

"No. You're the nice cook."

"Let's go see the nice baker."

"Who's that?"

"Benny. He'll give us coffee and donuts. He'll fix everything up."

"No, it's too late for the bakery. I live just up the next street."

"Which street?"

"India Street."

"I like India. Lot's of rice."

"That's right."

My eyes tried to focus on the bricks in the sidewalk, but they couldn't; I could only make out my feet darting in and out of the frame of my vision, and then Kelly's feet, which seemed much more deliberate. "Your feet are smarter than mine."

"Why's that?"

"They know which direction to go."

I stumbled up the stairs of her house.

"Be quiet," she hissed. "The family on the first floor's asleep."

"No problem. Just tell me when to start."

"You can start being quiet now."

"Okay. Now. Shhh." And immediately I tripped through the doorway.

We felt our way up the stairs and into her room. She turned on the overhead lamp.

"Please, no lights. No lights."

"How's this?" she said, turning on the bathroom light somewhere in the vast tundra of my periphery.

"Much better," I replied, exhaling the words in gusts. I lay in the warm refuge of her bed, breathing heavily, taking in her odors. The room spun softly with the wafting torque of a pinwheel in light breeze.

"Here, drink this. It'll make you feel better." She helped me sit up and gave me a big glass of water, which I slurped down, spilling some on my chest. The water cleared my eyes a little. For the first time I noticed the surroundings, a typical island room with Cape decor—flat braided rugs, antique furniture, cut glass lamps, ladder-back chairs. I ran my fingers over the chenille bedspread, and thought of my grandmother, long dead. She would have been very comfortable in this room. How ironic that a sexy young woman lived here.

Kelly walked in from the other room with a tray and cups. I watched her from my supine position among the shadows on the bed. "Here's some chamomile tea. It's pretty mellow."

Steam rose toward her chin, burrowing into her dark hair. I smiled. She smiled, stepped back, then removed her cotton sweater. Kelly always wore big, rumpled sweaters which made her look cute. She continued disrobing in front of the doorway, cast in its shroud, a brown silhouette. Her jeans fell to the floor, then her shirt, bra, and panties.

"You're very beautiful," I said, not for the purpose of flattery, but because my feelings were riding close to the surface of my consciousness, evaporating quickly into the air through my mouth. She turned in the light, profiling her breasts. They looked like the breasts of a French model, sacrificing size for the beauty of their contour. "Those are your breasts."

"Yup."

She lit an oil lamp on the dresser and turned out the electric light. An amber glow swam through the room.

"Where do you want me?" I asked.

"Right there." She came to the bed on soft paws. I had been watching the scene transpire as if it were on film, but when she touched me I realized that I was confronting another woman's nakedness in a bed. My emotions cross-circuited; I felt like a train at a track crossing, not sure which way to go, but moving forward, inexorably.

"I wasn't planning on sleeping with you."

"Neither was I, but I've had a little crush on you all summer, and now that the summer's almost over . . ."

She kissed me in the mouth, repeatedly; I had the sensation of food being forced into a full stomach. Light waves of nausea washed down my throat.

I couldn't stomach the sex until it reduced itself to a geo-metric level: breasts, hips, and legs forming abstract shapes that had no emotional affiliation to the woman I knew.

As she ground into me I searched the room for a focal point, some frame of reference I could anchor my sobriety to, that wouldn't be washed away by the undulations of her brown body —stroking up and down, as we floated on a raft of wet flesh. I saw the window and clung to it with my eyes. Night slammed against the glass, like the dark rum in my bottle. I held this vision until my head sank back, drowning in the rain of her hair.

31

I anticipated the approach of our party more like a wake. On Saturday I awoke feeling morose, and spent the morning watching the waves cresting in the distance. It was cold on the sand; a light rain had fallen. I walked along the sepia beach until I came to an inviting piece of driftwood and sat down. The air hung with the medieval density, slowing the flight of gulls. At the surf line the ground dropped off sharply, churning the water. I did not find anything to lift my spirits in the ocean, just a steel-gray sheet cut by the horizon. Letting my eyes sail forward I strained to see the shore of Spain. *It is all right to sleep in today, my friends. Go back to bed. This is not a day worth greeting. I hope it is better on your side.* I thought of the many brilliant sunsets that had catapulted over like meteors this year. My skin still radiated their warmth. Sand trickled over my brown ankles. Buttoning my denim jacket, I listened to the retching sea, the way you listen to someone speaking a foreign language. Every so often you hear a word that you think you recognize. But the harder you try to listen, the less you seem to understand.

The first people started arriving in mid-afternoon. Grant and his gang came with several cases of beer. "This is just for starters," he said. "Let me know when you need more."

Friends filled the house like warm coals. We received so much food and beer that people grabbed the coolers from their cars to hold the overflow.

210

Around four the sun came out and illuminated the sign we had hung from the deck, which read:

CLOSE TO THE EDGE PARTY
(Clothes Optional)

Larry had attached some empty beer cans and an old bikini top to it.

Everyone we invited had come, except Tammy, and Dave—both of whom I didn't really expect. Our friends who had never been to the house were amazed at the size of our living quarters and our picturesque seat on the edge of the sea. The place was ideal for a party. The main living room made a club-size dance floor; people spilled out onto the deck, the yard, and down to the beach.

After a couple of hours of drinking and dancing we announced the start of the clambake and led a procession down to the beach. Easy Al and Mark had borrowed, or temporarily stole, a bunch of pots and utensils from the Lobster Trap, and Al volunteered to be master chef. "Who's going to make the fire?" he asked. "We didn't bring the stove."

"Guy will," Larry told him. "It's time to make all those homosexual years as a Boy Scout pay off."

"You were a Boy Scout?" Al asked.

"Where did you think I learned to cook so well."

"Stick to arson."

I lit the fire in the dying sunlight. Flames bit the air with the clang of gold rings. Everyone began to weave around each other, following the will of the sand. People tend to stand stiffly at gatherings between walls; outside they sway with the earth's rotation. If each person had had a cord attached to him, we would have woven something insane by the end of the evening.

The wind droned under the current of our voices. Someone turned on a portable tape player. The volume of music fluttered in intensity. A couple of girls holding beer bottles undulated in their jeans and loose white shirts. As I crouched over the pit I had dug for the fire, I reflected on the myriad contingencies that had brought me to this point in time, this position on my knees.

It would never be possible to duplicate this moment, yet it unfolded as the most perfectly natural occurrence; each second passed like a vibration in harmony with the tonic chord of the island, resonating with ineffable overtones of predetermination.

The sky glowed with cobalt vividness. It made me feel like we were cartoon characters, painted against the sand. The flesh of my companions rang with bronze light. It seemed to me, at that instant, that we had evolved into a new race, that the strains of our previous lives had extinguished genetically, that we had mutated, like the transmuting light around us, into more vibrant beings, alive to a point well-beyond our previous capacities. I was now a man who could run with horses, lift great weights, climb jagged mountains, sire orchards of children, command ferocious beasts, achieve anything. This sky held no limits.

Such feelings may be endemic to life by the sea. Would the Greeks have conceived the idea of hubris had they not been a sea-faring nation? I felt the pulse of the waves in my heartbeat. Where at first the tides had served as the timekeeper of my environs, they now had become my body's clock, pulling my blood back and forth through arteries and veins in lunar surges.

The sand lay warmly beneath our bare feet: the breath of the sun exhaled, solidified, and then settled all around us.

Al steamed lobsters in huge pots over the coals. He also prepared corn-on-the-cob, steamers, and baked potatoes. We had a Romanesque feast—gorging ourselves as we lay on the sand. It was an honest meal—not synthetic, like restaurant food. It didn't taste like the thousands of dishes most of us had labored all summer to prepare or serve. The food was satisfying in a visceral way, not composed of calories but of the elements: it felt like we were actually imbibing the earth and the sea.

We had uncovered the midden of our existence, here on the beach. The point where everything breaks down into its ultimate deliquescence. All we had left as the sun crumbled into the sea were the bones and shells of our meal, the grit of sand between our teeth. Each grain a potential pearl. The sand the clams had ingested, we ingested, threading through each intestinal tract from species to species, again and again.

I lay under the blanket of sky, and for the first time in my life, felt the pull of the womb below me. A vast, undulating, nearly imperceptible suction. And as I looked over the ocean a seiche appeared on the skin of the water.

"Red sky at night, sailor's delight," someone said behind me, as the light dissolved in a faint, bloody smear. From down the beach we heard a guitar being played. I sat up. Dave approached slowly, strumming, his dog lagging behind.

"You made it."

"Of course I made it. You invited me."

"How'd you find us?"

"*Wasn't hard,*" he hummed to the chords he struck. "*It's a beach party. And this,*" he sang, swinging his body and guitar around slowly, "*is the beach.*" He ended with a cascading blues riff down the neck of the guitar.

We built the coals into a bright fire. People brought down more beer from the house, and we all sang with Dave. When some of the girls started to get cold I ran to the house to get blankets. Parked cars lined the road. The house looked ominously empty from outside. Only the kitchen window gave off light.

From the deck I could see the fire burning on the beach. I inhaled the stained, purple air, then opened the kitchen door. At the table sat Tammy, writing.

Suddenly I couldn't breathe. She looked up with a weak smile. "I was leaving you a note. I'm leaving the island tomorrow. I wanted to say good-bye, but not at a party."

Moments ticked by. Words flooded my mind but clogged in my throat. "Where are you going," I finally managed.

"Home. It's time to go. I've got to start lining up my job interviews. Time to think about the real world."

"Hell, it just occurred to me that this is the real world." She smiled fully.

"Yeah, but you know what I mean. A real job, career, all that."

"Yeah." I sat down. The clamp around my esophagus started to loosen. I couldn't bear the superficial nature of our conversation any longer. "I don't know how to say this, and I know it's not going to change anything, but I'm really sorry. I mean, I was wrong, and I don't blame you for hating me. . . ."

"I don't hate you. I did, but I'm over that. It's something else now."

Something lifted in my body as she spoke those words. My eyes followed the arc of her arm down to the table. "What did you write?"

"*Dear Guy.*"

"That's pretty straightforward."

"I'm shooting from the hip."

"You didn't say that?"

"No."

"Is there anything else?"

"Yes." She looked back at the paper. "*I didn't know what to say to you, so I'm writing this note. You're right, we should say good-bye. . . .*" She paused. "*I have been avoiding you, but now I'd like to talk. Please call me at home*—and that's as far as I got."

"I'm glad you feel that way. I don't know what I'd have done if you just left without saying anything." I tried to read her emotions, but couldn't. Her face looked tightly serene. I wondered if she was enjoying my awkwardness. "D-Do you have any feelings about where we stand now?"

"Do I have any feelings? I've been asking myself that a lot lately. At first I had no feelings, other than hurt. I thought you were so different, special. I thought I loved you—I did love you. Then *blam* you laid me out. And everything went flat. Totally flat. You were a monster."

"Yeah."

"But I talked to a lot of people, and to make a long story short, I talked to a lot of people and then realized that all that hate was hurting me, and that I should talk to you, and try to clear out the poisons and make something good out of something bad."

"I'm glad you feel that way." Just then a bunch of people tumbled in, drunk and giddy. One of the girls exclaimed, "We need more refreshment!" The wall that had been slowly dissolving between us suddenly returned to its previous thickness.

"Help yourself," I said, pointing to the refrigerator. More people came in, looking for blankets. My gaze flowed toward Tammy in the wake of their traffic; my eyes widened in absorbency. She rose.

"This isn't the time."

"Yes it is. Let's talk. I'll drive you home."

"No, that's okay. I can walk. You've got your guests."

"Fuck my guests."

Tammy clicked comfortably into the slot behind me. I drove the cycle through the village slowly because of the late hour. On the main road I accelerated into a dark blur. She pressed close to me, just like old times. I squinted into the opaque wind without the protection of my helmet and visor. They seemed so pointless now.

When I zipped past her house she squeezed my ribs. "Hey, where are you going?"

Sankaty Head Lighthouse grew on the hill as we shot down the empty road. Its light revolved at matronly speed. I downshifted to slow the bike without braking. Thinking of Dr. Wu, my old Tai Chi teacher, I realized that if one could master the art of momentum, he would never have to use brakes to stop throughout life. Yes, control is the mother of speed. . . .

The smooth deceleration felt like the outstroke during intercourse. By the time we reached the fence surrounding Sankaty, the bike was at the appropriate speed to make the right turn and negotiate the hill. We passed a sign which read "No Vehicles." Tammy said, "What are you doing?" In answer, I accelerated up the hill, over the gravel, and onto the grass. She hugged me tight as we skidded over a ditch and bit into a steep bank of grass. I took the bike past the lighthouse, straight to the fence at the edge the cliff. The wheel nudged the aluminum links. Surf hit the shore in darkness hundreds of feet below us.

We climbed off the bike. "Here we are."

"Thanks. But you overshot my house by a bit."

"Isn't it great up here? It doesn't even feel like we're on the same island with the rest of town. This is the raw edge of this whole fucking place. I mean, look out there. There's nothing. Not even a boat. Just the wind gnawing away at the cliff. In a few more years this lighthouse will be in the sea."

Tammy walked to the fence and looked out at the void of ocean. Then she turned and looked at the lighthouse.

"I want to show you something." I said, walking.

"Inside?"

"Sure."

"We can't. It's locked."

"No it's not. Look." I took her over and pushed the door open. A spiral staircase rose through the throat of the tower. "Let's go up. You game?"

"Why not."

We climbed round and round up the iron stairs until we got to the top floor. The beacon revolved in a glass house in the center of the room. The light almost blinded us.

"No view from up here," Tammy said. The room was so bright we couldn't see outside.

"I guess that's the secret of a lighthouse. Everyone can see you, but you can't see anything."

The room was too hot and bright to stay in for long, so we spiraled back down the stairs. It took a minute for our eyes to adapt to the darkness. I saw the hammer blow of each star poke through the tin skin of night, until it appeared we stood in the center of an immense lantern lit by Sankaty Head.

Tammy drew nearer. Something unfolded inside me. Kissing her, I could have been running my tongue through a waterfall.

Later, standing on her porch, she said, "It's late. I've got to pack and catch the first ferry. I'd like it if you'd come visit me."

"Where?"

"At home, in Connecticut. If you'd like to—"

"I'd love to. When?"

"Whenever you can. How long are you staying here?"

"I could be leaving sooner than I thought."

"Good." She smiled and kissed me on the cheek.

"Do you want me to stay with you tonight?"

"Not this fast. This is going to take a little time for me." She took a pen and paper out of her purse. "Here's my number at home. Call me when you're coming. You know my family. There's always room at our house."

I walked her to the door. She kissed me again. The porch grew brighter as the wind wrapped us in cashmere.

"I'll see you soon, Tam." She opened the door. "So where are you going to be interviewing?"

"Looks like San Francisco's my best shot. My father has a friend there with a company, and they need an entry-level marketing person. Sounds good. It's a great city, too. And after living here, there's no way I could stay at home, or go somewhere like New York."

"Yeah. Yeah, I agree."

She went inside. "See you soon. . . ."

Back at the house I stood alone on the deck. Each crash of the surf brought my departure a moment sooner. Larry came up to me. "Where've you been?"

"With Tammy."

"No shit! What happened."

"I don't know, but something good. Sometimes you shouldn't try to analyze things. You just play it as it lays."

"Yeah. I hate it when everyone gets bogged down with details."

"Well, it's about time I gave my notice at the Tourist Trap."

People crowded out onto the deck. Someone said, "Guy, Benny's roasting marshmallows."

"What more can a man ask for in a day, Lar? He gets his girl back, and he gets to roast marshmallows!"

"I dunno. Another cold-boy?"

38

The week went by quickly, the days cascading in waves. I made all the preparations necessary to leave the island. Buff only asked me to work until the Sunday before Labor Day, so I planned to take off that Monday.

I spent most of my time traveling to my favorite places, trying to absorb as much as possible to augment my less than photographic memory. As my remaining shifts were dinners I managed to cover a lot of ground during the daytime, riding the desolate roads glazed with sunlight, sand, and dust, listening to the gravel hum of my engine, stopping to clear my eyes and sit by the ocean, like a student attending an ongoing tutorial. The light shone less sharply now, the shadows appeared grayer. The sea sounded louder as it evolved into a winter animal.

One morning during the middle of the week I saw strange shapes ahead of me as I walked along Dionis beach. Tall boards and driftwood stuck out of the ground in a circular arrangement, along with a wild assortment of other items: oars, bottles, tires, surfboard parts, diving gear. Some of the objects were nailed to the boards, others were placed on mounds of sand. String and seaweed hung between some of the standing objects. The arrangement exuded a drunken artistry as well as a sense of pagan spirituality. It impressed me as having been made with serious intent by humorous people. One of the planks had been fashioned into the shape of a cross, with a naked baby doll impaled upon it. Someone had scratched the words "Miss

Spindrift

Nantucket" above it on the wood. In the middle of the circle on a sand hill were the words "Endless Summer" written in seashells. Empty beer bottles crowned the hill. I noticed there was no litter among this Stonehenge of the beach. Whoever made it left only their footprints for a signature.

It is all here within the libidinous spin of this circle, the radiating energy of a summer on Nantucket, caught in the frozen wink of a doll's eye. I have been riding on a plane of light, gliding on its metal fabric. Below me, a corked tide of sea foam struggles to ejaculate itself free of the sand. I may as well jerk off right here in the sultry glare of the doll; it's all the same to me: the touch of the sun, a woman's flesh—I can't feel the difference anymore.

However, I can feel the effulgence of the sky weakening, just as I can the shadow of Tammy's absence spreading across the island. Every day there is less to keep me here. The force of gravity is dying under me. Each moon labors to shift the tide. The wind blows my hair back, and I notice the arm of the little doll is pointing westward.

Later that morning I go to the Indian Room for breakfast. It sits at the foot of the Overlook Hotel, a hulking monster of a structure by Nantucket standards, built in the days when its three stories constituted a skyscraper. The Overlook is inconspicuously situated off North Water Street, away from the main tourist artery. I hope to have a quiet meal there.

I enter just about at eleven when the place is set to close. I don't look very affluent in my kneeless jeans and bandanna, but the perennially cheerful hostess seats me graciously, as if I'm her most valued customer.

"It's good to see you again," she says.

"Thanks. It's great to be here." I'm so happy to get such a friendly reception I could lift her in the air; but I don't, I just head for my usual table in the back corner by the window.

She comes over with an urn of coffee and fills my cup. "You still working at the lobster place?"

"Yes," I say, impressed that she remembers. "But not for long. I'm leaving on Monday."

"Going to school?"

"No. Done with that."

"I thought so. You look a little older. My boys are all grown and working in Boston now." Her eyes dart through the window, then settle back on me. "I'll get you a menu."

"That's okay, I know what I'm having. I'll have the fried bread dough, sausage, and a muffin." She smiles and takes the order to the kitchen. I'm grateful not to be treated like a tourist. Just a hungry person.

One part of the Indian Room is full of antiques such as a spinning wheel, Indian busts, harpoons, and other sea-faring relics. Dainty glass bottles sit on top of the half-wall dividing the restaurant from the antiques. The dining area doesn't have much decoration. It's merely a succession of surfaces, high and low, for eating and walking, with ugly trapezoidal tables made of blond wood—the color used in kindergarten classrooms to lower the anxiety of children in unfamiliar surroundings. Maybe that's why kids are always so docile in here, and explains why the glass bottles have survived so well.

I pick up the corn-yellow cup and finish the coffee. It ignites my dormant taste buds, mixing with the sour juices that have marinated overnight in my mouth, culminating in a dull rainbow of flavors: cinnamon, evergreen, mist, and lazy sunshine.

The door swings open and in walks the hostess with my breakfast.

"Here you go. And here's a little bon voyage drink on the house." She sets down a glass of orange juice.

"Thanks." I take a sip. It's a stiff screwdriver, to my surprise.

The breakfast crawls into my stomach like a warm cat.

There's only one couple left near the front of the restaurant. The guy looks to be about thirty, although he has the round face of a cute little boy. His hair falls over his ears, and he wears a red baseball cap, purposefully crooked on his head. I can tell there's something special about him; his girlfriend is much more attractive than he is, and he's sitting in his chair as if he were reclining on a couch. They're talking in jocular rhythms—too fast to have been on the island more than a few hours. They have not correlated to the tenor of the Nantucket yet, but through the echoes of their city laughter I can tell they are happy to be here. When the hostess brings more coffee she tells me, "He's a photographer. He's just had his book published and he's going to have a show in New York next week."

His fingers lace through the woman's. They smile, spin, laugh, and joke with the hostess. She laughs. I smile, vicariously lifted by their ebullience. Here is a man who rides life, lucky—or smart—enough not to be ridden by it. Watching them, I imagine a string of bridges swinging in the wind over brilliant waters. A line of smiling toll keepers bow with majestic sweeps, chanting, "Go right on through." I am driving a red convertible down the highway of America, past green fields full of insouciant cows, while daisies spring out of the yellow centerline, picked by sixteen-year old girls in creamy saddle shoes, who run back to their porch swings and sing, "He loves me. He loves me not. He loves me. . . ." I stop at country stores with tinnient doors in every town, run by pleasant sole proprietors named Ed. I order coffee and a cheese sandwich every time, and they always say, "Sit awhile and tell me your life story." As the sun wanes they speak proudly of their daughters studying hard in school. I pull out into the cool night air, turn on the radio, and hear James Cotton or Charlie Parker on the radio. I never run out of gas until I get to the next town. I watch myself cross America, until I end up on a cliff overlooking the ocean at Big Sur. I see a log cabin and a dog by the fire. And I'm inside, living a fulfilling life, fueled by creativity. . . .

"More coffee?" the hostess asks.

"No, I'm perfect."

I pay and walk out the door, satiated, like someone coming out of a good play or movie.

The streets have filled with tourists, moving past me in currents of color through the aquarium light of an overcast afternoon. Shoppers penetrate doorways, money pours out like semen, customers leave pregnant with burdens . . . I've seen this a hundred times yet it all seems so strange now, constricted in this slice of existence, on this short, ancient street. Cappy sits a few benches away, conducting his business through the fog of his distilled mind. Runo continues selling his over-priced food and abusing his staff. Angelic au pair girls stroll by. A dusty carpenter makes his way to the hardware store. I'm sure Mrs. Walsh is mumbling about the "invaduhs" as she zestfully picks up litter. A race of failed farmers turned whalers now selling T-shirts to survive. It makes sense in a surreal way.

The man in the suit is walking up the street again. It looks like he hasn't changed his clothes since the last time I've seen him. Same black shoes, starched shirt, and intensely vapid expression.

The island is meant to be enjoyed, but there's no patent on who can enjoy it. If a guy wants to come from Chicago, run around in black socks and shorts, and overpay for meals prepared by some mercenary cook like me, then fine! Salute him as he disembarks from the ferry. It's okay. When we erect a statue we don't tell the birds they can't rest on it. Let them shit all over it, the statue doesn't care. Let the masses come. . . .

An ocean passes between us as he takes each step up the street. It is time for me to find a tombolo in the other direction. The water is rising on every side. White shadows burn the ground. Tines of light dance with the breeze. The moist luster of the moment swells until I can sit on the bench no longer. I will follow the gulls out of this vortex as they circle the ferries headed for the mainland, crapping on the heads of the tourists.

39

All my belongings are packed in a duffel bag on the bed. I just have a few papers to look through. It's a beautiful Labor Day. Behind me the sea is a sparkling junkyard of memories. I've decided to get an early start so I won't have to navigate the poorly marked roads of the Cape in the dark.

I come across the letter my friend had sent me about the job in New York. Without thinking I crumple it up. A quick look at the other papers—mostly bills and a bunch of poems I had written over the summer—then I ball them all together and throw the lump in the trash can. I pick up the duffel and go to the living room.

"Larry, I'm out of here." He comes in with a beer.

"How about one for the road?"

"There's always room for one more."

We go out on the deck.

"So Lar, you're gonna do the masters?"

"Yeah. I'm not lookin' forward to next week."

"I don't think I could go back to school after all this time."

"Hey, why deal with reality when you can read about it?"

"Cheers buddy." We drank. I looked at the ocean. "Here's one for you, Old Man," I yelled, then threw my bottle at the water. "Time to catch that ferry."

We walked down to the bike, and I strapped my bag on the rack.

"So," Larry said. "What are your plans?"

"I've got an uncle in San Francisco who owns a publishing company. Crazy Uncle Max. Incredible guy. Hangs out with Allen Ginsberg, all those aging beatniks. Publishes some interesting stuff: literature, sociology, poetry—good shit. No fucking cat books. He once offered me a job when I was in college. I blew him off for Wall Street. Wasn't my thing then. But it seems like a perfect job for me now. 'Bout time I gave him a call."

I started up the bike. "I'll write you when I get settled."

"Sure thing. Thanks for everything, man." We shook hands.

"Oh Lar, and if you wanna get laid . . ." I let the clutch out. "Do some laundry."

As I pulled away, Larry yelled, "And thanks for the onion rings."

I rode up the hill past Grant's place. He was sitting on the roof. I waved. He saluted me with his beer bottle. He had told me that they were going to stay on the island until their place got too cold, then they'd all move back to Boston. Grant had an apartment on Newbury Street, and his friends all lived in the neighborhood. I imagined all six of them living together as old men and women—white-haired, vivacious, still carrying armfuls of beer bottles, dropping some occasionally, but never losing the thirst for each other's company.

As I rode along Sconset Road bits of fog stuck to the moors. My eyes watered, stung by the wind. All around me, floating pigments of atmosphere, circling in the manner of choices through the mind of a painter.

I thought of everything I would be leaving behind. A way of life unlivable on the mainland.

I tried to picture all that I had been taking for granted:

The daily sweep of the gnomon over the side of the house, ticking silently.

The sparkling deliria of moths under the deck light.

The array of stars scattered every time God shattered a bottle on the floor of the sky.

The dirty monologue of the sea.

The step of martial clouds, heralding storms.

The olive skin of dusk along the beach.

Spindrift

The moon hauled by an ox across the tides.
The weaving scrim of gulls at dawn.
The stippled friction of light, cleansing the island every day.
The volcanic sunrises.

Rounding the Rotary, shooting toward town, I thought about saying good-bye to the people I hadn't been able to see the past few days, like Ted, Mrs. Walsh, and Dave, but I decided against it. Why prolong the inevitable? Instead, I drove to the Hub and wrote my name on a piece of paper, then the number "86", and "See you in San Francisco!" I tacked it on the board next to an old sign advertising dishwasher positions.

The Steamship arrived against the dock with the serenity of a hippopotamus. Ferry hands threw lines to the shore. The ramp connected to the ferry making the whirring sound of a dentist's drill. Cries of goodbye mixed with joyous greetings in the oil and water exchange of passengers I had witnessed so many times.

I drove the motorcycle into the hold, then ascended to the top deck to watch the departure.

People swarmed erratically below as if scattered by the wind. All around me on the deck passengers pulled out cameras and nylon jackets.

A horn sounded. The ship moved slowly. Voices echoed in the vacuum between the ferry office and the metal hull.

Everything began to shrink as we pulled out of the harbor; the houses became toy cottages of gray shingle and white trim. The Brant Point lighthouse looked almost comic—like it had come from a child's railroad set. A few kids stood on the rocks around it and waved. I waved back, thinking of the many times I had observed this scene from their perspective.

As the wind picked up gulls started to follow the ferry. People held food for them to snatch out of their hands. Sunlight illuminated the blue intensity of water to the point where it looked as solid as the ground. A sailboat passed us heading back to the harbor, bouncing through our massive wake.

We reached the end of the long arc of the jetty, which I hadn't seen since the day Mark took us waterskiing. Nantucket receded into a flat scar on the water. Soon, other than the T-shirts and suntans we were wearing, the gulls were our only remnant of the island.

I walked to the windward side of the boat where few people were standing, and leaned over the rail. Amazingly, a lone windsurfer sailed by us, hurled by the violent wind. He came from the direction of the open sea on a tack to the landless horizon. He appeared to be using all of his strength to handle the sail. I feared for his safety. But as his face became visible I could see a lustful look of enjoyment on it, and on he sailed, as if he would never have to stop.

We slid into the warm arms of America at the dock in Hyannis. I felt numb walking ashore. The sunlight had lost its vivid reality. Crowds of people scurried to station wagons and big, awkward city cars. Parents greeted disheartened sons and daughters. Husbands struggled with heavy suitcases. The smell of gasoline and car fumes raped the air.

I rode the bike across the street and walked into the first bar I saw. It was nearly empty. A young waitress worked at setting the tables for lunch. I ordered a beer and started talking with her.

"You worked on the Cape all summer?"

"Yup. How 'bout you?"

"Nantucket. For about half-a-year. You have a good time?"

"No, just okay. There wasn't a lot going on. It got pretty boring after a while."

"Take some advice from an older guy. Try the island next year. I guarantee, it'll be a different story."

"That's what I've heard."

I drove through Buzzard's Bay and up the shoulder of the Cape. The sun hung high in the sky behind me. The numbness I experienced upon landing dissolved in the wind. I felt myself moving closer to Tammy with every mile.

Cars filled with vacationers raced alongside of me, the highway pulsing with exuberant holiday traffic. Everyone smiled and waved as we passed each other. A girl leaned out of a window and offered me a can of beer. I took it, lifted my visor, and drank. She blew me a kiss.

As we moved inland, each overpass was filled with young people waving and cheering for us, as if we were heroes returning from a war. They hung signs over the sides which read: "Life is a beach!" and "See you next year!" Cars honked. I tooted my horn and waved back. A cheer rang out from the bridge above me when I stood on the bike and saluted. The moment stretched before me as my arm rose toward the bridge, caught the sunlight, and I sailed toward a new dawn in the west.

Photo by Jeff Breland
(Thanks to Anchovies, Boston)

Stuart Sheppard grew up in Pittsburgh, graduated from Kenyon College, and currently lives in Boston. *Spindrift* is his first novel.

A Typical American Town

A Typical
American Town

J OHN M ADDOX R OBERTS

ST. MARTIN'S PRESS ——⌒—— NEW YORK

Design by Judith A. Stagnitto

Library of Congress Cataloging-in-Publication Data

Roberts, John Maddox.
    A typical American town / John Maddox Roberts.
      p. cm.
    "A Thomas Dunne book."
    ISBN 0-312-11359-5 BT 20.95|11.40 11|94
    1. Private investigators—Ohio—Fiction. 2. City and town life—
Ohio—Fiction. I. Title.
PS3568.O23874T97 1994
813'.54—dc20
                                   94-3777
                                      CIP

First Edition: November 1994

10 9 8 7 6 5 4 3 2 1

For Beth, who was the inspiration, the encouragement,

my helper,

critic and proofreader

and because it's our twentieth anniversary

April 23, 1993

BOOK ONE

The Model

glanced into my rearview mirror and the Columbus skyline wasn't there anymore. I wasn't sure when it had stopped being there, and that bothered me, because I had been keeping track of things like that: inconsequential comings and goings, when the terrain changed, crossing state lines, all the chain of nothings that make up a long road trip. All of it holding the great big nothing at bay. Had it been three days? Four? I wasn't sure, and that bothered me, too.

I'd left California behind in the awful desert heat-haze and crossed the tip of Nevada during a night broken by the neon hallucination of Las Vegas. After that, I wasn't so sure. There had been Utah and Colorado and the unbelievable flat sameness of Kansas. I was pretty sure Missouri had been in there somewhere, and Indiana and Illinois, but I wasn't sure which had come first. Eventually, it was Ohio. When the exhaustion had hit me I'd slept in roadside rest areas where the engines of the big semis had chugged away all night long.

The exhaustion had been good, too. It was full of tossing and turning and noise, the itchy seediness of a long road trip in summer, even the most disagreeable sensations helping to keep the big, black nothing at a distance. Now all that was left was a little bit more of Ohio and then I would be in Cleveland, where an old friend had offered me a haven. The little bit more of Ohio was too much.

The off-ramp came up on the right. I didn't bother to read the name of the nowhere town it gave access to. The road it led to crossed the highway I was on a quarter mile ahead, supported by a bridge resting on concrete abutments and stout concrete pillars. It was the right-hand abutment that interested me. It looked good and solid, unyielding and built to last centuries. Back in L.A. I had seen innumerable motor vehicles stopped by such abutments, wadded up like a handful of aluminum foil. I had the road all to myself. Nobody was going to crack up because of me. I still had that much sense of citizen's duty. I aimed the Plymouth at the abutment and floored it.

The concrete came up fast, gray-white like a tombstone. I knew I should have done this sooner instead of putting it off, adding to the shame of my life. It felt great. Two more seconds, then the big, black nothing could have me. Of course I chickened out. I always did.

The abutment loomed up and it seemed like something else took control of my hands, twisting the wheel to the right, making the tires squeal, making the abutment slide off to the left as the Plymouth lurched over the curb, the tires biting into turf, just missing the guard rail and swerving onto the exit ramp, then fishtailing to the top where I hit the brake without putting in the clutch. There might be something coming along the country road, unsuspecting.

The Plymouth stalled, kicking and bucking to a stop. Then it was quiet, except for the tick and ping of hot metal. For a while I couldn't do anything. My heart was a trip-hammer in my chest, but it seemed like no blood was getting anywhere important. My windpipe seemed to be too constricted for anything to pass, but my lungs were getting painfully overinflated. When I regained control of myself, I pounded the steering wheel with hammered fists, tears of rage and impotence squeezing from the corners of my eyes. Couldn't I even do this one, supremely simple, thing right? Apparently not.

I sat there, gradually calming down, wondering what to do next. I couldn't stay there on the ramp. I saw no point in going on to Cleveland, or anywhere else. I scanned in all directions, more from habit than anything else. A couple of cars and a truck were on the interstate. No highway patrolmen suspicious of my car or the marks I'd left on the turf back there. No traffic on the country road that crossed the interstate. Then I raised my eyes over the steering wheel and saw the sign. MONTICELLO, it said. An arrow pointed right, to the east.

If I hadn't been so numb my scalp would have been crawling. Monticello. My brain wasn't functioning too well. Was this a sign? I'd stopped believing in that sort of thing back when I was a kid. God didn't care and God didn't send signs. Then why was I here? Why had I picked this overpass out of all the hundreds along my route to waste myself on? No answer. So what to do now? It was clear that I didn't have the guts to do what really ought to be done. Cleveland? It was a million miles away and didn't interest me. I had no life waiting for me there. But Monticello, that was different. If nothing else, it offered a sense of symmetry. Beginnings and endings. I hit the ignition and the machinery fired right up, despite its rude treatment. I pulled out onto the crossroad and turned east. Toward Monticello.

The drive wasn't a long one, maybe twenty miles, but after the last twenty-nine years of my life it was like a visit to another planet. The country rolled in hilly waves, but it never got steep. It was as green as one of those movies about Ireland. Everywhere I saw black-and-white cattle doing their best to reduce the green. After a while I remembered that they were called Holsteins. This was dairy country. Every few miles there would be a little mom-and-pop store that sold gas and convenience-store food. I stopped at one and topped off the tank.

Inside, I looked over the stuff behind the counter—fish hooks, shotgun shells, car air fresheners, insect repellent, cigarette papers, pipe tobacco—it looked like a commercial time warp. On the counter, next to a stand of candy, chewing gum, and mints was a plastic canister full of ten-inch pretzel sticks as thick as my forefinger, studded with pebbles of salt. They lay tilted obliquely, so that when you lifted the lid and the bottom came up the pretzels fanned out for your selection. I wondered when was the last time I'd seen one of those. Probably the last time I was in this part of the country.

"That'll be sixteen fifty-two for the gas. Can I help you with anything else?" The woman was about sixty: smiling, open, trusting. I was willing to bet that this place had never been held up. I turned and looked at the refrigerator chest. Behind the glass door I could see stacks of beer in six-packs, the condensation gleaming on their aluminum sides, the green and brown bottles like oblong jewels. I made myself look away.

"No, thanks. That'll be all."

She hummed a little as she made my change. The cash register beeped and flashed red electronic numbers. At least that was new. I went out and got into the Plymouth. It was only a little hot, despite sitting out in the sun. It was still summer, but fall wasn't far off. The colors would be beautiful, then. Back in Southern California the hills would be green for a while, then they'd turn brown. Sometimes it would rain, mostly it wouldn't. There was more variety here, I remembered that.

I drove past farms out of Currier and Ives. They looked like there should be bearded guys in straw hats working them with horses, but this wasn't Amish country. The men I saw in the fields mostly wore baseball caps, and beards were optional rather than compulsory. I was still in the country when I passed the sign.

WELCOME TO MONTICELLO
Pop. 14380
Elevation 990
A TYPICAL AMERICAN TOWN

Just past the sign was a whitewashed wooden frame covered with the insignias of all the local civic and fraternal organizations, lodges, and churches painted on metal plates cut in various shapes. The grass around the signs was clipped better than my lawn had ever been. They were surrounded by planter boxes that were bright with flowers. I didn't know their names. I began to pass houses with fences and lawns. None of it looked familiar. I didn't know this area and that seemed strange. It hadn't occurred to me that there were parts of Monticello I had never known. I wasn't even sure what direction I was approaching from. After a short stretch of semirural residential road, things began to be organized in blocks. I passed a few stores and fast-food places, then I saw a restaurant sign on a corner and I finally got the first flash of the recognition I had been waiting for.

MAISEL'S
est. 1927

Suddenly I had my bearings. I'd gone to school with Jimmy Maisel. His parents had run the restaurant back in the fifties and early sixties. I turned left and began to head north. To my left I passed the old A&P that everyone called the Victory Market when I was a kid. But it wasn't a supermarket anymore. Somebody had converted it into a gym. Half a minute later I reached the square.

Every town in this part of the country had a square. Like most of them, Monticello's featured a rectangle of businesses and public buildings fronting on a circular island, with a Civil War monument in its center. I nosed the Plymouth into a parking space beneath a twisted old oak and turned off the engine.

When I got out, the first thing that struck me was the quiet. It wasn't deserted. Far from it. A bunch of teenagers had a spirited Frisbee game going on the grass. A kid in camouflage fatigues and spit-shined boots was loading a duffle bag into the trunk of a battered old Honda. He wore a maroon beret; a paratrooper winding up his leave and heading back to Bragg. A bunch of younger kids made a fuss over him, an older guy shook his hand, and a woman sniffled into a handkerchief. But all the activity went on without raised voices, and even the cars that circled the square did it quietly. There wasn't a loud muffler to be heard anywhere. The town was a Norman Rockwell painting come to life; a Frank Capra movie in 3-D and color.

The north and east sides of the square were just as I remembered them. A pair of Corinthian columns flanked the entrance of the Masonic lodge. Next to it the drugstore still had the huge vases of colored water in its window. The lamp store hadn't changed, and the weird, thirties-style diner still stood on the corner of the street leading west. Its facade was shiny orange and cream tile and the long, chrome-lined windows had rounded ends.

The south and west sides came as a shock. The movie theater was gone, along with the doughnut shop next to it and the town's other drugstore, that stood on the corner opposite the diner. All three had been replaced by a single, huge bank. Its redbrick facade was blank and soulless. On the east side, the old LeMay Hotel was gone, too. It had dated from the 1880s and had had the ritziest dining room in the county. There was a new LeMay on the same spot: a galleried, three-story motor hotel. I doubted that its restaurant enjoyed much of a reputation.

It was all coming back to me now. The entire town was a thousand mnemonic triggers. In another place I could have sat and thought for hours, trying to dredge up memories of my childhood here—not events but details of experience—and couldn't have come up with a fraction of the memory wash that deluged me by my just standing in one spot, glancing around. Many things were unchanged. Others, like the bank, were jarringly wrong.

Near the monument I spotted a water fountain and walked over to it. When I had lived here, the water fountain in the square was a turn-of-the-century cast-iron tulip. Its stream had bubbled perpetually, so that in winter its rim was encased in a thick layer of ice that curved inward to the hole through which the tiny geyser erupted. It always reminded me of those pitcher plants that let insects in, but that are too slick inside for them to climb back out. Its replacement stood in the same spot, a wedge of pebbles set in cement, doling out water stingily by manipulation of institutional hardware. The hardware itself was cheap and tacky, the chromelike paint peeling away to reveal plastic beneath.

Facing south I looked down the length of Main Street. Somewhere a few blocks down the street crossed the river and the railroad tracks. The facades of the buildings lining the street looked exactly as they always had. Or was my memory playing with reality, making it look as if I had stepped back into my hometown of thirty years ago? Having nothing better to do, since it looked as if I wasn't going to die that day, I crossed the street that ran around the square and began to walk south along Main.

The rich smell of leather hit me before I realized that I was standing in front of the shoe store. Its doors stood open and I looked down the center aisle, flanked by chairs and those slanted footstools they use in shoe stores. Something was missing there at the back of the store, and then I remembered the fluoroscopes. Back in the fifties, they were the saving diversion in the onerous task of trying on new shoes. The scope was in a wood-framed pylon like a lectern and you stood with your feet stuck into a slot in its base. Looking down through the eyepiece you saw the ghostly, green image of your skeletal feet. You could even wiggle your toe bones, a fascinating sight. My father and the clerk would peer through the other two ornate, bronze eyepieces, looking like two men watching an 1890s peep show.

Next to the shoe store was the jewelry store that had always had a clever clockwork display that fascinated me as a child. The display changed every few months and it was like something out of Gepetto's workshop, with little human and animal figures going in and out of miniature buildings, dancing, playing instruments. It looked like the art had been lost. The window featured only the usual watches, rings, and necklaces.

On the next block was the Cove. My twitching stomach was rebelling at a continent's worth of fast-food and I hadn't eaten anything since early that morning. I opened the door and went inside. The old lady behind the cashier's desk by the door looked me over without favor. I couldn't blame her. I looked pretty seedy. Then a puzzled look took over her face.

"Do I know you? Didn't you used to live here?"

"It was a long time ago," I said. Something twisted in my chest. I couldn't believe that this old biddy could see the sixteen-year-old boy inside the revenant in front of her. I tried to picture what she must have looked like thirty years ago, but I couldn't bring up anything.

"I never forget a face." Now she was smiling. I turned and looked around so that she wouldn't see my face. I was in the front room. They'd changed it into a dining room. Years ago it had been lined with glass candy cases. The Cove had made its own candy, and they sold the richest, most wonderful fudge in the world.

"You've changed things," I said.

She came around from behind the desk, holding a menu. "Yes, but I never approved of it. When all that health nonsense started up people stopped buying so many sweets and the owners figured they'd make more money by putting in more tables." She led me into the old dining room. I had it all to myself at that hour. A waitress who was only slightly younger than the cashier took my order.

The food took a while to arrive, and I ate it slowly, relishing the feeling of having absolutely nothing to do. It was a feeling I'd experienced rarely in my life. The dinner was plain but absolutely perfect: pork chops from a pig that had lived its brief life within ten miles of this spot, vegetables that had never seen the inside of a can, mashed potatoes that probably hadn't even been peeled before I ordered them. They had the tiny lumps, the unevenness of texture, that said they were made from actual potatoes rather than dry, white flakes that looked like fake snow on a movie set.

I finished and left a generous tip, paid my bill and went outside. The dinner had mellowed me and my nerves were no longer jumping around just under my skin. It was a good feeling, the best I'd had in a long time. I continued walking south. The last block before the river had been gentrified. It had once passed for the bad part of town, a stretch of seedy bars and poolrooms, now featuring artsy-craftsy New Age shops and expensive boutiques.

It struck me that for the entire length of the street, both sides, I hadn't seen a single empty storefront. It was a rare sight these days, with old downtown businesses unable to compete with the malls. Somehow, Monticello had been able to evade the curse.

I crossed the river on the road bridge. To my left, a hundred feet upstream, kids played all over the old railroad bridge, jumping from its iron truss into the lazy, brown water below, screaming and splashing. The concrete abutments of the bridge had been a favorite fishing spot for my friends and me. When we heard trains coming we'd run and put pennies on the track just to see how the massive wheels would flatten them. For some reason we found this endlessly fascinating.

With a start I realized that the track was gone, even though the old bridge still stood, freshly painted. I looked across the road and the rambling old train station was still there, the steel-wheeled luggage carts standing on the platform by the Railway Express office. I crossed the street and went up the steps into the waiting room.

A bronze plaque by the door proclaimed that the building had been converted into a community center, dedicated by the Monticello Historical Society, with a generous grant from the Cohan family. A bulletin board listed a program of activities from the Senior Citizens Activities Group to the Boy Scouts. There was a Disabled Veterans meeting coming up.

One wall was devoted to the history of Monticello. History hadn't been generous to the town, but a few notable things had happened there. There was a copy of the town's original charter, dating from the 1820s. A yellowed copy of the Polk County Times of 1860 gave an account of a fiery abolitionist speech that had almost touched off a riot. There were tintypes of townsmen setting off to the Civil War. A group photo showed gawky, patriotic young men about to entrain from this very station for the training camps of World War One.

A slightly less yellow front page of the Monticello Tribune revealed the destruction wrought by the tornado of '33, which had devastated the western end of town. There was a panoramic photo of the victory parade of the boys coming back from

World War Two. I tried to find my father in the picture, but the scale was too big to make out individual faces.

A final framed front page from the now merged *Polk Times-Tribune* blared out the story of the Cohan Chemical robbery of December '65. That had even made the news in Los Angeles, where I was living by that time. It was a daylight, payroll robbery and four men were killed. Two of the robbery gang were killed, along with the county sheriff and the cashier, who was carrying the payroll. The two surviving robbers made off with a reported two and a half million dollars. A string of follow-up articles dated over the next two years revealed an ever-decreasing likelihood of a break in the case.

An editorial dated December '75 gave a tenth-year anniversary synopsis of the case and the investigation. The name at the bottom of the editorial caught my attention: Lew Czuk. We'd been close friends as children. I'd last seen him one drunken evening in Florida, where he was working for a Miami paper. I was an MP at the end of a thirty-day leave before shipping out for Viet Nam. I had already been accepted by the LAPD Academy, to join as soon as I was discharged. I was going to be a one-man crime-busting phenomenon. Lew was going to be a crusading investigative reporter and snag a Pulitzer before he was thirty. So he had come back home. Still no Pulitzer and not much prospect of one in Monticello. Well, I hadn't put a big dent in L.A. crime, either.

On my way out I passed a row of photographs of local dignitaries, Angelica Cohan with her photography group, other members of the Cohan family cutting ribbons and making dedications. A last picture stopped me. It was a color glossy of a woman standing in the middle of a mass of flowers of almost hallucinatory color and brilliance. Walking past, glancing across it, something jerked my eyes back for a closer look. For an instant I thought I knew the woman, a strikingly pretty middle-aged blonde, but the more I looked the less she resembled anyone I knew. A strip of blue tape was below the photo, identifying the woman as Edna Tutt with her prize-winning flowers at the state fair in '87. The name meant nothing to me. I decided it must have been the extraordinary colors that grabbed my attention.

It was getting late. The streetlights were beginning to flicker on. The kids had abandoned the railroad bridge. The flush of nostalgia was welling away and I was just tired. I walked slowly back to the square, passing closed stores. Monticello had always been one of those towns where they roll up the sidewalks at six o'clock.

I got back into the Plymouth and pulled over to the LeMay. The man at the desk gave me the now familiar once-over. "Long trip?" he asked.

"Longer than you'd believe," I told him.

You couldn't go anywhere in Monticello without tripping over evidence of the Cohan family. They liked to remind people that they owned the place.

After breakfast at the hotel coffee shop, I went out to the square and began walking east on Central. Central Avenue crossed Main Street at the square. It divided the town north-south the way Main divided it east-west. The street sloped gently upward, paved with red brick. The townspeople had resisted repeated efforts to asphalt their brick streets. It might get slick in winter, but it was prettier than blacktop. The houses were set back from the sidewalk behind well-tended lawns, most of them separated from the walk by picket fences or low walls made of stone or brick. A few of them had carriage steps by the curb; odd little stone steps usually carved with relief decoration for getting into horse-drawn carriages. I'd forgotten about them.

At the top of the hill I passed Holy Name Hospital, where I was born during what nobody realized at the time was the beginning of the great post-war baby boom. Next to the hospital was St. Anne's, where I had gone to elementary school and my first two years of high school. It looked completely unchanged. It was quiet and deserted, the kids still on summer vacation. I crossed the street and went into the playground.

The swings and jungle gym were in the same place, their legs buried deep in the asphalt. The yard was on two levels with a steep dip where Mike Regen had taken a header during a rough game of touch football, breaking his arm and his front teeth. That made him a celebrity for a while and we all admired the stainless steel Bugs Bunny teeth he got as replacements until he was old enough for permanent caps.

I went to the entrance and peered in, shading the door window so that I could see more than my reflection. It opened onto a landing. On the right side a short stair went up to a corridor lined with classrooms. On the left another went down to an identical corridor, this one with the cafeteria and beyond that the gymnasium at one end.

Everything looked the same, but it didn't fill me with nostalgia. I'd hated going to school there, every day of it. Going to public school in California had been like getting out of prison. The nuns had delivered a decent education, though, I couldn't deny that. Then I saw a sign on the wall of the upstairs corridor. It said, "Computer Room," with an arrow pointing to the left. Some things had changed, after all.

I went up Central for another couple of blocks, past the old convent, then turned right on Maple Street. All these residential streets were lined with maples, buckeyes, and oaks. Some were huge, old trees. Others were smaller, planted in the last three or four decades to replace the stately trees that had died in the chestnut and elm blights.

At the corner of Maple and Wright, I stopped to look at a two-story house with a porch that wrapped around two sides, restrained gingerbread trim decorating its eaves. We had lived in it for six years, after my father was earning enough at Cohan Chemical to afford a better place than the one we had been living in down by the river. I saw a sign in a front window saying, "Room For Rent," followed by a phone number. The house had been white when we lived in it, but it was now a pale gray with white trim. The lawn had been transformed into a rose garden.

I walked around to the back yard, a small area between the house and the garage, where an apple tree had stood when I had lived there. The tree was gone, and the yard had been turned into another garden, this one filled with flowers I couldn't name. I thought I recognized hollyhocks and hibiscus, but I wasn't strong on the subject of gardening. The beds were divided by two graveled paths meeting at right angles. Where the two paths met, where you would expect a bird bath, there was a concrete pedestal topped by a sculpture of what seemed to be a nude goddess. Things had changed since my boyhood. My mother had what she called a "brown thumb." She couldn't keep weeds alive.

After a long look, I left the house and continued along Maple. Next to the garage was an alley running through the block, then the huge grounds of the Cohan estate.

It came as something of a surprise, in the midst of this middle-class residential district, but this wasn't L.A. There was no Beverly Hills here, no Bel Air. The local big folks lived right in town with the rest. Which is not to say they lived *like* the rest. The house was one of those Victorian structures, all turrets and cupolas, set in the middle of the grounds and plantings, with a cluster of outbuildings behind it. I'd always thought of it as the *Magnificent Ambersons* house from the time I'd seen the old Orson Welles movie on the WBNS late show. I thought it looked just like the house in the movie.

About fifty feet past the garage of my old house, near the sidewalk, was my favorite climbing tree. During my Tarzan phase, I'd spent a lot of time in it. It had a stout branch at just the right height for me to grab with a short hop. After I'd scrambled up on that, the rest of the branches were easier to climb than a ladder. I'd spent some wonderful hours in that tree. It was a place to go to be alone with your thoughts. The desire to do that had been enough to set me apart from most kids I knew.

The tree had smooth, gray bark, perfect for carving initials. Subsequent generations of kids had obviously discovered this, because the lower trunk looked like a fence on L.A. gang turf. Every square inch of it was covered with penknife graffiti. New carvings were sharp and clear. Older ones were getting blurry. I thought for a long time. Then I looked up and down the street, as if I was going to be embarrassed if someone saw me. I walked over to the tree and reached up. To my surprise, I didn't have to jump to reach that lowest limb. I stretched my arms and got my fingertips over the smooth, dusty bark, then hauled myself up onto the limb.

This wasn't as awkward as it would be for most men of my age. In my former profession, a lot of my job had consisted of chasing pachucos and homeboys over the fences of the barrios and the 'hoods. I'd made a point of keeping in shape, specially emphasizing the upper body strength so necessary in that sort of urban gymnastics.

I climbed the branches, not so much from my own conscious recollection as from a sort of muscular memory that took me to the spot I needed to find. Then I sat on the branch and looked at the trunk where I'd sat one hot afternoon and carved on the smooth, gray bark. Once, the letters had stood out, big and proud:

G T
+
L C

That had been almost thirty years ago. Now, where the carving had proclaimed my love to the world, there was an irregular, rectangular patch of brown keloid. I ran my fingers over the tree's scar tissue, trying to find the love of my youth, but it was gone, devoured by the tree's need to heal itself. The rough patch of bark blurred in my vision.

"They disappear after a few years."

The voice came from below me. I looked down. A woman was standing there. I didn't have to see her. I knew her voice. She was looking up, her hands stuck into the pockets of a short skirt she wore with a tank top.

"Hello, Lola." I fought to keep the tremor out of my voice.

"Hi, Gabe. I was in the house and I saw you out here looking up at the tree. I told myself you'd climb up there and you did."

I clambered down the branches and dropped in front of her. It came as a shock, seeing how short she was. She barely came up to my chest now.

"I knew you wouldn't stay away," Lola said. "What's it been? Twenty-five years?"

"Closer to thirty. How'd you know me from so far away?"

"A lot of things. I couldn't see your face, but no two people move quite the same. I knew it was you. What brings you back, Gabe?" Her face was broad and triangular, dominated by the eyes. My mother had called her, without favor, "that girl with spooky eyes." Lola Cohan had eyes with gray irises so huge that almost no white showed. Her pupils were small, even in subdued light, so that most of the time her eyes looked like featureless, gray balls. Ophthalmologists have a term for it. It didn't detract from her beauty.

"I had an urge to visit the home town. You know, middle-aged angst sort of thing."

She smiled. It put lines in her face, but that made her even more beautiful. It wrenched something inside me. I couldn't be coming back here to start this all over again, could I?

"You left all of a sudden back then," she said. "It shocked me."

"Wasn't my idea. The folks said we're going to California and we went. What have you been doing?" The absurdity of the question hit me the moment it was out of my mouth. How have you spent the last thirty years? Tell me briefly.

"I've kept busy. College. Three marriages. A fashion business. You?"

"Pretty succinct," I commended. "As for me: College, a war, a marriage, more college, a career, now back here."

She zeroed right in. "What kind of career?"

"Cop," I told her.

"You? Somehow I never pictured you that way."

"I was a lot younger last time you saw me."

"Weren't we all?" The years hadn't been hard on her. She was tanned and athletic looking, her hair unfaded. She was barefoot, her toes working unconsciously in the well-tended grass. Her parents had never been able to keep shoes on her during the summer. They came off as soon as the last snow melted. There was no ring on her left hand. Marriage number three hadn't worked out any better than one and two, it seemed.

"When did you come back?"

"Yesterday. I drove in about four in the afternoon, spent the night at the LeMay."

"How long will you be staying?"

I realized suddenly that I didn't know. "Oh, a couple of weeks, I guess. I want to look around, see a few people."

"Come on to the house. It's getting hot out here." She smiled, open, welcoming.

"I'd be glad to."

We walked over the springy turf beneath the huge, ancient trees. A dark, Mexican-looking man was driving a riding mower over the lawn. I looked at the cluster of outbuildings in back and pointed to them.

"What's changed?" I asked her.

"We pulled down the old carriage houses to put in the tennis court and swimming pool."

I remembered them. We'd gone in there as kids. There had been buggies and shays and a formal coach, even a huge old sleigh that probably hadn't been used since the 1890s.

"What did you do with the old sleigh? It belonged in a museum."

She shrugged. "Dad sent it to Dayton. I think it's in a museum there."

We went up the front steps and into the entrance hall. It was dark—paneled, lined with portraits. It struck me that I had never been in this house. From an ornate frame, a hard-faced man glared at me as if he'd just as soon I didn't come in now, at least not through the front door. He was dressed in a black suit, the lower half of his face framed by the high, stiff stand-up collar of the early nineteenth century. His mouth was clamped into a tight, straight line below a smashed-in nose.

"Back in L.A. I busted people for looking at me like that," I said. "Is that old Patrick?"

She laughed. "That's him. Our Founder."

Patrick Cohan was an Irish immigrant who had turned up in Monticello shortly after the town was chartered and started up a gunpowder factory. He had prospered, then the Civil War had come along and business had exploded, so to speak. He'd made millions out of the war, and later wars, branching into other explosives after Nobel invented dynamite, then into other chemical operations. The Cohans had become bush-league Du Ponts, the biggest employer and property owner in the county.

"Balzac said every great fortune began with a crime," she mused, looking at the portrait. "I wonder if he knew Patrick. They were contemporaries."

"I thought he was just a canny businessman," I said.

"That's the official line, but I'm not so sure. He fled Ireland during the Famine and arrived in Boston without a nickel. A month later he was here, with fifteen hundred dollars to invest in his powder mill."

"Maybe he was just a good poker player," I said, "like Scarlett O'Hara's father."

"Maybe so," she said. "Last honest man in the family if it's true."

She led me down a hall lined with photographs. They were striking western landscapes, so dark that they almost looked like negatives, but with every outline bright and clear.

"Did your mother take these?" I asked. Back at the old train station I'd seen that Angelica had a photography group.

She laughed again. "She wishes she had." We stepped out into a glassed-in porch, its decor light and cheerful in sharp contrast to the house. "Those are Ansel Adams studies. Mother worships his developing compounds. Adams, Weston, Bourke-White, Steichen, she loves them all."

To me, photography had been something that was done to record crime scenes. Something about the odd name struck me.

"Ansel Adams? Is that how your brother got that name?" Ansel Cohan was a few years older than I and he'd left Monticello about a year before I did under some sort of cloud.

Rumor in the high school had it that his father banished him for too many run-ins with the law. There were darker rumors, too. "Yes. It was Mother and Dad's biggest fight and the only one she won. He wanted a son named after him. What would you like?" She went to a wet bar that ran most of the length of one wall and opened its diminutive refrigerator. "We have beer and wine, white and rose, and lots of other stuff. Iced tea, lemonade, and coke if it's a little early for you."

"Iced tea, please." I looked over the sunroom. Its windows looked out on the lawn we'd just crossed. The ornamental curtains were patterned white and green, identical to the upholstery on the rattan furniture. The tables were rattan topped with disks of thick glass. "What do you hear from Ansel?"

She paused with the pitcher poised to pour, looking puzzled for an instant. "Hear?" Then her face cleared. "Oh, I remember, he was still away when you left. He came back, let's see . . . it must have been about '69, when Dad knew he had cancer. Ansel settled down and took over the family business."

"What was he doing all that time he was away?" I took the glass from her and she poured herself a goblet of white wine.

"He never talked about it and I never asked." She said it casually, but you don't handle as many interrogations as I have without getting a feel for those things. She wasn't being truthful with me. I shrugged it off. None of my business, anyway.

She clinked her glass against mine. "To your homecoming." We sat at one of the tables and she was silent for a minute, looking out over the lawn. "After you left," she said, a little hesitation in her voice, "did you ever write me?"

That took me by surprise. "Yes, I did. You never answered."

She sighed and nodded. "I never got your letters. Dad must have intercepted them." She shook her head. "Such a long time ago. It's hard to remember now, being so young and powerless. What did you write?"

I took a drink. The tea was cool and easy on the throat. "Like you said, it was a long time ago. Another world. We were different people."

"You're right." She glanced at my left hand, holding the tea glass. "Where is your wife? Did she come with you?"

I set the glass down and twisted the ring. "She died. Somehow I've never been able to bring myself to take the ring off."

She looked stricken. "Oh, I'm so sorry. I didn't mean to bring up something painful."

"It was quite a while ago," I assured her. "I should've taken the ring off years back, but it was my father's and . . ." From the sunroom I could see the circular driveway that ran in front of the house. A white Rolls was pulling in between the eagle-topped pillars that flanked the entrance.

Lola caught the direction of my gaze, and turned to see. "There's Ansel now. You'll get to meet him."

This, I thought, should be interesting. I'd seen him around town when I was a kid, but I was too young to be in the same crowd. Ansel Cohan had been the town's prize juvenile delinquent, hanging out with the Skinner kids, always in hot water for a series of petty offenses, always getting off because of family pull. He was the burden of Sheriff Fowles's life. Fowles's boy Mark used to tell me how his father longed for an excuse to shoot Ansel. Not to kill him, just to teach him some manners. Usually, though, Ansel confined his misbehavior to the city limits. The Cohans always owned the chief of police.

The front door opened and closed. "Ansel, come out to the porch. There's an old friend here I want you to see."

Ansel stood in the doorway, looking at me with a puzzled expression. If Lola had changed amazingly little, her brother was as transformed as any human being I had seen. The Ansel I remembered had been a weasely, pimple-faced lout with a greasy, duck's ass pompadour and skinny sideburns of early Elvis vintage, wearing jeans and a white T-shirt with a cigarette pack rolled into its sleeve, and a black motorcycle jacket, weather permitting.

This Ansel was as distinguished as a man could get. His weasel features had hardened into aristocratic aquilinity, relieved by a close-trimmed, salt-and-pepper mustache. He was around fifty, but his hair was still thick, dark on top with silver wings sweeping back above the ears. The suit he was wearing probably cost more than four months of my pay. His Italian shoes might have been carved from obsidian. He came in, holding out a beautifully manicured hand.

"An old friend? I'm afraid I don't . . ."

"Ansel, this is Gabe Treloar." She beamed at me. "Gabe used to live in the house where Mrs. Tutt lives now, back when we were children. He's just come back for a visit."

Something flickered in his eyes when he took my hand. I figured he was trying to place me. He had a firm, politician's handshake.

"Treloar?" I could see wheels spinning behind his eyes. "Oh, I remember now. I don't think you and I ever ran around together, but wasn't your father Ed Treloar, used to work for my father out at the river plant?"

"That's right," I said a little tightly, being put in my place.

"I believe your family had moved away by the time I took over the business, but I used to see your father's name a great deal, going over the finances from the interwar years."

"Interwar?" I said.

"Between Korea and Viet Nam," Lola said, taking another drink. "We Cohans mark the time from war to war. Those in-between spells are the doldrums for us."

Ansel turned to her and smiled. "National belligerence has been good to us." He turned back to me. "So what have you been doing with yourself all this time, Gabe?" He went to the bar and began to fix himself a scotch and soda, picking up the ice with little tongs and letting them fall, tinkling into the heavy glass.

"Living in Los Angeles, mostly."

"Gabe is on the police force," Lola said.

"LAPD?" He pronounced each letter, separately and distinctly. "Are we safe?"

"Ansel," she said.

"We're only dangerous when we run around in packs," I told him.

"Are you on vacation now?" Lola said brightly, shooting Ansel a warning look.

"Actually, I've left the force. I was on my way to Cleveland to meet with an old friend. He's invited me to join his firm. PI work. That's private investigator." I could see what Ansel was thinking: Why would a cop who's spent a career learning his territory and building up a network of contacts and informants leave to start over in a new city?

"Well, I'm glad you decided to take time to visit your home town," Lola said.

"I lived in southern California for a while," Ansel mused. "Wonderful place. I almost hated to come back, but duty called." He took a drink and unconsciously ran a finger along the edge of his mustache.

I heard a faint click of heels on the parquet hallway and a moment later a woman came into the sunroom. She had a slightly worried look, but the instant she noticed me a formal smile clicked into place.

"Children, I . . . oh, how do you do?" She held out a delicate, fine-boned hand and I took it.

"Gabe Treloar, Mrs. Cohan," I said. Her hand trembled slightly, which must have played hell with her photography. "You probably don't remember me. I used to live near here."

"Oh, yes," she said, "Edward's boy. It has been some time, hasn't it?" Nothing wrong with Angelica's memory. She was in her seventies somewhere, silver hair drawn back tightly from a face that had once been world-class beautiful. Traces of it still remained, among the lines, ruptured blood vessels and the dark eye-circles. She had the look of a lush who was going about it in a careful and deliberate fashion.

"Are you ready, Mother?" Ansel asked. "The Rolls is out front."

"Lola, dear," Angelica said, "I do wish you would come. You do have obligations, you know." Not wheedling at all, but irritated in a queenly fashion.

"I've sworn off political functions, Mother. There are better ways to lose weight than throwing up."

"Come along, Mother," Ansel said. "Lola isn't about to go anywhere she'll have to wear shoes."

Angelica turned to face me again. "We must run. So good to

see you again, Mr. Treloar." Her smile was as brittle as Noel Coward dialogue.

"No doubt we'll see you again, Gabe," Ansel said as he ushered his mother out into the hall.

"No doubt," I said.

"Don't mind them, Gabe," Lola said when the front door closed. "They're just . . ."

"They're just Cohans," I said.

"So am I."

"You were always different."

"I know." She got up and refilled her glass. "I even tried to get a different name. I was Lola Van Zandt for a while, then I was Lola Perlstein. Last time I was Lola Holliman. But each time I changed my name back to Cohan, because that's what I am."

"That doesn't sound like you," I told her. "Whatever Lola wants, Lola gets. That's what you always used to say. Everyone else said so, too. Except for your father."

"He was wrong about a lot of things. You don't walk away from a family like mine."

It seemed like a good time to switch subjects. "What's this about politics? It's hard enough picturing Ansel sitting in a boardroom."

"Oh, my brother's become quite the wheel in the local Republican organization. Tonight's a fund-raiser for our congressman's re-election campaign. Ansel's very cozy with the state house, too."

"Any ambitions in that direction himself?"

"He won't come out and say it, but tonight he's going to drop hints that, if everyone really insists, he wouldn't be averse to running for senator. But only if they twist his arm."

Ansel Cohan? With the greaseball haircut and the James Dean T-shirt?

"I take it you don't approve?"

She put her feet up in another chair and crossed them at the ankles. "I don't like sleaze. I don't like sweaty, two-faced men who laugh too loud at each other's jokes. I can only take so much greed."

She didn't have to tell me about world-weariness. She looked into her glass, saw the bottom and shook her head.

"A hot day and an empty stomach. That's a bad combination. This stuff is getting to me. I was so happy to see you out there in the tree and I didn't mean to cast gloom all over your visit. Shall we get together when I'm in a better mood?"

"I'd love to. Dinner tomorrow?"

"That would be wonderful." Her smile was genuine.

"Is the Lodge still the *in* place? Out by the lake?"

"It's considered a little stodgy these days, but it's still my favorite."

I got up. "Shall I come for you at seven?"

She got up too. "Don't be late." She got up on her bare toes and kissed my cheek.

Five minutes later I was back beneath the old tree, wondering where my life was taking me. The Mexican-looking guy was still mowing the lawn, giving me an occasional, curious glance. A lawn that size, mowing it was an all-day job, even with a riding mower.

I thought maybe I'd stay a while, a month or so, just give things a chance to sort themselves out. One thing was for sure: If it was going to be a long visit, I couldn't afford to stay at the LeMay. I needed someplace cheaper.

That was when I remembered the room for rent sign in my old house.

could hear music coming from an upstairs window, something classical. Two soprano voices twined around one another, playing sensual games with a heartbreakingly beautiful melody. I knew I'd heard it before, probably background music in a commercial or something. I pushed the doorbell button and heard chimes from somewhere inside.

"Hello?" The voice came from the same window as the music. I stepped back off the porch and looked up. I could dimly make out a form behind the screen.

"I've come to see about the room you have for rent," I said, smiling and trying to look respectable. "Is it still open?"

"Oh, yes. Go on in, I'll be right down."

A house you lived in as a child always looks smaller than you remembered. I was a lanky teenager when we moved away, but I still remembered it the way it seemed when we first moved in. I'd thought it was huge back then. The entrance hall, with the stairway to the second floor on the right, seemed downright cramped. I walked into the living room.

Oddly, it didn't seem all that familiar. The layout was the

same, but everything else was different. So much of what I remembered had been the furnishings, rather than the house. Even the paint and the wallpaper had changed. I remembered the room as rather dark and somber. Everything was in light colors now. Much of one wall was taken up with a book case. I walked over to take a look. Most of the books were about gardening or antiques. Some were coffee table books that had seen a lot of use. Several were about Deco period art and architecture.

A couple dozen figurines stood on top of the case, on the tables and shelves. They were variations on a single theme: each was a nude woman. Some were in dancing poses, others leaned against tubes that were obviously meant to hold something. Most had tiny holes all over their bases. I noticed that the ones without the tubes had their arms in a circle. They were all intended to hold something.

"You like my frogs?" She stood in the hall doorway. White female, five-four, hundred ten pounds, fiftyish, blond hair that didn't quite go with the dark eyebrows. She was dressed in a sweatsuit and sneakers. Her face was flushed and damp, and her breathing was a little heavy. Had I interrupted a midday tryst?

I said, "They don't look like frogs. They look like naked ladies to me."

"Everybody says that," she said, smiling. She had a wonderful, luminous smile. "They're flower holders. Florists call them frogs. These are Deco pieces. The nude figurines were very popular in the twenties and thirties." She picked one up. It was one of the dancing figures with a bronze green finish. "I just love them. I find them at flea markets and garage sales."

"I know you," I said.

The smile went off. "You do?"

"You're the flower lady. I saw your picture down at the old train station."

The smile reappeared. "Oh! I forgot about that. My garden is my claim to fame."

But I felt I really did know her from somewhere. I'd had the same impression when I glimpsed the photo in the train station.

I felt that I'd seen her a long time ago. I tried to picture her much younger. She'd been a beauty, that much was clear. Her body was compact and looked well conditioned.

She blotted her damp face with a sleeve. "Please forgive the way I look. I was working out when you rang the doorbell."

"I'm sorry I interrupted."

"Oh, I was just about finished. Those last hundred sit-ups are killers."

Last hundred? I thought. "I like your workout music."

"Isn't it beautiful? Do you enjoy opera?"

"I can recognize *The Ride of the Valkyries* when I hear it. That's about it. What was that?"

"The duet from *Lakme*. That's an opera by Delibes. It's pretty undistinguished except for that one song. The record is a CD I just bought. That's Lesley Garrett singing both parts." She shook her head. "Excuse me, I'm getting old and I ramble on. I'm Edna Tutt." She held out a hand and I took it. Her nails were short and the skin of her hands was a little rough. Apparently, she didn't believe in gardening gloves.

"Gabe Treloar. I'm going to be in town for a couple of months and I need a place to stay. I saw your sign and it seemed like an omen. I used to live in this house."

"You did? When was that?"

"From '54 to '63. That's when we moved to California. This is the first time I've been back since we moved away."

"Well, what a coincidence." There was a very faint southern tinge to her voice. "Would you like to look at the room? It's over the garage." She led me into the rear hallway, which had been converted into a utility room, and took a key that hung from a nail on a cord.

We went through the back door into the little yard that was now a garden. As she passed the sculpture on the pedestal she patted its bare bottom. "This is the biggest frog I ever found. They were almost never made this large. It must have been a showpiece in a florist's shop. It's solid bronze. I found it in a junk shop in Columbus, being used as a doorstop."

The nymph or goddess, or whatever she was, stood on

tiptoes, her back arched, holding a Greek-looking vase over-head like an offering to the sun. It was maybe twenty-four inches high.

"That looks too valuable to just leave out in the open," I said.

She sighed. "We didn't used to worry about things like that in Monticello," she said. "But we started having break-ins a few years ago and I had her bolted down to the pedestal. I think the whole thing would be too much trouble for a casual thief to move."

"They're not all casual," I said.

"If a thief is really determined, I'd rather he stole it out here than come into the house to get it."

I laughed. "You have a point."

An outside stairway led to the upper floor of the garage. She went up the steps as easily as a teenager, with no hesitation, puffing or groaning. It was plain she took her workouts seri-ously. She stopped at the top landing and turned around.

"You don't smoke, do you?"

"I quit ten years ago," I told her.

"Oh, good. I just couldn't rent to someone who smoked." She unlocked the door and I went in after her. "I tried a ciga-rette just once. I was eighteen and my boyfriend persuaded me to take one. It was a Lucky Strike and I was taken with the pack. I loved Deco design even then, and it was so pretty; dark green with a red circle inside a black one. I took two puffs and I was sick for hours." Then she turned and gave me that dazzling smile again. "But don't worry, I'm not a health Nazi. I won't complain about anything you care to eat or drink, and you can have women of loose morals up to visit if you like. I draw the line at cigarettes and loud rock music."

Inside it was a little musty and hot, and she went around opening up windows to air the place. It had been a storage space when I'd lived there, but someone had converted it into an effi-ciency apartment, with a fold-out sofa bed and a kitchenette. One end had been partitioned into a tiny bathroom with a cur-tained shower.

"When I bought the house there was an artist living in here. The owner before me converted it to an apartment."

"I like it. How much?"

"Two hundred a month. I ask first and last month's rent, plus a hundred dollars damage deposit."

I looked around, pretending to think it over, but I'd already decided to take it. My finances would stand it. In fact, I'd expected much worse. "Does that include utilities?"

"Uh-huh. Assuming you don't abuse them, of course."

"Then you have a deal. Can I move in this evening?"

"Do you have much to move in?"

"Everything I own is in my car. I closed my bank account when I left L.A., but I can go cash a few traveler's checks and bring you the money for the rent and deposit. Will that be okay?"

"Fine. There's a telephone jack over by the bed. If you want to install one, they can usually do it in a day or so. Everything else is on. Oh, just a minute." She opened the closet. There was a circuit box inside and she opened it and flipped a switch. "There. Now you'll have hot water in an hour or two. The water heater's in the garage downstairs."

I looked at my watch. It was past three o'clock. "I hope the bank's still open."

"The town bank closes at two, but there's a branch bank out at the mall. It's open till five."

"Then I'll be back in an hour."

We went back down the outside stairs.

"I'll have your receipt and key ready." She gave me that wonderful smile and turned to go back into the house. After a few seconds, I left the garden. The naked lady on the pedestal gave me some sort of benediction as I went.

The mall came as a surprise. It wasn't big as malls go, but it seemed out of place, like a chunk of California set brazenly defiant in the pristine landscape. Then I remembered what had been there before: an auto junkyard littered with rusting hulks and prowled by stray dogs. So maybe the mall was an improvement, after all. Inside it was like every other mall anywhere in America: the same shops, the same music. I found the bank and cashed a few checks, then stopped at a car wash near the old railroad bridge and treated the Plymouth to a much-needed bath.

I found a supermarket and laid in a supply of basic groceries, picked up a couple of cheap pans and a tea kettle: bachelor domesticity. I bought a copy of the Polk Times-Tribune. It was a daily, despite its generally rural content. Most people relied on the Columbus papers for their national and world news, but I wanted to know what was happening locally.

It was almost dark when I pulled into the driveway in front of the two-story garage. Walking to the back door, I could hear music coming from inside the house; classical, but not opera this time. I knocked and the door opened.

"Come on in, Gabe. I have everything ready." Edna Tutt was scrubbed and smelled faintly of scented soap. She was wearing a yellow terrycloth jumpsuit, thong sandals on her feet. "I took some linens and pillows and a couple of blankets up to your room."

"Thanks, that's very thoughtful."

"Setting up housekeeping isn't something you can do in an afternoon. Do you need plates and glasses, things to cook with?"

"I picked up a few items. I'll probably be eating out, mostly."

"Well, if you need anything, just ask."

"I couldn't have asked for a more helpful landlady," I said.

She gave me that smile again. "It'll be good to have someone staying here again. I get lonely, sometimes."

I didn't know what to say to that. "Well, I guess I'll go on up."

"Here's your key and your receipt. I hope you sleep well."

I thanked her and went out. It was hard to imagine someone of Edna Tutt's sunny disposition being lonely or lacking for company. I carried my worldly goods up to my new lodgings, spent a half hour putting things away and making up the bed, then sat down, wondering what to do next. I set the kettle on the stove and made a cup of tea, then picked up the paper.

According to the masthead, Lew Czuk was now owner and editor of the Times-Tribune. I decided I would look him up.

When we were kids, Lew's father had owned a combined news-stand and tobacco shop on one of the side streets off Main. I was a reader, and Lew's parents had been tolerant of my constant browsing. Even better, Lew had his own key to the place. At night, we'd go in through the back and go into the stock room. By the light of its single bulb, we'd go over all the skin mags. They were mild by modern standards, but a real education to a hormone-laden adolescent in the fifties. We marveled at the infinitely varied conformations of breasts and nipples, the rich contours of female buttocks, the smoothness of airbrushed flesh. Ah, youth.

There was local election news. Some of the names sounded vaguely familiar. Sheriff Fowles was running for reelection. That gave me a start, because Sheriff John Fowles had been killed in the Cohan Chemical robbery in '65. Then I realized it had to be his son, Mark. I'd known Mark only slightly. He wasn't a Catholic so he didn't go to St. Anne's. For a while we were in the same boy scout troop and we'd palled around a bit. A couple of times I'd gone with him to his father's office, and the Sheriff showed me the little arsenal in a locked room that opened off his office where he kept the brass knucks, black-jacks, switchblades and pistols confiscated from men he and his predecessors had arrested, mostly rowdy drunks. He'd allowed me to hold the department's Thompson submachine gun; a legacy from the Dillinger era, when the outlaw gangs were robbing banks all over the Midwest.

Most of the news was of the smalltown sort: school sports, promotions and transfers of local kids in the armed services, notices of church functions. The Cohan name appeared in some capacity or other on nearly every page. I finished my tea, folded the paper and lay back on my bed by an open window. I stared for a while at an old water stain on the ceiling, where there had once been a leak.

It took me a while to become conscious of the sound. It was something out of place in the quiet night. It was the sound of a woman sobbing, muffled, as if she held her hands or a kerchief over her face. I looked out the window, straining to hear where the sound was coming from. Below me was the flower-filled back yard. Could it be Edna? But all the lights in the house were off. In a minute or two the sobs quieted, and I wondered if it had been someone's television, or whether I had imagined the whole thing.

I lay back and turned the light off, so I wouldn't have to stare at the stain on the ceiling. Why had I come back? What could there be for me in a town I had left thirty years ago? There was nothing here but the past; the age-distorted memories of a boy who was a stranger to me now. Was I trying to find something, or was I just behaving like some wounded animal, crawling home to die?

I did have one thing: Tomorrow evening, I would have dinner with Lola Cohan.

4

When I woke up I had no sense of disorientation; an oddity upon waking in a strange bed, in a strange room. The light coming through the window seemed familiar in a way California light never had, even after almost three decades. I got out of bed, washed up, shaved, and dressed. My reflection in the mirror was looking pretty good, considering. I didn't feel bad at all. I thought I might start running in the mornings again.

I went out and down the stairs, into the back yard. Edna was kneeling on one of the walks, trowel in one hand, digging. She was wearing sweatpants and a halter top and one of those transparent green eye-shades, like the bill of a baseball cap without the top. When I got to the bottom of the steps she looked up at me from under her eye-shade and smiled.

"Are you going out?"

"I thought I'd look up an old friend or two." I looked at her tanned shoulders; no freckles or liver spots. "Don't you know you're not supposed to expose yourself to so much sunlight? Cancer and skin wrinkles and all that bad stuff."

She sat up on her heels, spine erect, brushing her hands on

her thighs. No gardening gloves. "I run on solar batteries and I need to recharge them before winter sets in. We won't be having many more days like this. I get very run-down and gloomy toward the end of winter. Then the sun comes back in spring and I charge up again. To tell you the truth, I get tired of hearing that yet another innocent pleasure is dangerous. I put on just a little sun screen and leave it at that."

"Good for you."

Her smile widened. "I inherited good genes for keeping the wrinkles at bay, and at my age I don't worry much about cancer. People act as if they can be immortal if they'd just deny themselves everything enjoyable. I think that's sad. I see young people in their twenties who're terrified of chocolate cream pie!"

"No smoking, though," I reminded her. "And you're a fiend for exercise."

She grinned, showing a tiny space between her front teeth. "I wouldn't mind people smoking if the smell didn't make me sick. And I enjoy exercise, always have. But I do it mostly at home. When health clubs became popular I joined one, but I quit after going just a few times. You know why?"

"Why?"

"They were full of people sweating and grunting and looking grim as death. They hated every minute of it. They were doing it because they felt they had to. It was terribly depressing."

I nodded. "When I was a kid going to St. Anne's we called it mortification of the flesh. In the old days they wore hair shirts under their clothes and flogged themselves and fasted until they dropped. God was supposed to like it. Now we diet and exercise."

"I hadn't thought of it that way. I was brought up Protestant, but our church was plenty puritanical. I guess it never took. When I was young I indulged myself every way I could think of. I enjoyed it at the time and haven't regretted it since. Don't you think that's healthier than all this worry about poundage and longevity? Why should I trade sunshine for another year or two of dotage?"

"I couldn't agree more."

"Good. That's my speech for this morning. I won't keep you any longer. I hope you find lots of old friends."

I walked away knowing I wouldn't find lots of them. There hadn't been that many in the first place.

I went to the Plymouth, then changed my mind. She was right; it was a beautiful morning. I walked past the Cohan grounds and turned right at the Y-shaped intersection onto Poplar Street. In the Y there was a triangular traffic island where there had once been a big stone fountain surrounded by a goldfish pond. Another landmark gone. Once on Poplar, it was three blocks downhill to Main.

By the time I reached the middle of town, I was hungry. The Cove didn't serve breakfast, but on the first block of Poplar, west of Main, I found an unpretentious little cafe where a record store and a seedy little pawnshop had stood before. I took a table by the window and a waitress brought me a menu. I caught myself automatically studying the fruit plates and bran muffins, as if God really worried about my cholesterol count and blood pressure. I thought to hell with it and ordered steak and eggs with a side of waffles and maple syrup.

While waiting for the food to arrive I started on a pot of strong black coffee with cream and lots of real sugar. When breakfast arrived I devoured it like a starving wolf. I left a tip, paid at the counter, and went back outside feeling a foot taller and ready to look life in the eye again.

Across the street was the old newsstand Mr. Czuk had owned. I crossed and went inside. The smell of cigars and pipe tobacco was fainter than it had been, and the interior had been completely remodeled. The stock room of fond memory had been converted into a little office. Through its open door I saw a glowing computer screen. I didn't recognize the fat guy sitting behind the counter, a science fiction paperback open in front of him, his T-shirted belly hanging over his belt buckle.

"Can I help you find anything?" He wore thick glasses and a ruff of beard. He looked thirty going on fifteen.

"I used to live around here. Do the Czuks still own this place?"

"No, I bought the store from Lew in '73. He publishes the

Times-Tribune now." I looked closer. Make that forty going on fifteen. He held out a hand. "I'm Scott van Houten."

I took the hand. "Gabe Treloar." His handshake was surprisingly firm.

"You a friend of Lew's?"

"Years ago. Where can I find him?"

"The Times-Tribune building's on Central, two blocks east of the square. It's right across the street from the county court house."

"Yeah, I remember now." I looked the shop over.

"I used to spend a lot of time in here when I was a kid. It looks different now."

"Yeah, the book and magazine business has changed a lot in the last twenty years. It's hard to compete with the chain stores in the malls."

"You seem to've done pretty well." The walls held current magazines and the serried ranks of paperback racks were well filled.

"Well, I didn't do it trying to sell more copies of Danielle Steel than B. Dalton's. C'mere, I'll show you." He slid off his stool and went through a door that hadn't been there before. Nothing better to do, I followed him. The adjoining room was bigger than the one we'd just left. The walls were covered with posters advertising classic movies. Filling the room were rack after rack of comics and magazines, most of them individually packaged in zip-top plastic bags. A couple of teenaged boys were browsing through them. I looked over a few racks. Most were titles I'd never heard of, but some of the older ones I remembered. I picked up a bagged issue of *Plastic Man* I remembered reading in that very store. It was a little tattered at the corners. The label said it sold for fifty dollars.

"Now that one would be really valuable in mint condition," he said.

"My mother threw all mine away when we moved from here," I said.

"Everybody's mom did that. It's why these are worth so much. What you see now is my current stock, but if you're looking for any particular number of an old comic or magazine, let me know. I can usually lay hands on it within forty-eight hours."

We went back out front and he gestured to the little office. The computer sat on a desk, its screen lit up with columns of words and figures. "I used to have to spend weeks at shows and conventions to find anything," Van Houten said, "but now the whole trade's linked by nationwide networks."

"I'll keep you in mind," I said. I thanked him and we shook again and I walked out. Just when you think the world has no more surprises in store, something new comes along.

East of the square was an area I hadn't spent much time in as a kid: The court house, the police station, the county sheriff's; grownup territory. My sole visit to the Times-Tribune building had been on a school trip in ninth grade and all I remembered about it was the noise of the presses and the overwhelming smell of inks and solvents.

The court house was one of those Classical revival buildings that pre-Civil War America thought to be the only properly dignified style for public buildings. It was redbrick with a white-columned portico and had a huge clock on its central cupola. The clock had Roman numerals and it played Westminster chimes before tolling the hour. On clear evenings I had been able to hear it from my bedroom window. It could be an ominous sound late on Sunday nights, knowing you had to go back to school in the morning.

There was a reception desk just inside the glass front door of the Times-Tribune building. It was a relatively modern structure, two-storied, pale brick with mostly glass in front and the name of the paper spelled out on top with big aluminum letters. The woman behind the reception desk looked up and smiled professionally. The smile didn't hide the once-over. I knew she made me for a cop.

"May I help you, Off—I mean, sir?" The slip was deliberate. Very coy.

"Is Lew Czuk in?"

"May I ask the purpose of your visit?" The little sign on her desk identified her as Sharon Newell. She was small and dark-haired, with the sort of full, white throat that always suggested voluptuous appetites to me. I don't know why.

"It's personal."

"Well, I'll see if he has a minute." She fiddled with her intercom. I could just imagine how busy a newspaper publisher must be in a town like Monticello. Those late-breaking stories from the Senior Citizen's Club could be real nail-biters.

"Go right in, sir," she said, wondering who the hell I was. "Mr. Czuk's office is upstairs, all the way to the end of the hall, straight ahead."

Lew looked up when I opened his door, blinking behind his glasses. He showed a lot more scalp than I remembered, and the flesh at the sides of his face was a little loose, but there wasn't much change otherwise. He began to stand.

"Hello? I don't believe I . . ." he let it trail off into uncertainty.

"Hello, Lew." I stuck my hand out. My voice must have tipped him.

"Gabe? My God, Gabe?" He grinned and came around the desk, grabbing my hand and pumping it with both of his. "My God, how long's it been, Gabe? Twenty years? No, twenty-four, almost twenty-five! In Florida, when you were on your way overseas. Sit down, Gabe. What brings you back here?"

"Oh, just a wild hair," I waffled. "I was on my way to Cleveland and saw the sign pointing to Monticello and thought, what the hell. So I drove in."

He sat back down, shaking his head. "You're the last person I thought I'd see coming through that door this morning." He put his feet up on his desk. It looked like they were up there a lot. "Did you just get in?"

I shook my head. "Night before last. I spent yesterday kind of looking around and finding a place to stay."

"Then you're going to be here a while? Great! How long?"

"I'm not sure. A month, maybe. I'm sort of at loose ends."

"Then we'll get to spend some time together. God, we have a lot to catch up on. While you were overseas you sent me a letter that you were getting married. Is your wife with you?"

"She died."

"Oh . . ." he reddened. "Oh, I'm sorry, Gabe."

"It was a while ago. You?"

"I never married. A couple of times . . . well, it never worked out. Kids?"

I shook my head. "No. We tried."

"Yeah," like he knew all about trying. "Lots of things don't work out." He frowned, then brightened. "What're you doing this evening? Like to get together for dinner? A few drinks?"

"Previous engagement. I'm taking Lola Cohan to dinner this evening."

That took him aback. "Kind of taking up where you left off, aren't you?"

"I hadn't even been thinking about her," I lied. "I just kind of ran into her yesterday. I met Ansel, too. Is he really getting into politics?"

"Absolutely. Hard to believe, isn't it? He's been running Cohan Chemical so long now most local people have forgotten what a hood he was when we were kids."

"He wasn't just a hood, if some of the stories about him were true. They weren't the sort of stories a man running for office would want to have dredged up."

"Look, Gabe," he got serious, frowning again, "You want to walk a wide circle around Ansel Cohan. He's ambitious and he owns this town and most of Polk County. He's a heavy, *heavy* contributor to the state Republican Party. He has lots of friends in the State House and on the National Committee. Nobody around here is going to dredge up those old stories. Ah, Gabe, why this interest?"

"When he saw me with Lola yesterday he didn't exactly radiate warmth."

"No," Lew mused, "he wouldn't."

"Why? She told me she's been married three times. It's not like he's afraid I'm going to snatch his baby sister from the cradle."

"It's a strange family. They don't go by the same rules as the rest of us. It's pretty certain he's angling for her to marry Ted

Rapley. He's a state prosecutor with his office in Columbus. From here originally. He spends a lot of time in Monticello."

The name seemed familiar. "Rapley. Big jock over at the public high school when we were at St. Anne's?"

"That's the one. He's tight with Ansel, real tight with Lester Cabell, the Chief of Police. They were on the team together here, and later at State. Not so tight with Sheriff Fowles."

"A political alliance in the making, huh?" I'd been a cop long enough to be wary of ambitious DAs.

"It's made. But it would be cemented if they were in-laws. So step carefully. If Ansel wants you out of town, he'll set Lester on you."

"On what pretext?" I asked, knowing what a foolish question it was, even as I said it.

"Oh, come on, Gabe. You know how it works. It's easier when he wants some parolee to take up habitation somewhere else, but he'd find something. Harassment, if nothing else. We're a long way from Los Angeles. I doubt you'd be able to appeal to his fellow feeling as a brother officer."

"I'm not with LAPD anymore. I've . . . retired. I was on my way to Cleveland to join a PI firm run by an old friend when I decided to make this side trip."

"I'm glad you did. I . . ." his intercom buzzed. "Mr. Czuk, the gentleman from the town planning commission is here to see you: Mr. Fullbright."

"Okay, send him up, Sharon." He looked up at me. "Sorry, Gabe. Look, if dinner's out, how about lunch? Noon at the Cove?"

I got up. "Fine. I have some errands to run, get a phone installed, things like that. Is the library still in the same place?"

"Still the reader, huh? No, one block west, across the street from the old place, in a new building. By the way, where are you staying?"

"You won't believe this. It's my old house on the corner of Maple and Wright. Well, the apartment over the garage."

"Right in Ansel's back yard," he said, shaking his head. "Who lives there now? Oh, the lady who grows the flowers.

Sharon writes her up once a year when she wins a prize at some garden show."

"Sharon? Your receptionist?"

"Receptionist, reporter, circulation manager, you name it. I can't afford a big staff here."

Somebody knocked on the door, we shook hands and I left, pledging to meet with him at twelve sharp. Outside, a pudgy man waited, a load of rolled-up charts under an arm. I went down the hall and down the stairs and Miss Newell smiled brightly at me stretching her lips wide enough to show a gold crown back at the corner of her mouth. I smiled back, not so wide.

"Come see us again, Mr. Treloar," she said as I went out. Very cute. I hadn't given her my name going in. I'd have to remind Lew to be more careful about that intercom. Then I remembered that Lew had only used my first name. I was going to have to watch out for Miss Newell.

Outside, I looked across the street. The county sheriff's office was in the court house, the chief of police in the town hall next to it. Time was when small-town chiefs lived and worked in isolation, barely connected even to the state police. Now the office computer gave them practically instant access to police files all over the country. Cabell could be checking up on me right now. Some homecoming.

I found a pay phone and arranged for a telephone hookup the next day. Then I went to the library. I found it across the street from a huge new YMCA building that had apparently replaced not only the old library, but also a beautiful Victorian mansion. I wondered if the old place had burned down.

Inside, the new library smelled just like the old one. The library had been my place to get away. It showed me a world far wider than Monticello, Ohio, and I never ran into any of the people I didn't like there. But this time I wasn't there for recreational reading. I asked the librarian if they had back issues of the Columbus papers.

"Yes, we have them on microfiche back to the twenties.

You'll need to go to the central library in Columbus to find them earlier than that."

"This will be fine," I assured her. "I just need to look at the past few years."

She led me to a room off the main reading room. Against one wall was a big case of steel microfiche drawers next to a viewer that wasn't in use. Other walls had glass-fronted cabinets holding old phone books, county histories, high school year books back to the forties, genealogical tables, city directories and so forth. Even a small town can accumulate a lot of records in a century and a half. She showed me where the Columbus papers were to be found and gave me a rundown on how to use the viewer, even though I assured her I already knew how. She wasn't taking any chances.

I couldn't begin to count the hours I'd spent doing this sort of scut work. Thousands, probably. Taking police science classes at USC, doing case investigation at the Department, most of it was the most boring drudgery imaginable. But that much experience gives you a feel for the work. One by one I loaded the strips into the viewer and ran the eye-straining images up the screen, stopping only when I caught one of the key names. It wasn't difficult. I could ignore most sections of the papers. Everything I was interested in would be on the first two pages of the front section or the local news section. I wasn't doing any sort of exhaustive research, just trying to get a feel for what was going on. The names I was looking for were Cohan and Rapley. It didn't take me long to find them.

Ted Rapley was riding on top of a string of successful prosecutions. He grabbed the splashiest cases that came along and proclaimed himself a big fan of the death penalty. He was a champion of small-town, Midwest values and spent a lot of time deploring the disappearance of Ohio industrial jobs overseas, although this had very little to do with the office of state prosecutor.

Ansel was right in there, too, mostly running political functions and lobbying against environmental legislation that cramped the chemical industry. He was more prominent politically than as a business wheel. Cohan Chemical was big stuff in rural, primarily agricultural Polk County, but Ohio is a heavy industry state and it wasn't a major player by state standards.

There were quite a few pictures of the two of them together, giving speeches and gladhanding it at state Republican rallies. I turned the machine off, blinking and rubbing my eyes. I refiled the tapes and went out to the front desk. There were a few patrons in the main reading room, being very quiet.

"All finished?" the librarian asked.

"Yes, thank you." I glanced out the front door at the new Y. "What happened to the house that used to be across the street?"

Her face hardened and her mouth clamped into a straight line. "That was such a shame! The old Paisley home was one of the most historic buildings in the county. Architects used to come from all over the country just to study it. They tore it down to make room for that awful YMCA! And there was plenty of vacant land they could have used for the Y. That was when we formed the Historical Society, to keep that sort of thing from happening again." She said all this in a sort of vehement whisper. "This town has always been run by utter Philistines; no sense of history or culture or aesthetics! If it isn't making money, they don't want it."

"I know what you mean," I told her.

It was getting near noon and I walked back to the center of town. The aged waitress came up to me the moment I entered. "You've come to join Mr. Czuk? He's in the back room. Just come with me." I followed her through the front room where the candy counters had been and to a small dining room that opened off the main one. Most of the tables in the place were occupied by the lunchtime crowd. Lew sat at a table with a martini in front of him. I sat down and the waitress gave me a menu.

"May I bring you something to drink while you read the menu?"

"Just some water, please." She walked off and I turned to Lew. He was getting near the bottom of his glass. "I didn't expect to find you here, Lew. How'd you end up back home running the local paper?"

He gave a self-deprecating little chuckle. "Oh, you know how it is. I was going to be a hotshot investigative reporter down in Florida. Gave it a try for a few years, but then Watergate came along and *everybody* wanted to crack the next big story." He tossed back the last of his martini and signaled the waitress for another. "Some of those kids just out of journalism school had multiple rows of teeth. I found out that I didn't have the real killer instinct.

"But I was good at desk work, especially editing. Anyway, I was getting tired of Florida so I came back here. Old Ed Perkins—he'd been publishing the Times-Tribune forever—was getting too old to do everything himself and I became his assistant. After a few years of doing all the work, I sold the old newsstand and cashed in some stocks my Dad left me and I bought old Perkins out."

"I met the new proprietor of the newsstand."

He laughed. "You've met Scott? He's a character, isn't he? He started working for my Dad when he was still in high school. Crazy about comics and magazines. Dad was pretty careless about stripping unsold copies and returning them. If he only had one or two of a particular issue, he sometimes didn't bother. Our cellar and garage were full of them. Anyway, he let Scott have any of them he wanted as one of the perks of a low-paying job. Had no idea they could be worth anything."

The waitress brought his martini and we ordered. "When I decided to sell the place," he went on, "Scott offered to buy it. I asked him how he could afford it. Turned out he had a mint condition issue number one of *Playboy*, along with some comics dating back to the thirties. He sold them for enough to buy the newsstand and the florist shop next door."

Our orders arrived and we talked about old friends and teachers and half-remembered incidents, catching each other up on some things, but not talking much about events of the past few years. It was easy, and we didn't fall into any of those awkward silences that you usually experience when you've hashed over old times with a friend you haven't seen in years, when you've come to the end of the common experiences and realize that neither of you is that kid anymore and you really have nothing in common now. I knew we probably would eventually, but not just yet.

"So now you're taking up with Lola again," Lew said after the dishes had been cleared away. He was midway through his third martini.

"I wouldn't call it that. I don't know her after all this time. We're having dinner at the Lodge. I suspect we'll both be pretty cautious."

He nodded solemnly. "Good idea. I don't know much about her, really. She keeps pretty much to herself."

"When half the news in your paper involves the Cohans in one way or another?"

"That's mostly the company, and Ansel. Angelica's pretty active socially. Lola doesn't seem to have much to do with them."

"But she still lives at the mansion."

"Who wouldn't? It's not exactly tract housing. And I guess she'll probably inherit it some day." The alcohol had greased him up and he was getting pretty loose.

"Because Ansel is unlikely to marry and have kids? If he's ambitious politically, he just might. Men have been known to bite the bullet and do the respectable thing when there's a lot at stake."

Lew looked around as if someone might be eavesdropping. We had the little room to ourselves.

"Well, I doubt it. See, those stories about him when we were kids? Well, they were true, all right. Back in those benighted days, before we got all enlightened and sensitive about personal lifestyle choices, we would've said that Ansel Cohan is as queer as three left feet."

"We may have become pious about gay rights, but that's still enough to sink a political career."

He shrugged. "Who's going to talk? Nobody around here, that's for sure. Ansel's preferences are common knowledge and this is the conservative center of middle America, but you can overlook a lot in a man whose name is on half the paychecks in the county."

He glanced at his watch, maybe deciding he was talking too much. "Oh, hell, I'm running late. Sharon'll be sending someone after me pretty soon." We got up and shook hands and promised to get together again real soon.

I prowled the town for a while, picking up a few items I needed. I even bought a pair of running shoes. Late in the afternoon I walked up Central, past the hospital and the school. In the next block was a big old house I remembered as the convent. Somebody called to me from its porch.

"Gabriel?"

I looked up, surprised. In the shade of the porch an old woman sat on a rocking chair. She wore the old-fashioned habit and wimple of the teaching order that staffed St. Anne's. I went up the sidewalk, studying the old face, trying to take away the effect of the years.

"Sister Margaret Michael?"

She smiled, further creasing her fine-boned old face. "You were always observant, Gabriel."

I climbed up on the porch. "I'm amazed that you knew me. It's been a while."

"I was expecting you."

"How did you know I was in town, Sister?"

"Mrs. Cekola dropped by about an hour ago. She works in the school, they're getting ready for the beginning of the new year. She got a call from that snoop Sharon Newell at the newspaper. She wanted to know about someone named Gabe who was at St. Anne's at the same time as Lew Czuk. Gabriel isn't a common name, it didn't take her long to find you."

So that was one little mystery solved. Sister Margaret Michael had taught fifth and sixth grades at St. Anne's. Later, when we were in high school, she had taught music; a birdlike little woman who talked nonstop when she got excited, which was often. We'd liked her because, unlike the other nuns, she'd had a sense of humor. Also, she didn't spend half the day telling us what irredeemably evil little beasts we were.

"Are you still teaching, Sister?" I asked gallantly.

Even her laugh was birdlike. "Heavens, no! I retired years ago. When was it? About the time they changed from the Latin liturgy to English." She sighed. "That almost broke my heart.

And for what? If people wanted to be Protestants, why not just join a Protestant church?"

"But you didn't say that, did you?"

"Oh, of course not. We all felt that way, but obedience is one of the vows."

"Sometimes you have to put up with the whims of your superiors, even when you know they're wrong."

"I'm afraid we never taught you that in school."

"It's one of those things you learn on your own. I think it sank in when I was in the Army. By the time I was doing police work, it was second nature."

"We can't blind ourselves to it, though." She looked past me and her voice wandered a little. "We have such responsibilities. Teachers, policemen . . . we have other people's lives in our hands, don't we?"

"That's right," I said, maybe a little brusquely.

She didn't notice. "So you went into police work. That doesn't surprise me. You were always a serious boy, Gabriel. I knew you would choose a serious path. So many take the easy way."

It was an odd compliment, but it had been a long time since I'd had one. "I guess they do."

"But it never makes them happy." I knew there was a homily coming on, but she turned her head at the tinkle of a bell from inside. "That's vespers," she said, getting up from her rocker. "I have to go to chapel now. Gabe, it's been so good to see you again. Please come by and see me before you leave."

I took both of her delicate, spidery hands in mine. They were no more substantial than dry leaves. "I will, Sister."

She turned and shuffled inside, disappearing into the interior dimness like a fading memory.

5

The big, circular driveway was intimidating, as it was meant to be. It made the Plymouth seem mean and shabby. It should have been a Rolls, a Cadillac, a coach-and-four. At least there was no sneering doorman to soil his white gloves on my plebeian door handle. Even for the Cohans, the days of doormen were long past.

Lola opened the door before I could knock. She was wearing a brief summer dress of green silk held up by spaghetti straps and reaching to mid-thigh. There wasn't much of it but what there was looked expensive. She held a matching clutch purse and a silk shawl draped over her elbows and behind her back. She wasn't quite barefoot, wearing sandals with minimal heels and a web of thin, leather straps giving her feet plenty of air.

I held the car door for her and when she climbed into the passenger seat her hem slid up nearly to her hip. If she noticed, it didn't seem to bother her. Women usually know how much they're showing. I got in and pulled away from the house.

"Most men can make that more flattering," she said.

"Make what more flattering?"

"Giving a woman the once-over. You looked like you were sizing up a suspect."

"Old habits die hard." I put the car in gear and pulled away. The tires made that odd humming noise, going over the red bricks. Outside of town the brick gave way to asphalt and the tires quieted. The country road was twilit, peaceful in a way only midwestern country roads can be. We passed a garage I vaguely remembered, with fifty years worth of Mobil flying red horse signs nailed all over it. A little past that a side road went off to the left, toward the lake.

The Lodge looked like a sprawling, ramshackle barn with a garish, neon sign on top. I parked in the graveled lot and helped Lola out. We walked to the entrance and I inhaled the smell of the lake. It lacked the overpowering, fecund reek of the ocean. Instead it was a wet, muddy, marshy smell that went with the peeping of the frogs and the chirping of the crickets.

Inside, the place was as classy as any joint in Bel Air. They had let the exterior deteriorate for the sake of contrast. The maitre d' led us to a table by the windows that made up one wall, overlooking the lake. The lights of the houses surrounding the lake were doubled by the water and the moon was up, adding its own shimmering reflection. Somewhere across there, I remembered, was the old Cohan summer cottage.

"The boathouse is still there," she said, reading my mind.

"More unfinished business," I said. A waitress came with big, leather-bound menus and asked if we wanted to order cocktails.

"Vodka martini," Lola said. I just shook my head.

The menu was extensive and expensive. "What do you recommend?" I asked Lola.

"I'm partial to the halibut, but the smoked duck here has a reputation." She stroked her cheek with a sharp fingernail, those spooky eyes looking out over the lake. "We used to be able to see this place from the cottage, remember? We wondered what went on here. This was grown-up territory."

"And what a disappointment when we found out, huh?"

"Most grown-up things turned out to be disappointments. Not everything, though."

"No," I said, "not everything."

The waitress came and took our orders. Lola had the halibut and I opted for the duck. We spoke polite nothings for a while, circling around each other, trying to find things out without giving away too much, like a couple of lawyers cutting a plea bargain. It said a lot about the lives we'd lived since last seeing each other that we were so wary.

"So who's this guy Rapley?" I said, tiring of it.

"Gabe! You've been checking up on me!" Just then our orders arrived.

"In a town like this, who needs to snoop? Just keep your ears open and you hear everything sooner or later."

"I don't believe that. You've been playing policeman." She tried to sound indignant, but she seemed a little flattered that I'd gone to the trouble. "Well, if you must know, Ted is an old political crony of my brother's."

"And Ansel wants you to marry him?"

"I don't get married just to help his career." She tried the halibut. "I didn't the first three times, anyway."

The smoked duck was excellent. "But Ansel is going for the big time now, isn't he? Prospects like that can make a man lean pretty hard."

She sat back, blotting her lips with her napkin. "Gabe, this would be a lot more pleasant if you sounded motivated by concern. You sound like one of those movie cops interrogating someone."

"I'm sorry. It's just"—I fumbled around, trying to explain why I was acting this way—". . . it's just that we broke off so long ago, and it was so sudden. I've felt ever since that something was left unfinished."

"Two kids, so many years ago. Should it be important now?"

"Here we are," I said. "I'm back in town, and you wanted to come to dinner with me. Why, if you're going to marry this Rapley guy?"

"I didn't say I was going to marry him," she said, a little tightly. "Maybe I just wanted to catch up with an old friend."

I told myself to stop acting like a prize jerk. "I'm sorry.

Like I said: old habits." It was pretty lame, but she seemed to accept it.

"Well, it looks like we've both been through the marriage mill. Children?" The same question Lew had asked.

"No, but we wanted them. You?"

Old pain made tiny lines around her eyes. "I had a little girl, Julia, by my first marriage. She died when she was six, of leukemia. After that I was terrified to try to have more children. I couldn't go through that pain again. I had my tubes tied and that's really why Sam and I split up. He wanted a houseful, preferably boys."

"I'm sorry," I said. What else are you going to say?

"So you lost a wife and I lost a daughter. Our lives didn't follow such differing paths after all."

"Have you lived here the whole time?"

"Goodness, no! A lifetime here would have finished me long before now. I met Sam when I was at Vassar and we lived in Boston. After Julia died I just couldn't stay there and I ended up in Houston for a while, and I spent a lot of the seventies in Paris."

Nothing about husbands two and three. I thought it best not to inquire. We talked for a while about the long intervening years, but we stayed off the really serious subjects after her revelation about her daughter's death. Something kept me from talking too much about myself. There was a sort of wariness there that wouldn't let me give too much away.

When dinner ended we were no more intimate. The conversation turned to banalities of the sort people do turn to when they need time to sort things out, think matters over, decide whether this is something they really want to pursue seriously. It was time to wrap up the evening.

On the drive back she said little, enveloped in her own thoughts. They must have been pleasant thoughts, because the corners of her mouth wore a tiny smile.

There were a lot of lights on in the Cohan mansion when we got back. I walked Lola to the door.

"It's been a lovely evening, Gabe," she said, "but I don't

think it would stay that way if I asked you in. Mother and Ansel are home. Let's do this again when we have lots of time to ourselves."

She took my hands and I leaned forward for the obligatory kiss on the cheek, but one, or both of us, steered wrong because my lips touched hers instead. She let them stay there, hers a little parted, not turning it into a passionate matter of tongues and teeth, but making it a good deal more intimate than an ordinary goodnight peck. Then she pulled back, but slowly.

"Good night, Gabe."

"Good night," I said. I went back down the steps and opened the car door.

"Gabe?"

I paused and looked back at her. She stood in the shadow of the deep porch, almost invisible. "Yes?"

"That night at the boathouse? I wish we hadn't stopped." Then there was a flood of light as she opened the door and I saw her silhouette for a second, then the light was gone and the door was shut. I climbed into the Plymouth and drove the few hundred feet back to my old house.

We were sixteen. Lola and I had known each other practically since we were born, since my father worked for hers and the two men conferred pretty frequently at the Cohan home, going over financial matters that were a complete mystery to me. We never went to the same schools, because Andrew Cohan, Patrick's son, had renounced his Irish heritage and joined the Methodist church, Monticello's largest and most respectable.

When we moved into the house on Maple, I saw her practically every day. During that time she underwent that miraculous transformation from girl to young woman—a young woman of almost eerie beauty. My mother never liked her and my father was oddly reluctant for us to be together, but she lived just on the other side of our fence so there wasn't much they could do about it. I was hopelessly in love with her for my last couple of years in Monticello.

Later I realized that she knew about it the whole time, but back then I knew nothing about women. I was a shy, awkward teenager, like a million others, and I was afraid even to hold her hand, for fear she would be offended and banish me from her presence. In the meantime she showered her attentions on other boys. To her credit, she never went for the jocks. There was nothing of the cheerleader about her. She set her sights on the intelligent and talented ones and, even then, her slogan was "whatever Lola wants, Lola gets." She got a lot of mileage out of that old song.

But that last spring things were a little different. We were all more serious. The Kennedy assassination the previous November had awakened us to the terribly real, irreversible importance of things, and that made us very earnest, for a while. Lola was upset when her brother Ansel, on his twenty-first birthday, was banished under some sort of cloud.

The party was a yearly affair, thrown by James Cohan for the families of his senior employees. It always took place on Memorial day at the Cohan cottage on the lake. James, a big, portly man, shook hands with everyone as they entered, and Angelica, looking brittle even then, was a gracious, if somewhat cool, hostess. The younger children played on the big lawn and I went immediately to find Lola.

We were the only ones there of our age group, so I had her all to myself for a change. I found her wandering among the trees by the lakeside, barefoot, and wearing a tennis outfit; a crisp, white blouse and short, pleated skirt. She smiled when she saw me and took my hand and didn't let it go for a while. My heart started to thud. We talked about serious teenage matters and I thought I was being brilliant, but I could never afterward remember what I had said.

Dinner was a huge buffet on the lawn, and by nightfall everyone was well into the booze and getting very loose. It wasn't at all difficult for us to slip away after dinner and go down to the boathouse. Inside was the Cohan's small cabin cruiser. The cruiser's seat cushions had been taken out and set on a bench that ran along one wall. We sat on the cushions and were suddenly quiet, by ourselves in the darkness.

We sat side by side, her knee and shoulder touching mine, the usual barriers down. I didn't know what body language was then, but it's something understood on a visceral level anyway. I knew she was ready.

I'd fumbled around with a few other girls, so I knew where the noses went. Besides, she knew more about it than I did. The first kiss was a long one, with lots of exploration with lips and tongues. I was lost in the textures of her mouth, until her body pressed against mine and I remembered that I had hands.

I slid a hand up her flank, my fingertips rippling over her ribs, until it cupped her breast. I marveled at its hard-softness, deliciously yielding. She sighed and pressed harder against me. I had never been so excited, wanting to keep on, to discover all her secrets, terrified that she would make me stop, slap me for my presumption.

Sheer hormonal urgency won out. I began to unbutton her blouse, ashamed not at what I was doing, but at the fumbling awkwardness of my fingers. My hand went inside, touched the tender skin of her belly, working hard with her panting breath. I cupped her breast again, then my fingertips trailed across its pale upper surface, just visible in the moonlight that came in through the dusty windows. My fingers flexed, dipped inside her brassiere, and scooped out the soft half-globe of flesh. Her nipple was a dark circle, wonderfully resilient.

Lola's head dropped back, lids hooding her eyes. My own head dipped and I kissed her breast, then took her nipple between my lips, tugging at it lightly, flicking my tongue across its tip. It thickened and hardened in my mouth and she moaned. I couldn't believe that she wasn't trying to stop me. Girls then weren't supposed to be aggressive, but she gripped my thigh near the knee, then slid her hand upward, stopping just short of my crotch, her fingers flexing as her teeth closed lightly on my ear.

Reluctantly, my hand released her breast and slid back down her belly. I was completely beyond thought or discretion, drunk with new sensations and the sexual chemicals raging through my bloodstream. My fingertips stopped at the waistband of her skirt but she sucked her belly in and they slid under it, beneath the elastic of her panties and plunged through the forest of tight-curled hair until I held her mound cupped in my hand, marveling at its multitude of textures; its plumpness, its humid heat, the deep separation of her labia.

She groaned and ran her hand over the erection that bulged the front of my pants and I almost came at that second. She tugged for a while at my belt buckle, her fingers as clumsy as mine had been. I wanted to help her but that would have meant releasing my prize. My other hand was behind her back, supporting her shoulders. Slickness began to coat my fingers as I massaged her and she got my belt loose at last. She tugged and pulled and suddenly I felt free and unconstrained by the strangling cloth, the air abruptly cool on me and I stopped breathing. Then her fingers clasped around me and our mouths were together again and we were moaning into each other.

Not releasing our mutual grip we fell back until we were lying on our sides, hands working rhythmically, mine growing wet and working inside, hers sliding loose skin against hardness. Neither of us had said a word since the first kiss and that was just as well, because I could never have thought of anything to say. We had gone beyond our teenaged verbal skills and were in the realm of the purely tactile.

With a wrenching effort I let her go for a half-second, pulled my hand out of the waistband of her skirt and reached up under it, tugging her panties down to her knees, starting to move over her, need driving me blindly.

Her breath stopped in mid-groan and her eyelids snapped open. Her strange eyes were blank as steel marbles in the moonlight, but on her face was an expression of pure terror.

"No! Gabe, stop! We can't do this, Gabe! Please stop!" She pushed at me and began to beat on my shoulders with her palms, then with hammered fists.

Shocked and bewildered, I backed off. "What? Huh . . . I . . . what's wrong?" It wasn't my most sparkling conversation, but I was up to my eyeballs in male hormones and her abrupt change was too much for what little mind I had left. A few seconds before she had been writhing with a need as great as my own. Even in my inexperience I knew she wasn't faking that. Now she acted like she had just seen a werewolf.

"This is wrong. We can't do it. I'm sorry, Gabe, we just

can't." She was sitting up on the bench, pulling her panties up, shrugging her bared breast back into its cup, buttoning her blouse, all so quickly that our passionate intimacy seemed like a dream.

Of course it never occurred to me to try to force things. I would have been shocked at the suggestion. Boys weren't supposed to do that. I rearranged my own clothes, an awkward task since I had an erection I was sure would never go down.

She stood up. "I have to go back." Her breath still came in pants. "You wait here for a while. We shouldn't go back together." I wondered why, since we hadn't really done anything. She went to the door, then turned back. "I'm not a tease, Gabe. I just . . . just can't." Then she was gone.

I got up and lurched to the door. She was a pale shape against the trees, then she disappeared among them, leaving me with nothing but a deep ache in my groin and the scent of her on my fingers.

I pulled up to my garage apartment, cut the lights and shut off the engine. I sat there for a few minutes, listening to the cooling noises the car made. Then I got out.

"Hello, Gabe." It was Edna Tutt, in the back yard by the bronze goddess on her pedestal.

"Don't tell me you're gardening at this time of night."

"No, I was just talking with Flora here," she patted the statue's bronze backside, "but she doesn't say much. Would you like to come in? Have a cup of tea and some conversation?" Her voice was tinged with melancholy, as if she were the one in need of talk. I almost begged off, but what was there to do except go to my room and stare at the ceiling? For the first time in a long while I felt the need for some real, human contact.

"I'd love to," I said.

I followed her inside. She was wearing a powder-blue jumpsuit with a wide, falling collar and a white leather belt. Something classical was playing on her stereo. I realized that I hadn't seen a TV in the house, but then I hadn't been upstairs.

"Have a seat, I'll just be a minute." She disappeared into the kitchen and I heard things rattle and clink.

I sat at the coffee table and began to leaf through one of her big books on Deco period design. It was full of things I half-remembered from my childhood: radios and vases and furniture, all of them featuring straight lines and circles, arcs and interrupted arcs and jagged, lightning-like motifs. There were elegant nudes and elongated animals. The dominant color was a rich, bronze green. In the architecture section I saw a few L.A. buildings I recognized, leftovers from an era as remote to Angelenos as the Tower is to Londoners.

"I thought you'd stop at that one," Edna said, looking over my shoulder at the bizarre building with its rows of porthole windows.

I put a finger just below the building, on the sidewalk. "I made my first bust right there: a hooker named Babycakes, I don't remember her real name. She had a rap sheet for prostitution going back three years. She was sixteen."

Edna set out a tray of cookies and tiny sandwiches and went back into the kitchen. A minute later she brought out a tea pot and cups.

"Sixteen," she said as she poured. "That's so tragic. The world is so full of tragedy. Sometimes you just have to stop thinking about it or it breaks your heart. What ever happened to her?" She sat down and took a cup.

I stirred some sugar into mine. "She lasted, let's see, another two years. While she was a juvenile she always managed to get back to her corner. After she graduated, her pimp would always bail her out. A john beat her to death one night."

She closed her eyes and shook her head a little. "How . . . awful. I hate to keep using the same words: awful, terrible, tragic, but there are so few words and so much evil. I lived on the coast for a little while, a long time ago. There were some rough places, but nothing like now. It was before drugs were everywhere. Runaways were mostly girls from the South and Midwest trying to break into movies. People didn't just . . . abandon children, or let them run away and never look for them." She looked up beneath her blond bangs and smiled a little sadly. "Or am I just idealizing the past? Do I just think it was better because I was younger?"

"That could be," I said. "Looking back, I sometimes catch myself getting nostalgic about the Army, even about Viet Nam. I hated it all then, but when you're past forty-five, anything that happened when you were twenty takes on that rosy tinge."

"I suppose so." She sipped at her tea, then looked into the cup for a while.

"But you're right," I said. "L.A. is much worse than it was thirty years ago, when I first moved there. But then, it's much bigger. Plus drugs, illegal immigration, bad economic times—there's a thousand factors making it like it is. Big urban areas all over the country are in the same shape. Some of them worse."

"We always want to think our own times are uniquely bad," Edna mused. "But London in Dickens's day was probably just as bad, or New York in the 1880s."

"Big cities and bad times are a rough combination. You probably made the right decision, coming here to live."

"Oh, you can't get away from evil," she said. "Monticello is such a peaceful, dull, quiet place, but it has its secrets."

"Every place has," I agreed.

"Gabe, I don't want you to think I'm nosy. I hate to pry, but it's just that . . . I like you, and you seem to be a terribly unhappy person. I have the feeling that something awful has happened to you and you've come back to the place you came from to say goodbye. Only someone very old and ready to die should do that. Would you like to talk about it?"

It was the sort of thing that always made me draw back. "You don't need to hear about my troubles."

"Of course I don't. But maybe you need to talk about them. You're still young, Gabe, even if you feel middle-aged, and you're a fine-looking man. Depression robs things of proportion, and holding things in makes them worse. Sometimes talking helps put things in perspective, helps you get over the things that are past and can't be helped." She wasn't just talking platitudes. She spoke with real concern and she had human warmth of a sort I had all but forgotten existed.

"You wouldn't want to hear this," I said, a little desperately. "It'll just sound small and sordid and ugly."

She actually laughed. "Gabe, do you think anyone's tragedies are glamorous? Mine certainly aren't. I'd be willing to bet my experiences have been as sorry and shameful as yours. Most of us reach the point where it seems things just can't get worse and we want for it all to be over. You have to get past it."

Then I knew that I wanted, *needed* to unburden myself to this woman. I started slowly, hesitantly, but it all came out, first in broken sentences, then in a rush, then in near-serenity.

"It was my partner . . . he was . . . no, it began with Rose, my wife, and my drinking, and . . ."

"There's no rush, Gabe," Edna said, refilling my cup with steaming tea. I hadn't even noticed that I'd finished the first one. "Start at the beginning. Start back before all the troubles, if you like. That might make it easier."

I took a sip and leaned back on the couch. "Right. Well, my family moved to L.A. in '64. I never found out why, but I think my father had some sort of argument with old man Cohan. Dad was an accountant at Cohan Chemical. Anyway, we went out there and he got a job at a chemical firm and did okay, but he started to drink, something he never did before. So did my mother. It killed them both, finally. Dad drove over a cliff on the coast highway when I was nineteen. It was ruled an accident so we collected his life insurance, but I knew different. Mom just drank more and got more vague. She died when I was in the Army."

Edna didn't say anything, but her silence encouraged me to keep on.

"I graduated from high school in '65 and for a couple of years I took college classes and did the usual kid jobs: drove a Chicken Delight van, ushered at Grauman's Chinese, that sort of thing. Then, in '67, I joined the Army. I'd gotten interested in police work, so I volunteered for the MPs. I knew it would give me a leg up in a civilian police department when I left the service. I went to Viet Nam in '68 and that was where I met Rose, my wife."

"Your wife was Vietnamese?"

"Uh-huh. Rose Nguyen. She was a convent-raised Catholic, that's why she had that first name. I was in the 18th MP Battalion and she was a secretary in Battalion headquarters. She was always there when I delivered reports from my company and she was the most beautiful thing I'd ever seen, had a smile like yours."

"Thank you."

"I wheeled and dealed for months to wangle an assignment at headquarters so I could be close to her. We were married just before I ETSed. That means went back to the States. The Army didn't like it, but they couldn't stop us. Some of the guys in my outfit said Vietnamese women only married soldiers so they could get to the States and get citizenship papers."

"I suppose there are always people who say things like that."

"Well, they were wrong," I said fervently. "I separated from the service and went straight into the LAPD Academy. Rose got a job as a waitress. Those first years were rough. We both worked and went to school at the same time, sometimes nights, sometimes days. We never saw enough of each other, but I got onto the force and she earned her teaching certificate, started teaching second grade. We worked hard and we were happy. My promotions came along regularly, I finally got my diploma, Rose got her Master's, she built up seniority, I picked up a few citations. Things were good." I sort of trailed off.

"It sounds like a good marriage," Edna said. "Children?"

It took a second to start again. "No, though we tried and tried. And then we found out why. Ovarian cancer."

"Oh, dear," Edna whispered.

"We tried everything; chemotherapy, radiation, but it was too late. In the end, we just prolonged her dying. Her last months, she looked like something from a Nazi death camp."

"Oh, Gabe, that is so dreadful."

"It was," I said, brushing at my eyes. "The strange thing was, she talked me through the whole thing, when it should've been me comforting her. It was God's will, she said, I wasn't to mourn. She told me to remarry and have all the kids we couldn't have." I stopped talking for a couple of minutes and swallowed some tea. Edna didn't prod me.

"Anyway, my partner, Murray—I'll have to tell you all about Murray, some other time—Murray was a rock. I never would've made it through without him. Sometimes I just sat beside him in the car like a zombie and he carried the weight for both of us. I thought I was getting over it, but I wasn't. I couldn't stop brooding about Rose. I moved out of our house and took an apartment, thought seeing our place wouldn't let me forget. But it didn't help. She was in my head and she wouldn't leave. I didn't *want* her to leave.

"What I did was I got so I could pretend to be back to normal. I could put a good face on it, hang out with the other guys and laugh, but when I got home, by myself, it was still the same. One thing helped and that was drinking. Every night I drank myself to sleep. At least I slept.

"For a long time it didn't interfere with my work. There were a lot of hung-over mornings but I did my job. Sometimes, when things were really rough, feeling miserable gave me the mean edge I needed, dealing with the gangs. The promotions stopped and the commendations slowed, but I didn't really care.

"It wasn't anything sudden, but after a while I was drinking on the job. Not often, but sometimes when I needed to get through an especially rough day. Then it was more often. After a while it was every day. But Murray covered for me. He made excuses and took up my slack." I hesitated, then pushed on. "He must've really loved me, because I was wrecking his career, too, and he still stood by me. I did this to us for two or three years. Even now I can't believe it."

"We're often strangers to ourselves, Gabe," Edna said, her eyes shimmering.

"Then one day we were working on a fugitive warrant, guy wanted for three armed robberies. Just a routine questioning of the guy's wife. We'd talked to her three or four times already that month. She had a little house in South Central. We parked at the curb, just as usual. Murray went up to the door alone. He left me in the car because it was late afternoon and by that time I wasn't even talking straight."

Of course she knew what was coming, but it didn't make saying the next part any easier. "This time the guy was at home. He shot Murray through the screen door, twice in the face. I got out of the car—stumbled out, is more like it—almost dropped my piece trying to get it out from under my coat. The guy came out and shot at me twice, hit me once but I didn't even notice. His car was across the street. He jumped in it and burned rubber. I emptied my piece at him, hit him in the throat by sheer luck. He got about two blocks and plowed into a guard rail. He was D.O.A. at the hospital.

"I was a real sight when the black-and-whites got there, holding Murray my lap and bawling like a baby, not the kind of picture they run on the six o'clock news. I had so much of his blood all over me nobody noticed I'd been shot, not even me."

I looked at Edna and I wondered if she would be so kind and gentle, now that she knew what I was. "There was nobody this time to tell me it was God's will. The Department hushed it up. They'd had enough bad publicity; I'd killed the perp and he was a multiple offender, all violent crimes. I'd managed not to bag any innocent bystanders doing it. But they knew what had happened, and they were through with me.

"So was I, really. I tried to kill myself the first night, drive over a cliff like my Dad. But he'd had the guts and I didn't. I tried a few more times, always chickened out. The last time was the day I came back here. I guess I'll get it right sooner or later."

"Gabe, I can understand your pain," Edna said. "Self-hate is the most vicious kind, because there's no one to forgive you. But you've let your conscience destroy all proportion in this. Your wife must have been a wonderful woman, and your partner was a fine, loyal man but the world is a brutal place and none of us leaves it unscathed. You've become so wrapped up in yourself that you think you must be responsible for everything. So much is just not in our hands, believe me."

"God may have killed Rose," I said, bleakly, "but I did it to Murray. I killed him."

"No, Gabe. He was murdered by a killer. Do you think you could have saved him if you'd been sober? Shot like that without warning, knocking on a door for a routine questioning? Policemen are killed like that every day, and it always happens so quickly that it's over before anybody knows what happened."

"I should have been with him. You never let your partner go

up to a known haunt alone like that, not when there's a violent offender involved. He did it because he didn't want me disgracing myself and the Department, not even in front of some cheap hood's woman."

"It was his choice. If you had died, maybe he'd be the one in a suicidal depression now. We can't know. I know I've . . . well, maybe some night I'll tell you."

Maybe if I'd pressed her she would have given me her story, but suddenly I was awfully tired. I got up. "Thanks for listening, Edna. Think you can stand having me for a lodger now?"

She smiled that wonderful smile again. "Of course, Gabe. And I don't think you've got it all out of your system yet. Don't hug it to yourself as if it were something you treasure. Don't let it become old sin."

"Old sin?"

"That's a term my mother used. She was a very religious woman. Old sin was the thing that was buried, but never forgotten or forgiven. It's the deadliest thing in the world, and it never stays buried. It always comes back. My mother used to say it always destroyed the sinner, because he chose to turn away from God; chose to live with his sin instead.

"I stopped believing in a vengeful God a long time ago, but I know she was right on an instinctive, intuitive level. It's a way that we destroy ourselves, and it can ruin those around us. Don't let it happen to you."

"I think it already has," I said.

"You're too young for despair," she said, exasperated. "Give yourself a chance." She got up and walked me to the back door. "But promise me, before you do anything awful or think about drinking again, you'll come talk to me."

"I promise," I said. "Thanks, Edna."

She put her hands on my shoulders. "Good night, Gabe." She stood on tiptoe and kissed me lightly on the cheek. It was my second kiss of the night. I stepped outside and she closed the door behind me.

I walked back to the garage and up the steps and went into my room. As I undressed I realized that I really did feel better. Edna had that rare warmth and empathy that can absorb other people's pain like a sponge. I had no idea what it cost her, but it couldn't have been easy.

I was about to turn out the bedside lamp when I saw the folded paper on the floor by the entrance. Someone had pushed it beneath the door and I hadn't noticed it when I went in. I picked it up and carried it back, unfolding it. I sat on the bed and read its single sentence.

Meet me at the boathouse tomorrow night at ten.

There was no signature, but it didn't need one.

6

I slept late. It was after nine-thirty when I got up, splashed some water on my face and brushed my teeth. I hadn't slept so well in longer than I could handily remember. I put on my new running shoes and went out.

No sign of Edna, no music drifting from the house. I went south on Maple past the Cohan estate, starting at a fast walk, stepping up the pace until I was moving at a steady jog. Across Poplar, Maple sloped sharply down to the river and that part was easy, going downhill.

At the bottom of the hill, I turned left and began running along the river road, and before long I was beginning to sweat. It had been a while since I'd done anything like this. After about a half-mile the town sort of petered out. Across the river was the area we called Skinnertown Flats, a disorderly cluster of shabby houses, shacks and trailers. Amid the squalor of rusted cars, abandoned refrigerators, and disassembled motorcycles, a classic Airstream trailer gleamed like a silver teardrop. Skinnertown was named for the Skinners, a family of low-lifes who had been a fixture of Monticello life for generations. The Skinner kids were the ones your parents always told you not to play with.

I was winded by the time I was a quarter-mile past Skinner-town. Going back, I alternated running and walking, feeling the long muscles in my thighs burning and knowing my knees would give me hell. It felt good.

Back in my room I showered and shaved, then made the phone call I'd been putting off. I had to dig through my wallet to find the card, then I punched in the number and listened to the ring from the other end.

"Carson Investigations, may I help you?" It was a woman's voice.

"May I speak to Kit, please? Tell him it's Gabe Treloar."

"One moment, please." There was a wait and the sound of conferring voices, then a man's voice on the line.

"Gabe? Where the hell are you? I was expecting you a day or two ago." Randall "Kit" Carson had been a cop in L.A. and I'd worked with him quite a bit over the years. About ten years older than me, he'd retired a few years earlier and taken up PI work in Cleveland, joining an old friend from *his* younger days on the force. Now he owned the agency and he'd kept up with his old L.A. contacts. He thought I'd gotten a raw deal, called up and offered me a job. With no other prospects and not caring a whole lot, I'd taken him up on it.

"I kind of got side-tracked, Kit. I'm in Monticello. It's in Polk County, about sixty . . ."

"I know where Monticello is. What're you doing there?"

"It's my old home town. I sort of drove here on impulse, and now I'm in a few things that're gonna take some time." Pretty lame, I thought, but he'd gotten along for a long time without me. It wasn't like he was desperate for my company.

"Sentimental journey, huh? Well, when're you gonna get here?"

"I'm not sure. It may be a few weeks."

He paused. "Is everything okay? You're not in any trouble, are you?"

"No, no, nothing like that. It's just . . . there are some things I have to do. Is it all right by you?"

"Sure. It ain't like you need my permission or anything."

"I just don't want you to think I don't appreciate your offer, or that I'm undependable. I'll get up there pretty soon."

"Okay. The job's still open. You doing all right for money? I could advance you a little."

"No, I'm doing okay. Thanks, though, I appreciate it."

"Well, all right. Keep in touch, Gabe. Let me know when to expect you." He clicked off and I hung up. As I glanced up I saw Edna crossing the street toward the red-and-blue post office box that stood catty-corner to her house. She put in some sort of big envelope and then returned to the house. I thought I saw her glance up toward my room. I thought she looked sad.

But I was thinking about the coming night, and how to kill the time until then. It made for a long day.

I walked around aimlessly, not wanting to talk to anybody. I visited old haunts, saw things that triggered memories long lost, trivial incidents from childhood, some of them not so trivial. Much of it was like those landscapes you see in dreams, where everything seems somehow familiar but you can't call up any specific memory of them. It wasn't quite deja vu, but it felt just as spooky.

Somehow I got through it, my palms sweating, getting a ticklish sensation in the pit of my stomach, wondering why the hell I was acting and feeling like a lovesick teenager. I was a grown man of long experience going to meet a three-times-married woman, neither of us exactly untouched by life and the world. Maybe, I thought, I was being like one of those grown kids who go back to live with their parents and immediately revert to whining, moody teenagers. I had come back home and it was as if the past thirty years had been swept away, leaving me the same gawky, inexperienced boy I had been when I left. And I was about to resume my interrupted relationship with Lola.

I had an urge to go talk to Edna about it, but she was my landlady, not my shrink. Besides, I thought, I really didn't want to talk to anybody. Just to Lola.

The Cohan place at the lake had a big stone wall and a wrought-iron gate and I wondered if I was going to have to climb it. I got out of the Plymouth and walked over with a flashlight, shining it on the lock. It was locked tight, and looked as if it hadn't been opened all summer. Was I supposed to wait for her to come let me in? Somehow I knew that wasn't the idea.

I remembered that there was a state bird refuge next to the Cohan property, with a path leading down to the lake shore about a hundred yards from the gate. I drove past the end of the wall and onto the hard-packed, grassy ground beyond. I cut the engine and lights, picked up the flashlight and got out. It was quiet except for the breeze in the long grass and the sounds of night: insects, frogs, an owl or two. This had been a popular parking spot for the high school kids but it looked like the kids no longer bothered to seek privacy for that purpose anymore.

I switched on the flash and found the trail, still plainly marked. It was clear enough to see by moonlight so I turned the light off. It seemed like an intrusion, somehow. Going down the path was like climbing the tree had been. I didn't really need my eyes. My feet knew the way. Still the sweaty palms, still the fluttery stomach.

I went in under the trees and the moonlight was cut off, but I still didn't turn on the flashlight. The sounds were closer beneath the trees, and the smell was marshy. The leaf-rot underfoot made my steps all but soundless. Somehow I knew I wasn't going to run into a tree or have a branch swat me across the face. Moonlight began to filter down in tiny beams and patches, then I was out of the trees and the lake was in front of me, sparkling with the lights of the houses and docks around its periphery. Brightest of all was the multicolored sign atop the Lodge on the other side of the lake, with the lanterns lining the rail of its waterside deck where a few diners were undoubtedly savoring a late dinner beneath the moon and stars.

I turned right and began to walk along the shore. The gravel crunched faintly to my steps. The line of trees I remembered was gone and I could see the broad lawn slanting uphill to the cottage. There wasn't a light to be seen anywhere. I wondered if she was pulling some sort of sick joke on me.

Then the boathouse loomed in front of me. The tarry, mossy smell of it was like an old friend. I went up the steps to the door, turning the knob. It swung open easily and I went in. The big, lakeside doors were open and I saw a boat in the dock. It wasn't the same one, naturally enough. There was a faint scent of exhaust in the air. Then there was another scent.

"Gabe?" She was a pale shape on the other side, beyond the hulking outline of the cabin cruiser. She laughed, a girlish giggle that ended in an abrupt catch, almost like a sob. "You're going to have to come over to me, Gabe. I'm blind in here. My pupils don't dilate right, remember?"

I set the flashlight on the floor and walked around the little dock and she was standing in front of me, dressed in something pale, the tan of her skin like a shadow. I put my hands to her waist, she gripped my arms and we held each other at a distance, warily.

"Why'd you make me walk?" I asked, keeping my voice steady.

"I wanted to see if you remembered, and I didn't want this to be too easy for you." She was being cool, but her voice was thick, almost furry.

"I haven't forgotten anything. And none of this is easy." I pulled her close and her arms went around me as her face tilted up. We kissed, then broke apart for a moment and I looked to see if the cushions were on the bench this time. She laughed again, this time a little more throatily.

"We can do better than that now. Come on." Holding my hand, she stepped over to the boat and felt for its rail with her foot. I stepped down into it, reached up for her waist again and lowered her feet gently to the deck. Then we were together again in the gentle wash of moonlight that spilled through the double doors.

There was no awkwardness this time, no teenage fumbling. We were grownups with more than a few miles on us. The dress she wore drifted off of her. Her hand slid up my chest and my shirt fell away. Then there was nothing but air between us. Soon there wasn't even that. She was a rich armful now, not the adolescent of my memory. The hard cupcake breasts were now full and had an easy sway, and her belly had gained an undulating softness. I ran my hands down her spine to her hips, then cupped her buttocks. They were firm and taut in this age of the gym.

"Not sixteen anymore, Gabe. Sorry." Her own hands traced the odd bumps and ridges that decorated my back.

"You'd be shocked to see me in daylight," I said, my voice beginning to shudder. "I've been shot six times. I caught some shrapnel in Viet Nam. Worked over with knives once."

"Character, just character," she chuckled. "I want to see them all, soon. Come on, we've waited much too long for this." She tugged at me and we padded into the little cabin.

The bed inside was larger than I would have thought, sweet-smelling and deeply cushioned. She sat on it and drew me down to her. Lola Cohan was mine again, as she had almost been so briefly, so long ago. Gone was the spastic groping and the frantic urgency of children just growing into new bodies and new feelings. We came together with perfect grace and assurance, as if we'd been lovers for a long, long time. Maybe we had been, in our minds.

Without surging and plunging, with only the gentlest, loving violence, we brought each other to the exquisite, lingering moment when pain and death disappear and there is only unbearable perfection. For the first time in more than ten years, in that penultimate moment before I collapsed into pulsing, quivering helplessness, the woman beneath me didn't turn into Rose.

I woke to swaying and creaking. For a second I was disoriented, then the smell of the boathouse brought me back. I could smell Lola, too, faintly. I reached out for her, but she wasn't there. I touched the button on my watch and the display lit up: 3:30 A.M.

I rolled out of the bed and went out of the cabin, the morning air cool on my naked skin. Still no Lola. Had I dreamed her? Then I heard a gentle splashing from the stern of the boat and I walked back and leaned over the rail.

She was in the water, her hair plastered to her head, holding on to the rudder. She looked up at me and her smile was white in her shadowed face.

"What's this, an undine?"

"I swam all the way out to the middle of the lake," she said. "I haven't done that since I was twenty. I used to come out here on vacation with some of my sorority sisters and we'd skinny dip on summer nights. I didn't know how much I missed it."

She reached up and I reached down and hauled her into the boat, wet and slippery as a mermaid. There was a folded towel on one of the cruiser's side benches and I rubbed her down.

"How could you see to swim?"

"Out there, with the moon reflecting off the water, I could see. It was beautiful." She shivered a little and came into my arms. My toweling began to warm her skin.

"Suppose somebody'd been out there? You might've been picked up by someone out trolling."

She shrugged. "So what? They'd have brought me back here, or anywhere else I wanted to go."

"Whatever Lola wants, Lola gets," I said.

"Uh-huh. That's how it is." Her eyes gleamed eerily and she raised her head, standing on her toes to lick at the base of my throat. I started to grow excited all over again, but she pushed me gently away. "No, Gabe. It'll be light soon. We have to go, and I don't want anyone to see us together just yet."

"Why?" I asked her. "You don't mind being found naked in the middle of the lake, what makes me so embarrassing?"

She put her fingertips against my chest. "It's not that, Gabe, don't be like that. There are things happening . . . in my family. I have to be very careful right now. But it won't be for long, I promise. Just humor me in this, all right?"

I took a deep breath. "All right." She was already getting dressed. I did the same, slowly and reluctantly. She came back into my arms and we kissed one last time.

"Soon, Gabe," she said.

I left the boat and went out through the door, leaving it open behind me. The walk along the lake shore seemed shorter than before and I was back under the trees before I remembered the flashlight. But I didn't need it anyway. I walked through the dark like I was floating, as if a huge weight had been lifted from me. My car was right where I'd left it. Somehow, my keys had stayed in my pocket which was lucky, because I hadn't thought to check for them when I'd gotten dressed. I backed out onto the road, switched on the lights and began to drive back toward town.

I never thought to ask her why she'd panicked, all those years ago. It didn't seem important any longer.

It was still dark when I pulled into town. The place had an unreal, ghostly feeling at that hour, everything brightly lit by streetlamps, everything utterly deserted. I drove north up Main and turned east on Poplar. When I turned north again on Maple, I saw the lights: the surreal red-and-blue strobing of police vehicles, lots of them.

Accident, I told myself: fender-bender, busted water main, maybe a heart attack. But I had that sinking feeling. I knew it was something bad. There were so many emergency vehicles I couldn't park in front of the garage, so I pulled up down the street and got out. Walking toward the corner, I could see uniforms going into Edna's house.

There's something about those lights, the way they light up everything so fitfully, flashing their multiple colors, making the crowd that stood all around look like visitors from space. Then there were the sounds: approaching sirens, and the startling hiss, crackle and loud, intrusive voices from the police radios. I had lived much of my adult life amid those sights and sounds, they ought to have been like home to me. But I was a civilian now, cut off from that uniformed, disciplined world with its specialized jargon and practices, and the scene filled me with dread.

The neighbors always gather in the street and on the sidewalk and peer from the surrounding windows. At this hour they were mostly tousle-haired, their clothes hastily thrown on, blinking, unshaven or hair in curlers. They all looked shocked, transported to another world. I walked up to a woman who clutched a bathrobe around her skinny body, the flashing lights reflecting from the thick lenses of her glasses.

"What's happened?" I asked her.

"Somebody said Mrs. Tutt's been killed, but I don't know.

The police won't tell us anything." She put her spidery finger-tips over her lips, a picture of disbelieving shock.

I felt a lurching deep below my stomach, not bothering to tell myself she had to be wrong. It had to be true, to raise this much pandemonium. There were town and county cars all over the place. Even as I watched, a couple of state cars arrived, sirens screaming. There were blue and brown uniforms in the yard, trampling all over Edna's garden, and I was briefly furious, not just at the desecration, but professionally, at their small-town ineptitude. They were fast obliterating any evidence that might have been out there, and were undoubtedly doing the same inside.

I asked a couple more neighbors and got the same response. I walked over to the back yard, where most of the traffic was. Some of the men wearing khaki or blue glanced at me curiously, but nobody tried to stop me. This kind of thing happened so seldom that they didn't have any practiced procedure for dealing with interloping civilians. I saw a small, khaki-clad man coming out the back door, a clipboard in his hand and a grim, almost sick look on a face that looked pale even in the eerie light. I went through the back fence and walked up to him. He looked up at me with no recognition whatsoever.

"Mark?" I said. "Mark Fowles? I'm Gabe Treloar, remember me? I used to live in this house."

He had the slightly stunned look of a man too preoccupied to shift mental gears. "No, I don't . . . look, I'm awfully busy here."

"Is it true? Has Mrs. Tutt been killed?"

He looked around, then back at me, irritated. "Look, I can't talk right now. You'd better go on back . . ."

"I live here. I mean, I've been renting the apartment over the garage from Edna."

"What do we have here, Mark? Return of the native?" I looked up and saw a big man standing in the doorway, blue-uniformed, wearing an old-fashioned Sam Browne belt. The belt carried no paraphernalia except a military-style .45 automatic and a clip pouch. He was at least six-four, wide in the shoulders, going big in the gut, with curly, yellow hair and square, white teeth set in a massive jaw.

"His name's Treloar, Les. Used to live in this house when we were kids. Says he's renting the apartment over the garage."

The big man came down the steps. "I'm Lester Cabell, Chief of Police, and I don't guess you were up there when all the excitement happened because we checked and nobody was in that apartment when we arrived."

"I was out from nine o'clock on. I just now got back. Look, I'm a cop. I could help you . . ."

"That's not what I heard," Cabell broke in. "I like to keep track of who takes up residence in my town. You left the L.A. police a while back sort of suddenly." Checking up on me for Ansel, no doubt.

"Listen to me," I said. "These guys out here are tearing up evidence, and there are more arriving every minute. You haven't cordoned off the area, you don't have officers out taking statements from witnesses, you . . ."

"We don't need any help, thank you kindly," Fowles said, glaring.

"Oh, I don't know," Cabell said, drawing his words out, "maybe we could use a little advice from a veteran officer of a major metropolitan police department."

Fowles shrugged. "Your jurisdiction." He leaned forward and tapped me on the chest with a corner of his clipboard. "But I want to talk to you, in my office, as soon as I'm through here. Don't go anywhere."

"I don't plan to."

"Come on," Cabell said. "Tell me what you think of this." He went back inside, his big shoulders almost brushing the doorframe, sticking a big cigar into his mouth and firing it up. The utility room was a mess, the washer and dryer open, boxes of soap powder spilled. The kitchen was worse, all the cabinets turned out, cannisters overturned, bottles, cans and jars removed from the shelves and set on the counter or floor with odd precision.

"Your men do any of this?" I asked him.

"Uh-uh. It was all like this when we found it."

"Who called it in?" I asked him.

"Mrs. Joseph, from across the street. She doesn't get much sleep nights, her bedroom faces the street and she keeps her window open in the summer. She heard some funny noises, clattering, loud footsteps on the stairs, then someone running out and the front door slamming. She figured a burglary since there were no lights on in the house and she called us."

We went into the living room. The pictures were off the walls, the upholstery was cut up, furniture overturned. The little figurines were lined up neatly on the floor, covered with white powder. At least somebody had been dusting for prints.

"Just one runner?" I asked.

"That's all she was sure of."

"Hear an engine start up?"

"She didn't mention it. I'll have to ask." He puffed on his cigar, releasing a noxious cloud.

"Edna didn't like smoking in her house." I said, inanely.

He took out the cigar and contemplated it. "I'm afraid Edna's a little past caring now, and when we get upstairs you'll be grateful for the smoke."

It was the same story in the hallway, the same orderly wreckage. Three cops in town uniforms came down the stairs, white-faced, one of them weaving a little.

"If you have to throw up, get outside to do it," Cabell told them. Their feet made strange sounds on the steps and I took a look. Every tread had been pried up from its riser. I took a handkerchief from my pocket and wrapped it around my fingertips, then lifted one. It came up about two inches. They hadn't been pried far enough to admit a hand, but enough to see inside, if you used a penlight. I took a deep breath and went up the stairs.

The curved bannister had been dusted for prints. At the top landing was the rolled-up carpet somebody had removed to look under the steps. To the right was the room that had been my bedroom, years ago. It was fitted up as a home gym. There was no elaborate machinery, just a mat and a few pieces of simple apparatus and some small dumbbells, no more than five pounds. There was also a stereo with big speakers. Not much destruction here: the speakers had been opened up, the records taken from their jackets and set on the mat along with the CDs.

"In here," Cabell said, standing in the doorway of the bedroom that had been my parents'.

Twenty years of professional experience doesn't brace you for the utter horror, the unbelievable awfulness, when it's someone you know, someone you liked and cared about. There was a photographer taking pictures, and an elderly, white-coated man was squatting beside the bed where Edna Tutt lay.

She was naked, spread-eagled, her violated body making an X against the blood-soaked bedding. A cloth gag bound her mouth. Her eyes were unnaturally wide, staring, I thought, straight at me, begging me to help her. The smell, as Cabell had predicted, made me grateful for his smoke. I closed my eyes, breathed deep a few times, through my mouth, and made myself look, putting aside my feelings.

Edna had been ripped wide open. The wound started at her sternum and made a long arrow all the way to her lower abdomen. It pointed to her pubis, where the hair shone startling, inky black despite the blood soaking it. I remembered how her dark eyebrows hadn't quite gone with her hair. Her thighs had been deeply gashed and all the blood made it impossible to see what lay between them.

There were small, triangular burn marks all over her. Only her face was left untouched, although the gag was blood-soaked. Bitten tongue, I guessed. People often bite their tongues under torture. The white-coated man prodded at her, mumbling inaudible notes into a tiny recorder. He looked sad, but I guessed that was his habitual expression. Otherwise he was impassive. The docs usually are, even small-town coroners who rarely have to deal with murder. They make their covenant with horror in med school and then confront it for the rest of their professional lives. The most demented murderer can't match Mother Nature in that respect. No Nazi sadist ever did anything worse than what nature did to Rose.

"What've you got for me, Doc?" Cabell asked.

The man looked up glumly, blinking behind his heavy-framed spectacles. "I won't say anything official until I've had a chance to conduct a complete autopsy. Unofficially, I think the cause of death was asphyxia, probably caused by blood from a bitten tongue, or from swallowing the tongue. Prior to death she was tortured with a red-hot object, leaving distinctive burn marks."

"Soldering iron," I said. "Those are soldering iron burns."

The coroner looked at me without a word, then at Cabell, his eyebrows raised. The chief clapped a hand on my shoulder.

"This is my colleague, Mr. Treloar. He's assisting in the investigation. Mr. Treloar, this is Doc Appelhof, our county coroner and head of surgery at Polk County General Hospital. Go ahead, Doc."

"The larger wounds are almost certainly post-mortem, and that is all I am going to say at this time." He spoke with a very faint German accent.

"It'll do for now," Cabell said. "It provides us with plenty of food for thought. Doc, send me a copy of your report as soon as it's prepared." Appelhof nodded curtly, saying nothing.

"Seen enough, Mr. Treloar?"

"Yes." I looked my last at a woman who had known nothing about me, and then had known more than enough, and had been the soul of kindness through it all. She hadn't deserved this.

I followed Cabell down the stairs and out through the front door, onto the wraparound porch. It was startling to see that it was light outside. Morning had come. Most of the police cars had cleared out. Only a few neighbors gawked. Cabell flicked ash onto the lawn, then sat on the porch rail, half-leaning against a support post, his arms crossed, legs stretched out and crossed at the ankles.

"Okay, Treloar, talk to me."

"Am I a suspect?"

He grinned. "Not yet, but I'm going to tell you what Mark told you: Don't try to go anyplace. I guarantee, you won't get far."

"I'm staying right here," I told him.

"Good. Ever work homicide, out in L.A.?"

"Four years as a detective," I said. "But I ran into murders practically from my first day out of the academy."

"Things are a little more sedate here, more laid back. We've had maybe ten in the whole county since I've been chief. Usually it's some drunk beats his wife to death. Once, a carload of junkies on their way from Pittsburgh to Indianapolis stopped by long enough to rob a drugstore and kill the proprietor, over near the college. A thing like this . . ." he shrugged and spread his hands a little, ". . . it's something new. Let me run a few thoughts by you, maybe you can point out where I'm thinking wrong."

"Go ahead." I figured he'd taken me inside, let me see Edna, so he could watch my reaction. I didn't know what he'd read, but he was still feeling me out.

"I see it as a junkie killing. People need money for drugs, they're capable of anything. This man, only I figure it was more than one, thought Mrs. Tutt had money, came in here and tied her up, worked her over with a soldering iron . . . you're sure it was an iron?"

"I've seen the marks before."

"Worked her over with the iron, and loosened the gag once in a while to let her talk. But she didn't, maybe couldn't, tell them anything, and finally she died. They cut her open to make sure she didn't survive, then ransacked the house, looking for money. Something panicked them, the phone rang, or maybe they thought they heard someone coming back, and they ran. How's that sound to you?" He puffed on his cigar.

I saw someone talking to the sheriff on the corner. It was Sharon Newell, Lew's assistant from the paper. Cabell followed the direction of my gaze. "I don't want you to say a thing about what you saw in there to that woman. If you do, I'll find an excuse to lock you up."

"I know who she is," I told him. "Lew's an old friend of mine. Don't worry, I know how it's done."

"Good."

"It was probably more than one. Edna wasn't young, but she was in top physical shape for her age. Even taken by surprise in her sleep, she'd have put up a hell of a fight. She was overpowered by more than one man or else by someone very strong. I think the torture and the search were concurrent. She was worked over for a long time, and the house was gone over pretty thoroughly. I don't think there was time to do both one after the other, unless it was a whole gang."

"You think dopers are likely?"

I shook my head. "They usually trash a place looking for drugs or money."

"It's pretty messed up in there," he said.

"It was searched by someone who knew what he was doing. Things were spilled that had to be spilled—powders, cereals, things that had to be dumped to search the containers quickly. Everything else was moved in an orderly and efficient manner. The steps were only pried up enough to see under. Junkies take anything valuable. Did it look like valuables were taken?"

"We won't know for a while, but they may've ignored the little stuff and gone for the big score."

"What big score?" I asked.

He grinned, showing his big teeth. "This is where I have the advantage over you, Treloar. This is a small town. Mrs. Tutt kept pretty much to herself. Nobody knew her very well. That's enough to get the boys in the biker bars talking. Pretty soon, somebody says he heard she's got big money squirreled away and someone decides to come look for it."

"That makes sense as far as some of it goes," I said. "But the cutting was the work of a head case."

"So, do we have one burglar and one psycho sadist?"

"They usually like to hear their victims beg, hear them scream."

"You ran into some hard customers out there on the coast," he said.

"Enough of them. But it still bothers me. The torture was brutal, but it looked methodical. Whoever did it was thinking ahead—he brought a soldering iron along, and used it carefully. The ripping, though—that was done by someone in a total, insane rage."

"It doesn't add up."

I rubbed a hand down over my face, feeling the whisker stubble. I was tired and the day was just starting.

"It won't," I told him. "Not for a while. Not until you have all the facts. That's when it'll start to make sense."

Fowles finished talking to Sharon Newell and walked up toward the porch. "You through with him, Les?"

Cabell grinned. "For a while. Gabe here's been a real help. I think we might just crack this thing with him on our side. Say you knew him when you were kids?"

Mark nodded. "That's right."

"Well, you two go on over to your office and talk about old times. I'm expecting some state people here pretty soon, but I want to talk some more with Gabe, soon as you're done with him."

Mark's eyes narrowed. "Who'd you call?"

Cabell didn't lose his grin. "Just people who'd show up anyway. The TV crews from Columbus are gonna be here in a few minutes. You know how they love to get in front of those cameras at a big crime scene."

Mark Fowles spoke each word clearly, distinctly: "When that grandstanding son of a bitch Rapley shows up, you keep him out of my way." Sharon Newell was scribbling furiously on her pad.

Cabell's grin slipped a little bit at the corners. "Sure thing, Mark. Of course, Ted pretty much goes his own way. He wants to talk to you, I don't doubt he'll figure out a way to do it."

Mark spun on his heel. "Come with me, Treloar." Sharon Newell started toward me, a big smile on her face and her ballpoint poised. The sheriff jabbed a rigid finger at her, stopping her in her tracks. "No. Not a word. I'm going to take his statement. You can try to catch him later, if I don't decide to lock him up."

"Mark, you're such a sweetie. To think I let you get away and Margaret snagged you instead. Some nights I cry myself to sleep over that." She turned her feral smile on me. "Later, Mr. Treloar."

7

The clock in the county courthouse steeple sounded West-minster chimes as we were getting out of Mark Fowles's car. Murray, my partner, used to say they were the most famous eight notes in the world, bringing in the hour on every BBC broadcast worldwide, Big Ben sounding as permanent as the British Empire had once seemed. He said that it was more fa-mous than the four notes that introduced Beethoven's Fifth Symphony, even more famous than the four notes at the begin-ning of *Star Trek*. Then the bell tolled seven o'clock.

We walked through the front office where a dispatcher sat in front of her mike. The other desks were empty. The woman looked up at Mark as if she were going to ask him something, but he shook his head. I followed him into his office and he closed the door behind us.

"Want some coffee?" he asked, sounding marginally warmer.

The smell from the coffee maker hit me and suddenly I needed it like a junkie needs smack. "Please."

He poured two cups and handed me one. "There's creamer and sugar here if you want it."

"I take it black."

He sat behind his desk and I took a chair on the other side. It was a big, old, mahogany desk, heavily scarred with scratches and gouges and cigarette burns. Amid a clutter of papers and other desk paraphernalia sat an odd object: It looked a bit like a battered film canister, a flat metal disk about ten inches wide, its top smashed in, a smear of lead, white with age, in the center of the depression. One side was split partially open, brass tubes gleaming inside like a grin full of gold teeth.

"Where were you last night, Treloar?"

I knew better than to lie. "I was with a woman who'd rather not have her name mentioned."

"Edna Tutt would've preferred not to be murdered, too. We don't all get our wishes." He looked down into his coffee cup and swirled its rainbow-glinting surface.

"I think you wouldn't want to bring her into this, either."

That made him stop his swirling. "Is she important enough to go to jail for?"

"Look, Mark, if you want to charge me with something, go ahead and book me and I'll get a lawyer and I'll talk to him about an alibi for last night. In the meantime, I'll say this: I last saw Edna alive yesterday morning around eleven. She left her house and walked across the street and mailed something, then she went back in. I spent the rest of the day wandering around. I didn't really talk to anybody except a couple of waitresses. I was undoubtedly seen by a lot of people.

"About nine last night I drove out to see the lady in question. Early this morning I returned to find the scene at Edna's house, when you saw me. That's it."

He looked at me for a long, hard time, saying nothing. I knew the technique. I'd used it myself plenty of times. It's still just as intimidating when you're on the other side of the desk. Finally he broke eye contact and took another drink of his coffee.

"Okay. For now. You're not in the clear yet as far as I'm concerned, not by a long shot. You blew into town Monday after an absence of almost thirty years. Tuesday you rented a room from Edna Tutt. Late Thursday night and the early hours of Friday morning, Edna was tortured and murdered in a fashion never before seen in a century and a half of Monticello history." He'd been doing some quick checking up on me. I guessed Sharon Newell as his informant.

"It looks bad," I admitted. "This is a small town and I'm the interloper here."

"Don't flatter yourself," Mark said. "You're not Sidney Poitier in that old movie. There's several people here in town I'd rather see behind bars than you." He pushed away from the desk and leaned back, making the ancient, wooden, roller chair squeak. "No, I just don't see you doing anything this crazy and then just walking up to the police investigating. Granted, my acquaintance with psychos is pretty slight. Maybe that's how they always operate. What did you tell Lester?"

I ran through my conversation with the chief, and Mark nodded. "That makes three of us, then. I don't think it was one man working alone, either, and that's another piece in your favor, but don't take it to the bank just yet."

"Mark, just who was Edna Tutt?" I asked him. "What did she live on? Was she a widow? Did she have any family around here?"

"I intend to be looking into all that for some time to come. I know she moved here in the mid to late sixties. She kept pretty much to herself. Nobody ever complained about her. She paid her fees and taxes on time. As for her income, that was between her, her banker, and the IRS. As long as she didn't steal it, she never came under my purview. More than fourteen thousand people in this town alone. More than triple that for the county. It's not big, but the ones who give me trouble keep me plenty busy. I don't trouble the ones who mind their own business and keep on good terms with their neighbors. Until last night, Edna Tutt never brought herself to my attention."

"I didn't know her long," I told him, "but I liked her. She was a good woman and she shouldn't have died like that."

"Nobody deserves that. It happens anyway. This time it happened in my county and I intend to find out who did it, and why, and put them away."

"I want to help," I said.

"I want you to keep out of the way. What brings you back here, Gabe?" At least he was using my first name.

"I was on my way to Cleveland to meet an old friend from the L.A. police, Randall Carson. He has a PI firm there and he has a position for me."

He nodded. "Heard of him."

"I was heading up I-71 and saw the sign pointing to Monticello. I hadn't even been thinking about it. I drove in on an impulse and decided to stay a while. That was Monday evening. Wednesday I called on Lew Czuk. We were pretty close in the old days. And I talked to Sister Margaret Michael at the convent. I planned on looking up a lot of my old friends and acquaintances, take it easy for a few weeks, then go on to Cleveland."

"And one of these old friends was the lady you spent the night with?"

"I could tell you I met her in a bar yesterday, but I won't."

"Just as well, because I wouldn't believe you. Men don't stick their necks out for bar pickups."

My eyes went back to the bashed-in canister thing on the desktop. I touched it with my fingertip. "That's the magazine for the old Thompson, isn't it?"

He looked at it, gimlet-eyed. "That's right. You heard about the robbery in '65?"

"It made the news in California. We were sorry to hear about your father. My father was awfully upset about Raymond Purvis. They'd worked in the same office for years."

"Dad shouldn't've even been out there that day. It was a deputy's job. But there were only three deputies back then, and there was a big flu epidemic, and all three of them were down with it. And, hell, Dad just liked to get out with that Thompson. There were four robbers out at the plant. The company driver tried to get away but they shot him. Dad got out of the car and he got two of them with the Thompson. But one of them scored a lucky hit on that magazine and jammed it. Then the two still on their feet killed Dad and Purvis. They got away with the payroll. Never been caught, though I've never given up hope."

I didn't have to tell him how remote that possibility was. "Who were the two killed?"

"One was Jarvis Skinner. The other was a small-timer named Stanley Kincaid. He'd done time with Jarvis in the state pen. No history of violent crime but I guess he was working his way up." He got up. "All right, I guess you can go now. I'm going to have a busy time of it, the next few days."

"I'd still like to help."

"Gabe, I want you to go back to your place and stay there and don't go messing in any of this. You're still a potential suspect. And I don't want you telling Lew Czuk or Sharon Newell about what you saw in that house. I think Lester was a fool to take you in there but he's probably playing some game of his own. He usually is."

How he expected to keep things quiet after half the city and county cops had tramped all through the house I couldn't imagine, but I wasn't going to argue with him in his own office. I got up and shook hands with him and went out through the outer office. All the desks were full now and the phones were all ringing at once. The workers all looked me over as I left. There were reporters in the corridor outside, but I pushed my way through them and got out of the courthouse intact.

I was worn out, but I didn't want to go back to my room just yet. The police would be all over the grounds for the rest of the day. While I was trying to decide what to do, a stretch limo pulled up to the curb a few yards away and the cameras converged on it. A passenger door opened and a man got out: white male, five-eleven, one-seventy-five, brown and blue, impeccably tailored in a cream silk suit, three-piece with a Phi Beta Kappa key. I knew the face from the papers I'd been studying. Ted Rapley, ambitious state prosecutor, had arrived.

I couldn't hear what he was saying to the press and I wasn't interested. It would be on the evening news, anyway. I caught him glancing my way, giving me the once-over without breaking the pattern of his speech. He only needed a second to dismiss me as someone of no importance.

I walked down to the cafe across from the old newsstand and had breakfast. That made me feel a little better. As I left, I rubbed a hand over my bristly chin. I still didn't want to go back to my apartment, but I needed a shave. My chin whiskers had been going gray, and nothing makes you look like an old wino more than a silver stubble. I couldn't afford to look seedy just then, so I treated myself to my first barbershop shave in years.

I was feeling almost human when I left the barbershop. I hadn't even had time to decide which way to turn when a car pulled up in front of me and the passenger door opened.

"Climb in, Gabe," Chief of Police, Lester Cabell said. I knew I'd just have to get used to it.

I climbed in. "Your office for a questioning?" I said as he pulled away from the curb.

"No, I just want to socialize." He went around the block and turned south on Main. "Did we ever run around together as kids? If we did I don't remember, and my memory's pretty good for such things."

"No, we didn't," I said. "I was at St. Anne's, you were at the public school."

"That's right," he said. "We didn't run around with you mackerel snappers much." He grinned when he said it, to show he was just kidding. The grin didn't help and I didn't think he really meant for it to.

"Where are we going?" I asked him. We crossed the river and he turned east up the curving river road.

"Skinnertown: Monticello's own third world. Out in Los Angeles you have your Mexicans and your niggers and your Vietnamese and whatnot. I, for my sins, have Skinners. You know much about 'em?"

"Just that we weren't supposed to have anything to do with them when I was a kid."

"Wise advice. They came up here not long after the town was chartered. They still have kinfolk all over West Virginia and Tennessee. In the 1840s they were horse thieves. They were bootleggers in the twenties. During World War Two they ran counterfeit ration tickets. This generation grows pot and deals coke. The men are mostly bikers and the women mostly hook. Been in this town a hundred and fifty years and they're still hillbillies. I guess every town has a family like the Skinners."

"It keeps things simple," I said. "Are you going to round up the usual suspects?"

"Just going to let 'em know I'm thinking of 'em. They wouldn't understand if I didn't. This sort of keeps the world on an even keel."

He turned onto a dirt road that ran down to the riverside. We began to pass the shacks and trailers that straggled along the bottom land. The weedy yards held about equal numbers of unkempt children and rangy dogs. We pulled up in front of the most substantial house in the area; a frame structure with real shingles on the roof instead of tar paper. It looked as if it had been painted within the last seven or eight years. About fifty yards away, next to the bank that sloped up toward the river road, was the old Airstream I'd seen on my morning run the day before. It was hard to believe it had been only twenty-four hours ago.

"Welcome to Maison Skinner," Cabell said. "This is Earl Skinner's place. He's paterfamilias of the clan."

"What do they do here when the river floods?"

"They get wet. Then they collect state and federal money. I honestly don't know why Earl never got a teaching job over at the college in the economics department. He knows more about the welfare system than any professor they have."

As we climbed out of the car, people were leaving the shacks and trailers or standing out on porches, watching us warily. A woman stepped out of the Airstream. About five-four, with striking red hair, she had a physical address that caught my eye. She stood at the bottom of the steps with an easy, relaxed alertness; weight on her left leg, the right bent, the ball of that foot just behind the heel of the other, arms at her sides, an inch or two clear of her hips. She could have been modeling for a Classical sculptor. I guessed sports, gymnastics, maybe ballet or modern dance training. She had a sort of classy-trashy look that's hard to describe, except to say she looked like she rated better than her surroundings, but not all that much.

A big man came out of the house, with a slatternly, used-up-looking woman behind him. He was easily as big as Cabell, square-built with a big pot gut and the sort of blunt, heavily scarred hands you often see on mechanics. Bald and clean-shaven, he moved very slowly, as if he'd made a lot of wrong moves in his life and age had made him careful.

"Good morning, Earl," Cabell said, all false joviality. "Fine morning, isn't it?"

"So far," Skinner said. A younger replica of Earl came out of the house, bearded, wearing biker drag: leather vest, Harley-Davidson logo T-shirt, Levi's, boots, one of those biker wallets that are connected to a beltloop by a short chrome chain, a snap-top pouch for a heavy folding knife on the belt. He didn't pay much attention to Cabell, who must have been one of the more familiar sights in his world, but he gave me a long, careful study with his piggy, little blue eyes.

"I guess you heard about what happened in town last night," Cabell said.

"I heard some woman got killed. That's all I know about it." Earl spoke with a heavy mountain twang, hardly a trace of central Ohio in it.

"Her name was Edna Tutt, lived on the corner of Maple and Wright. She was worked over for a long time before she died."

"Sorry to hear it, but I never heard of the woman." His face stayed flat and impassive, but that meant nothing.

"Would you happen to have a soldering iron, Earl?" Cabell asked, smiling.

"Probly half a dozen around here. Why?"

"Whoever did what was done to Edna Tutt had a fondness for soldering irons."

"Then you'd best look for it in the river," Earl deadpanned.

"I suppose that's correct. Any experienced felon knows enough to ditch the evidence." He looked at the younger Skinner. "Why, hello, Jesse. How does freedom agree with you?"

"Suits me fine," Jesse said, glaring. He hadn't learned to control his expression like Earl. "Who's he?" He nodded in my direction.

"Well, where's my manners? Folks, this is my friend Mr. Treloar, formerly of the Los Angeles Police Department. He's generously volunteered to assist me on this case. Gabe, this is Earl Skinner, his wife Lou, and their youngest son, Jesse." Nobody stuck out a hand, nodded, or acknowledged me in any fashion. I saw that more of the community had drifted closer. The men all had a strong family resemblance and the younger ones affected biker fashion. The women mostly shared a weathered, abused look. The ones in their twenties could as easily have been in their forties.

The redhead was a vivid contrast. I caught her studying me from a few feet away. I hadn't seen her approach, but she stood in that same statuesque pose. From this close I saw that her face was dominated by large eyes, startlingly brown. They were cool and detached, but her full-lipped, pouty mouth robbed her face of class and put her more in harmony with her surroundings. Her shorts and halter top left a lot of dead-white skin bare. At least she didn't have any tattoos showing.

"We don't know yet what the killers wanted," Cabell announced to the tribe at large, "but we'll be looking for anything taken from that house. If anything turns up here, if any of you hear anything, you'd better come to me with it, pronto. Believe me, you don't want me to come looking for you."

"You accusin' anyone here of anything, Chief?" Earl said.

"We didn't apprehend anyone red-handed, Earl, so I'm not putting out any accusations yet. But we have a real splashy murder here, and there's a state's attorney in town with a real hard-on for the death penalty. I find out anyone's hiding anything, some real hurt's gonna come down. You understand?"

"I got you, Chief," Earl said. "But nobody here's gonna be mixed up in anything like that."

"Why I know you wouldn't, Earl," Cabell said, grinning at Jesse and the rest, "but you know what this younger generation is like. They weren't brought up to be gentlemen the way we were." He turned slowly, his hand resting on the butt of his .45.

He carried it like an expert, with a round in the chamber, the hammer cocked and the thumb safety set, what the aficionados call condition one. A trained man can get off a shot in less than a tenth of a second from that carry. I suspected that Cabell practiced a lot.

He finished his full turn. "I'll be seeing you, Earl." He got back into the car and I got in beside him. He started up, put it in gear and made a wide, dog-scattering circle, heading back toward the river road.

"Aren't they a bunch of sweethearts, though?" he chuckled.

"Who's the redhead?"

"Noticed her, eh? That's Ann Smyth; Ann with no E, Smyth with a Y. She's Mel Skinner's woman. Mel's doing a little stretch for possession with intent to sell. He found her somewhere down where the Skinners find their women. Tennessee, I think. Isn't she a hot little piece?" He grinned and winked. I've always detested men who wink.

"What does she do? Aside from pining away for the absent Mel?"

"She strips at the Lido."

I almost gaped at him. "Monticello has a strip joint?"

"Even this town feels the hand of progress. It's over near Granville, catches a lot of the college trade. Of course, there's nothing very sophisticated about the art of striptease as practiced at the Lido. Mostly the girls come out in short little dresses and get out of them quick. Then they shake their tits and ass to a lot of loud jungle music. Little Ann's better than most. She tries to actually dance a little." He caught my look and winked again. "Got to keep an eye on these sleazy places. One of the onerous duties of the job."

"Chief . . ."

"Call me Lester. Everybody does. Except for Skinners."

"Lester, what do you know about Edna Tutt?"

"Somehow I'm not surprised you asked that. Truth to tell, hardly anything. She was a quiet woman, never caused anyone any trouble, paid her bills and taxes. I looked into her records a bit this morning. She never even had a parking ticket, never kept a dog, never had a complaint filed against her. That's a lot of nevers, but there you are."

Almost exactly what Mark Fowles had said. "She was an unperson. Doesn't that seem strange?"

"Maybe in California, not here. There must be three or four thousand people in this town exactly like her. People are left alone here, as long as they don't cause trouble."

"Where did she come here from?"

"I don't know and she was probably never asked. Fact is, you don't need a passport to change residence in this country."

"But if she applied for an Ohio driver's permit, she would've noted her last state of residence."

His eyes went wide and his mouth dropped open in mock surprise. "Why, glory be! A small-town cop like me never would've thought of a thing like that! I just knew you were gonna be a big help."

I could feel my face coloring. "Hell, I didn't mean . . ."

He laughed and slapped my knee, making a joke of it. "Just kidding. I've already started the wheels on that, but we're talking about twenty-five or more years ago. I've notified the bank where she had her charge and savings accounts to see what they can find in her records. We're looking over the papers in her house, to see where she got mail from, but you know what? I'll bet we don't find a damn thing anywhere."

"Why do you say that?"

He took out one of his cigars and fired it up, all one-handed. He spoke almost pensively as he drove. "Sometimes, someone has a bad experience, a bad marriage they want to get away from, something like that, they'll just pull up stakes, go to a place where they're not known, and start a new life. It's easy to do in this country. I've got a feeling Edna Tutt was like that. As far as she was concerned, her life started the day she moved to Monticello. If she made a clean break with her past, we may never know who she was. She was just a lady who grew her flowers and never harmed anyone."

He pulled up in front of the courthouse and let me out. "I'll be in touch, Gabe. Let me know before you plan on going any-where."

"Thanks for the ride," I told him. He grinned and waggled his cigar at me, then pulled away. The crowd of reporters was gone. The street looked as quiet as usual. I thought about the little episode, about how he had watched me when he said we were going to Skinnertown, how he had scanned the Skinners while we were there. Probably looking for a reaction from me and from them. I didn't like him, but he seemed to have good cop instincts.

I walked across the street and into the Times-Tribune build-ing. There was a serious-looking, bespectacled young man at the reception desk this morning. The name tag on the desk identified him as Morley Gerber. "May I help you?"

"Is Lew in?"

"He went out to cover the big murder story earlier today. May I take a message?"

"I'm a friend, Gabe Treloar. He'll want to see me."

He looked doubtful. "Well, this time of day he usually has lunch at the Cove. You might try . . ."

"Thanks," I said, already out the door. One advantage of a town like Monticello is that you can get almost anyplace by walking no more than ten minutes. It took me only five to reach the Cove and I found Lew at the same table as before. He looked happy to see me.

"Gabe! I've been trying to find you. Sit down, sit down." He gestured a waitress over to us. "Helen, take Mr. Treloar's order, put it on my tab." It hadn't been that long since breakfast so I ordered a fruit plate, just to have something to occupy my hands.

"What can you tell me, Gabe?" he said eagerly when the waitress was gone.

"The chief and the sheriff both told me to keep my mouth shut," I told him. "How much do you know already?"

"I know that sometime last night Edna Tutt was murdered. Sharon snagged Thad Selner—he's one of the county depu-ties—when he staggered out of the house and ran back to the bushes to throw up. Between heaves he just babbled. Is it true she was tortured and cut open? 'Gutted like a goddamn catfish' was Thad's phrase."

"It's true."

"My God!"

"Come on, Lew. You must have seen worse in Miami."

"Sure, but that was Miami. Things like that just don't happen here. We're a long way from drug wars and we've never had a psychotic murderer before. Do you know if she was raped?"

"That'll take a lab report. The coroner on the spot looked like he knew what he was doing, but forensics can take weeks. They don't like to be rushed."

"They'll rush if Ted Rapley wants them to," Lew said.

"I saw him in front of the courthouse when I left Mark Fowles's office. Looks like a slick piece of work."

"He is. I talked to him an hour ago and he scents blood, to coin a phrase. I think he wants to ride this one."

"Lester Cabell was saying as much to the Skinners this morning."

"You've been getting around."

So I told him about my experiences of the last twenty-four hours, not being very specific about the hours just before I came back to find the chaos at Edna's house.

Lew let out a long breath at the end of it, reaching for his martini. "You're playing an awfully dangerous game, Gabe, covering for Lola when you're practically a suspect."

"I never mentioned that name," I said.

"Neither will I, but let's be grownups here. A teenage crush is one thing. You're going way out on a limb for a woman who hasn't given you a thought in decades."

I didn't like that, but he was right. "No big risk. Is Ted Rapley going to want his intended's name all over this? Would that make Ansel Cohan happy?"

"Lord, this is complicated, isn't it? Okay, Ted and Ansel may want to keep that quiet, and Lester will do whatever they tell him to, but not Mark Fowles."

"Why is he different?"

"You've seen what an uptight, straight-arrow he is. He was an easygoing kid, but that all changed when his father was killed. He's a deacon of his church and he thinks the Cohans and their tame police chief are the center of corruption in his clean county."

"Why is that?"

"Local politics, suspected fiscal irregularities on the part of Cohan Chemical, a lot of things. But a fireplug is the soul of loquacity compared to Mark. I think he's biding his time, collecting evidence."

"What's happened to Cohan political control?" I asked him. "Why haven't they had him ousted?"

"The voters are happy with him and they've never been able to dig up a thing on him, although they've tried. And he's never attacked them openly, so they have to leave well enough alone."

"Maybe they'll cancel each other out on this," I said. "Lew, I want to find Edna's killer, or killers. She was a good woman. I liked her. And I'm still a cop, in spite of everything."

His eyes were owlish behind his glasses. "You just can't stop asking for trouble, can you, Gabe?" He paused and took a sip from his glass. "Okay. I'm with you."

I smiled, really smiled, for the first time that day. "Great! I need everything you can find about Edna Tutt, from the time she showed up in Monticello. Before that, if you can."

"I'm already working on that; background for the story and its follow-ups. But why? You don't think it was something random or spontaneous?"

I sorted through my own feelings and instincts. "Something just doesn't feel right. I knew her for three days, but I felt like I'd known her a long time. She was a warm person with an open disposition, but she seems to have had no friends. There was a sadness in her that got to me. I kept thinking I'd seen her before, but for the life of me I couldn't call up a real memory. And there are some things about her murder that are way off base for something spontaneous."

"Things besides what you told Mark and Lester?"

"Uh-huh. But this is strictly between us, right?"

"You think I'm going to quote you? I couldn't even call you a reliable source."

"Okay, okay, I just want it understood."

"Understood. So tell me."

The waitress brought my fruit plate and poured me a black coffee while I collected my thoughts. When she was safely out of earshot, I began.

"Lew, they didn't touch her face."

He was quiet for a few seconds. "Go on."

"Remember Injun Joe in *Tom Sawyer?*" When we were around twelve we'd gone through a Mark Twain phase, reading *Tom Sawyer* and *Huckleberry Finn,* whittling corncob pipes. We'd even built a makeshift raft and somehow managed not to drown ourselves in the river.

He thought about it for a minute. "He slit women's noses, didn't he? And notched their ears?"

"Right. And Twain knew what he was talking about. Edna was tortured at least partially to tell where something was hidden. The place was ransacked. Now, when you torture a man to make him talk, and you want him to talk fast, you go for his balls. There's no way you can cause him any greater pain, plus there's the psychological torment of knowing his manhood is being destroyed.

"With a woman it's a little different. Attacking the face causes tremendous pain. The nerve endings are most densely packed in the fingertips and the face. And women fear facial disfigurement more than men. Knowing their looks are being wrecked is a special trauma."

He looked pretty shaky. "This is rough stuff, Gabe. And now you've got me confused. We have cold-blooded torture, maniacal evisceration, what looks like an attempted robbery, and Edna's face was left untouched. What's it mean?"

"If I knew that I'd go to Mark Fowles with it and he'd bust somebody. The torture may have been primarily to force Edna to talk, but the way she was mutilated after she died looks like revenge. I think we're dealing with two men, and they're both torturers and murderers and they had two different motives. And to one, if not both of them, Edna's face had special significance."

He promised to search all the files he had access to to learn what he could about Edna's history. I'd investigate my own way and we'd pool information. By the end of it he was getting a little animated, like he was recapturing some of the old young-reporter spirit. He didn't even order another martini.

From the Cove I walked back up to my rented garage apartment. The police cars were gone, but not the cameras. There was a crew standing around, talking and smoking, but not shooting anything. Then I saw the three men standing by the back yard fence.

Lester Cabell saw me first, said something and nodded in my direction. Ted Rapley and Ansel Cohan turned to look at me. It was hard to tell whether Rapley or Cohan was the better-dressed. As I walked up to them, Rapley took a step forward and shook hands. The camera crew looked uncertain whether to start shooting.

"Mr. Treloar, Chief Fowles has told us that you've been a help to him in this case." He wasn't exactly gladhanding it, but he didn't seem hostile.

"Yes," Ansel said. "I've, er, recommended that he allow you to assist in any way you can." Ansel looked upset and distracted. "I didn't know Miss Tutt very well, but it's . . . it's horrifying to have something like this happen almost in my back yard. When I heard about it . . ."

"We'll catch whoever's responsible, Mr. Cohan," Cabell said, cutting him off. Rapley put a hand on Ansel's shoulder.

"You know Chief Cabell always means what he says, Ansel. And I'm sure Mr. Treloar has dealt with many such cases."

I looked over the back yard. Edna's beautifully tended garden looked as if an army had marched over it. There were cigarette butts and scraps of paper all over. While I watched, a punk-haired cameraman, apparently with nothing better to do, went in and got some footage of the flower carnage. Satisfied, he took the dangling butt out of his mouth, dropped it and ground it out on the once-immaculate walk. He looked up, caught me glaring at him and looked around as if to see if I really meant someone else. Didn't have a clue.

"I want to help," I said to Rapley, the line already sounding old to my ears. "I didn't know her long, but she befriended me.

I feel if I'd been here, maybe it wouldn't have happened." I waited for him to ask why I hadn't been there, but he didn't.

"People always feel that way after something terrible happens. But it's past and can't be undone. Now we have to apprehend the killers." He fixed me with a practiced, steely stare. "I want to see arrests in this case, and I will seek an indictment against the felon or felons, I will prosecute and convict, and I will demand the death penalty, if I have to get an amendment to the state constitution to do it." I knew I could tune in the evening news and hear him reciting the identical words to the cameras.

"Ted, those men are as good as dead," Cabell assured him.

"Yes, ah, Chief," Ansel said, still stumbling a little but recovering smoothly. "We want these people caught without delay. Anything you need in the way of funds, equipment or manpower, come to me. I'll see that you get it."

"I appreciate your help, Mr. Cohan."

Rapley glanced at his Rolex. "I have to go now. Come with me, Ansel?" Ansel nodded and Rapley stuck his hand out to me again. "I'm glad we had a chance to meet, Mr. Treloar. I hope to hear from you soon."

"Doubtless you will," I said. He and Ansel got into his limo. Cabell threw me a sardonic salute and got into his city car. When they were gone, the camera crews packed up and left. Abruptly, eerily, the place was as quiet as it had been the day I came in to rent the room. It looked almost the same, too, except for the trampling and the crime-scene tape everywhere.

I went up the stairs and let myself into the apartment. It looked almost as bad as Edna's house had. Drawers had been opened, things overturned, my mattress slit open. I knew it would be the same story in the garage downstairs. They had been searching in here, too. No crime-scene tape. The police hadn't thought to look in here. I shook my head, disgusted. Small towns. For all they knew, the killers were hiding in here, watching them. Unlikely, it's true, but I've known criminals to do dumber things.

I took a couple of hours to get the little apartment back in shape, then bagged up my laundry and drove to a laundromat. I wanted to go back into Edna's house for a careful look, but that was going to have to wait until late one night. I didn't want Lester Cabell breathing down my collar while I was doing it.

The sun was getting low when I got back. I'd been through an emotionally exhausting day with almost no sleep, but I knew I wasn't going to be able to sleep for a while. So I pulled on a set of sweats and my running shoes and went out. I ran without any aim, just jogging down streets, turning corners or doubling back, breaking into sprints on flat stretches.

After twenty minutes I broke into a heavy sweat. Coming to a low hill, I turned around and backpedaled until my thigh muscles began sending out serious distress signals. I went forward again, my body getting loose, my lungs working hard, flooding my blood with oxygen, sending it rushing to my brain.

A long time ago I'd learned that this was a good way to get the mind working when it was overloaded. I felt like a boxer who got overmatched and took too many hard punches to the head. It helped to clear away some of the fog and get things lined out, but there were still too many missing connections for anything to make much sense. I knew sleep would help. So would time. Sometimes, you just have to let go, allow your subconscious to work on problems, back there in the primitive parts of the brain where insight and mystery and religious enlightenment dwell.

It was fully dark when I trudged back up my stairs. I was sopping wet, more exhausted than I could remember being in years. I'd skipped dinner and hadn't missed it. All I wanted now was to shower, collapse into bed and sleep about ten hours.

But it turned out that the long, long day wasn't over yet. I opened the door, went in, closed it behind me, and I knew there was someone else inside. I went very still. By blind instinct my hand slowly moved toward the gun I no longer wore, then stopped. I tried to picture the place in my mind, where there might be something I could grab as a weapon. Then the light by the bed went on.

"Hello, Mr. Treloar." It was Sharon Newell. She sat on the bed, her back propped against the headboard, shoes off, black-stockinged feet crossed on the spread. She had a pad in one hand. The other was still on the light switch.

I stepped over to the chair and collapsed into it. "You dumb twit," I said, too tired for real anger. "I might've brained you with a tire iron."

"You have to take the risks to get the stories," she said, stretching her red lips back in that tooth-baring smile. She was wearing a dark-blue suit with a tight skirt, the jacket's shoulders lightly padded. Her white blouse was buttoned up to her neck, with a fall of lace cascading from that full, white throat over an outstanding bosom. "Besides, I just knew when I saw you that you're a man who keeps himself under tight control."

"If you thought that," I said, picking up a towel from my pile of clean laundry and mopping my face, "then what you know about men can be engraved on the head of a pin in letters a foot high."

"Oh, come on, you needn't be so modest. Give me points for initiative."

"How did you get in?" I was still mopping.

"Old-fashioned locks like that are easy. I used my gold card."

"It's late, Miss Newell."

"Call me Sharon. I've found that fatigue lowers the natural resistance to questioning." She picked up a gleaming Cross pen. It rested in the nest of her two-inch nails like a stick insect in the jaws of a Venus flytrap.

"You can go ahead and take a shower if you want, but I wish you wouldn't. You're going to smell just yummy for the next couple of hours." Now she smiled with her lips closed, a look ripe with insinuation. "I know more about men than you suspect."

"Why don't you get out of here, Sharon?" I said, my voice leaden.

"It's not all that bad an experience, coming home and finding a strange woman in your bed." Her face was white and powdered even whiter. It made her black eyes glitter in their almond frames of artfully applied cosmetics.

"Right now, I'm not interested in any woman, in my bed or out of it."

"Yes, tell me about you and Lola Cohan."

"You know, Lew could fire you for listening in on the intercom like that."

"Who needs to eavesdrop? You two were seen at the Lodge Wednesday night. Rumor links socialite Lola Cohan with rising State Prosecutor Ted Rapley. Who is the mystery man squiring the heiress around after a thirty-year absence? Sharon scents a story." She inhaled deeply through her long, elegantly arched nose.

"We're old friends," I said.

"To say the least." She wiggled her bottom, making the bedsprings squeak. "You weren't in *this* bed last night, when ghastly events were taking place next door."

"Sharon, I've put up with you this long because Lew is my oldest friend. Don't try me."

She leaned forward, letting her lower lip drop a little as she spoke. "I'm not kidding, Gabe. I smell a story here and I intend to ride it onto a major paper the way Ted Rapley is going to ride it into the Governor's Mansion, and I don't intend to come back here the way Lew did. I've lived all my life in Monticello and I know all about the ugly little things that tunnel beneath the well-tended lawns and gardens here. Just yank up a piece of turf and you'll see things you never dreamed of wiggling away from the light."

She got out of the bed smoothly, swiveling on her butt, placing her feet into her shoes without looking, standing all in one motion. There wasn't a wrinkle on the suit that wrapped her compact, lush body. Not a strand was out of place in the tight bubble of dark hair. She stepped close.

"And you haven't had enough of me yet. You haven't had a bit of me yet." She picked up her shoulder bag with one hand. With the other, she drew a long forefinger nail along the top of my collarbone and came away with a drop of sweat. She touched it to her tongue. " 'Night, Gabe." She turned and walked to the door, opened it and left.

When I got out of the shower, dried off, and collapsed onto the bed I could smell her perfume, and it was still warm from contact with her body.

8

The first thing I did the next morning was go out and buy a heavy-duty broom. Then I started cleaning up the walks crossing Edna Tutt's garden. I went all over the garden and lawns, picking up cigarette butts like an Army recruit. I thought about trimming off the broken branches from the hedges, but I wasn't sure how to do it and I was afraid I might kill them instead.

I didn't know what to do about the trampled flowers, but I didn't have to puzzle over them long. A station wagon pulled up and three women got out. They ranged in age from around fifty to sixty, all of them dressed in work pants and shirts and sun hats. Two came over to the fence while one, a squat, sixty-ish woman with her hair in a bun, unloaded boxes through the tailgate.

A tall woman of about fifty looked over the garden. "Oh, this is awful!" Then she saw me. "Well, I'm glad somebody is straightening up."

I walked over to them and introduced myself. They eyed me a little suspiciously. I was a stranger, after all, and Edna had died violently.

"I'm Muriel Todd," the tall one said. "This is Nancy Luce," that one was small and spare, around sixty, with iron-gray hair, tightly curled, "and Cora Lee," the squat one. "We're with the Monticello Flower and Garden Society. We were so shocked about what happened to Edna, but we felt we ought to do something about her garden. It meant so much to her, and look at what those people did!" She looked it over like a civilian seeing his first battlefield.

"That's a lovely thought," I said. "I've done what I could. I know how she would've felt about all those cigarette butts. But I know nothing at all about flowers."

"I don't know," the thin woman said, doubtfully. "Lester Cabell might not like us tampering with the scene."

"Lester Cabell can go piss up a rope," said the squat woman, barging through the gate with a basket full of tools. "I never liked him anyway, and if he doesn't catch that killer quick the town should fire him."

"Cora!" Muriel said. Then, to me: "Are you any relation to the Treloars who used to live here?"

"My parents were Edward and Brigid Treloar."

"I thought so. It's such an uncommon name. Your mother used to come to our house on Wednesday evenings for bridge. My mother was president of the bridge club."

"You're Muriel Zinn?" More memories floated up from wherever they had lain.

"That's right," she said, smiling. "We lived two blocks down on Poplar, the old Jamison house."

"You left for college about the time we moved to this house. I remember your parents coming here for dinner a few times."

"It's so unfortunate you came back for a visit just when this happened." She pulled on her gardening gloves, looking at the house as if she couldn't believe such a familiar sight was the scene for events so grotesque. It was an understandable reaction. The other two were already on their knees, pulling up ruined plants with ruthless efficiency.

"We can save some," said Nancy Luce, the thin one. "Replace others. It's late in the summer, but we can get it into some sort of shape. I know Edna would have wanted it." Her voice was conversational, but tears ran down her wrinkled cheeks.

"How long did you know Edna?" I asked, addressing the group at large.

"Let's see," Nancy said, not faltering in her uprooting rhythm as she spoke, "I guess Edna joined the Society around '68 or '69. She didn't know a thing about gardening then, and she wanted to do something with this yard. The old apple tree there," she pointed with her trowel at the pedestal, "was dead. We cut it down and dug up the roots and helped her landscape this place. She was a real natural when it came to gardening. Lord, her peonies this spring were marvelous." She sniffed and blotted at her face with the back of her glove.

"Was Edna ever married?" I asked. "Any children?"

"She never said," Muriel told me. "Edna didn't socialize much, though she was friendly and everyone liked her. She was a very private person. I never knew her to go out with a man. That seemed odd, she was such a pretty woman, but she seemed satisfied to stay single."

"I always had the impression she'd had an unhappy relationship and swore off men," Nancy said. "Nothing definite, just an attitude she had. And why not? She was independent, she didn't really need a husband. She had her house and her garden. It seemed to be enough for her."

"Husbands are an overrated commodity, if you ask me," the toadlike Cora put in. She straightened and sat back on her heels, nodding toward the bronze goddess. "I remember it caused a neighborhood scandal when Edna set that oversized frog in the middle of her garden. Van Rijn—he was the Dutch Reformed minister—came up to her right in this garden while we were helping her set out some new rose bushes, and he said that frog would corrupt public morals. You know what she said? She said, 'People have to look at you every day. Who wouldn't rather see a beautiful, naked woman than an ugly, clothed man?'"

The others laughed softly. "She was so quiet, but she wouldn't be pushed around," Muriel said.

They worked like a well-drilled team and I helped out where I could. They tolerated me and got over their initial reserve. I think being a native helped. If I'd been a total stranger, they would have been sure I was the murderer. Muriel made a list of plants that could be replaced. It was too late in the year to set out any new flowers, she said, but they would all contribute flowering plants from their own gardens. Apparently this was a difficult task and they discussed the logistics like military tacticians.

I let them know I was an ex-officer, helping the police with the investigation. That made my questions about Edna less suspicion-raising, but they thought it strange that I was concentrating on her rather than the killer.

"Do you think it could have been someone she knew?" Nancy asked.

"It usually is," I told her.

"Oh, that may be true in Los Angeles, but people aren't like that here," Muriel said, earnestly.

"Edna surely never associated with any of the town riffraff," Cora asserted, "those people who hang out at the bars and pool places on the other side of the river."

"She used to take trips once in a while," Muriel said. She looked at me. "Do you think she might have become involved with somebody somewhere else and he followed her here?"

"It's possible," I said. "Where did she go?"

"She'd take little vacations," Muriel said, "just a few days at a time. She mentioned Chicago, Boston, Knoxville, places like that. She went to flower shows, garden tours. She loved to prowl flea markets and antique fairs. That's where she picked up all those little frogs and the Deco pieces she was so fond of."

"It's something to look into." We talked a while longer but I'd reached a dead end. It was the same story: These women, who had known Edna for so many years and had shared something close to her heart, knew nothing about her past or her private life. I cast around for possible sources.

"Do you know where Edna had her hair done?" I asked them.

"The Emerald Beauty Room," Cora said. "It's on West Central, across from the post office. Ask for Sue. She owns the place now. She always did Edna's hair."

Muriel looked up from her note pad and smiled, her eyes still sad. "Women always talk to their hairdressers, is that it?"

"It's worth a try," I said.

A little while later they left to haul off the dead plants and fetch the ones they were going to transplant. The garden was looking better. The bare spots were forlorn, but at least it was tidy. I put up my broom and gave the house a long look, deciding I'd go in that night. I walked all around the place, getting the last of the cigarette butts, looking at all the doors and windows. A set of storm doors gave access to the cellar, closed by a hasp and secured by a padlock that was rusted solid. Getting in would be no problem. As Sharon had noted, the old locks were a joke.

I drove out of town on the Mansfield road, looking for a place to have lunch where I wouldn't run into anyone I knew. I found a little roadside restaurant and picked up copies of the *Times-Tribune* and the Columbus paper. Over coffee and a BLT with french fries, I studied the articles on the murder.

The Columbus article featured a large photo of Ted Rapley in front of Edna's house, looking stern. The article, next to one on the latest Serbian atrocities, was headlined: *Horror in Monticello.*

The text began about as I would have expected: *The sleepy rural Ohio town of Monticello was visited by horror in the early hours of Friday morning when resident Edna Tutt was tortured and slain by an unknown assailant or assailants. Details of the murder are being kept confidential by police for purposes of investigation, but unconfirmed reports indicate bizarre circumstances. In answer to questions whether evidence of ritual or cult-like murder had been found, Monticello Chief of Police Lester Cabell would say only: "We have no comment on that at this time." County Sheriff Mark Fowles indicated that a break in the case was expected momentarily. State Prosecutor Ted Rapley, who reached the crime scene late Friday morning said: "I want to see arrests in this case, and I will seek an indictment against the felon or felons, I will prosecute and convict, and I will demand the death penalty, if I have to get an amendment to the state constitution to do it."*

I just had to smile at that. It went on: *Tutt, 57, had been a Monticello resident for more than twenty-five years. Noted for her beautiful garden and her many prizes at fairs and flower shows, her bizarre slaying came as a total shock to friends and neighbors.* There followed the usual quotes from neighbors: *"I just don't understand it!"*, *"She was such a quiet person. Who would have thought this would happen?"*, *"How could something like this happen here?"*, all the inane things people say when the Martians show up and blast their little community to smoking ruins.

There was no mention of me, and no mention of the Cohans, no pictures of Ansel, even though he'd been there that morning with Rapley and Cabell. Strapped for copy, the paper ran accounts of similar crimes in other parts of the country. If I'd taken newspaper reports seriously, it might have added to my confusion.

Fifty-seven. Edna had been a little older than I'd judged, but then she'd kept herself in terrific shape and seemed to have no bad habits at all, so that wasn't so surprising.

Sharon Newell's article in the *Times-Tribune* was more inclusive, with more quotes from neighbors, a little more background on Edna, not that it amounted to much, and a respectful account of Ted Rapley's string of successful convictions. She dropped lots of hints about inside tips and upcoming, shocking breaks in the story. She had style, I was forced to admit it.

I drove back to town and parked on West Central. The Emerald Beauty Room was situated between an antique shop and a tea room that offered palm and tea leaf readings. As I went in, a young woman was seeing an older one out the door.

"I have you in for the twenty-ninth at one, Mrs. Dawson," the girl said. She was pretty and blond and couldn't have been more than nineteen. She smiled brightly at me. "May I help you?"

I stepped through the door and was hit by that powerful, ammoniac, beauty salon odor that women never seem to notice. "My name is Gabe Treloar," I said. "Are you Sue?"

A woman came from a room in the rear. "I'm Sue Olden-burg." Her brown eyes were red-rimmed beneath straight, dark brows. "I've been sort of expecting you." That threw me. She turned to the younger one. "Tina, we don't have any more appointments today. You can go on."

The girl looked concerned. "Are you sure you're going to be all right?"

"I'll be fine. Mr. Treloar and I have some things to talk about."

"Okay, then. See you Monday morning." She looked at me doubtfully, then went out and closed the door behind her.

Sue Oldenburg went to the door and locked it, turning the open/closed sign around and pulling down the shade. Then she turned again and faced me. "Come on in back."

I followed her past the chairs, mirrors, and sink into a little room equipped with a desk and chairs, a small table with a coffee machine, a microwave oven and a tabletop refrigerator. The walls were lined with shelves holding beauty shop supplies. She looked me over frankly as she took a cigarette pack off the desk and shook one out.

She was in her mid-forties somewhere, medium-tall, dressed in a white smock over white pants and blouse. Her hair was oddly coarse, almost bushy, and fell to her shoulders in crisp, tight, little waves. With her dark eyes, heavy brows, and olive skin she might have been Latin, but the wide cheekbones suggested an Indian ancestor, some Cherokee or Potowatamie, who had hidden out and avoided the Trail of Tears. Her front teeth pushed out a little at her upper lip, so that she needed a little effort to keep them covered. It was a good, strong face but at the moment it wasn't friendly.

She lit her cigarette and sat, toeing her shoes off and putting her feet up on a stool. Beauticians have chronic foot pains. She waved to another chair and I sat. She blew out a long stream of smoke.

"Who are you, Mr. Treloar?" Her eyes were hard, calculating, and intelligent. They were also red from what looked like hours of weeping, but that didn't weaken them any.

So I went into the story again, telling as much as I could, leaving out what I judged best to keep to myself. She listened and nodded. I wound up with: "The garden club ladies said you were Edna's hairdresser. What can you tell me about Edna?"

She looked at me for a long, uncomfortable time, smoking her cigarette. Then: "Okay, I'll buy it for now. What do you need to know?"

"Tell me how and when you met Edna."

She raised her eyes, looking at the ceiling. "I've known her—knew her, I guess I should say, longer than anyone in town, because I met her the day she came to town. That was in '66. I was just starting here, had the same job Tina has now, when Emerald Reedy still owned the place.

"She came in on the bus. We didn't have a real bus station then. The bus stopped up at the Central Cafe," she gestured in the direction of the diner with the tile front and the rounded windows, "to let off passengers and pick up others. I was out front there, time on my hands, when the Trailways stopped and this woman got off. It was early, about eight-thirty. It was late winter and she was wearing a blue cloth coat with the collar up and a scarf over her hair and big sunglasses. I thought she looked like one of those movie stars, Katherine Hepburn and Lucille Ball and them, who always dressed like that in public, like they didn't want to be recognized.

"Anyway, she looked all around and saw the beauty shop sign and she walked straight over and came in. She asked me if anyone else was there, and I told her I was holding the place down until afternoon. She asked if I'd do her hair and not tell anybody. I said sure, it was none of my business. I locked up and pulled the shade like I just now did and she finally took off that scarf and the sunglasses and coat."

Still looking at the ceiling, she blinked hard and put another cigarette in her mouth and lit it. She took a few puffs, and went on.

"You saw what a pretty woman she was. Well, let me tell you: In '66 she was drop-dead gorgeous. I thought she really must be a movie star but I could have recognized them all back then and she wasn't one of them. That skin, and that face, and the thickest, shiniest, blackest hair you ever saw. I'd've given anything to have hair like that, instead of this straw.

"Well, she wanted me to cut that hair short and dye it blond! I tried to talk her out of it, but she wasn't going to have it any other way. I about bawled when I cut that beautiful hair, but it didn't bother her a bit. We worked all morning to get her hair blond, and it wasn't easy with the colors we had back then. It was like trying to turn ink white by pouring milk on it. But I finally managed it and it was a real transformation. I didn't think she looked nearly as good, and I told her so, but she was happy with it. I did her hair for her like that just about every week for twenty-seven years." The tears spilled out the corners of her eyes as she looked back along all those years, not seeing the ceiling.

"Did she ever say where she'd come from?"

"She never did. She had kind of a southern accent when she got here, but it came and went, like she'd practiced to lose it. You could hardly hear it at all the last ten years. Sometimes she talked about places in California like she was familiar with them. But I'd try to talk about her past and she'd steer the talk in another direction."

"Family? Men?"

"She sometimes talked about her mother, nothing real specific, just that she was religious, and her first husband died and she remarried. A couple of times Edna mentioned a brother and it was like she loved him, but he exasperated her. I remember she said she'd 'had' a brother, like maybe he was dead."

She blinked away the tears and her mouth firmed a little. "As for men, she was just as cagey about that. But I think she was with a man, from time to time."

That snagged my attention. "How is that?"

"Sometimes she'd come in and her manner was a little different, more relaxed, happier. I read it as a satisfying night with a man. Other times, I could tell she'd been crying, and if a woman doesn't have kids, it's usually men that make her cry. And I think she sometimes spent those trips of hers with a man."

"Tell me about that."

"Well, she wasn't seeing a man on all of them, because I took a few of them with her. We'd go spend a couple of days going to the garden shows and antique places she liked to visit, and the clothes places I like to go to, and just have a good time. She always enjoyed them so much, like she really needed to get away from here. She used to write letters and postcards and send them off from wherever we were."

"Do you know who she wrote to?"

She shook her head. "I never looked over her shoulder. It was always short notes. She'd dash them off and drop them in the nearest mailbox. But sometimes she'd come back from a trip she'd taken alone and be moody, either unhappy or just tired."

"Did she take any of these trips with anyone else?"

"No. As far as I know, I was her only real friend in town. We had lunch together a lot. For a while we went to a women's health spa. Edna took better care of herself than anybody I ever saw. We used to use the sauna and the whirlpool." Her eyes grew even more distant. "I couldn't believe it when the paper said she was fifty-seven. I thought she looked younger than me, and I'm forty-six. She had a better body than Tina out there, and that girl was a cheerleader last year."

"So you really don't know who she was, either?" I said, letting the bitterness come through.

She sat straight up, her eyes almost wild, her lower lip quivering. "Edna was—the sweetest, kindest—oh, God, I can't believe she's never going to come through that door again!" Then she broke down, sobbing and heaving, doubled over, her arms wrapped tight around her middle, in convulsions that were actually painful to see. Her face went scarlet and mucus ran in strings from her nostrils.

I went out front and grabbed a handful of tissues and went back, held her around her spasming shoulders, blotting at her face with the tissues, until she began to get control again.

"I'm sorry," she wailed in a little-girl voice. "I've been crying since yesterday morning and I can't stop."

"It's all right," I said. "I know what it's like to lose someone you love."

Slowly, she got her breathing under control. Then she looked up at me with eyes that were red, but almost dry. "You under-stand, then?"

"Uh-huh. And for what it's worth, I'm glad to know she had a friend like you. I was beginning to think she had no one."

She took a deep breath and settled herself. "All right, then. Now I've got something for you, but I have to know something."

She'd said that she'd been expecting me, but I hadn't wanted to push it. "What is it?"

"Tell me what you found in her house that morning. Tell me what happened to her."

"Look, I don't think you're in any shape."

"I can't hurt any worse. Tell me. I can't stand the hints they let out in the paper."

So I told her, and through the whole awful description her eyes stayed dry and hard. When it was finished she sat for a full ten minutes, saying nothing, lighting yet another cigarette and smoking it down to a butt and stubbing it out.

"Okay," she said at last. "I'll have nightmares for the rest of my life, but at least I know." Still sitting, she reached to the desk, yanked a drawer open, and took out a big, brown enve-lope. I flashed to Edna on Thursday morning, crossing the street to mail something.

"This came in this morning's mail." She pulled a smaller brown envelope from the first. It was heavily taped, and it had a white sheet of paper clipped to it. Sue unclipped the paper and handed it to me. It was a short letter written with a felt-point pen in an easy scrawl.

Sue, dear:
Something bad is happening. I may not see you again. If you hear that something has happened to me, please give this packet to Mr. Gabriel Treloar, who is renting the apartment over my garage. This is terribly important. Sue, I am sorry to end twenty-seven years this way, there is so much I would like to tell you, but things have caught up with me and I am just out of time.

Thank you for being such a wonderful friend,
                              With all my love,
                              Edna

"She knew it was going to happen, didn't she?" Sue asked.

"She knew something was going to happen. I can't believe she sat and waited for them to come and do that to her."

She gave me the envelope. It was about half an inch thick and felt heavier than if it contained ordinary paper. I had an urge to tear it open, but I didn't. Instead I got up and I could see the disappointment in her eyes.

"Thank you, Sue. I'll keep you posted, but this is something I need to look at alone."

She got up, terribly weary, and walked me to the door. "I want you to let me know what you find out."

"I will."

"Let me know what I can do to help. I hear a lot in this place."

"I appreciate it."

She unlocked the door, but didn't open it, letting her hand rest on the knob. "Mr. Treloar, have you ever killed anybody?"

The question took me back. "Yes, I have. In Vietnam, and twice in L.A., in the line of duty."

"Good. I'm glad you've had the practice," she said, and that long-dead Indian was looking out at me through those brown eyes. "Because I want you to kill some more. Keep in touch, Mr. Treloar." And she opened the door and let me out.

I got into my car and drove away, the envelope seeming to mock me as it lay on the seat next to me. Was the answer in there? Of all the bewildering turns that this insane affair had taken, this was the strangest. Could she really have known what was coming?

I pulled up to the garage and cut the engine, then I got out and stood for a while, quiet, just listening to the sounds of a late afternoon in the summer: lawnmowers, barking dogs, kids playing a game somewhere. I walked around the grounds. The ladies had been back and had planted their flowers. The new plantings stood in depressions dark with water. The garden looked almost as pretty as Edna had left it.

I checked the streets, the nearby windows. Nobody seemed to be watching. I went back up to my little apartment, closed the door and locked it. I sat with the fat envelope in my hands, and they trembled a little. Then, very carefully, I tore the tape away and opened the flap. I pulled out a stack of eight-by-ten photos.

The one on top was of a naked woman in a classic fifties cheesecake pose: kneeling, sitting back on her heels, lower body in profile so the swell of her thigh concealed the pubic area, the upper body half-turned so you got a three-quarters view of perfect breasts, hands behind the head, elbows raised and the face straight into the camera. The background was cheap photo studio paper, but the model was a heart-stopper. Every line of her body was vibrant, wonderfully alive and controlled. The bodily control and perfect eye contact, the way she dominated the camera so that she became the artist, rather than the photographer, were the qualities of a genuinely great model.

And that face, framed within the black, black pageboy hair, was illuminated by the radiant, sunburst smile I had come to know so well.

Below her right knee had been written, in the same easy scrawl as Sue's letter, with the same felt-point pen: *To Gabe: Have a wonderful life! Love, Edna.*

That was when I knew who Edna Tutt was.

BOOK TWO

Old Sin

$\mathcal{S}$ally Keane?" Lew looked at the photo, then up at me, then back to the photo again. "Are you telling me that Edna Tutt was really Sally Keane?"

"That's right." When I saw the pictures I knew I had to share this with Lew. I'd found him working late in his office, Sharon safely out of the building. I'd checked to make sure his intercom was off, anyway.

That first picture had transported me back to those long-ago nights in Lew's father's stockroom when we'd pored over the forbidden magazines. The models were mostly just pretty girls earning a few dollars in front of the camera, many of them hoping, somehow, to break into show business. You rarely saw the same girl more than once.

But there were exceptions. A handful of models were outstanding enough for us to know by name, because they were in virtually all of the magazines: Bunny Yeager, Diane Webber, a few others. And, of course, Sally Keane. She was the queen of the lot.

"Sally Keane, my God!" He whispered it almost reverently. "And all those years she lived just a few blocks away."

"It explains why she changed her hair," I said. "In '66 she'd probably have been recognized. I don't remember when I last saw a picture of her. I went into the Army in '67. Army barracks are always full of skin magazines and I don't remember seeing her during those years."

Lew examined the other photos, one after another. There were twenty of them. Some were nude or seminude, others were costume pieces, with Sally wearing garter belts and bustiers and spike heels, or silly French maid get-ups, or hokey, jungle girl outfits made of fake leopard skin.

In every one of them, she dominated the camera effortlessly. In the cheesiest surroundings, wearing the tackiest accoutrements, she gave the viewer that same look of complicity in twenty different variations, like she was having fun and wanted to share it.

"You know what always struck me about her?" Lew said. "I mean aside from being perfect? She was almost absurdly wholesome-looking, like a Mouseketeer gone bad. It was like Annette decided to give up Disney and go into the skin mags."

"Doreen," I said. "Doreen Tracy was always my favorite Mouseketeer."

He looked up at me again, over the rims of his glasses. "I don't get it. Why did she send you these?"

"I don't know. That's what I have to find out. She was trying to give me something, Lew, something important."

"So what do you do next?"

"I'll have to research Sally Keane. At last I know who Edna Tutt was before she came to Monticello." I took back that first picture and shook my head. "But how do we track down a model who was an underground celebrity thirty years ago?"

"I know who can help," Lew said.

It was a slightly seedy neighborhood to the west of Main Street, near the river. My family had once lived near there. I hadn't remembered the houses being this small, or so close together, with smaller yards than the places east of Main. Across the street stood some tall grain elevators. The house was two-story, white with aluminum siding. There was a fanciful covered gingerbread porch in the L formed by the main part of the house and a small wing.

We stepped beneath the porch light and Lew knocked. A girl of about seventeen opened the door. She had short, jagged white hair that stood up in little spikes.

"Oh, hi, Mr. Czuk," she said cheerily. "Come in." She held the door open and stood aside.

"Hello, Marty. This is Gabe Treloar. He's an old friend of mine. Is your dad home?"

"I'll get him. How do you like my new hair?" She turned around so we could admire the back, which was shaved from ear level down.

"Uh, very nice, Marty. I think it looks a lot better than the green and black."

"Thanks. I thought so, too." The girl had the gym-toned look so popular of late; completely without fat but with too much muscle for true anorexia. She dashed off to fetch her father. Half a minute later Scott van Houten, the man who'd bought Mr. Czuk's newsstand, came into the living room.

"Hello, Lew, Mr. Treloar. What's up?"

"Scott," Lew said, "we've got a little problem we'd like you to help us with and we'd like you to keep it quiet for a few days."

He looked puzzled. "Sure. What is it?"

Lew handed him the pictures and he took them over to a coffee table. "Have a seat, gentlemen." We sat and he spread the pictures out and studied them, then he looked up at me. I'd removed the one she signed.

"Sally Keane. You a collector, Mr. Treloar? These are nice prints."

"No, it's something I'm working on. I need to find out about this woman."

"I know she was a top model for a long time, then she disappeared sometime in the late fifties or early sixties. It's sort of a mystery."

A woman came from the kitchen and was introduced as Mrs.

van Houten. She rivaled her husband for girth, had a pleasant face and didn't seem to think it at all strange that three men were sitting in her living room with pictures of a naked woman all over the coffee table. She offered coffee and snacks, but we declined.

Marty came in and looked the pictures over. "She had a waist problem, didn't she?"

"Marty," Scott said, "in the fifties this woman was a goddess. Back then a woman wasn't supposed to look like a fourteen-year-old boy with boobs."

"The fifties," she said, like that was when dinosaurs roamed Ohio. Her mother came back in with a platter of brownies, cups and a pot of coffee. Apparently, she understood that men only turned down food out of misguided politeness. The brownies were excellent.

"You don't know any more about her?" Lew said.

"Not me. But I can ask someone who does."

"Who's that?" I asked.

"Irving Schwartz. He publishes the Sally Keane newsletter."

I couldn't believe it. "You mean Sally Keane has a *fan club?*"

"Sure," he said, looking at me like I must have been living on the moon or something. "It's called *Neat-O Kean-O,* comes out two or three times a year. It's devoted mainly to her, but has articles on other models of the period and related subjects."

"I guess the world is a stranger place than most of us imagine," Lew said. "Can you put us in contact with this guy?"

"Sure. Is it all right if I fax him these pictures? If any of them are ones he hasn't seen, he'll want to talk to you."

"Go ahead," I said. "And let him know it's urgent."

"Anything about Sally Keane is always urgent to him. I can send this out from here. Unless he's out of town, I should have something back from him tomorrow."

He took the pictures upstairs and we chatted with Marty and her mother while Scott practiced the mysteries of his profession. He came back down and returned the photos and I gave him my new phone number. He promised to let me know as soon as he got an answer from Schwartz. We said our goodbyes and left.

"You know, Gabe," Lew said, "this story is getting so strange! There could be a Pulitzer in it. I never thought anything like this would come my way. I'd given up." No doubt about it, the young reporter was coming back.

He dropped me off at the Times-Tribune building where I'd left my car and I drove to a shopping center where a drug emporium stayed open late. I bought a penlight and a pair of rubber surgical gloves, then went back to my apartment. I studied the photos some more, looking for answers, but all I saw was the beautiful, young Edna Tutt/Sally Keane of thirty-odd years ago.

When it was late enough, I went out and crossed the garden. There were summer night sounds, but nothing else. I went up the steps to the back door and took out my no longer needed L.A. public library card. The lock was a cinch. After a few seconds of probing, it clicked open and I was inside.

An empty house is always still, but one where the owner has died somehow seems even quieter. I stood still for a few minutes, letting my eyes adjust to the dimness. It wasn't quite dark. All the curtains were open and light came in from the streetlamp on the corner.

Very slowly, I went through the ground floor, giving each room ten minutes or so. Everything was as the police had left it. Nothing had been put away. The searchers had been very thorough here. Everywhere, the indirect light gleamed eerily from fingerprint dust. I was wearing the surgical gloves so I wouldn't leave any of my own behind. A side-effect of the AIDS scare is the ready availability of surgical gloves.

There was nothing on the ground floor. I went up the stairs. The loosened treads were loud beneath my feet, but nobody was listening. I checked the home gym, and another room Edna had fitted up as a sewing room. Nothing. Then I took a deep breath and went into the bedroom where she had died.

The bedframe was empty. The bed clothes and mattress had been taken away for lab testing. There were ugly stains on the floor, everything was overturned. It took less than five minutes to determine that there was nothing there for me to find. I got out, feeling as if I'd held my breath the whole time I was in there.

Next stop was the attic. A narrow flight of stairs took me there. It was a long, narrow room, its walls angled by the pitch of the roof. The pen flash showed me that a lot of boards had been pried up. Long ribbons of fiberglass insulation hung from the ceiling. I poked around for a while, figuring I was wasting my time just as they had. Whatever they were looking for wasn't very big, it was an old, frame house, and Edna had had close to thirty years to learn all its crannies and hiding places.

I went back down to the kitchen and from there down the steps to the basement. It was gloomy and dank, the air stale. Its smell took me to the days when I had played there, pretending it was a dungeon, a castle, Frankenstein's laboratory. A waist-high brick wall defined a coal bin, left over from the days when all the houses in town had coal furnaces. Even when I'd lived there it had electric heat. A bewildering warren of old conduits snaked overhead, remnants of old heating systems. They'd been pulled down and pried open for a look. The killers had been awfully busy that night.

I left the house and carefully locked the door behind me. Whatever they'd been looking for, they hadn't found it. What was it? And why hadn't Edna told them where it was?

Of course, it was likely that she hadn't told them because it didn't exist, maybe had never existed. It wasn't the pictures she had sent me, I was sure of that. There was nothing in them worth killing for.

I decided to have a look at the garage. It wasn't even locked. Edna had an elderly Toyota, white, with seventy thousand miles on it. There was nothing of interest in its glove box. I popped the trunk and found only a spare tire and a cardboard box full of old magazines: *Look, Collier's, Saturday Evening Post, Redbook,* all from the thirties and forties: a flea-market prize. On the off-chance, I took the box out and closed the trunk. There was always a possibility that something was hidden in a magazine, but I'd wait until I had them upstairs and in a good light.

There was nothing else in the garage. I carried the box up to my room, turned on the bedside lamp and blinked in the sudden light after more than two hours of straining my eyes to see in the dimness.

One by one, I flipped through the magazines, holding them spine-up so that anything loose would drop out. Nothing. Just a lot of articles and photo essays of events long past, people long dead, ads for products long off the market. Historical curios. Another dead end. I closed the last magazine and dropped it on top of the others.

I undressed, got into bed and turned out the light. Sleep wasn't long in coming, but all night I dreamed, tormented by a black-haired woman and another with gray eyes that had no whites. They led me on and teased me, promising unearthly delights but disappearing the second I embraced them. Toward morning the three of us were in a car driving along the old coast highway. It was an old, familiar dream, one filled with dread and guilt, but this was the first time I'd had two naked women with me. Usually, I was alone. They laughed and pointed to the spot where I was supposed to drive over the side. Obediently, I turned the wheel and plowed through the guard rail. It parted like tissue paper and with a final laugh the women disappeared, just as the hood nosed down and the broad Pacific flashed by and there was nothing in the windshield but the jagged rocks at the base of the cliff, coming closer with terrifying speed.

I jerked awake with my heart thudding, guilt pressing down on me with suffocating weight. I sat up and forced my heart to slow down. It was an old routine. I'd been having the dream, with variations, ever since Dad took his header off the coast highway in '66. It had been almost a month since I'd last had the dream, so I wasn't surprised that it had come around again. But why were Lola and Edna there? I decided that they were just on my mind so they made themselves at home in my old nightmare.

The sky was getting pale and I saw no sense in going back to sleep, so I pulled on my sweats and running shoes. I ran the block north to Central and turned west, past my old school and the church, the hospital, all the public buildings and down into town, around the square, then south on Main, across the river and out of town.

The houses thinned out, then there were a few bars and road houses, among them the Lido Lester Cabell had mentioned. I finally stopped out in farm land, in front of a huge old barn, rust-colored, with Mail Pouch chewing tobacco advertising painted all over it in big, yellow letters. Directly across the road from it was a prefab building housing Monticello Custom Cycles, an establishment I was certain must be frequented by many Skinners.

I walked around, getting my breath back, then I ran back, retracing my steps. It was Sunday morning in Monticello, and I could have run down the middle of Main in perfect safety. Church bells were starting to ring, and in Monticello they were real bells, not recordings. I smelled incense as I ran past St. Anne's, remembering Sunday mornings long ago when I was an altar boy there, and the way Father Daugherty winced because he hated the taste of the Communion wine.

Back home I showered and climbed into clean clothes, then wondered what I could accomplish on Sunday. I decided that what I needed most of all was some coffee, and I was in no mood for instant. I walked down to my by-now-familiar cafe and ordered breakfast. From there I picked up the Monticello and Columbus papers and walked back home to read them. I got there just as a red Jaguar pulled up.

"Good morning, Gabe," Sharon Newell said.

"What do you want, Sharon?"

"Want? Aren't you interested in what I have?" She held up some folded papers.

"All right," I said, "but you can't come in. You'll ruin my reputation."

"I happen to have here," she waved the papers at me, "some Xeroxes from a friend who owes me a favor and works in the Sheriff's office."

"Let me see," I said.

She held on to them. "Now this," she peeled one off, "is from the Social Security Administration. It states that Edna

Tutt was born on May 5, 1936, in Los Angeles, California. She applied for a Social Security card in February 1966. Funny, isn't it? Waiting until she was thirty to apply? I got mine when I was fifteen."

I shrugged. "It happens. A woman marries and keeps house and never gets a job, or she stays home and takes care of Mother, or she's a wealthy heiress."

"Oh, sure. Now here," she peeled off another, "is a Xerox of a fax from Queen of Angels Hospital in L.A., Edna Tutt's birth certificate."

"And the other one is the one that says Edna Tutt died on May 6, 1936, right?"

"The seventh, actually. You peeked."

"It's an old dodge. You want to change identities, you find someone who died in infancy around the time you were born and you get a copy of the kid's birth certificate. That way you can apply for a Social Security number without running into the real person's application. With that you can get a passport and everything else you need. It's not as easy as it used to be, but it's still done."

"Would an innocent woman have known how to do it back in '66?"

"If she read a lot of spy novels. Ian Fleming was big back then."

"What've you found out, Gabe? There's something about you that makes my antennas stand up and quiver."

"Don't know a thing, Sharon." I pretended to study the front page of the fat Sunday paper.

"Come off it. Lew's acting like a teenager with the hots for the cheerleader. I want to know what it is."

"Just keep up the good work, Sharon. You get any more stuff from Mark's or Lester's offices, bring it by."

She smiled sweetly. "How's Lola?"

"I haven't seen her in a while."

"Nobody has."

"What do you mean?" The woman could get under your skin like an IV needle.

"Lola Cohan hasn't been seen anywhere since Thursday afternoon. Are you keeping her somewhere?"

"If I was, you'd've found her by now. She's probably taken a trip: Cape Cod, New York, Machu Picchu, somewhere like that."

"Am I going to have to tempt you with my body?"

"See you around, Sharon."

She gave me a final, acid smile and put the Jag in gear. She peeled away, scooting down the redbrick street like she smelled a story somewhere to the north.

I killed the morning reading the papers. The murder was page-three news by now. It was agreed by all that an arrest was imminent, but otherwise there was nothing to report. I was just finishing the funnies when the phone rang.

"Hello?"

"I'm trying to reach a Mr. Gabriel Treloar." It was a male voice, oddly eager.

"Speaking."

"Mr. Treloar, I'm Irving Schwartz. I'm calling about those Sally pictures I was faxed yesterday evening."

"You don't waste any time, do you?"

"Not a chance. How many people have you contacted so far?"

"Nobody. I didn't know there was anybody to contact until Scott van Houten told me about you last night."

There was a pause like I'd thrown him a curve. "You mean you didn't know about *Neat-O Keane-O?*"

"I didn't even know anyone remembered Sally Keane except for me and an old friend."

Schwartz laughed incredulously. "And to think I've got you all to myself! Look, Mr. Treloar, I'll make you a very good price for those pictures. Seven of them I've never even seen before! I'll run a special issue for this."

"I'm not in the picture-selling business, Mr. Schwartz."

"You aren't? Then why . . ."

"Which one do you want the most?"

"Uh, I guess the French maid pic. That's from a Venice Photography Club shoot in April '57 and I thought I had a complete collection, but . . ."

"It's yours, no charge, if you'll give me some information."

"Hey, information I got. but I still want to buy the rest."

"We'll talk about it later."

"Okay. What do you need to know?"

"First off, when did Sally quit modeling?"

"She was very active from '55 to '63. After that she did a little work for professional photographers and a few of the clubs, but she was tapering off. Finally, sometime late in '64, she quit for good."

"Do you know why?"

"Nobody knows, but I'm guessing she just got tired of it. She was making a good living, but for good reason she was extremely proud of her looks and probably didn't want to show her body past her prime. The last year it's believed that she only posed for Bunny Yeager because she trusted Bunny to take only the best pictures of her."

"Wait a minute. I thought Bunny Yeager was a model."

Again that pause. He just couldn't believe my ignorance. "Of *course* Bunny was a model! She was one of the greatest! But she also turned pro and made her reputation as one of the best figure photographers. She wrote a famous book on figure photography."

"If Sally wasn't modeling all the time, what was she doing to support herself?"

"She worked as a secretary at Warner Brothers for a while, and she worked other jobs at the film and TV studios. She was always trying to break into the movies and TV, but she never caught on. She did some bit playing in a few movies, danced in a chorus line on the Sullivan show, things like that. She went to New York a number of times to pose there and work in the variety shows like Sullivan's. But, her theatrical career was obviously going nowhere, and I think that's another reason she finally quit.

"See, for my money she was the greatest model who ever lived, but she only did it to support her acting lessons and dancing lessons and voice lessons so she could do 'serious' work. Everybody that knew her said she was the hardest-working woman in Southern California. Classes at Pasadena Playhouse followed by a six-hour shoot on the beach at Malibu, then night classes at USC, every day like that for years."

"Was she ever married?"

"No, at least not after she got to California. She dated, had a number of boyfriends, but none for very long, which is understandable when you think about it. I mean, no guy she went with ever saw much of her with that schedule. She was married to her career, at least, what she hoped was going to be her career."

"Did you know her personally?"

He laughed a little sadly. "Don't I wish. No, I was only about twelve when she quit modeling. I discovered her in my twenties, when I got into the magazine collecting business. Some collectors asked for pictures of this great model from the fifties and I looked her up and fell in love."

"Does anyone know where she went?"

"Mr. Treloar, from the day she left to this, nobody has seen or heard from her. Nobody was looking for her at the time. It wasn't until years later that this underground Sally cult got started, and by that time the trail was cold." He paused, then said a little wistfully: "To be honest, nobody's looked very hard."

"Why is that?"

"She was a goddess—a fantasy figure. I think we all want to remember her the way she was. Why make her mortal? She's probably living someplace, married to some guy who has no idea what she used to do for a living. I yield to no man in my affection for Sally Keane, but if I knew where she was, I wouldn't bother her. What would be the point?"

"One more thing and you've got your picture."

"Shoot."

"Is there someone I can talk to who was close to her when she was modeling? Was there a friend or roommate or employer still around?"

"Sally did most of her work for the Bloom Photo Service.

Irma Bloom still runs it. Her husband, Sam, died some years back. He took most of the early Sally pictures." He gave me an L.A. number to call.

"Thanks, Mr. Schwartz. You've been a great help. I'll send that picture out today."

"Look, Mr. Treloar, I really need that horseback pic. There are only two nude horseback photos of Sally, both from a shoot in the San Gabriel Valley in '58, and she's riding a bay in those. This fax looks like maybe three years earlier and she's on a palomino . . ."

"We'll talk about it later, Irving," I told him. "Goodbye, now."

I punched in the number he'd given me. A woman answered on the fourth ring.

"Bloom Photo Service, may I help you?" The voice was that of a woman in late middle age and sounded tired.

"Am I speaking to Irma Bloom?"

"You are."

"Mrs. Bloom, my name is Gabe Treloar. I'm calling to ask you about a model who used to work for your agency: Sally Keane."

She sighed loudly, her breath gusting across the mouthpiece. "Look, it's Sunday and I'm just in the office to catch up on some work. If you want to talk about Sally Keane, the man you want to talk to is Irving Schwartz, he publishes your fan magazine. I can give you his number."

"I just spoke to him and he gave me yours. I'm not a Sally fan, Mrs. Bloom, I'm a detective." Feeling a rush when I said it, feeling good, knowing it was true.

"A detective? Look, if you're one of the ones trying to find out where she disappeared to, I can't tell you. I don't know myself."

I took a deep breath. "Mrs. Bloom, I'm calling from Ohio. Sally Keane was living here under an assumed identity from the time she left California. In the early hours of Thursday morning she was murdered. I have reason to believe that the crime was connected in some way with her past and I need any information about her you can give me."

"Murdered? My God! Are you certain it was her?"

"There is no doubt as to her identity."

"Well—this is hard to believe. I mean, I don't know why it should be, I live in L.A. and people are murdered here every day over nothing. My God! I had a card from her just this last spring. May, I think, maybe June." The usual California vagueness about seasons.

"Did the two of you correspond often?"

"I could never write her back. Three or four times a year I'd get a card or a short letter. Never a return address, always mailed from a different town, usually in the Midwest or South somewhere."

I remembered Sue Oldenburg describing Edna writing letters and cards during their trips together. "What did she write you about?"

"They were always short and just said she was doing well, she'd taken up gardening, best wishes, that sort of thing."

"Nothing about problems, someone from her past showing up unexpectedly, anything like that?"

"Never. And it was clear that she'd taken up a new life and didn't want to be bothered."

"Do you know if she wrote anybody else out there?"

"If so, nobody ever told me."

"Okay, I need background. When did you meet Sally?"

"She came here in '55. She'd only been in California for a few months and she was working as a waitress, trying to break into films the way all the pretty ones did. Someone at the Maury Spielman Agency gave her one of our business cards and she showed up one day. Sam, that's my late husband, God rest his soul, took some trial shots that day and she had a job. The kid was such a natural."

"How long did she work for you?"

"Longer than any of our other models . . . eight or nine years. By the end of her first year with us she was in constant demand—the magazines, the clubs, the art photographers, they all wanted her, and she obliged."

"Was there jealousy over that?"

"Some, I guess. But she was so sweet and friendly, I don't think anyone held a grudge for long. See, most of the girls modeled as part-time work and they didn't put a lot into it, but she loved it. She could put her whole heart into every shoot. You know the costume bits? The maid, the jungle girl, the cowgirl? She made all her own outfits. She even designed her shoes and boots and we had them made for her by a house in Burbank."

"Was she making good money?"

"Very good, unlike the other girls, because she was getting so much more work."

"What did she spend it on?"

"I figured she was socking it away, because she lived very frugally. She didn't just sew her costumes, she made all her own clothes. She was careful what she ate. She didn't party, even though the other girls thought you had to to meet important people in the movie business. She was very strictly brought up and it showed. She never smoked or drank, and I never even heard her use a swear word."

"But she posed naked for strangers."

Irma chuckled. "Mr.—Treloar, is it?—she was a nice, beautiful girl who simply had not a single hangup about her body. Nobody ever had to coax her out of her clothes. If she had a real fault it was vanity about her looks. She worked out every day in a gym, and this was in the fifties, mind you, when nobody but professional athletes did that. I think she could've been a pro athlete if she'd wanted to.

"But you asked about how she spent her money. Well all those classes she took must have cost, and I know her brother cost her."

"Her brother?"

"Yes, he showed up from time to time and lived with her here. He was in the Navy for a while, I remember that. He used to drop her off at work and pick her up. I met him a few times, a real polite, good-looking Southern boy, but he was a no-good, always in trouble; she had to go downtown and bail him out more than once."

"What was he in trouble for?"

"Little stuff, mostly: drunk and disorderly, barroom fighting, petty theft. I think car theft once. He'd be away for a year or two at a time but he always showed back up."

"Do you remember his name?"

"God, it's been so long . . . Steve or Stan or something like that."

"What about other men? Boyfriends? Suitors?"

"She dated. With her looks, she had plenty of offers, but she always thought she was going to break into the movies and that came first."

"Do you know if she had any bitter or violent breakups? I'm asking this because the circumstances of her death suggest somebody obsessive; someone who nursed a grudge for a long time."

"Oh, God. Look, she didn't work here the last year or two she was living on the Coast. We met for lunch a few times. I know she was seeing a man, maybe even living with him, and the way she talked it was sort of rocky. I think he may have been some guy involved with her brother, but that's about all I can tell you."

"It'll help," I said, hoping it was true.

"She has a fan club, you know. Do you think it might have been one of those deranged fans you hear about now? Like Hinckley or the man who shot John Lennon? One of those weirdos might have tracked her down."

"I hope not, because then he's going to be hard to find. Look, Mrs. Bloom, something's been bothering me, talking to Irving Schwartz and now to you: Sally was so beautiful and she tried so hard for so long to break into show business. Why didn't she make it?"

Irma paused a moment, then chuckled sadly. "Mr. Treloar, she was a beautiful kid, but Hollywood is a place where people are beautiful for a living. She tried, but she just wasn't very good. She could dance a little, but she was an athlete and a gymnast, not a dancer. She couldn't sing, couldn't even stay in key. As for her acting, walk-on bits were all she was good for. When she got here she had a Tennessee accent, you could stick a fork in it and it'd stand up. And she could never lose it, no matter how many speech classes she took. She got it smoothed out a little, but even if she'd made it in movies she would've been stuck in Southern character roles all her life, and that wasn't good enough for her. What Lucy was, was a great model and that was it."

I felt like I'd tripped over a brick. "Wait a minute. Who's Lucy?"

"Who've we been talking about? You didn't think Sally Keane was her real name, did you?"

"I hadn't thought about it," I said, stupidly. It should have been the first thing I asked.

"No, Sam made that up for her when she first came here. A lot of our models used professional names. Lucy was saving her real name for when she got her big break, and that never came. She was Lucinda Elkins, from Holston, Tennessee. That sticks in my mind because there's a big Eastman plant in Holston and we always got a lot of photographic supplies from there."

I wrote the name down. Edna had more layers than an onion. "Was Sally . . . Lucy, that is, ever in any trouble with the law?"

Irma laughed. "I doubt if she ever got a parking ticket. She was always so embarrassed when her brother got in trouble. I guess it was a part of her upbringing. She about had a breakdown during those Senate hearings."

"What? Senate hearings?"

"Uh-huh." Now her voice turned bitter. "You remember Senator Kefauver? He was always investigating something or other in those days. This, you'll recall, was when J. Edgar Hoover swore up and down that there was no such thing as organized crime, but something had to be to blame for all the bad stuff that was going on, so Kefauver and his friends decided it was comics and quote pornography unquote. They summoned Sam, which I am sure shortened his life, and they summoned Lucy, because she was our top model and at that time she was famous for a series of shoots where she wore corsets and six-inch heels, also stockings and garter belts, which everyone thinks of today as S and M gear, but back then was just women's underwear.

"Now you have to understand, Bloom Photo Service was always strictly a mail-order business. In those days you couldn't show so much as an exposed female nipple on material sent through the U.S. Mail. We dealt mainly in movie portraits for the fan clubs, celebrity photos, movie stills, that sort of thing, plus the glamour shots and cheesecake Lucy and the other girls did. It was nothing like you see in the magazines now. Lucy did her nude posing for the photo clubs and professional photographers, although they sometimes used our facilities here.

"Anyway, we were the biggest cheesecake operation in the country then, so those buffoons grilled poor Sam for hours, trying to make him out as some sort of pervert and corrupter of youth. I mean, can you imagine! Every rock musician these days has an act more salacious than anything we ever did, and they put it on TV! Even the figure work Lucy did looks innocent now. Anything full-frontal had to be airbrushed before they could run it in the girlie magazines.

"Okay, I'm running a little off the subject. I always get mad when I talk about that time. Lucy never got called in to testify, she just sat outside the hearing chamber with her purse in her lap. But she was terrified and she almost quit modeling over it, until she got over her scare and got mad at the sheer injustice of it all. Then she came back to work."

"Mrs. Bloom, you've been a terrific help. If you can think of anything else that might have some bearing on this, please call me." I gave her my number.

"I'm so sorry to hear about her death. I really missed that girl. The world is turning into such an awful place."

"That it is, Mrs. Bloom. But I think you may have aided the investigation more than you know."

"Will you drop me a line when you've solved this?"

"I'll send you a copy of my report," I promised.

After hanging up I sat a long time, staring out my window overlooking the garden. The little goddess gleamed in the sun, the flowers made their colorful display. I thought about obsessed fans. Could one of them have tracked her here, found a middle-aged lady instead of the twenty-year-old goddess he was seeking, and taken a terrible revenge? There were always people like that out there—the ones without their own lives or personalities, who latched onto an image and could not distinguish between fantasy and reality. Celebrities went in fear of them every day.

But the obsessed fans were solitary brooders, unable to form attachments with other human beings. I was looking at more than one, and somebody had been looking for something. I scratched the obsessed fan from the list of suspects with a sense of relief.

Lucinda Elkins, of Holston, Tennessee. I went out to the Plymouth and got out my road atlas. I found Holston on Highway 23, just south of the Virginia state line. I could drive over to Columbus, catch 23 there, and be in Holston in six hours. I had a hunch some of Edna's trips had been visits home. I might find her family there, old friends, people she had been in contact with recently, anyone who might have another piece of this maddening puzzle.

It felt good, getting back into it. I was doing real work—important work, and it was pushing back the ghosts, making the old guilts and cravings back off, leaving my mind clear for important things.

I could feel myself coming back to life again, and for that if for nothing else, I owed Edna Tutt/Sally Keane/Lucinda Elkins a big debt, and I planned to pay in full.

had too many questions, not enough answers. Why Edna, of all people? True, she had once inhabited the sleazy half-world of skin magazines and scuffling, show-biz wannabes, but she had left that far behind so long ago. What had she done, what had she been involved in or just known about, that made her the target of someone's violent rage?

And where was Lola? She hadn't contacted me since our night in the boathouse. Was she with Rapley?

I sat, idly thumbing through the old magazines, when my phone rang again.

"Mr. Treloar?" It was a young woman's voice this time.

"Right."

"I'm Ann Smyth? That you saw out in Skinnertown the day before yesterday?" She had that rising Southern inflection that turns most sentences into questions.

"I remember you."

"I got some information you might like to have. Confidential, like?"

My palm started to sweat on the phone. "What is it?"

"Uh-uh. You want it, you pay for it. Let's get together, then we can talk about what I know and what it's worth to you."

"Okay. Do you know where I'm staying?"

"No, you come here, or no deal. The Airstream?"

"I saw it. When?"

"I'm not working tonight. Eleven?"

"I'll be there."

"See you then." Click.

It looked like my stupidity index was going to be put to the test. Skinnertown was no place I wanted to be in daylight, much less in the middle of the night. But something about the woman intrigued me, and the prospect of foolish risk was curiously attractive, just as having the case to work on was making me come alive. It might be a trap, but so what.

I thought about telling somebody. Mark Fowles? Bad move. Lester Cabell? Forget it. I called Lew and told him what I'd learned so far that day.

"This is amazing!" he said. "So now we're looking for a girl named Lucinda Elkins, born somewhere around 1935, in Holston, Tennessee."

"She wasn't necessarily born there, but it seems to have been her last home of record before leaving for the coast. If I can get away without Mark or Lester noticing, I plan to go there, maybe tomorrow, and nose around—see what I can turn up. It's only about six hours from here."

"They don't have any roadblocks out. If you leave while it's dark you should have no problem."

"I'm going over to Skinnertown tonight. A woman there wants to meet me. Says she has some information to sell. I may have to tap you for the money if she has something and it's steep."

He didn't say anything for a minute. "Anything special you want in the obituary?"

"Don't be dramatic. The Skinners don't know me from Adam."

"One, don't assume that. Two, they saw you there with

Lester Cabell on Friday, asking about the murder. And three, nearly every major crime in this county for a hundred years has been Skinner-related. Don't assume they aren't involved."

"I've got to risk it if she has something."

"No you don't. If she wants the money, she'll come to you."

"True. But I'm feeling itchy and restless. So far I've just been receiving information. I don't think I'm going to get much more this way. I want to go out and shake the trees, see what falls out."

"Is it the kind of thing you used to look for on the streets, back in L.A.?"

I thought about it. "Yeah, I guess it is."

"Well, you're likely to find more than you want in Skinner-town."

The place was quiet when I drove up. Nobody was hanging around outside as I passed the shacks and trailers. A few dogs investigated, but they didn't raise much fuss. The Airstream was a pale shape, the moon reflecting as a big, white blob on its domed roof. I pulled up in front of it and got out. Fifty yards to my left the river made faint noises as it flowed by. The frogs and crickets serenaded. There were still some lights on in Earl's house.

I walked up to the door and a fuzzy, white figure appeared on the other side of the screen door.

"Treloar?" She opened the door and looked around outside. "Come in."

I stepped up into the trailer and the door shut behind me. Ann Smyth pointed to a chair next to a tiny, formica table. "Make yourself to home."

I sat, studying her. She was wearing a sleeveless T-shirt cut off so short that the undersides of her small breasts showed. That was her major article of clothing. Other than that, she wore a pair of panties, consisting of a tiny triangle of white cloth held up by a couple of strings that snaked up over her prominent hipbones.

"What do you have for me, Ann?" It wasn't my business to tell her how she should receive guests.

"No need to rush. Relax. Be sociable. Want a beer?"

"No, thanks." She remained standing, leaning against the minimal kitchen counter.

"Think I'll have one." She turned to open the refrigerator. There was even less of her panties in back than in front. She pulled out a long-necked bottle and twisted off the cap.

"Where are you from, Ann?"

"Tennessee."

"What part?" I was hoping for a connection.

"Memphis." She said it with the ghost "L" people from that part of the world often employ: "Melmphis." I was disappointed. Holston was in the northeastern part of the state, Memphis in the extreme southwestern corner, as far apart as they could get and still be in the same state.

"How did you get here?"

"I met Mel when I was workin' in a club in Memphis. He brought me to this hole and then he got busted for possession." She smiled cynically. "I can pick 'em, huh?" She took a swallow of beer, slowly inserting almost the whole neck into her mouth to do it, keeping her eyes on mine the whole time.

"I take it you don't like Monticello?"

"It's noplace and nothing happens here and a Skinner's woman ends up looking like my mama: used up and toothless before she's forty. I like the city. Mel's gonna be away for a while, so now Jesse and some of the others're sniffin' around here."

"So you want out."

She nodded. "Uh-huh. And I need money to travel on." She leaned back, one bare foot on the floor, the other propped on a cabinet door below the counter, throwing her pelvis into prominence. The little white triangle was almost at my eye level, making it hard to take my gaze off it. Just above it, on the right, an old appendectomy scar made a silvery centipede on her dead-white abdomen.

"What do you have to sell, Ann?"

She smiled lazily. I couldn't tell if the come-on was part of a package she was offering or just second nature to her. Maybe, I thought, it was her way of establishing control over men. I had to admit it was effective.

"Mel, he used to talk a lot when he was drinking, which was most of the time. Liked to talk big, let on like he knew things. I once asked him if he knew anything important or just liked to run his mouth. He said he knew somethin' would blow this town apart if he talked, but he couldn't talk 'cause it was a big Skinner secret an' the others'd kill him, blood kin or no blood kin."

Outside the frogs and crickets were quieting down for the night. "What did Mel tell you, Ann?"

She ran a palm down her hip, making the skin shiny with condensation from the bottle, raising tiny goosebumps as the moisture evaporated.

"He finally got drunk enough to talk some, though it wasn't easy to follow. See, his daddy was Jarvis Skinner."

"Jarvis . . ." someone had mentioned the name recently.

"Uh-huh. He was killed in that big robbery here, before I was born, when Mel was just a baby. Sheriff Fowles's daddy shot him with a Tommy gun."

"Interesting story, Ann, but I'm looking into Edna Tutt's murder, not ancient history." Still, I felt that little tingle you get when something important starts coming in from nowhere.

She gave me that lazy smile again. "You think the two wasn't connected? There was another . . ."

The door jerked open and something big and hairy barreled through. Jesse Skinner loomed over me, eyes bloodshot and stinking of beer. I got up quick, the chair going over backward. He twisted his head to stare at Ann. She didn't change expression.

"You redhead slut, I tol' you what I'd do if I caught you peddlin' your tail while Mel's away! I'm gonna cut you so no man'll want you again." He turned to glare at me and his hand went to the pouch at his belt. He unsnapped it, pulled out the knife and shook it open all in one move. Light gleamed along its well-honed edge. "First I'm gonna cut him so he knows what happens when you mess with a Skinner's woman."

There was no place for me to run and my eyes searched for a

weapon. He was big and mean and more than half-crazy and, in his condition, he'd have to be hit hard to feel anything. I'd faced men like him before, but then I'd had a gun and baton and Mace and I wasn't alone.

He started for me, I measured a shot to his jaw, then Ann reached into a kitchen drawer and came out with something that gleamed dull silver. She laid the short barrel of a revolver right in Jesse's ear and thumbed back the hammer. He stopped dead at the feel of the cold steel and the multiple click of the rotating cylinder and the sear engaging at full-cock. There were limits even to a drunken Skinner's craziness.

"Jesse, you just stop right there. It would surely grieve me to blow your brains all over my pretty Airstream but I swear I'll do it." Her hand was rock-steady. I recognized the gun: a Ruger SP 101, no bigger than the little snub-nosed .38s that detectives used to carry, but a full-powered .357 Magnum. A potent handful, not that any great firepower is called for when a gun goes off inside a man's ear.

"Lay down the knife, Jesse."

Slowly, he lowered the knife and dropped it to the floor. "You're gonna regret this, Ann."

"Hell, Jesse, for two years I been regrettin' I ever heard of you Skinners." Her hand raised abruptly over her head and she sapped Jesse behind the ear with the solid little gun. There was a meaty smack, a grunt, and he fell to his knees. She hit him again, just as hard, in the same spot. This time he went down on his face, still on his knees. She braced a bare foot against his shoulder, her butt against the counter, and shoved. Jesse shot backward through the door and sprawled on his back in the weedy yard beyond.

"Guess we'll talk another time, Mr. Treloar. They'll be coming around to see what the commotion is. I'll tell 'em he come over here drunk and tried to get into my pants. Won't be the first time. Bring five hundred in cash when we get together again."

I started to leave, then turned back. "Ann, tell me something."

"Make it short." Doors were slamming someplace.

"Those panties you wear: Isn't it uncomfortable, having a string up your rear like that?"

"Uh-huh, it is. I like the feeling. Now get."

I climbed into the Plymouth, started it up, and pulled away. As I left, Ann was standing over the inert Jesse in the same pose I'd seen her in on Friday, only now she had a gun dangling by her thigh. A couple of Skinner women blinked at my car as they made their way toward the Airstream. Maybe the women were the only ones sober enough to have heard the uproar.

The primary tool for a detective, private or police, is the telephone. I went to work with mine on Monday morning. A call to information for the 615 area code got me the number for Holston County's main high school. A few questions got me routed to a secretary with access to records.

"Miss Breckenridge speaking. May I help you?"

"I hope so. I'm trying to trace a woman from Holston who would have graduated from high school sometime between '51 and '54. Do you have those records?"

"All our old records are on computer now. What name are we looking for?"

"Lucinda Elkins."

"Let me see . . ." I heard tapping sounds. "Elkins is a pretty common name around here. I'm bringing up a lot of them." A short pause. "No, not a single Lucy. Are you sure about the dates?"

"Not exactly, but it has to be somewhere in that range. Might she have been in another school?"

"There was only one high school in Holston until the early sixties, but these files have the records from all the county schools back to the teens. Of course, not everyone went to high school, especially in the rural areas."

I thanked her and hung up. Another dead end. I'd been hoping for an easy trace and it was disappointing. Wondering who to call next, I flipped through an old *Life*. It was World War Two vintage, the photos grim and real despite obvious propaganda censorship, the lighter articles strangely otherworldly.

The advertising seemed remarkably unsophisticated, almost naive.

I turned over a page and saw an ad and my brain did one of those flip-flops that you have when you see or hear something terribly contradictory and you don't know what it is. It took up an upper corner on a page of "Life Goes To the Movies," where the pictures were of Dick Powell and Myrna Loy. Like so many of the ads in the magazine, it had a military setting. War sold products then, like sex does now.

The picture showed a GI in a foxhole, impossibly clean and well-groomed. He was smiling broadly and he held up a pack of cigarettes. The pack was white, with a red dot in the center. The ad copy read: *"Lucky Strike Green Has Gone To War!"*

Something was all off. I flipped to the cover. Dated August, 1942. I looked back at the ad. Seven days before, Edna had stood on the steps outside and asked me if I smoked. What had she said?

"I tried a cigarette just once. I was eighteen and my boyfriend persuaded me to take one. It was a Lucky Strike and I was taken with the pack. I loved Deco design even then, and it was so pretty: dark green with a red circle inside a black one."

I grabbed for the phone, so anxious that I fumbled and almost dropped it. My first call was to a supermarket. I got a clerk and asked him to grab a pack of Luckies and read me the name of the company that sold them.

"American Tobacco Company, sir," he said, like he was used to such questions.

A call to information in North Carolina got me American's headquarters, and a few minutes of shunting got me a man in the publicity department.

"Marvin Collins here. Can I help you?"

"Could you tell me when Lucky Strike changed over from a green pack to white?"

"Oh, that's easy: the beginning of 1942. That dark green color was extremely popular in the twenties and especially the thirties. You saw it everywhere back then. Collectors and decorators refer to it as 'Depression Green.'"

I remembered the bronze green finish on a number of Edna's frogs.

"Anyway," Collins continued, "the dye was copper-based, and after Pearl Harbor, copper was declared crucial war materiel and that color disappeared from the civilian market. The military used copper for everything from artillery shells to camouflage paint. We even got an advertising boost out of it. Somebody came up with the slogan, 'Lucky Strike green has gone to war.' "

"How long would the old green packs have been on the shelves?"

"Most places they'd have moved almost immediately. Of course, we had stocks of the green paper, and we used those up, but I'd say that no green packs were seen for sale after June '42."

"Thanks, Mr. Collins, you've been a big help."

I hung up and sat for a moment in stunned wonder. I'd been a bit surprised to read that Edna was fifty-seven when she died. But unless her memory about the cigarette pack had played her false, Edna Tutt had been closer to seventy years old!

I dialled the 615 number again and got Miss Breckenridge back on the line. "I think I made a mistake. Lucinda Elkins may have graduated in '41 or '42. Could you look it up?"

"Certainly." There was a pause and a bit of tapping, then: "Here we are: Lucinda Elkins attended Holston High from September '38 to June '42."

I felt a triumphant rush. "Great! She may have had a brother who graduated after her by a few years. Do you have a Stanley or a Steven Elkins somewhere from '42 to the mid-fifties? I'm sorry I can't be more specific, but I don't know what their age difference was."

"No problem," she said cheerily. "These computers make it so easy." She tapped for a few more minutes, then: "I'm sorry, but I don't find a Stanley or Steven Elkins anywhere between '40 and '60, although we got a ninth-grader named Steven in '61."

"Can't be the same one." It was a minor disappointment. "Thank you, Miss Breckenridge. I plan to come to Holston in the next day or two to do some research and I'll be calling on you. Would you mind asking around for me and see if anyone there remembers Lucinda? It's a very important matter. Police business."

"Oh, dear. Why, yes, I'd be glad to." She sounded like she needed a little excitement.

"Then I'll be seeing you."

I hung up, then gathered my shaving kit and a change of clothes and threw them in the car. I wanted to call Ann, but she wasn't in the phone book and I hadn't seen a phone in her trailer the night before. I decided her story, if any, could wait. One thing couldn't, though.

I drove around the corner and pulled up in front of the Cohan mansion. I rang the bell and waited a few minutes. I was about to give up when the door swung open. It wasn't Lola.

"Yes?" Angelica Cohan said. "Oh, it's Mr. Treloar, isn't it?" She seemed vaguely courteous, with a chilly edge.

"Yes, it is. I'm calling for Lola. Is she home?"

"Please come in."

I stepped inside and Angelica remained where she was, leaving the door open. Presumably she felt more in control with both of us inside her house.

"My daughter is away on a trip. She won't return for several days."

"Where did she go?" I asked, feeling Patrick Cohan's cold, hostile eyes on me.

"She didn't specify. Ansel tells me that you are investigating that woman's death." It seemed an unsympathetic reference, considering that Edna had been her next-door neighbor, but then the rich calculate distances differently from the rest of us.

"Yes, I am. Did you know Edna well?"

"No. We moved in different circles. Have you found any ... clues, as it were?"

"I'm looking into a number of leads." I could be vague, too.

"Excellent." She paused, as if the next words were an effort. "Mr. Treloar, I would advise you not to place great hopes on any sort of future with my daughter."

Well, that was plain enough. "With all due respect, Mrs.

Cohan, Lola is forty-five years old and so am I. We're grown-ups and we can work out our lives by ourselves."

"Nonetheless, she is still my daughter, and she is not as strong or as stable as you seem to think. I tell you this for your own good as well as for hers." There was steel inside her outer fragility, and it was showing.

"Look, if it's because of Ted Rapley . . ."

"It isn't him!" The bitter hostility in her face shocked me. No love lost between her and old Ted, that was for sure. "Lola has been hurt terribly, many times. It has left her uniquely vulnerable. You seem to be a decent man, Mr. Treloar, and such men have been rare in my daughter's life. Her judgment in men was never the best."

"I'm flattered. What is your objection to me?"

"Oh, to you, none at all. It's just that Lola may place . . . an exaggerated value on your better qualities."

"And I could never measure up?"

"I doubt that anybody could. I will not detain you longer, Mr. Treloar." And I was out the door, wondering what that was all about. Was she serious? Was there an underlying message? Was this just the way Cohans talked to underlings? Or was it just the maunderings of an old woman's pickled brain, and she wouldn't even remember it next time we met?

I got back in the Plymouth and headed out of town, toward Columbus. I didn't get far. The flashing red-and-blue lights in my mirror reminded me that I should have waited until night. I pulled over and watched as a bulky shape climbed from the police car.

"Going somewhere, Gabe?" Lester Cabell asked, leaning on my open window.

"I need to talk to some people out of town."

"Out of state?" he grinned.

"That's right. But I won't be gone long. I'll probably be back by tomorrow night."

"You're asking me to trust you?"

"Look, am I charged with anything?"

"No, no," he chuckled. "I'm just being cautious." He

slapped the door of the Plymouth. "Okay, Gabe, I'm gonna trust you. Go talk to your people and tell me what you found out. 'Bye, now." He shambled back to his car and climbed in, still a schoolyard bully throwing his weight around. But I had to admit he was giving me plenty of leeway to do my work, considering his legitimate suspicions. I made a useful cat's paw and he knew how to run me.

Columbus took an hour, then south on 23 to Portsmouth, where I crossed the Ohio River into Kentucky. The highway skirted the Kentucky-West Virginia border, two-lane for much of the way as the terrain grew mountainous until it was like wadded-up paper, a landscape of high, razor-edged ridges and dark valleys that would have looked like the moon if it hadn't been so green. It was Skinner territory and it seemed to go on forever.

In the southeastern end of the state the signs pointed to names like Hazard and Harlan, resonant of long-ago coal camp wars. Then there was a long, steep ascent and I went over a mountain pass and before me the view opened up into a breath-taking series of hills and valleys marching away in range after range to the distant Blue Ridge. The shadows were long and sharp in the light of the setting sun. It was a rugged landscape, but it was beautiful after the narrow, cramped hollows I had spent four hours traversing.

I pulled over to a wide spot where a convenience store sold gas and sundries and offered travelers their first chance to buy Virginia lottery tickets. A big sign by the road informed me that I was now in Virginia and a smaller historical marker recorded three Civil War skirmishes fought in the little mountain pass, one of them led on the Union side by future U.S. President James Garfield. Plenty of bloodshed in these hills.

I bought gas, and the proprietor told me that Holston was a little over an hour away.

It was fully dark by the time I crossed the little corner of Virginia and passed into Tennessee. Minutes later I was in Edna Tutt's home town, where a teenaged girl named Lucinda Elkins had graduated from high school fourteen years before showing up at Sam and Irma Bloom's photo agency, to earn a sort of immortality under the name Sally Keane. That was a lot of years to account for.

n daylight, I found that Holston, Tennessee, was a pretty, medium-sized city situated on a picturesque river. There was a pungent chemical smell in the air and I remembered what Irma Bloom had said about the Eastman plant. I left my cheap motel and drove past a big paper mill and several large printing facilities and saw signs pointing to an Army ammunition plant. Chemicals seemed to be Holston's stock in trade.

The main high school was a sprawling, brick and glass structure dating from no earlier than the seventies. I was watched as I got out of my car and walked to the main entrance. Strange adults are objects of suspicion around schools these days. I followed the signs to the school office. A receptionist led me to a cubicle where Miss Breckenridge worked at a desktop computer. She was a plump, gray-haired woman who smiled as she took my hand.

"I'm Gabe Treloar. I called you yesterday about Lucinda Elkins."

"Well, you didn't waste any time, did you?"

"I'm working on a tight schedule. Were you able to learn anything beyond what you called up yesterday?"

"You know, I just asked around in the teacher's lounge yesterday and Mary Jackson said if you wanted to talk about Lucinda Elkins, you should come see her."

I couldn't believe my luck. "She knew her?"

"I couldn't say. She just said come see her." She glanced at the clock. In the corridor outside a bell rang. "That's her last class of the day letting out now. Mary teaches mornings on Tuesday. If you want to come with me, I'll take you to her room."

"Lead on," I said.

We went through corridors bustling with students who might have been the ones I went to high school with, except that we would have thought these came from Mars, going by their clothes, hair styles and makeup. They looked exactly like high schoolers in L.A. The regional differences are disappearing fast. It's all MTV coast to coast, these days. We went into the sudden silence of a classroom deserted except for a woman gathering up papers. She looked up as we entered.

"Mary, this is Mr. Treloar. He's the one asking about Lucinda Elkins."

"I'm please to meet you, Mr. Treloar." Mary Jackson surprised me, for no good reason. She was Asian, and looked a little bit like Rose, but with the subtle differences that told me she was of Japanese ancestry. She appeared to be about forty, but my confidence in judging women's ages had just been given a severe jolt.

"Miss Breckenridge says you can tell me about Lucinda Elkins."

She studied me coolly.

"Well, I'll just run along," Miss Breckenridge said, taking the hint. "Nice meeting you, Mr. Treloar."

When she was gone, Mary spoke. "My mother and Lucy Elkins were lifelong friends. Police business was mentioned. Is this something bad?"

"As bad as it can get, I'm afraid. Five days ago the woman you know as Lucinda Elkins was murdered. I have a feeling that she was killed because of something in her past, and I traced her as far as Holston. It hasn't been easy, but I had a few breaks."

Her fingertips went to her lips and her eyelids dropped. "Oh, my God! Mother is just . . ." She shook her head.

"Does your mother live here in Holston?"

"She lives with me. I'll take you to speak with her, but please be easy with her. She isn't as strong as she used to be."

"Don't worry. I'm not interrogating anybody. I just need to know about Lucinda."

"Do you have a car? I usually take the bus home."

"It's parked in the lot out front."

She didn't say anything more until we were in the car. As I drove, she gave directions.

"My mother was a teacher here for almost forty years. It's become a family tradition."

"She lived here all her life?"

"Yes, except for a few years during . . ." her voice caught a little, ". . . during World War Two. She and Lucy were class-mates from grammar school on."

"Did you know her personally?"

"Yes, but Mother is the one you need to talk to."

We stopped in front of a cozy little one-story house on a resi-dential street, its front porch boasting a swing, its railing over-run with a riot of honeysuckle. A brown mongrel got up suspiciously at our arrival, then went into an ecstasy of tail-wagging when it caught Mary Jackson's scent. She scratched behind its ears as we walked to the front door.

"It's all right, Boofer. This is a friend." Boofer didn't even know I was on the same planet. "Mr. Treloar, I'm going to talk with Mother first. This is going to be awfully hard on her."

"Any way you want to play it," I told her. The dog stayed outside when we went in. It was dim and cool inside the house. We were in a living room or parlor with a piano and framed photographs. Mary went into the rear of the house and I stud-ied the pictures. There was a Victorian photo of a middle-aged couple in traditional Japanese clothing. There were others, doubtless friends and family. One stopped me cold. Two teen-aged girls sat on the fender of a vintage De Soto, cokes in hand, identically dressed in white sweaters, long skirts, bobby socks and saddle shoes. One looked much like Mary Jackson. The other was a very young Edna Tutt. Her hair was pulled back, exposing a rather high forehead, and her face had not grown into its full beauty, but the smile was unmistakable.

I heard a sharp gasp from the back of the house. There were no more pictures of Edna, nor was there any sign of a Mr. Jackson. A bookcase on one wall held what seemed to be a complete collection of Holston High yearbooks from the thirties to the present. I itched to pull them out and rummage for Edna's old pictures, but I couldn't do it without permission. I felt that somehow I was close to grasping the most elusive woman I had ever known.

Mary came out of the back. With her was an older copy. Unlike her old friend, this one looked her age, about seventy. She was white-haired, with the authoritative bearing natural to a woman who has spent her life facing down classrooms full of young hellions who would much rather have fun than gain an education.

"Mr. Treloar, this is my mother, Jane Okamura."

I took her hand. "I wish this could have been a happier occasion, Mrs. Okamura."

She was composed but full of sadness. "When Mary said yesterday that someone had called asking about Lucy, and that it was police business, I felt that something terrible had happened. Please, sit down." She looked like she needed to sit a lot worse than I.

"I'll make some coffee," Mary said.

We sat. "You don't seem terribly surprised that she was murdered," I said.

The old woman shook her head. "Sad beyond measure, but no, I can't say I am surprised. I loved Lucy like a sister, and I knew her perhaps better than anyone else. She was not a happy woman, Mr. Treloar, although she could make anyone else feel good."

"For what it's worth, I liked her very much, the short time I knew her."

"Most people did. But there was great sadness in her life, and if I may be melodramatic, I think her life was touched by genuine evil."

I knew I was getting close. "That's what I'm here to learn about. But let's hear it from the beginning. I need to know who Edna . . . who Lucinda Elkins *was.*"

"Let's see . . ." Her dark eyes grew distant. "My parents emigrated from Yokohama just after the First World War. My father found work in Rochester, New York, with Kodak. He became a film technician and was transferred to work in the plant here. I was born here in '23, the same year as Lucy."

So it was true. Sally Keane was thirty-two when she first took her clothes off for photographers. I wondered what Irving Schwartz and the readers of *Neat-O Keane-O* would think of that little fact.

Jane Okamura gathered decades of thoughts as her daughter brought in the coffee and poured cups for the three of us, then she went on.

"I don't even remember when I met Lucy. It was probably in the first grade. Holston was a much smaller town then; just another lazy little Southern town where everybody knew everybody else. We were the only Japanese family in town and we were a bit exotic and this was, after all, the South, but it wasn't disagreeable. Prejudice against Asians was nothing like it was against black people.

"Anyway, it certainly made no difference to Lucy. I doubt that she even noticed until we were in our teens. She was a very high-spirited girl, extremely active, excellent at sports. She would have been considered a tomboy except that she was also so feminine. She was always having trouble with her mother, who was very, very religious. Mrs. Elkins wouldn't permit her to go out for the swimming team, because she thought the suits were too immodest. Dancing, of course, was unthinkable, as was wearing makeup. Movies were forbidden, too. Lucy had to sneak out to them with me or with other friends."

So movies were the forbidden fruit. That could explain her show-biz ambitions.

"Lucy insisted on going out for the track team, and her mother couldn't object too strongly. In Tennessee, as long as it is connected to sports, it has to be all right. Anything else is almost treasonous.

"Her father worked at one of the printing facilities, but he was ill much of the time, some sort of heart condition. He died when Lucy was about nine. Her mother remarried just a few months later, and Lucy never got along with her stepfather. Her mother was strict, but her stepfather was abusive. He was an ignorant, fanatical preacher, and I know that he beat her more than once for little things; absurd trifles like wearing lipstick or listening to swing music on the radio. She was determined to leave home as soon as she was old enough."

She took a deep breath. "But overall, our lives weren't terribly different from those of other girls our age at that time. We agonized over school and grades, we talked about the boys we liked or didn't like, we resented the cliques that wouldn't let us in, and we formed our own with students of a like mind. We considered ourselves more intelligent and independent. It was the sort of life they celebrated in all those silly movies back then, the Andy Hardy things and those Frank Capra celebrations of small-town American life. If you'd gone into Holston High back then, you wouldn't have been surprised to see Mickey Rooney and Judy Garland in the corridors."

She looked up at the photo of her younger self and Lucy Elkins seated on the De Soto. "Of course, all that changed in December of 1941."

"It must have been a terrible time for you," I said.

"It was more than awful. I had never thought of myself as Japanese. I was a Tennessee girl. Suddenly, I and my whole family were enemy aliens. People wrote horrible things on our house, on the sidewalk out front. My little sister was beaten up coming home from school. Our dog was shot. In the end, we were shipped off to a concentration camp. And that's what it was, don't let anyone tell you different.

"Sometimes I feel a little ashamed for being so bitter about those years. Compared to the sufferings of others, ours were minor. People died horribly by the millions all over the world, and at least ours weren't death camps. But it was all so unnecessary, just wartime hysteria. Still, citizens of German ancestry weren't harassed. People with names like Eisenhower weren't sent to camps."

She waved a hand in front of her face, clearing away a fog. "I'm getting off the point. Please forgive me. The point is that it needn't have been terrible for Lucy, but it was. Lucy had an easily outraged sense of justice. She stuck by me every day until we were sent away. When other students cursed at me in the halls, she turned on them. She had a gift for sarcasm that was hard to credit.

"On the most notable occasion, a dreadful boy—he became mayor some years later—passed a remark concerning the well-known misconception about Asian female anatomy. I was so mortified that I couldn't speak, but Lucy could. She said, loudly, and I quote: 'What would a needle-dick pissant like you know about it? You've never even seen a white woman's!' Please excuse the language, but Lucy knew no moderation when she defended me."

"I've heard worse," I assured her. "This must have made her unpopular."

"You can't imagine. Of course her parents heard of it and that led to more beatings. She was forbidden to see me and she ignored that. But the worst came when the removal order came and Lucy insisted on protesting at the weekly school assembly. She started out being calm and reasonable, but all the hoots and catcalls made her angry and she ended up denouncing the principal as a coward too spineless to protect one of his own students."

"I'm amazed they let her graduate at all," I said.

"I think the faculty were all a bit ashamed of themselves, knowing that this girl was taking a principled stand while they acquiesced to a weaseling, hypocritical policy. Luckily, by that time, the school year was almost over. I don't believe anyone at the school said a word to Lucy from that assembly to her graduation. I didn't see her again until after the war."

"Yet you came back here."

"Where would I go. The hysteria wasn't local, it was nationwide. I wasn't about to leave the country, so I came back to the place I knew. I was married by that time—my husband was a decorated veteran of the fighting in Italy. Those years abounded in irony. I went to Eastern Tennessee State University and in 1950 I began teaching in my old high school."

"That must have seemed strange."

"Many of the same people were still teaching and working there. For years they wouldn't meet my eyes when we spoke. It was a sort of revenge for me, I suppose."

"When did you see Lucy again?"

"It was in '51. She came home for her brother's high school graduation. We had a very tearful reunion. Of course, she berated me for working with the people who had treated me so shabbily, but we were very different people by that time."

"What had she been doing during the war years and after?"

"She worked at several jobs in Knoxville—during the war there was always plenty of employment. But despite her unwillingness to hate me for my ancestry, Lucy was as patriotic as anyone else. She tried to join the WACs, but she couldn't pass the physical, if you can believe that—something to do with her eyes, I think. So she ended up joining the USO. She toured all over North Africa and Europe until late '46. She was never with the big-name acts—Bob Hope or any of those—but she loved it. Everyone did everything on those shows, so she sang and danced and shifted the props and operated the lights and microphones.

"She came under fire a few times, and once the truck she was riding in took a wrong turn and she was almost captured by the Germans, and she loved it all, the danger and the attention, the applause, the excitement—Lucy was in her element.

"But when she left the USO in '46, jobs were hard to come by. Plus, she wanted to get into show business, so she worked as a waitress and a hotel maid in New York, trying to get on the stage all the while. She found that producers and New York audiences were a bit more demanding than USO officers and GIs. And, God bless her, she just wasn't very talented in that way, although she'd never face the fact.

"When I saw her again, she was planning her move to California. She was sure that movies would be more promising than the New York stage. Of course, it was the same story. About once a year she came back to visit, then it was every three or four years, after she left California and changed her name. She wrote frequently, though."

"Does the name Sally Keane mean anything to you?" I asked.

For the first time she laughed. "Of course! Lucy loved to scandalize me with those pictures. I don't know how it survived her upbringing but she was the least body-conscious person I ever knew. I suppose like most stage-struck people she was an exhibitionist at heart. And she was always able to convince people she was at least ten years younger than her real age."

"She convinced me," I told her. "I had her pegged closer to twenty years younger than she really was."

"I used to tell her," Mary Jackson said, taking part for the first time, "all she had to do to be a millionaire was write a book with her pictures and birth certificate in it and pretend she knew how she did it. She'd blow Jane Fonda off the charts."

"She said that it was just 'good genes, clean living and regular scheduled maintenance,'" Jane said. "In the early fifties she did a bit role in one of Buster Crabbe's children's television programs. She said Crabbe was the same way—in his fifties by then but looking barely thirty."

"Did she say anything about why she gave it all up and changed her name?"

"It was the one part of her life that she kept a complete secret," Jane said, disappointing me. "She said only one woman knew her secrets and she didn't talk."

Who was this? Sue Oldenburg? Unlikely. Some other old friend tucked away in some obscure corner of the country? More likely. Or just an enigmatic utterance by a woman who had clamped down tight on her life? Most likely of all.

"When did you last see her?"

"In March. She came down here and said she was going to get my garden in order. I confess she could get tiresome on the subject of gardening. I told her she would do no such thing, I preferred to let it grow wild."

"Was she acting differently from before?"

"It's hard to say, her visits were so infrequent. She was less ebullient, more introspective. A number of times I thought she was finally going to tell me what had been troubling her for so many years, but she thought better of it. I know it was something that went far back, and I suspect it involved a man, or men. And it was something terrible, to make a woman as strong as Lucinda give up her dreams and go to live in obscurity under an assumed name."

"Did she ever tell you where she was living, or what the name was?"

"Never, although by little inferences over the years I gathered it was in Ohio. Her car had Ohio plates and once an envelope fell from her purse addressed to an Edna Tutt." She hesitated a moment. "And . . . it's only a feeling, but I had the impression that she was still living close to the evil that blighted her life. She hadn't truly run away from it."

I looked over at the case of yearbooks. "May I see Lucy's old pictures?"

"Oh, certainly."

I went over to the case and began pulling out the '38 to '42 volumes. Freshman, sophomore, junior, senior: a pretty, dark-haired girl growing prettier by the year.

"You say her brother graduated in '51?" I took down the book for that year.

"Yes. He was in one of my classes during his senior year. A quiet boy, but difficult to teach. I suspect that Lucy's stepfather was very brutal toward him. I know Stan gave her a lot of grief, after he moved in with her in California."

"So I heard." I flipped to E in the senior pictures, but no Stan Elkins. "I don't see him. Did he miss the photo session that year?"

"I'm sure he's in there." Jane rose from her chair and came over to look at the book. "Oh, Stan wasn't an Elkins. He was Lucy's half-brother by her stepfather." She flipped a few pages. "There's Stan."

A moon-faced teenaged boy, vaguely handsome, his half-formed features as yet unmarked by character and experience. Just like a million other teenaged boys. But the name below the picture came up and slapped me in the face: Stanley Kincaid.

Four days before, in Mark Fowles's office: "*One was Jarvis Skinner. The other was a small-timer named Stanley Kincaid. He'd done time with Jarvis in the state pen. No history of violent crime but I guess he was working his way up.*"

Edna Tutt's little brother was killed in the Cohan Chemical robbery of '65.

12

I was at the Monticello library when it opened in the morning. I'd driven back from Holston the night before, slept four hours and woke up more energized than if I'd slept twelve hours and had a handful of uppers for breakfast. I brushed past the librarian who opened the door and went straight for the microfiche room.

I took out the tapes for the Monticello and Columbus papers dated December '65. I knew that, somehow, brother Stanley was the key. But where did he fit?

The robbery had taken place on December 1st, too late for the morning papers. The Columbus afternoon paper missed it as well. The Monticello paper for the 2nd, the one I'd seen in the old train station, carried its biggest headline since Pearl Harbor:

4 SLAIN IN COHAN CHEMICAL ROBBERY!
Sheriff Fowles, Raymond Purvis, Two Robbers
Killed in Hail of Gunfire
Cohan Driver Sturdevant Wounded, May Not Live

The story went on, a little breathlessly:

In a daring, daylight holdup that went terribly wrong, four gunmen robbed Cohan Chemical Company of a record payroll. Their well-planned criminal operation went awry when Sheriff John Fowles took a hand, at the cost of his own life (see Obituary, p. 5).

Eyewitness accounts conflict, but the sequence of events seems to have been as follows: Four gunmen, their faces concealed by stocking masks, drove through the gate of the Monticello plant at 8:30 AM, entered the gatehouse and overpowered gate guard Harmon Gilchrist, then concealed themselves in the gatehouse until the car carrying the payroll arrived at 8:45. The robbers' car, with two of the bandits inside, sped from behind the gatehouse to block the way and the remaining two robbers rushed out to take control of the payroll car.

At that moment the operation, reminiscent of the famous Brinks Armored Car robbery, began to go awry. According to one eyewitness, the Cohan driver, Bill Sturdevant, put the car in reverse and tried to escape. At that instant, he was shot by one of the robbers, who emerged from the passenger seat of the robbers' car and opened fire with a shotgun. Shotgun slugs struck Sturdevant in the head and chest. Sturdevant is currently in Holy Name Hospital in intensive care.

At the first shot Sheriff Fowles, who had been seated in back on the passenger side, emerged from the car and engaged the robbers with his Thompson submachine gun. He sprayed the robbers' car with bullets, killing the driver, who was in the act of emerging from the vehicle, gun in hand, as well as the shotgun-wielding passenger (see diagram, p. 2).

Sheriff Fowles then aimed across the top of the payroll car at the two surviving robbers. Tragically, a chance bullet fired by a robber struck the magazine of the submachine gun, jamming the weapon. The two robbers ran around the payroll car and fired at Sheriff Fowles, striking him repeatedly.

At some time during the brief but terrible exchange of fire, a bullet, deliberately or by chance, struck Cohan Chemical accountant Raymond Purvis in the forehead, killing him instantly (see Obituary, p.5). The surviving robbers then took the payroll, contained in several canvas bags, from the payroll car and transferred it to their own. They then entered their car and sped away, leaving their companions lying dead on the pavement.

The whole action, from the arrival of the payroll car to the escape of the felons, occupied scarcely three minutes. The robbers' vehicle, described variously as a late-model Pontiac or an older Buick, black in color, was seen turning onto the Fredericktown Road but was not subsequently spotted.

The shotgun-wielding robber killed by Sheriff Fowles has been identified as Jarvis Skinner, a Monticello resident with a history of violent crime. The driver, also killed by Sheriff Fowles, remains unidentified. The escaping robbers are described as white males, one tall and bulky, the other smaller and slender of build.

Police throughout Ohio have been put on all-points alert and federal authorities have been contacted.

Another story on the same page carried a title in slightly smaller type:

COHAN CHEMICAL ROBBERS NET STAGGERING 2.5 MILLION DOLLARS

James Cohan, owner of Cohan Chemical Corporation, has confirmed to this reporter that yesterday's robbery, in which four men were slain and another left in critical condition, netted the robbers a staggering two and a half million dollars. Questioned about the extraordinary amount, Mr. Cohan replied:

"The payroll carried in that car yesterday was not only

for the Monticello plant, but for our offices in Columbus and Chillicothe as well. The December payroll is always the largest of the year as it contains all the Christmas bonuses. I might add that it also contained my own yearly salary and those of my top executives. In keeping with the policy laid down by Patrick Cohan, our founder, everyone in Cohan Chemical, from the janitor to the owner, is paid in cash. I should long ago have considered what a tempting target it must be for thieves, but Monticello is such a peaceful town that one seldom thinks in such terms. I feel a deep, terrible responsibility for what happened yesterday."

The visibly distraught Mr. Cohan went on: "In Raymond Purvis and Sheriff John Fowles I have lost two close, dear friends. Bill Sturdevant is a trusted employee of many years' service and I have, of course, assumed responsibility for all of his hospital care and expenses. I have also posted a fifty thousand dollar reward for information leading to the apprehension, arrest and conviction of these murderers."

There was more in the same vein. The witnesses were plant employees and people who lived near the plant entrance, but my own experience told me how seldom eyewitness evidence has any value. Most people notice little enough in their everyday lives. Give them a situation entirely out of their usual experience and you have as many descriptions as you have witnesses. There was one witness here I wanted to look up, and I really had only one important question to ask him.

The rest of the articles over the next few days consisted of repeats and the stories of people who were just talking to each other. A *Times-Tribune* article on the 4th was headed:

SECOND COHAN CHEMICAL ROBBER IDENTIFIED

Authorities have positively identified the driver in the robbery of December 1st as Stanley Kincaid, a California felon with a long record of petty arrests, who recently served time in Tennessee for auto theft. Kincaid, a Tennessee native, was arrested as part of a car-theft ring running stolen vehicles from California to the Southeast. Jarvis Skinner, also killed in the holdup, served time at the same institution and the two are believed to have met there.

That was that. Just another small-timer killed in another robbery. But another article on the same page caught my eye.

SHERIFF'S DEPUTY KILLED IN HIT-AND-RUN

Tragedy struck the Polk County Sheriff's Department for the second time in a week when Deputy Richard Percy, 25, was struck by a hit-and-run driver in front of his house on Holly Street last night. Percy rose from his bed in spite of a lingering case of flu to help on the late shift. As he was unlocking the door of his car, a speeding vehicle lurched around the corner of Holly and Ridgecrest, sideswiping Percy's car, crushing the deputy between the two vehicles. The driver then sped off. No witness has been found to supply a description of the vehicle.

"I didn't want him to go to work tonight," said Percy's sobbing widow, JoAnne, 23. "But he wanted to help out the Department. They've been so shorthanded since Sheriff John was killed and so many out with the flu."

Services for Richard Percy will be held at the First Congregational Church on Saturday at 1:00 PM.

Somebody had been tying up some loose ends. Mark had said that all three deputies were out with the flu that day. I'd have bet big money that Percy had been the one scheduled to guard the payroll. Either he had really caught flu, or he'd used it as an excuse to back out of the job. The robbers had been expecting an accomplice inside the payroll car. They hadn't been expecting the Sheriff and his Tommy gun.

A look at the phone book showed that Harmon Gilchrist still

lived in Monticello, with an address on Tyler Street. I remembered that the chemical plant was at the end of Tyler, near the river. I called and the phone was picked up on the second ring.

"I'm trying to reach Mr. Harmon Gilchrist."

"That's me."

"Mr. Gilchrist, my name is Gabe Treloar and I'm researching the Cohan Chemical robbery of 1965. Are you the Mr. Gilchrist who was in the gatehouse that day?"

"You got the right man. If you have questions about that robbery, you just ask me." The voice was elderly, and the tone was eager to talk.

"Would it be convenient for you if I called on you now? I can be at your place in five minutes."

"Come on over."

A short drive along the Columbus road brought me to Tyler and I turned left. Gilchrist's house was in the second block. To the south, three blocks farther on, I could see the entrance to the chemical plant. I pulled into the driveway and got out. A tall, very thin old man stood on the porch.

"Harmon Gilchrist?"

"You got the right man. You're Mr. Treloar?"

"That's right."

"Would you be any relation to Ed Treloar, used to work for Cohan?"

"I'm his son."

He held out a thin hand and we shook. His hair was white and lay close to his skull, but he was erect and his voice was firm.

"What is it you need to know about that robbery? I know it all. I'm the only one that was there from beginning to end." I could tell that it was his one big story. He wouldn't need any prodding.

"I've been looking up the newspaper stories and they were pretty vague."

The old man snorted. "Them newspaper articles didn't get nothing right, hardly. Them reporters wouldn't listen to me." I could hear an old bitterness coming through.

"Why was that? You were there, you should have been the prime eyewitness."

"You'd'a thought so, wouldn't you? But people acted like it was someways my fault, like I should've took them robbers on by myself. Hell, all I had was an old .38, and there was four of 'em with serious hardware."

"There was nothing you could have done," I assured him, knowing his manhood still suffered after almost thirty years. "Hell, if John Fowles couldn't take them all out with his Tommy gun, how could you do it with a pistol, when they had the drop on you like that?"

"Damn right," he said, nodding. Then he looked up. "Feel like a walk?"

"Suits me."

"Let's go down to the plant. I'll show you how it went that day." We went down his walk and turned down the street toward the plant. "How come you're looking into that old robbery?" he asked. "You writing something about it?"

"No, I was investigating something else and the robbery kept cropping up."

"I think it was Mr. Cohan convinced them reporters I wasn't reliable. James Cohan, that is. He was owner then. It was like he thought it was somehow my fault. He acted like my word couldn't be taken seriously, like I was a drunk or something, and I never took more than a beer or two in my life."

"He must have been pretty upset."

"Upset ain't the word for it. 'Course, him and Ray Purvis was pretty close." He turned and looked at me. "It would've been your father in that car if he hadn't left—what was it? A year before?"

"About a year and a half. Dad was pretty broken up when we heard about Ray. It was on Huntley-Brinkley that evening."

"Yep," he nodded, exuding satisfaction, "made the news nationwide. There was reporters from all over, camera crews, the works."

The walk down the shady street was pleasant, the morning cool, the sunlight falling between the leaves in brilliant little points. We crossed a double set of railroad tracks and came to the plant entrance.

The plant covered several acres, full of hulking buildings and chemical storage tanks. I remembered it as a noisy, smoky place, but it had either changed its operations or complied with government emissions standards. There were only a few wisps of steam to be seen and the place seemed to operate in total silence. The grounds were surrounded by a chain-link fence, the entrance secured by a double, rolling gate, open at the moment. To the left of the gate stood the gatehouse, a one-room building with glass windows facing on the street. We walked through the open gate and a uniformed man came from the gatehouse.

" 'Mornin', Arthur," Gilchrist said.

"Hello, Harmon," the man said, boredly. "Back for another visit?"

"Just telling this young man about the big robbery," Gilchrist said, proudly. The guard shrugged and went back inside.

"Now that morning," Gilchrist began, "I was sitting behind my desk in there when this black Pontiac, a new one, pulls through the gate. Now, it was supposed to stop right there in front, but sometimes people don't notice the sign and go on in. So I got up and went out to talk to 'em. The work force was already inside the plant. Nobody comes in late on payday.

"I barely got out the door before there was a gun in my face and two men was shoving me back inside. You ever seen men with stocking masks over their faces? They look like something out of Frankenstein's lab."

"I've seen them," I said. "It's scary."

" 'Bout give me a heart attack. One of 'em snatched my gun out of my holster before I could make a move. They pushed me back in my chair—it was an old swivel chair—and cuffed my hands behind my back. Then one of 'em tied my feet to the chair with clothesline."

"They came prepared," I said.

"They knew what they was doing."

"Did they say anything?"

"First one of 'em said, 'Go back in and sit down.' Then while they were tying me up, one said, 'just sit there and be quiet and nobody gets hurt.' They kind of growled, like they were disguising their voices."

"What did they look like?"

"One was big, burly. Other one wasn't as big, kind of slender built." Just what the paper had said.

"Could you tell anything about hair or eye color?"

"Not through those masks. And they were wearing watch caps under the masks, so their hair didn't show."

"Did you see the ones that stayed in the car?"

"Not until the shooting started and they was killed."

"Okay. They barged in and tied you up. What then?"

"Well, I was tied up and still trying to figure out what'd happened when the payroll car got there. See, they set me in my chair right in front of that window. Anyone going by would see me and think nothing was wrong."

"Just a minute. The paper said the robbers got here at 8:30 and the payroll car arrived at 8:45."

He snorted. "They weren't there any fifteen minutes. Mr. Cohan just wouldn't believe they could cut it that close, and everybody listened to him, not me. They wasn't there more than five minutes before the car showed up."

Had somebody tipped the robbers when the payroll left the bank? The tighter they could schedule it, the less chance some late-arriving employees would stumble onto their caper.

"Then what?"

"Okay, this is the important part, the part the police and the reporters really got wrong." He glared like this had eaten at him for all the years since.

"Tell me."

"You read those accounts, they all say the shooting started when the driver, Bill Sturdevant, tried to get away. Well, that car was in park through the whole thing. I went over and took a look while the ambulance boys was taking poor Bill out. What happened was, the robbers' car pulled out from behind the gatehouse right there." He pointed and swept his arm, indicating the car's path.

"It stopped maybe ten feet in front of the payroll car. That

Skinner boy jumped out of the passenger side with a shotgun and he fired right through the windshield at Bill. There was no waiting, he come out of that car ready to open fire.

"Before that shot, the two in the gatehouse was running out." He took a deep breath. "Now you got to understand, this takes me a while to describe to you, but it all happened so fast, it was over in ten-twenty seconds."

"I know how fast things go down when the shooting starts," I assured him. "I was a cop for twenty years."

"Then you know what I'm talking about. Okay, when that Skinner boy got out with his shotgun, the driver piled out at the same time. He had a pistol, holding it like he didn't know what to do. I got the impression he wasn't expecting the shooting." That was Stanley Kincaid, Edna's brother.

"Now Sheriff Fowles got out on the passenger side, away from me, but I saw his head and shoulders come up over the top of the car real fast, before Skinner could pump and fire again. He had that old Tommy gun, and I saw him glance for just a second at the two running up from the driver's side of the car, then he opened up. He shot the Skinner boy first."

"The two in the gatehouse," I asked him, "how were they armed?"

"They both had snub-nosed pistols."

"So Fowles took out the shotgun first. Smart move."

"That's how I figured it. Then he shot the driver, that Kincaid fella. He just had to move his gun a few inches to do that. He turned to his left and tried to shoot across the top of the car at that bigger man, who was trying to run across the front of it to get a clear shot at the sheriff. Both of those men were firing at him as they ran. That must've been when a shot hit the big drum clip on the Thompson gun. I saw it jerk in his hands. He tried to fire, but both of the robbers ran around the car from front and back and they finished emptying their guns at him. He was hit five times."

"Did you notice when Ray Purvis was hit?"

"I sure did," he nodded, grimly, playing it out for effect. "That's another thing the papers and the radio and TV reports all got wrong, and I don't know why. When Sheriff Fowles was dead, those two men started grabbing the money sacks. Mr. Purvis was just sitting there, sort of stunned. I thought if he held still he'd be okay, but while the skinny one was carrying the money sacks to the getaway car, the big one took a little automatic out of his back pocket, leaned back inside and shot him through the forehead, cool as you please."

"Do you think he could have seen something, maybe recognized one of them?"

"I don't know how he could've seen more than I did, and they didn't bother to kill me."

I had one more question, and it was one I dreaded. "Mr. Gilchrist, the smaller of the two robbers who tied you up—is it possible that was a woman?"

"You mean a Bonnie and Clyde sort of thing?" He shook his head. "No, that one was smaller than the other, but they was both good-sized men, and no growling's gonna make a woman's voice sound like that."

"It was just a thought," I said, relieved.

"Even Mark Fowles never asked me if one was a woman."

"He's talked with you about it?"

"Every couple of years he comes to see me and we go over it. He thinks maybe I'll remember something new, but that ain't gonna happen." He shook his head again, looking up at the blue sky, brooding. "I've thought about that morning every day of my life since, going over it all. There's nothing else to tell. But his father's death hit young Mark hard. He wants them two men, wants 'em bad."

A big car rolled up to the gate, as another, similar car had rolled up on that morning in '65. This one was gray, with smoked windows. It brought the gate guard running and he touched the brim of his cap as the left rear window rolled down.

"Mornin' Mr. Cohan."

"Good morning, Arthur," Ansel Cohan said. He looked around and saw us. "Well, hello, Gabe, Harmon." He got out of the limo and walked over to us.

"I've been telling young Mr. Treloar about the big robbery," Harmon said, proudly.

"Well, you've come to the right man, Gabe," Ansel told me.

"Harmon saw it all." Then he cocked a graying eyebrow at me. "But I thought you were looking into Edna Tutt's murder."

"Oh, I was checking out some records from when Edna moved here and that wasn't long after the robbery. It was still in the papers. I never did get the whole story about that affair, so I decided to talk to Harmon about it. He seems to be the only surviving witness who saw it first-hand."

"That he is. A few people saw some of it from the plant," he nodded toward the buildings fifty yards away, "but they didn't look until after the firing began. Some people up the street came out when they heard the noise and saw the getaway car tearing off in that direction."

"I hear Mark Fowles is still looking for the two who got away," I said.

"Mark has a bee in his bonnet about the incident," Ansel said with a tiny shrug. "Understandable, with his father dying that way when Mark was so young and impressionable. But somehow I don't think those two will ever be caught, not after so many years, don't you agree?"

"It doesn't happen often." I said.

"They were just criminals, after all, and that sort kill each other, often as not," Ansel persisted. "With two and a half million in cash, 1965 dollars, how long would they have lasted, once their cohorts learned what they had?"

"It's a lot of money," I agreed.

"I wasn't here, of course, but later on I heard all about the legal wrangle with the insurance company. It was pretty fierce and took more than a year, but in the end they had to pay up."

"Must've been hard on your employees in the meantime," I noted.

"Cohan Chemical has always been blessed with a loyal work force," Ansel said. "We stick by each other in the hard times."

Harmon Gilchrist looked like he wanted to spit.

"Have you turned up anything on the Tutt murder?" Ansel asked.

"A few things."

"What did you learn on your little trip out of state?" Letting me know Cabell was keeping him informed.

"A few more things."

He grinned. "Like to play it close to the vest, eh?"

"I don't like to talk about my investigations while I'm still gathering information. It's too easy to make those intuitive leaps on insufficient evidence and I don't trust them. I should have what I need in a few days."

"Do you really think you're going to be able to make sense of that godawful business?"

"Things are starting to come together."

"You know, if you can crack this thing, Ted Rapley's going to be very impressed. He can always use good investigators, and he's on his way up. If you'd like, I'll speak to him about it."

"Let me think about it," I said. "I wasn't always on good terms with the DA's office, in my cop days. It would be a radical change."

He went serious. "Sometimes you have to put things behind you to turn your life around and get ahead. It's never too late in life to consider making a change. Think about it."

We shook hands and he got back into his limo. It pulled silently into the plant compound. I began walking back up the street with Harmon.

"What do you think of Ansel?" I asked him.

"Guess I like him better than I did his old man, not that that's saying much." He thought for a minute. "You know, there's lots of stories about him, and I'm not sure if they're true, but you sure never see him squiring the ladies around. But he don't act, you know, limp-wristed or faggoty, so I'm not sure what to think."

"But you don't really like him?"

"Cohans don't want to be liked. But they make sure you respect them. They about own the county, so they get all the respect they want."

I thanked him and drove back into town, thinking about events long ago, things dead and buried that come back to haunt you.

Lew spread out the Xeroxes of the pages from the high school yearbooks on his coffee table. He lived in a small, one-story brick house two blocks from the newspaper building. A bottle of beer sat on the table by the pictures, condensation flecking its sides. He studied the faces, Edna's and her brother's, like they were going to tell him something.

"What do we know now?" he said, rhetorically. "We have a line on who she was, from the time she was born up through her modeling days. And we know her brother did prison time, got mixed up there with Jarvis Skinner, and was killed along with Skinner in the holdup. But what happened in there to make her drop everything in California, change her name and come here to live? You'd think this was the last place she'd want to be."

"There's another link in there someplace," I told him. "There's more to it than just brother Stanley."

"Can we be so sure that the robbery and her murder are connected?"

"Things tie in too closely," I insisted. "The robbery in '65 and the murder last Thursday night; brother and sister linked by violent death in Monticello, Ohio. Her letter to Sue Oldenburg said things had caught up with her."

"That doesn't necessarily mean anything as far back as 1965," Lew pointed out.

"But it's what I've got. Ann Smyth was starting to tell me about Jarvis and his connection to the murder when we were interrupted."

"That little chippie is likely to say anything for money. And maybe all she knows is that Edna's brother was the wheelman. That could be common knowledge in Skinnertown, which might as well be the moon as far as the rest of Monticello is concerned. Has she tried to contact you again?"

"Not as far as I know. She might have tried to call but I don't have an answering machine and wouldn't use one if I had. Everyone from Lester Cabell to your girl Sharon would be making copies."

"Sharon's okay," Lew said, a bit shamefaced. "She's just a little ambitious."

I wondered if I could be reading his embarrassment correctly. "Lew, shame on you! She's young enough to be your daughter!"

"She's thirty," he said, defensively. "I'd have needed an awfully early start to be her dad. Anyway, I don't blab things to her."

Sure you don't, I thought, knowing now I'd have to be careful what I said to him.

"Let's get back to the point," Lew said. "Let's talk motive. What makes someone change a whole life and wait in one place for almost thirty years and keep it a secret from everyone?"

"The big ones," I said. "Love, hate, revenge." I thought of me and Lola, together again after all that time. What was that?

"Then who was it she loved or hated? Who did she want revenge on? This wasn't her beloved twin here." He slapped the picture of Stanley with the backs of his fingers for emphasis. "He was so much younger she must barely have known him when they were kids. He had a different father. When he came back into her life in California he was nothing but trouble. He got killed pulling a stupid robbery and the man who killed him died seconds later."

"Not much motive for revenge," I admitted. "Not for a woman with an oversized sense of justice."

"Love, then? Sue seems to think she was seeing someone."

"If so, she kept it as quiet as everything else in her life. And would she hang around that long for one man? That's something from a folk song."

"Maybe it was more than one." Lew picked up the beer and took a pull at it. "Maybe it was a series of discreet, well-heeled, married men. She couldn't have been living on her savings all those years."

"That would have called for a number of people, including some unhappy wives, to be awfully quiet."

"People keep things to themselves, especially in a town like Monticello. And she was getting on in years. I still can hardly believe that she was almost seventy! She held the advancing years at bay for an incredible time, but nobody wins that fight. Maybe her sources had dried up and she was resorting to blackmail."

I didn't like that. Viscerally, my being rebelled. "That doesn't sound like Edna."

Lew looked at me solemnly. "Gabe, I never thought I'd have to tell an L.A. cop this, but you're letting affection color your judgment. Hell, you're half in love with some decades-old pictures and stories about a young girl." He took another pull at his beer.

"You remember the kids you and I were at seventeen. Would we know those two boys if they walked through that door right now?" He gestured with the bottle. "They'd be strangers to us. They'd have the same names, we'd share a few memories in common, but otherwise there'd be no resemblance. We've had twenty-odd years of wars and careers and marriage and whatnot to shape us into different people. That amount of experience changes idealistic kids into disillusioned, middle-aged men. And Edna Tutt or Sally Keane or Lucy Elkins, or whoever the hell she was, had a *big* head start on us in that regard."

"I can't buy it," I insisted, stubbornly. "I didn't know her long, but I couldn't picture her as a cold-blooded blackmailer."

"No need for her to be an evil vamp. Just a desperate woman facing a lonely old age. It wouldn't take much for her to justify it to herself; those fat, respectable hypocrites who used her, then dumped her when they were bored or afraid their wives would find out. Maybe she tried to lean on them and maybe one of them was not a good man to push."

"There was more than one," I pointed out as he got up, went to his refrigerator and pulled out another beer. He sat back down and twisted off the cap.

"Hired help. While he amused himself torturing and killing Edna, the errand boy tossed the house for the love letters or incriminating pictures. Sally Keane would've known her way around a camera. Maybe she was saving a little insurance for a rainy day."

"I don't think so. She would've turned them over the minute he threatened her."

"Maybe they never existed and he wouldn't buy it. Life can be a nasty business, and it's easy for people to get in over their heads. No, Edna wasn't an evil woman. She might have been scared and made a foolish mistake late in life."

"Evil," I said, musing, letting the word spin me back into some memories. "It's not a word you hear much these days."

"Just in novels about the supernatural," Lew said. "Like it doesn't exist in the real world. But it does. We've seen it, haven't we?"

"Right," I said, still remembering. "You see so much of it in cop work that it does weird things to your head, to your whole outlook on life. I think of the things I saw and did in those years and I can't believe it was me."

"Like what?" he asked, the young police reporter coming back strong.

"Well, there was once . . ." I hesitated. This was one I never could have told my wife. But, what the hell. ". . . I was with my partner, Murray—I'll have to tell you about Murray sometime. Anyway, it was the middle of the night and we got a squeal about a domestic argument and shooting. Our unit got there first." The scene came back in my mind over the years: the flashing, red-and-blue lights, the sirens coming in from other directions, the huddle of neighbors standing around.

"We went into the house and it was a bad one. A body on the floor and one on the bed and there were two little kids in the bed with the body, unharmed. Not shot, anyway. It was a blood-on-the-ceiling scene. That's no exaggeration, Lew. It was actually dripping on us from the ceiling."

"I've seen the phenomenon," he said.

"The way we got the story, finally, was this guy and his wife had been arguing, and he was beating her around, and she retreated to the kids' bedroom, and she got the kids in bed with her because she thought he wouldn't hurt her with them there.

"So he comes into the room with his shotgun and he puts it to her forehead and orders her to come back to bed with him or he'll pull the trigger. She just hugs the kids closer to her and squeezes her eyes shut and won't do it. So he tells her the same thing a couple more times and she still won't do it. So he pulls the trigger." Lew looked at me without expression. It wasn't exactly an unusual story.

"Anyway, having blown his wife's head all over the wall, not to mention all over his kids, he gets all remorseful and sticks the shotgun under his chin and pulls the trigger again. That was the blood and hair and stuff all over the ceiling. About two minutes later Murray and I show up.

"So, we got the meat wagons there and someone to take care of the kids and so forth, and the amazing thing was, the guy was still alive. He'd flinched at the last instant and only blew half his face off. He lived to stand trial. Looked like something from a horror movie, which didn't do his chances with the jury much good.

"Finally, Murray and I were out in the front yard finishing up our questioning the neighbors when this paramedic came over and asked us if we knew where the guy's eye was."

"His eye?" Lew said.

"That's what *we* said. The paramedic said that one of the guy's eyes was missing, along with that whole side of his face.

He told us if we could find the eye, they might be able to reconstruct the socket and put it back in. It'd be blind, of course, but at least he'd have an eye.

"So we went back in. Everyone else was gone and we went into the bedroom and looked all around and sure enough, in one of the corners there was this perfect, blue eye on the floor, looking up at us. So we looked back at it for a while.

"Then Murray turned to me and he said, 'That guy was a real son of a bitch, wasn't he?', and I said yes he sure was. So Murray stepped on the eye. Squish. And it was just a smear on the floor."

Lew was looking at me now with his mouth a little open.

"The thing was, at the time it seemed like a perfectly normal thing to do. That's what police work does to you."

I thought about that time during the short drive back to my apartment. It was dark by then, I'd spent most of the afternoon and evening going over the unfolding Edna Tutt story with Lew. The sort of hardness I'd described to Lew, the nonchalance toward death and tragedy, was a necessity in cop business. Rookies turned green and got sick and had nightmares. After a while you got over that, except sometimes for the nightmares.

The hardest part was keeping the brutality of the job separate from your home life. Police marriages often fell apart for that reason. How do you go home and talk about how you spent your day after something like the scene in that house? Rose had been understanding about it. She'd lived most of her life in a war-torn country. She hadn't been raised to expect an Ozzie and Harriet life in the 'burbs. Still, it hadn't been easy.

That's one reason why cops tend to clannishness. They socialize with other cops and their families. Who else can understand the way they live? But that creates even more distance between them and the civilian population; more us-against-them mentality.

As I walked through my door the ringing of the telephone shook me out of my reverie. I snatched up the receiver.

"Treloar?" It was Ann Smyth.

"That's right."

"Where the hell've you been?"

"Away," I said, impatiently. "Do you have anything for me?"

"You got five hundred?"

"If you have something I don't already know. I've been picking up information on my own."

She was quiet for a moment. "Well, you sure as hell don't got this, or you wouldn't be talking to me at all."

That sounded promising. "Where do you want to meet? Forget Skinnertown."

"Yeah, that'd be sort of indiscreet, wouldn't it? Look, I'm dancing at the Lido tonight. I go on at ten and my last set's at half past twelve. We can meet after, in the parking lot."

"Twelve forty-five?"

"Okay. Why don't you come early, catch my act?"

"I think I saw most of what you have Sunday night."

"Naw, I was all dressed up then. 'Sides, you never saw it all in action."

"What do you do in your act, sap the customers with a pipe wrench?"

"Just the mean ones. Come on out." She hung up. I barely set the receiver down when it rang again. I was getting to be a popular man.

"Gabe?" It was Lola.

"Where have you been?" I asked, sounding just like Ann.

"I've had to work some things out. I need to see you."

"It's about time." I glanced at my watch. It was just after nine. "When and where?"

"The boathouse at eleven?"

"I can't be there until one or a little after," I told her, my insides twisting with frustration.

"Why?"

"Why have you been out of touch since Thursday night?"

"Actually, it was Friday morning."

"Whatever. Look, Lola, this can't wait. I have to see someone, and it may be someone with some answers, answers that I need."

"Answers about what?" she said, surprising me.

"About Edna's murder, of course."

"Aren't the police supposed to be handling that?"

Maybe she really had been out of town the whole time. "I'll tell you all about it tonight."

"All right. I'll try not to go to sleep before you get there."

"Don't you dare."

She made a kissing noise into the phone and hung up. I dialed Lew's number.

"Lew, Gabe here. Can you lend me five hundred? I'm a little short." I told him about my call from Ann, not mentioning Lola's.

"So the little chippie's going to sing as well as strip?"

"Damon Runyon couldn't have said it better. Do you have the cash?"

"Not at the moment, but we're getting near the end of the twentieth century and thank God for cash machines. Do you ever wonder what people did before cash machines when they needed cash in the middle of the night?"

"They used to hold up gas stations and liquor stores. Do you want me to come over and drive you?" I was worried he was too far into the juice to drive.

"No, there's one not two blocks from here. I'll walk. Come by in about an hour to pick it up. I want five hundred dollars worth of story for this."

"Play it right, you'll get your Pulitzer," I assured him.

"Okay, that'll do." He hung up.

It occurred to me that I hadn't eaten since breakfast and it looked like I had a long, long night ahead of me. I went out in search of a meal.

I'd seen the Lido on a couple of my morning runs: a low, windowless, cinderblock building with a dingy parking lot in back. It was located at the intersection of highway 13 and the Granville road. Granville was the college town just a couple of miles away. The location was a good one, catching the raffish college trade as well as the customers from staid Monticello.

At night it had the sleazy glamour expected of a roadhouse. The roofline, corners, and doorway were outlined in red, green and blue neon. Atop the roof a lightbulb sign blinked LIDO off and on through the warm summer night.

The parking lot held a good collection of cars and motorcycles. You can tell a lot about a place by the quality of the motorized transportation outside. I didn't see any garish pimpmobiles, and the bikes were mostly production models; no biker hogs with extended forks and ape-hanger handlebars. Granville College was regarded as one of the country's best small colleges. Catering to that trade, the Lido was offering only the illusion of low life. I found a space next to a Volvo with a Star Trek bumper sticker and went inside.

The interior was decorated in pure retro-chic, a look that had been all the rage in L.A. three years ago. Pictures and brick-a-brac mixed up the forties and fifties, either through ignorance or indifference, and apparently on the principle that any time is better than the present. A poster of James Dean from *Giant* and one of James Cagney flanked a wall display of lunch boxes featuring Hopalong Cassidy, Roy Rogers, Lash LaRue and other celluloid cowboys. Above a row of prewar Army campaign hats a portrait of a near-naked Johnny Weissmuller as Tarzan brooded over the place with solemn disdain. Old pressed-tin screen door signs advertising Coke and Wonder Bread were all over the walls.

The clientele ran to the young and callow. At two pastel-topped pool tables some boys made like hustlers and pretended they weren't paying any attention to the girl dancing on the stage at the far end of the long room. The music was over-amplified, the sort that I no longer really hear, although I can still feel the vibrations. I found a seat at the bar—an end seat closest to the stage, so that I had only one flanker to contend with. He was a little guy wearing, of all things, a tweed jacket. A dark-haired girl was leaning over the bar, talking to a college boy in a T-shirt decorated with the logo of some rock band I'd never heard of. She broke off her conversation and came down to my end.

"What can I get for you?" she asked, smiling.

"Plain Coke, please."

"There's still a five-dollar cover charge."

I looked at the stage. "Is the entertainment worth five bucks?"

She shrugged. "It depends on your taste." She brought me the Coke and accepted my money. At least she didn't act like a real man should be drinking something stronger.

I twisted around to watch the girl on the stage. She was dancing in approximate time to the music, and chewing gum slightly off-beat. She was wearing a spike-studded dog collar with matching halter top and G-string; minimal black leather and lots of chrome. She wore black lipstick and nail polish and her main prop was a leather whip she popped from time to time.

"Kind of sad, isn't it?" the guy next to me said. I looked at him. He was middle-aged, balding and had thick glasses perched on his nose. He was also wearing a red bow tie. I could hardly believe it. He grinned toothily and held out a hand. "Nathan Ames, Humanities." Apparently, where he came from, you introduced yourself by department.

"Gabe Treloar, Criminology," I said, taking his hand. "If you mean the degradation, this is pretty mild. You ought to see it where I come from."

"No, no, I mean this playing at decadence. These people lack both the age and experience for it. Besides, true decadence has always been the milieu of the elite. The masses really aren't equipped to appreciate it."

"It's this year's look," I said. "Next year it'll be something else."

"Undoubtedly." He took a pull at his drink, which looked a lot stronger than mine.

Another girl took the stage. As Cabell had told me, this one arrived in a short, tight dress and was out of it in no time. Thinking along those lines, I looked around to see if Cabell was in the place, keeping an eye on the dangerous elements. I didn't see him, or anyone else in police uniform.

"This one's a little more basic," my new companion said, gesturing toward the dancer. She was down to high heels and a G-string and a lot of silicone. "This type reduces the grammar of sexuality to a sort of sculpturesque symbology. It never works, because they try to bring a neolithic earth-mother archetype into line with modern body consciousness. The result is what you see: the Venus of Willendorf with liposuction."

I took a sip of my Coke, which was much too sweet. "Is this something you do a lot?"

He nodded. "It's a book I'm writing: *The Semiotics of Striptease*. It's one of the advantages of being an academic, you can hang out in places like this and tell people you're doing research." He was weaving a little on his seat, but his diction was perfect. As a conversationalist he was far better than some drunken redneck, but you really have to be drinking yourself to appreciate barroom chatter.

I switched to ginger ale and was tying into a cold one when the professor said, "Now this one is a natural." I could tell by his expression that he was seeing what he'd been waiting for all night. The neon reflecting from his glasses gave him a beatific look. I turned and saw that Ann Smyth had taken center stage.

"Isn't she a little skinny for this particular art form?" I asked him.

"It's all in the attitude. She was on earlier, before you came in, but she's always better on her second turn." A true connoisseur.

I could see that she put conviction into her work. Like the others, she came on in high heels, but she kicked them off first thing. After that, she prolonged the stripping process, managing to make even that tired, commonplace act provocative. The patrons watched her with rapt attention, occasionally hooting or clapping for their companions' benefit. If I hadn't had my mind on another woman, I probably would have appreciated her performance more. Her eyes were half shut and they swept over me without pausing. She didn't look at anyone else, either, or acknowledge her enthusiastic fans in any way. She seemed totally self-absorbed.

"She's a perfect narcissist-exhibitionist," Ames said. "She sucks in attention the way a black hole sucks in light. Nothing escapes. It doesn't matter to her that she has small breasts and bony hips, so it doesn't matter to the audience, either. She's making love to herself up there, and it communicates."

I couldn't disagree with that. Her slow strip segued into a rhythmic set of floor gymnastics—she was an eye-boggling contortionist—and as the music crescendoed she went into near-orgasmic gyrations that ended abruptly with the music. Amid wild applause she walked sedately off the stage: sweaty, unsmiling, completely self-contained.

I finished my ginger ale, giving her time to dry off and get dressed, listening to Ames babble on about the historic and mythic significance of his chosen performance art. I wished the professor good luck in his contribution to culture and the humanities and went out to the parking lot to wait.

Ten minutes later she hadn't shown up and Lola was waiting for me. I went back inside and walked to the back. Behind the stage was a black curtain and I pushed through it. There was a dressing room with the usual tables and mirrors, smelling of hair spray, perfume and sweat. The siliconed woman was making repairs to her makeup at a mirror.

"No men allowed back here," she said, without turning.

"Ann Smyth was supposed to meet me outside," I said. "Is she here?"

She blinked a couple of times, cogitating. "She left just after her last set. She got a phone call right after she came off stage and she went out that way as soon as she was dressed." She pointed to a door at the rear of the room. "I think someone picked her up." The door opened onto the south side of the building. The parking lot was on the west side.

"Who called?"

"She answered the phone, I don't know who was calling. Ann looked sort of upset." She turned back to her mirror and went to work on her lips.

I returned to my car, angry with Ann for leading me on then skipping, but most of all for wasting an evening I could have spent with Lola. I looked at my watch: one o'clock already. I drove off, wondering what Ann knew that was so valuable, wondering if she really knew anything at all.

Twenty minutes later I was at the old parking spot. The moonlight was still bright enough to see by. I threaded my way through the weeds and the trees, the low-hanging leaves brushing my face. They rustled in a sudden wind from the north. The fresh wind was cool in the sultry night. Fall wasn't far away.

The wind picked up and it riffled the surface of the lake by the time I came out of the woods, making the reflected lights shimmer like a mirage. The hard points of color gleamed steadily from the far shore. Distance made the sign on top of the Lodge less garish. Except for the wind and the leaves, there was utter silence.

I walked along the shore, the gravel crunching beneath my feet, my stomach fluttering, when I saw something that shouldn't have been there. At first I thought it was a log that had floated ashore, but that was the sort of automatic denial that cuts in when we don't want to believe what we know we're seeing. I walked closer and the bare feet wouldn't allow me to hold on to the illusion.

She lay face down, with her lower body on the rocky shore, her head and shoulders in the water. Her arms were beneath the water. I ran up, saw the back of her head turned black and matted with blood that was still fresh enough to gleam in the moonlight, to make a dark cloud in the water around her head.

"Oh, God, Lola!" I forgot all my cop instincts, ignored the sheer hopelessness of it as I crouched by her and grabbed her shoulders, feeling the fabric of her white blouse, turning her over, dragging her out of the water.

She was dead, of course. Her face had that inhumanly slack quality that even someone in a deep coma doesn't display. Her eyes were open, rolled up so only the whites showed. The whites of her eyes sent a sensation through my body and head that was a disorienting combination of horror and relief and cut me off in mid-breath. It wasn't Lola.

It was Ann Smyth.

I ran to the boathouse, knowing I was being a fool, but unable to stop myself. I had to know if Lola was in there. Not a trace of her, naturally. Jittery, my heart thudding, I sat on one of the benches to think. The cabin cruiser bumped gently against the padding of the narrow deck.

I knew I was being set up, crowded, herded toward some destiny I knew would be unthinkable. I cursed myself and tried to think my way through it. There had been a time when I was good at this sort of thing. Of course, my intimate personal involvement this time made things different. Ann, the Lido, the lake; they were all strands in the fabric. Where had they all come together?

My telephone.

The sweat came out on my scalp as I thought about it. How long had my phone been bugged? Who had been listening? At least there was no big mystery about how they had enticed poor Ann—a promise of money would have worked wonders with her.

Now the big question: What to do next?

My first impulse was to run, just drop it all and get as far from it as I could. I was pretty certain that I wouldn't get far. I could sneak back home, go to bed and pretend that I hadn't come to the lake, but that contingency had probably been covered as well.

I was left with a single option: Act like a good citizen. Be a public-spirited ex-cop who's just stumbled on a murder. Don't disturb the evidence and go notify the authorities. Then look for a good lawyer.

I got up and went outside and stood very still, listening. Nothing but the wind rustling the leaves. The water made little lapping sounds as the wind washed it around the pilings. There was more chill in the air and it occurred to me, absurdly, that I would have to pick up a jacket.

I looked up toward the house, thought about going in there and finding a phone. Bad move. It was probably rigged with an alarm and I'd look that much worse. I began to walk back toward my car. They couldn't get me for leaving the scene of a crime if I was going to notify the authorities. I had an excuse for touching and moving the body, since I'd had no way of being sure she was dead and I might have saved her from drowning.

By the time I reached my car I was feeling a little better. There was nothing to tie me to her killing, except having been in a remote area in the early hours of the morning. No problem there. I was through protecting Lola. And where was Lola and what was her part in all this? Somewhat to my surprise, nothing happened when I drove away.

Two miles up the road was a convenience store and gas station that, at more civilized hours, sold bait and other supplies to people coming to fish on the lake. It was closed, but there was a pay phone at one corner of the building. A mercury vapor light on a pole flooded the parking lot with a ghostly luminescence, the sort that makes the healthiest skin look leprous. The wind had died down and insects buzzed listlessly around the light. It was so quiet that the sound of my car door closing was like an explosion.

Standing by the phone, under that awful light amid that oppressive silence, I felt lonelier than I could remember; lonelier than the night Rose had died. At least then I had Murray and my friends on the force. When Murray was killed, I was so crazy and booze-numbed that loneliness was the least of my feelings.

Now there was nobody but me and the telephone. Lola had metamorphosed into something unknown. Edna was dead. And I was at a dead end, unable to find the final link that would solve Edna's murder and, I hoped, put her unhappy soul to rest.

What I really, really wanted to do was break into that store and grab a few bottles of something that would give me oblivion. What I did instead was dip into my pocket and fish out my change: two quarters. Spend them wisely, Gabriel.

First I dialed 911, no quarter required for that, and told the operator I had a murder to report and I wanted the County Sheriff's office. She connected me with someone holding down the desk and I gave my name, my location, and the situation.

"There's been an emergency out on Highway 36 and most of the units are out there, but someone will get to you as soon as possible."

Great. A night of wild excitement for Polk County. As I hung up the phone it occurred to me that, in my position, I'd be an utter damned fool to think that this emergency was pure coincidence. With shaky fingers, I dropped a quarter into the phone. The other end rang for a while and I almost gave up, then it was lifted.

"Hello?" The voice was thick, understandable enough considering the hour.

"Lew? It's Gabe. Big trouble, buddy. Ann's been murdered and I think I'm being set up."

"Huh? That you, Gabe?" Wonderful. It was the perfect night for him to go to bed drunk.

"Lew, Lew, listen to me, now. You know where the Cohan summer place is? By the lake?"

"Yeah, Cohan place by the—the lake, yeah, I know it. What's going on, Gabe?"

Only patience was going to work. "Ann Smyth was murdered there, Lew, near the path from the old lover's lane to the lake. She was supposed to meet me at the Lido and she didn't. I have to get back there and see what I can learn before the local police mess up the site the way they did at Edna's. Are you following me, Lew?"

"Yeah, yeah, Gabe. What do you want me to do?" He sounded like he'd be doing well to get his pants on.

"Come out here as quick as you can. I called Mark's office but there's some sort of emergency going on. God knows who's going to arrive or when, but I'd rather not be alone when they do. And I may need a lawyer." I was hoping, without great confidence, that he would retain at least one word in three.

"Okay, Gabe, don' worry. I'll be out there pretty soon. Murdered, huh? Gettin' to be like jaywalking around here."

"I have to go. Just get out here as quick as you can, and be thinking about a lawyer." I hung up, feeling my luck running out like sand through an hourglass.

Ten minutes later I was back at the lake. I had the penlight I'd bought to search Edna's house. It wasn't much illumination outdoors, but better than nothing.

I squatted by the body first. No extensive bruising that I could see. It looked like she'd been caught completely by surprise, sapped from behind by something blunt and heavy. That probably let Jesse Skinner off. He seemed to like his knife and I doubted that Ann would have turned her back on him anyway. Besides the white blouse she was wearing a pair of light blue shorts. No sign of rips in the clothing, just heavy blood staining of the blouse collar. No shoes in sight.

Next I scanned the ground around her body. No footprints except mine. Just wonderful. She was a small woman, and it was possible that her bare feet would have made no marks on the gravelly shore, at least none I could see by penlight. But I was betting that she'd been killed elsewhere and dumped here. Most likely, she'd been dumped from a boat.

Over the rustling of the leaves I heard voices. Flashlights and men were coming my way. They got closer and one of the lights shone on me.

"Why, good evening, Gabe. What have you got for us tonight?" It was Lester Cabell.

"I called the Sheriff's office," I said. "Where's Mark?"

"There was a little emergency out on 36 tonight. Every law officer in the county was there. I just happened to be by my car when the call came in. Decided to come out personally." He flicked the beam over Ann. "You sort of have a thing about murdered women, don't you, Gabe? There've been two killed in Monticello in the last ten years and you've been involved with both of 'em. All within a week, too."

It was a bad time to say anything, so I stayed quiet. There were three other men with Cabell and two of them began searching the weeds. The third walked over to stand by me.

"How do you happen to be here tonight, Mr. Treloar?" Ansel Cohan asked.

"I might ask the same," I said.

"That emergency Lester mentioned? It was a Cohan Chemical truck overturned on the highway. I was at the scene talking with Lester when this call came over his radio. Since this is my property, I felt I had better come with him."

"Mercury fulminate blasting caps all over the highway," Cabell said, squatting by the body as I had minutes before. "Tricky situation. They were the civilian type, a lot easier to set off than the military ones."

"Chief, I think you better come here," one of the cops called. He was poking among the weeds about twenty yards away.

"Poor Ann," Cabell said. "Looks like the Lido's going to be needing a new stripper. Now," he said, straightening up, "I can't say it surprises me she ended up here. The old lover's lane is still used occasionally, and Ann was known to turn professional from time to time. She couldn't very well take her customers to her trailer in Skinnertown."

"I think I'll buy that property and fence off the trail," Ansel said. "Every week in the summer my groundskeeper has to come out here and pick up the discarded condoms and wrappers."

"Take that as a reassuring sign, Mr. Cohan," Cabell said. "It's when he finds used needles and syringes we need to worry. If you two will excuse me, I need to go consult with my colleague over here." He walked off, sweeping his light from side to side.

"You never did answer my question, Treloar," Ansel said, quietly.

We weren't in front of the police so there was no need for me to play word games. "As a matter of fact, I came out here to meet with Lola. We were going to get together in the boat-house. It's an old practice of ours, goes back years. Where is she, Ansel?"

"I'm afraid my sister is out of town and you are deluding yourself. If you really need to solicit cheap whores you should have the discretion to keep away from my property." He was cool, unflappable, well-rehearsed.

"Sure, I'm deluded. Your property, huh? And your truck on the highway tonight. And a call from your sister." I stepped up close and had the satisfaction of seeing him step back. "What was Edna Tutt to you, Ansel?"

"Looks like we have a murder weapon here, gentlemen," Cabell said. He and his men stood over something in the weeds, shining their lights on it. Ansel turned and walked toward them. I followed close behind him. The beams illuminated the long, blood-caked object on the ground like spotlights. It was a flashlight of heavy, black-anodized aluminum.

"Just the sort of flashlight police officers use," Cabell noted.

And I knew just which ex-police officer's fingerprints were all over it. I felt like I was in one of those hokey old horror movies where the hero is strapped to a chair and the spike-lined walls start closing inexorably in on him.

"I think I'd better go look at my house," Ansel said. "I want to make sure everything's all right up there."

"Tony," Cabell said, "you go along with Mr. Cohan. Don't touch anything if it looks like the house has been broken into. Buck, you stay here, don't let anybody near the body or the murder weapon till I get back. I'm going to run Mr. Treloar back to town. We need to talk down at the station."

Tony and Ansel walked off. Buck took up his station next to Ann's body. "Let's go, Gabe," Lester said.

My mouth turned dry. I should have run when I had the chance. I walked a little ahead of Cabell, my eyes flickering from the lake to the wood line, trying to pick a direction. Not a chance. Maybe when we got onto the trail. The trees and bushes grew closer there. We turned from the lakeside and went in beneath the canopy. It had been benign, unthreatening before. Now it was a menacing place. I found myself wishing I'd had more bush experience in Viet Nam and knew how to duck into the brush and make myself invisible like the old boonie-busters could. Unfortunately, I'd spent almost all my time there in Saigon.

"Okay, Treloar, you can stop there." We were about halfway back to the parking spot. Up ahead, I could see the strobing red-and-blue where they'd left their cars with the lights flashing. There was a mutter of radio traffic.

"Does Ohio have the *Ley Fuga?*" I asked.

"The lay what?"

"It's the old Mexican fugitive law," I said. "It lets the police shoot a fleeing suspect without being accountable for it."

I heard a little rustling up ahead. Probably a possum. Time to decide right or left. Straight ahead was out of the question. I thought about Cabell's .45 in its quick-draw rig, wondered if I had a chance in hell. I braced myself.

The flash caught me by surprise. I knew you didn't hear the shot that hit you. I didn't feel a thing, but I hadn't felt anything the other times I'd been shot, either. The flash was awfully white, though. Muzzle blasts are usually orange. And shots aren't ordinarily followed by a mechanical whizz-click.

"Lester Cabell, where are you taking my sweetie?" cried a bright, chirpy voice.

"What the fu . . . Sharon?" Cabell was blinking the flash from his eyes, his hand on his pistol-butt.

"Can't put a thing over on you, can I Lester?" Sharon Newell came closer and took another picture, then stepped up next to me. "I hear you've found another murder, Gabriel. Where's the body?"

"Sharon, you get away from him! Treloar's a suspect and he's a dangerous man. I'm pretty sure he just killed Ann Smyth."

"Oh, don't be silly. Gabe's just an old pussycat." She hugged my arm and kissed me on the cheek. *"Keep your stupid mouth shut,"* she whispered. I needed absolutely no encouragement.

"What the hell are you up to?" Cabell demanded, his face gone white even in the moonlight, his eyes a little wild.

"Just my job, Lester, serving the people's right to know, freedom of the press, that sort of thing."

"Goddammit, Sharon!" Cabell barked. "You're interfering with a police investigation. I'll arrest you, too, if you don't get the hell away from here."

I wondered if I should point out to him that he hadn't arrested me yet, or read me my rights or any of that stuff. I decided to stay quiet. He could always say later that I was lying. For that moment I was grateful to be in any shape to be accused of anything at all. There was more pushing through the brush, more flashlights.

"I'll take charge of him, Lester," Mark Fowles said.

"I saw him first, Mark," Cabell said, his grin back in place.

"My jurisdiction," Mark said. "This is county territory. You passed the city limits a ways back." Four deputies came up behind him. He and Cabell stood facing one another square on, like two rival tomcats. Mark was a good deal smaller, but he wasn't alone.

"Now, Mark," Cabell soothed, "there's no need for us to be playing political games."

"I agree. Show me the body. Treloar, you come with us."

Cabell did a slow burn as we walked, but he was back to smiling and chuckling. Sharon and I dropped back a little. As usual she was impeccably turned out in tight skirt, jacket, lace and black hose. She'd put on flat-heeled shoes as a gesture to the terrain. Her makeup was on and every hair was in place, but she smelled sweaty. Sharon had been a busy girl, that night.

"Thanks," I said. "I owe you one."

"You'll pay," she promised.

"How did you do this so fast? Do you have a bug on Lew's phone?"

"That's both illegal and unnecessary. Who do you think picked up the phone when you called him?"

"Poor Lew," I said.

"But lucky Gabe. I got on the line to the dispatcher and found out where Mark was and put a call straight through to his car. I told him he had bigger concerns than a few citizens stepping on Cohan's prize products."

"Find out how that accident happened."

"Trade, Gabriel. What did you learn on your trip? Lew won't tell."

"Good for him." All this was in a fast, furious whisper while we walked back to the lakeside. When we reached the body, Sharon started snapping pictures.

"Publish those and I'll put you in jail," Mark said. "You men cordon off this area. I don't want the scene messed up worse than it is already. We'll wait until daylight to comb the area. It's not that far off." The chaos at Edna's house must have sent him back to his textbooks.

I didn't see any sign of Ansel. After a while Mark and Cabell were standing over the flashlight in the weeds, Mark instructing someone on how to pick it up and bag it. He had to shoo Sharon away again. The mournful Doc Appelhof showed up and his assistant set up floodlights next to the body and Mark came over to tell them how not to mess up the site. I looked around and Cabell had left. Mark came over to me.

"You'd better come to town with me, Treloar."

"Am I a suspect?"

"I'll tell you when you are."

"You understand you can't use anything I say before you've read me my rights in court?"

"I've heard of the law, yes."

"Then do you want a suggestion?"

"Go ahead."

I nodded toward the boathouse. "There's a boat in there. I think you should check it for bloodstains." It was a long shot, but I needed any help I could get.

"I'll do it. Now come along." We began to walk back to the path. Sharon was right behind us. Mark turned around. "Go away, Sharon."

"He's mine, Mark," she said, determined as a pit bull with its teeth sunk into its prey. "And you both owe me big, whether you know it or not." Then she turned her basilisk eyes on me.

"And I want in. All the way. You could be dead right now, Treloar."

"What the hell?" Fowles said, probably using the strongest language he'd employed in ten years. We were back under those trees that were getting all too familiar.

"All right, you're in. But it's still my call when to tell you what."

"Not good enough. Everything now," she insisted.

"My way or no way," I said.

"Treloar," Mark said, "right now you're an idiot to be talking to me, much less to her."

"Let's talk back at your office," I said.

A bevy of police cars waited at the old lover's lane, lights turning the night surreal. Mark gave his instructions, telling the city and state boys in no uncertain terms to keep the hell away from his crime site. Then he made arrangements for my car to be driven back to town. Mark and I got into his car and Sharon followed close behind in her red Jag. Mark was very quiet.

"Sharon's a bitch," I said, "but she's a gutsy bitch, I'll give her that."

"She'd cut your throat to get out of here and onto a big paper."

"Mark, I might as well tell you now: You're going to find my prints on that flashlight. It's mine." He turned and looked at me as if I'd just appeared beside him in a puff of green smoke. "But," I went on, "they won't be new prints. I haven't touched it in a week. There won't be any prints on the blood, and there's no blood on my hands. The prints are purely circumstantial evidence."

"People have been convicted on circumstantial evidence a lot weaker than that."

He didn't have to tell me.

The anteroom in front of Mark's office was heavily staffed for the hour. Ordinarily, only a dispatcher would have been on duty. But this wasn't an ordinary night for Monticello and Polk County.

"Sheriff," said a harried-looking man who looked like he'd

been dragged from bed to man his desk, "the state and the federal offices say they need to have every last blasting cap on that truck accounted for."

"Tell them to talk to Cohan," Fowles said. "As long as the highway's safe I'm satisfied."

"Has there really been another murder?" A secretary asked.

"Yep." Mark went into his office and I went in after him. Before I could even close the door, Sharon Newell was in.

"Mark, somebody has a bug on my phone," I said. "We need to get someone there and find it before they come and pick it up."

"What do you mean 'we'?" Mark said, pouring himself a cup of coffee. "Don't presume just because I haven't locked you up yet that we're some kind of colleagues. You're still prime suspect material as far as I'm concerned." He took a swallow, made a face, then looked at me and Sharon with disgust. "And I used to have a quiet little county," he muttered. Then: "I don't have anybody who'd know a phone bug if it bit them on the behind."

"I know how to find them," Sharon said. We just looked at her. She smiled, showing that gold crown in back. "One of my professors at college used to be in the Justice Department. That's what he did: wiretaps. I got him to teach me all about them."

"I'll bet you got a good grade from that one," Mark commented.

It pained me to do it, but I took the room key off my ring and handed it to her. "Go find it. Leave everything else alone."

She grabbed it. "Bless your little heart, Gabe. 'Bye now." She jerked her bubble hairdo in Mark's direction. "Don't tell him anything until I get back." She was out the door like a shot.

Fowles shook his head. "You should have joined a monastery, Gabe. Women are strictly trouble for you. Now," he got serious, "talk to me before Cabell comes in with Ted Rapley riding in his back pocket. Tell me about that flashlight and why you were out at Cohan's place tonight."

I told him about seeing Lola the night Edna was killed, and leaving my flashlight in the boathouse. I told him about seeing

Ann in Skinnertown and my run-in with Jesse Skinner. I told him about Ann's call that night and her standing me up at the Lido and going on out to meet with Lola again. I told it fast because I knew I'd have to clam up when Cabell got back with reinforcements.

"My God, Gabe," Mark said with wonder. "You don't need a monastery. You need to sit on one of those pillars in the desert for forty years and meditate on your sins. Go get yourself some coffee."

He brooded while I poured myself a cup. All of a sudden, coffee seemed like the most wonderful thing in the world. I sat back down across from him, the desk and the dented old Tommy gun clip between us, and he came out from his brown study.

"Talk to me some more, Gabe. Tell me why I should believe you. Tell me why I shouldn't book you now and lock you up."

Well, hell, I thought. Time to go off the deep end. "Mark, Edna Tutt's brother was Stanley Kincaid, the wheelman on the Cohan Chemical heist. Your father killed him."

For a long time Mark stared at the ruined drum clip on his desk. I thought I knew what was going through his head: The key to ending almost thirty years of torment was lying close to his grasp. He looked back up.

"Talk to me some more, Gabe."

He heard most of it by the time Sharon got back. She pushed in without knocking, closed the door behind her and reached into her purse. Her hand came out dangling a tiny, flat, gold chip on a thin, gold wire.

"Isn't it cute? It was right in the mouthpiece of your phone, Gabe."

"And you've put your fingerprints all over it," Mark said.

"Just the wire, dear. The little broadcasting unit's here in my purse. What do you want to bet you won't find any fingerprints anyway?" Carefully, she lifted the gadget out of her purse and set it on his desk. Just as carefully, Mark bagged it. He took a form from his desk, made notations on it, and stapled it to the bag. Then he got up.

"I'm taking this to the evidence room. You two don't talk to anybody until I get back."

"Don't you just hate bossy people?" Sharon said when he was gone. Then, "Gabe, why are your naughty pictures all of the same woman?"

"I suppose you just had to look. She's an old girlfriend. Couldn't you tell her hairdo was out of date?"

She perched herself on the arm of my chair. "I have a better body than hers."

"You'll never match her smile."

"She did kind of have a resemblance to the late Edna Tutt, if you allow for the years and the hair. Sue does my hair, too, but I can't get her to talk about Edna."

"Sue is a loyal friend."

She leaned close and hissed: "Dammit, Gabe, we made a deal! This story is getting weirder by the minute and I want to know what's going on!"

I pulled out my wallet and took out the five hundred Lew had given me hours before. "You have a note pad?"

"I'm a reporter, dummy." She took a pad from her purse and handed me a pen.

I wrote: *Lew: Ann won't be needing the money. Go ahead and tell Sharon everything. There's no keeping her out of it now.* I signed it and handed it to her.

She smiled. "You're so gallant."

"Find out about that truck," I told her.

"I'm on my way." She got up and made her quick, hip-swiveling way to the door.

"And thanks for jumping in when you did tonight."

She turned with her hand on the knob and gave me the gold tooth again. "Don't make me sorry I did, Gabe." Then she was out the door.

I took a sip of coffee, feeling unbelievably tired. A few minutes later Mark Fowles came back.

"We've got reporters converging on Monticello again," he said. "It seems we have a 'crime wave' in Monticello."

"Maybe it's been a slow week in Columbus. Are you going to be on my side in this, Mark?"

He swallowed some coffee. "I'm on the side of the law, Gabe." At least he was using my first name again. I took it for a good sign. "I won't pretend you don't look guilty. Under any other circumstances I'd have you booked and locked up right now."

"But now?" I prodded.

"Now, guilty or not, you're not the only one flouting the law in Polk County. Random crime is one thing. Conspiracy is another. Murder, wiretaps, that scene with Lester tonight . . ." He shook his head. ". . . it's gotten too big."

"I can break this case for you, Mark," I urged him, "but you're going to have to let me do it my way."

"I'm going to have my work cut out just to keep you out of Ted Rapley's hands. He'll be here ahead of the camera crews." He got up. "Look, I have to get back to the lake. I want you to stay here. Get some sleep. There's a couch in that room." He pointed to a door behind his desk. "If you set foot out on Central, you're in Lester's territory and I won't be able to do anything for you."

"I'll be right here when you get back," I said.

"Good. I'll leave orders that nobody is to come in here. Be ready to do some fast, convincing talking when I get back."

When he was gone I looked for a while at the telephone on his desk. I wanted to call Lew, but I was through using telephones in Monticello. I knew that I was groggy and suffering from reaction. Mark was right. What I needed more than anything else was sleep. I got up and wobbled back through the door behind Mark's desk.

 woke up disoriented, unfamiliar with the room or the couch under me. I lay still, afraid to move until I had all the events of the previous day logged in, in order, to the moment that I collapsed on the couch. I looked at my watch: almost noon. I'd slept for nearly six hours. I sat up, then poked around until I found a tiny bathroom that opened off Mark's office. I splashed my face and made what repairs I could to my appearance. I was looking a little seedy, but I felt far better for the sleep.

 The door to the outer office opened and for a second I could hear the uproar from the anteroom. "Treloar?" It was Mark.

 "In here," I said. "I'll be out in a minute."

 He shoved a small plastic bag through the half-open door. "Get yourself presentable. You're going to be talking to some people."

 The bag had a drugstore logo on the side and it contained a disposable razor, a can of lather, a sample-sized bottle of after-shave, a toothbrush, a tube of toothpaste and a comb. In ten minutes I looked almost back to normal. That was important.

It's one of the little secrets of police work that the grubbier a man looks and feels, the lower his resistance to interrogation will be. A big part of our self-confidence and sense of worth is tied up in our appearance.

I went out and Mark looked me over. He was looking pretty ragged himself. He nodded and pointed to a chair next to his desk. I sat. He shoved a cup of coffee in front of me and I slugged it down.

"Rapley's here with Lester Cabell and Ansel Cohan. They want to talk to you and I can't put them off without making things worse. Rapley will just get an injunction from a state judge and force me to hand you over. Lew Czuk is out there with a lawyer standing by: Chuck Holder. He's a good one, and he hates Rapley's guts."

"I'll cooperate where I can," I told him. "But I'm not spilling everything in front of those three."

"Tell the truth or keep your mouth shut. Just don't lie."

Mark opened the door and the three filed in, Rapley first, then Ansel, then Cabell. The police chief gave me his phony grin.

"You're not very sociable today, Gabe."

"I've got a lot on my mind."

"That I wouldn't doubt for a minute," Rapley said. He took a chair and so did Ansel. Cabell remained standing, looming over the other two.

"We have a few questions for you, Mr. Treloar," Rapley said, smooth and polished as ever, except for his shoes. There was a tiny rim of mud around the soles. He'd been out at the lake.

"Ask away."

"You have claimed that you went out to the Cohan property to meet with Lola Cohan, and instead found the body of Ann Smyth."

"That's correct."

"Yet, according to her family, Lola Cohan has not been in town for a week."

"Maybe she was at the lake cottage," I said.

"Furthermore," Rapley went on, "last night you were seen at the Lido, where Miss Smyth worked as an 'exotic dancer.'" He said it so you could hear the quotes. "Vicky Sutfin, who was tending bar last night, identified you. Professor Nathan Ames, who sat next to you, says that you and he discussed Miss Smyth at some length during her performance."

"Actually, he did most of the discussing," I said.

"Barbara Zinn, another of the Lido's entertainers, says that you came back to the dressing room after the performance asking for Ann Smyth."

"Did she tell you that Ann had already left, with someone else?" I said.

"She says Ann left," Cabell put in, "but she didn't know who with. For all we know you got Ann out to your car, then went back in to ask for her and cover your tracks."

Rapley held up a hand, cutting Cabell off. "Mr. Treloar, what was your business with Ann Smyth last night?"

"Yesterday evening she called me and told me she had information to sell relevant to Edna Tutt's murder. She told me to bring five hundred dollars and be waiting for her in the Lido's parking lot after her last performance. I did as she instructed but she didn't show. That's when I went back in and asked about her. Did Barbara Zinn tell you that Ann got a phone call and ran out the side door?"

"Uh-huh," Cabell said. "There's a pay phone in the Lido's parking lot."

"Zinn told me Ann answered the phone just as she came off stage. I sat talking with Ames for a good fifteen minutes longer to give her time to dry off and get dressed before I went to meet her in the parking lot."

"Barbara's a little fuzzy on the time factor," Cabell said.

"Look," I said. "I discovered a murder and reported it. That's all."

Rapley looked at Fowles. "Where is the murder weapon?"

"The flashlight's on its way to the lab," he said. "We don't know it's the murder weapon, just that it has blood on it. Sort of jumping to conclusions, aren't you?"

"I want the lab report on that flashlight," Cabell said. "It shouldn't take that long to get it dusted for prints."

"I'm following routine procedure," Mark said, his eyes

steady on Cabell. "Do you know something about that flash-light that I don't?"

"Let's stick to what we have," Rapley interrupted. "What we have is Mr. Treloar here, whose attention to Ann Smyth earlier in the evening coupled with his proximity to her corpse still makes him the most likely suspect in this case. It isn't at all un-common for a murderer to report the crime, hoping to avert suspicion."

"Why would I kill her?" I asked.

"Oh, come now, Treloar," Rapley said. "You were a police officer long enough to know that, in murder cases, motive is for television. People kill each other for no reason at all, or for the pettiest of causes, or out of compulsions no one else could pos-sibly comprehend."

"Maybe you asked her to do something really kinky and she wouldn't do it," Cabell suggested. "Even poor Ann must've had her standards."

"And I take particular exception to her being murdered on Cohan property," Ansel said. "I think Mr. Treloar wanted to embarrass us."

"Why would I want to do that?"

"Because you hold us responsible for your father's death."

"What's this?" Cabell said, eyebrows going up sardonically.

"When Treloar showed up ten days ago, acting rather irratio-nal and taking up his . . . shall we say quixotic pursuit of my sister, I began to look into the company records from those years, and I made inquiries with contacts on the West Coast.

"In '64 Ed Treloar was let go from Cohan Chemical. The family moved away to California and a little less than three years later Ed Treloar drove off a cliff. The official verdict was accidental death but all indications pointed to suicide."

I could feel the blood rushing to my face, but I let him go on.

"It seems that Gabriel here was well on his way to following in his father's footsteps. He left the Los Angeles police under a cloud—something involving a drinking problem and a partner who was killed as a result. For some time afterward he dis-played suicidal tendencies."

It's that way, now. If someone has the money and the pull, if he has the services of a top-flight investigator, he can find out anything he wants about you: job history, medical history, police record, credit record, the works. Forget that stuff about privacy. It's all to be had without getting out of your chair. Just a phone and a desktop computer will do the trick. That, and the money, of course.

"Isn't committing murder a little extreme just for the sake of the minor embarrassment it might cause you?" I asked.

"Nobody is accusing you of being rational," Ansel said.

"Why was old Ed fired?" Lester asked. He was still smiling, enjoying it all. Mark was watching me closely through the whole process. I was getting tired of it. I wanted the smile off Lester's face and Rapley's superiority taken down and Ansel squirming. You should always watch out for that kind of thinking. The dumbest thing you can do when you're being interrogated is let your feelings control your reactions. Unfortunately, cops are no more immune to it than criminals or ordinary citizens.

"James Cohan was angry because Lola and I got a little too intimate in the boathouse one night in spring of '64. The old man didn't want any employee riffraff playing around with his daughter and he fired my father."

Ansel surprised me. He looked vaguely astonished, then he chuckled. "Do you really think my father would have dismissed a valued employee over a little teenaged dalliance? I don't know how important your boyish hanky-panky was to you, Treloar, but I'm sure it was nothing to my father and probably meant less to Lola. To answer Lester's question, my father fired Ed Treloar for embezzling."

I felt like the rug had been pulled out from under me. My first urge was to call him a liar, but was he? It suddenly occurred to me how little I knew about those years. I was a kid with a kid's fixation on himself and his own problems. Kids operate on assumptions, and I had assumed that Dad's firing was somehow my fault. But I couldn't let it pass.

"You're full of shit, Cohan. My father never stole a nickel in his life."

"Oh, I don't blame you for thinking your father was a saint,

Gabe. It's always hard to see a father as something other than our childhood idol. But I'm afraid the figures were incontrovertible. My father decided not to prosecute. He had no wish to humiliate your family publicly. The sum wasn't vast, and he didn't want adverse publicity for the company. We were gearing up for the new war, lots of big government contracts being bid on, that sort of thing. So, my father just called Edward to the house, confronted him with the evidence, and dismissed him." Ansel sat back, satisfaction oozing like oil from his pores. "I spoke to my mother about the incident. She remembers the confrontation vividly. Poor Edward broke down in tears."

The image damn near unhinged me, and I knew it was meant to. I thought of my father as I had known him here in Monticello; my father as a boozer, slowly degenerating in a dead end job in L.A.; my father dead at the bottom of a cliff off the coast highway. I saw myself doing the same thing, fulfilling my decades-old nightmare.

"Sheriff," Ansel said, "I want you to arrest this man for the murder of Ann Smyth."

Mark looked back at him, unimpressed. "I'll arrest him, or someone else, when I think I have sufficient evidence."

Ansel looked like he wasn't believing his ears. "Goddammit! What do you want, Fowles? If you have any hope of reelection, you'd better arrest him right now! And you might as well throw in Edna Tutt's murder, too." He turned, looked up at Cabell.

"Lester, the Tutt murder was your jurisdiction. All of us know that Treloar must have done it. Go ahead and arrest him now." He was almost quivering with rage. Young punk Ansel was never far from the surface.

Cabell looked down at him, his upper lip twitching, suppressing a sneer. "One murder at a time, Mr. Cohan. If it looks like he'll beat the Ann Smyth rap, we'll get him for Edna." I could see what he was thinking: the flashlight. As soon as the lab report was in, I was nailed.

"You, too?" Ansel practically yelled. "What do I have to do to get some action? This man is a menace to me and to my family. I want you to . . ." Rapley reached over and touched his wrist. It was no more than that, just a light touch, but Ansel shut up.

"Ansel?" Rapley looked at him and Cohan calmed down. "Possess yourself. This serves nothing." His hand remained where it was, Rapley's long fingers against Ansel's fine-boned wrist. Cabell looked down at the point of contact where the two men were joined and the sneer came out, unsuppressed.

"Of course," Ansel said. "You're right." Then, to Fowles: "Sheriff, is this your last word?"

"No," Mark said, "but any more words will have to wait on the evidence."

"Sheriff," Rapley said briskly, "I will take charge of this case as soon as the paperwork comes in from Columbus. If you have a better suspect, you'd better produce him by morning." He got up, turned around and walked out, Ansel and Lester right behind him.

My hands were shaking a little when I turned to Fowles. "How long have I got?"

"I'll stall that lab report as long as I can, but once Rapley gets his people in Columbus moving, he'll have you with or without it. I'll make some calls, try to stall that as long as I can. I have a few IOUs in the state courthouse. I'll call them in. It still doesn't leave you much time."

"But you believe me?" I asked.

He gave me that evaluating stare. "I believe something's going on, and I want to know what it is. You may or may not have killed Ann. If you did, you won't get away from me. But I want everybody involved, not just a patsy." He paused. "I was watching you just now. That business about your father embezzling caught you by surprise, didn't it?"

"I still don't believe it. Dad kind of went to pieces there, toward the end. But he never stole. Cohan's covering something."

Mark looked down at his desk, touched the old Thompson magazine with a finger, making it rotate slowly. "I think so, too." He got up. "I'm going to trust you, Gabe. I'm going to go and pull every string I can to buy time. Meantime, there's some other people who want to see you."

"Mark," I said, before he could leave.

He turned at the door. "What?"

"I appreciate what you're doing. I know what a limb you're going out on for me."

"I might as well. If I don't put an end to this craziness, I'm through here anyway. And I'm not doing it for you. There's some very old business in this town that needs settling."

"I think I can find what we need, Mark," I told him. "I'm this close, I can feel it." I held up a hand, my thumb and forefinger a tenth of an inch apart. He nodded and went on out.

A minute later Lew came in with his lawyer and we talked about my increasingly slim chances. Chuck Holder, in his fifties, was a slightly rumpled, chubby man with an ancient, seam-sprung briefcase and a pair of sharp, steady blue eyes behind little, round lenses. He was the sort of small-town lawyer who knew everybody and kept up extensive contacts at the state courts. He didn't give me any song-and-dance about how I was going to waltz away, but he let me know that I'd have the fullest protection of the law. For whatever that was worth.

Holder left to get his paperwork started and Lew stayed behind. He was hesitant and had a hard time meeting my eyes.

"Uh, Gabe, about last night—I overdid it a little, I'm sorry."

"Yeah, I know how it is. I've been there myself. Sharon came through and it worked out all right." I didn't want to preach to him. I had a lot of other things on my mind, and I remembered a time when I'd been the same way and there had been nobody to bail me out. "But you're going to have to get it under control, Lew. That woman will eat you alive."

"I know, I know." He mused for a while. "But I don't think Sharon's going to be around much longer, one way or the other."

We sent out for lunch and were finishing up when Mark came back.

"I've just been to Skinnertown," he said. "They're pretty upset out there. Beating on their own women is one thing. They don't like outsiders doing the same."

"What about Jesse?" I asked.

"He's got an alibi. From nine last night until two this morning he was at the Harley shop working on his bike with Arthur Meath, the owner, and Jimmy Deur, the mechanic. Meath and Deur both confirm."

"Do you think they're trustworthy?" Lew asked.

"They might cover for him if it was a little matter of pot selling or stolen parts. Not for anything this serious. Funny thing, though: Lester hasn't been out to Skinnertown asking questions yet."

"If he's so sure about Gabe's prints on that flashlight, why bother?" Lew said.

Mark nodded. "Yeah, Lester's certainty about those prints is about the only thing keeping me on your side."

Sharon came in, beaming happily. "I've just been to the hospital and had a little chat with Gus Hanley, the driver of that Cohan truck." She sat down and smoothed her skirt over her thighs. "It turns out that shipment of blasting caps wasn't supposed to go out until next week, but there was a hurry-up order and it had to go out last night instead. Anyway, when he got to that sharp turn on the Newark highway a car pulled out in front of him, from that little rural road that forks off just where the turn starts, no lights showing until it was almost on the highway.

"Poor Gus swears he was under the speed limit for an explosives truck, but he had to hit his brakes and swerve, and guess what happened?"

"His right front tire came off," Mark said.

"Right you are! And somebody must have neglected to secure the lock on the back of the truck, because the gate came open when the truck overturned and those little blasting caps were all over the highway. I guess some heads are going to roll at Cohan Chemical, don't you? The company could be in for all sorts of fines over this."

"Where was the shipment going?" Mark asked.

"It was for the Houston Powder Company in Cincinnati. They get most of their detonators from Cohan, it seems. They are a major purveyor of explosives to the Appalachian coal mining companies."

"And he took the Newark highway?" Lew said.

"Uh-huh. That was another of last night's little mix-ups. See, usually Cohan trucks take 36 to Columbus, but somebody got the erroneous impression that a bridge was out on 36 and left a memo to that effect stapled to the transportation order. So the dispatcher told Gus to take Highway 13 south and pick up Highway 62 to Columbus and then take I-71 to Cincinatti the usual way. See, you can't send explosives on just any old road." She reached into her purse and came out with some papers, which she handed to Mark. "See, here are the forms filed with the Highway Department last night at 9:30 confirming the new route."

Mark took the papers. "I don't suppose there was a signature on that memo about the bridge being out?"

Sharon smiled brightly. "You know, somebody just plumb forgot! The dispatcher—that's Paulette Mauzy, she's a good friend of mine, we go to the same hairdresser—Paulette said it was such a rush order she didn't have time to track it down and get a signature. It only meant about thirty minutes difference in the delivery time and since it was going to arrive in Cincinnati in the middle of the night anyway it was no big deal. She just went ahead and made out the shipping order and filed the papers with the highway department." She turned her beam on me. "You're looking better all the time, Gabe."

"I'll be the judge of that," Mark told her.

"Where do we go from here?" Lew asked.

"I have to get out of here," I said. "There are some things I have to check into."

"I'm not holding you officially," Mark pointed out. "But you won't stay free a minute out on the street. And what do you plan to accomplish, anyway?"

I sat back in my chair, cradling a cup of coffee in my hands. I'd already drunk a pot and a half since waking. But I knew I had another long night ahead of me. I gave my next words some careful consideration.

"For the last ten days I've been getting to know Edna Tutt: Edna alive, Edna dead, Edna in her former life. I've been learning about her when she was Sally Keane and when she was Lucinda Elkins. I've talked to people who knew her slightly and who knew her well, old friends, lifelong friends, and even the head of her fan club.

"She was a private woman, to an extent most people would never dream possible, but I feel I've come to know her, and now I've gained a little insight into how she thought." I paused for a while, trying to think how I should put this next part.

"I met her when I was suicidally depressed, when I wouldn't have valued my life at half a bottle of stale beer. But she saw something in me worth salvaging. She knew that I was a detective, and before she died she left me something."

"She left you some girlie pictures," Sharon said.

"It was a gift. I think she could have told the whole story, but instead she gave me a key and left it up to me to find out where the keyhole was. I think I know now. If you can smuggle me out of here after dark, I'll go find what she wanted me to find."

"You mean," Lew said, "she did this so she could go out with one last good deed?"

"I think so," I said. "I think it was a problem with her all her life. She was a woman who loved too easily."

"Oh, God, now you're gonna make me bawl," Sharon said, giving me the fisheye that said that I, like most men, was a sentimental fool.

"I can get you out," Mark said. "But your car is impounded and I'm going to be busy right here all night, thanks to you."

"I'll pick him up," Sharon said.

"That red Jag of yours is pretty well known around here," Mark pointed out.

"I'll get you," Lew said.

"Then I'm coming along," Sharon insisted. "I want to be in at the kill." I wasn't sure whether she really cared who it was that got killed.

"I'll need some tools," I said. "A crescent wrench and a crowbar, at least."

"I'll bring them," Lew said. He seemed anxious to make up for his screwup of the night before.

"He'll be out back at 9:30," Mark said. "If any trouble starts, I don't want you two hanging around. I've had two murders to contend with this month, and I don't want any more. You'd better go on now."

They went out, and that left me alone with the Sheriff of Polk County, who had a stake in these matters that went back nearly as far as mine. He was quiet for a while, in his usual fashion, sipping at his coffee and thinking. He wasn't the sort to talk without thinking, and he'd been thinking for a lot of years.

"I was still a kid when Dad was killed. I thought it was straight cops-and-robbers stuff back then. When Dick Percy was killed by a hit-and-run driver I thought that was all it was. I didn't know him well. He hadn't been a deputy long. It was just days after Dad's death, that was all I could think about.

"By the time I was old enough to connect the two events, the rosters had been tossed or removed. I asked the others who'd been deputies then, but nobody could remember if Percy had been scheduled to ride guard on the payroll or not. Everyone had flu, they were all home sick for days.

"But I've been pretty sure for all these years that he was in on the heist. He was supposed to be guarding the money, and he got cold feet and backed out at the last minute. That means both of the surviving robbers didn't leave town after the job. At least one of them stayed behind to take care of Percy."

"And you know Harmon Gilchrist's story: that there was no hail of unaimed gunfire."

"Right. And I believe him. It was James Cohan who pressured the police and the papers to ignore Harmon's story. And Sturdevant, the driver, remembered nothing at all after going to bed the night before the robbery. Him I believe too. Traumatic shock can do that. For a long time I thought Cohan just wanted it to be a run-of-the-mill stickup that went bad, didn't want to believe his own employees could be involved. It would be bad publicity for the company, if nothing else. Now I doubt that was his only reason."

"The answers are all out there," I said. "Somebody's been trying like hell to keep them buried."

"Then you'd better find them," Mark said. "And you'd better do it tonight. You won't get another chance. None of us will get another chance."

The car was waiting in the alley behind the county police station. I felt like I ought to be bundled in a trench coat and hat and dark glasses, but I went out of the station as I'd gone in. Nobody looked up as Mark and I left his office and walked down a corridor past closed office doors and down a flight of steps to a steel fire door. He pushed the door open and I smelled air just washed by an evening rain storm.

"I'll be waiting to hear from you," Mark said.

"I'll have the goods when I get back," I promised him, trying to sound more confident than I felt.

He closed the door, leaving me on the wet pavement. Like so many of the streets and sidewalks in Monticello, the alley was paved with pattern-stamped redbrick of a sort nobody makes anymore. The streetlight that shone from the west end of the alley glistened off the infinitely repeated pattern of crosshatch-and-bull's-eye, for a few seconds almost mesmerizing me.

A rear door of Lew's Volvo opened. "Are you going to stand there moping all night?" Sharon demanded. "We have work to do. Get in." I climbed in beside her. There was a tool box on the floor, along with pry bars of various sizes.

"Where are we headed?" Lew asked, putting the car in gear.

"Back to Edna's house. But don't park on Maple or Wright. Drive on past to the east end of the block and come back down the alley behind the house."

"They tore that house up pretty thoroughly," Sharon said. "Have you thought of someplace they didn't look?"

"The places you have to look for are inside people's heads," I told her.

"There's a quote I can use. Do you have any other good ones for me?"

But I wasn't really listening to her. I was thinking of Edna as Lew drove three blocks east on Central, past Wright, then turned south on Bush Street. We crossed Maple, then, in the middle of the block, turned west down the tree-lined alley that divided the back yards of the houses on the north side of the block from the grounds of the Cohan estate, that took up the whole south side.

"Stop here," I said as we approached the garage. I rummaged in the tool box, came up with a pair of good-sized adjustable crescent wrenches, a small pry bar and a flashlight.

"Can I come with you?" Sharon asked, her teeth showing in the dimness.

"No, wait here. I shouldn't be long." She hissed a little but I ignored her.

I got out and stood looking over the roof of the Volvo. Through the trees on the south side of the alley I could see the soft glow of light coming from the windows of the Cohan mansion. Then I turned and went to the white picket fence that went from the back of the garage to the fence of the house next door. A low gate gave access from the yard to the alley. I opened it and went into Edna's garden.

I thought of Edna, the way she had gone about things, the way she had acted, the way I thought she thought. *Only one woman knew her secrets, and she didn't talk,* Edna had once told Jane Okamura. I passed between the rows of pretty flowers, glowing pale in the beams from the streetlight at the corner of Maple and Wright. I stopped in front of the little bronze goddess who raised her arms in eternal benediction.

It started to rain again, a gentle shower of warm summer drops. I ran the flash over the pedestal, then turned it off. First look beneath. I gripped the pedestal and wrestled it, scooting the square base from its position on the concrete pad in the center of the garden. It was heavy, but it only took a minute to move it aside. I shone the flash on the exposed square of paler concrete. No sign of a hole or a movable cover. I hoped I wouldn't have to break through it.

With one of the pry bars I levered the pad up a few inches, then lay down flat and shone the flashlight beneath it. Nothing there but bare, black dirt, fuzzy roots and the exposed channels dug by burrowing worms. I let it drop. Out of a sense of neatness I moved the pedestal back in place before I went to work on it.

Four lag bolts fastened the base of the statue to the top of the pedestal. I took the two crescent wrenches and adjusted them to fit the bolt heads and the nuts on the bottom of the platform. Then I carefully turned the bolts. They moved easily, as if they had been removed recently. One, two, three and four. I collected the bolts, nuts and washers and placed them neatly on the ground.

My breath was a little uneven, my stomach shaky, as I gripped the bronze goddess and lifted. She was heavy, reluctant to leave her altar. But she came up, and I looked into the black, black well she had covered. I set her gently down beside the bolts and aimed the flashlight into the hole.

There was a steel box inside, one with an airtight lid, like the cans military ammunition and explosives are shipped in. It stood on end, barely fitting in the round well. There was a handle on its end, and I reached in and pulled it out. It wasn't very heavy. I set it down, then I replaced the goddess, fastening the bolts securely. Before I left, I patted her shiny bottom as I had once seen Edna do.

"You were a good friend," I told her. Then I went back to the car.

"You found it?" Sharon said eagerly.

"It was where I thought it would be."

"Well, come on in and let's see what it is," she urged, practically wriggling on the seat with impatience.

"No, I'm tired of this sneaking around," I said. "Let's go up to my apartment. My rent's paid up."

"Why the hell not?" Lew said, laughing and seeming happy for the first time in who knew how long. "If they're looking for us, let's let 'em know where we are."

So we trooped up the steps and went inside and I turned on the light. It didn't look as if anyone had been there since Sharon earlier in the day. She had reassembled my phone neatly. I sat on the bed and she sat next to me, as close as she could get. She didn't take her eyes off the box at our feet. Lew took the chair.

I got my fingers under the flap at one end and pulled it up. The locking lever snapped up, springing the lid a little. Then I pulled the lid up and the rubber seal parted with a sticky sound.

It came open readily, although bits of rubber adhering to the rim showed that it had once remained shut for a long, long time. Somebody had pried it open recently.

On top were some rolled-up bags. I took one, so did Sharon and Lew. We straightened them and laid them flat on the floor. There were five of them; old-fashioned canvas cash bags, their tops fastened by heavy brass zippers. On the sides were printed the name of the Cohan Chemical Company and its logo.

"The money bags from the Cohan robbery in '65," Lew said, sticking his hand into one, coming up with a few paper tapes, the sort used for binding sheaves of bills. Sharon reached into another, came up with some more tapes, plus a few slips of newspaper cut into rectangles about two and a half by six inches.

"What's this?" Sharon said, holding them up.

"That's what this is all about," I told her. I took a thick packet out of the box, broke its string and unwrapped it. It was a stack of photos, hundreds of them. All were of Sally Keane, alone or with other models, clothed and unclothed. I wondered what Irving Schwartz and his cohorts would pay for this treasure trove.

"One bit left," Sharon said, eyeing the envelope in the bottom of the box, her eyes hot, but knowing better than to reach for it before I did.

"Uh-huh." I handed the stack of photos to Lew and took the nine-by-eleven brown envelope from the box. I opened the top flap and slid out two eight-by-ten glossies.

"Oh, dear," Sharon murmured. "So Sally Keane did hard core after all."

The first one was black-and-white, a little off-center, a tiny bit off the sharpest focus, signs that the camera had been set with a remote timer. There were two lovers on a bed, the man above the woman, propped up on his extended arms. The woman was Edna of almost thirty years ago, and it was definitely hard core, penetration clearly visible. The only thing that took it from the realm of ordinary porn was the radiant look of love suffusing her face.

The man was another matter. The James Dean d.a. and side-burns were gone; his haircut was early Beatles, but there was no doubt about his identity. It was Ansel Cohan.

"Oh, dear, oh, dear," Sharon cooed. "And here we all thought, without saying it, of course, that Ansel Cohan's taste was for less feminine partners."

"Edna's done nothing but surprise me since I met her," I said. "Why should Ansel be as simple as we'd thought?" I studied the second photo for a minute or two, savoring it, feeling things come together.

"What is it?" Sharon demanded, trying to look over my shoulder.

"This one is even better." I showed it to them. It was another black-and-white, perfectly composed, sharply focused. Sally Keane had learned how to use a camera as well as pose for one. In the center was Ansel, still with the Beatles coiffure, lying on a floor. He was asleep, drunk or drugged, but in any case un-conscious. Arranged neatly around him were the money bags with the lettering perfectly readable, and an *L.A. Times* dated December 2, 1965, with a front page article on the robbery. I remembered reading that paper myself.

"The news story's all yours, Lew," Sharon said, all but purr-ing. "I'm writing a book."

Lew pondered over the photos for a while. "What do we do now?"

"I've found out all I'm going to learn here," I told them. "The rest of the story is over there." I jabbed a finger toward the south-facing window. Through it we could see the trees of the Cohan estate.

"We're going over there?" Lew said, his eyes going owlish behind his glasses.

"No," Sharon told him, "we aren't." She turned and looked at me. "This is one place I don't want to follow you."

"Good, because I wouldn't let you. Lew, do you have a gun?"

"Why would I have a gun?" This from a man who had lived in Miami.

"Sharon, I don't suppose you pack one around in that purse?"

"But, sweetheart, that would be illegal. Would a can of Mace help?" She held up a little spray can, probably adequate for driving off unwelcome dogs.

"Thanks," I said, getting up. "I'll just have to do without." I went to the door.

"Gabe," Lew said. "How long should we wait for you?"

I thought about it for a few seconds, then shook my head.

"It doesn't matter." I went on out into the rainy night.

16

*T*he rain dripped softly from the leaves of the trees lining the alley that divided the block into halves. Some of the houses were dark. From others, warm light glowed through closed curtains. In some windows the flickering, multicolored ghosts of television images danced over the glass. I could hear distant traffic noises and a dog barking a block or two away. Otherwise, there was no sound except for the patter of raindrops. A cat darted across the alley in front of me, intent upon some feline errand.

I was feeling a little high, charged with that heightened intensity of sensation that you get when you knowingly head into those situations from which you know you may not come back. I had known the feeling powerfully during Tet '68, patrolling the streets of Saigon in the back of an open Jeep, manning a machinegun, knowing the fire could erupt from any alley or any building. I had known it again in L.A., those heart-thudding moments when you have to go into a dark alley after some armed psycho who just wasted six people in a liquor store or carved up a hooker with a straight razor.

Some people grow addicted to the sensation. They seek out the thrill over and over again, taking insane risks just to experience that drug-like heightening of the senses where every cell of your body comes alive and even the rocks and trees take on a life of their own and you see the world the way a primitive shaman sees it; as a living, teeming place with an agenda of its own, indifferent to your welfare. Only your own actions can bring you through alive.

I had never come to enjoy the feeling, although I knew that, for its duration, there was no thrill like it. It always left me wrung-out and sick and swearing never again, like a drunk after a three-day binge. But for now, in this alley, going where I was going, it felt good. I might not last long, but for this moment I was fully alive.

The glow from distant streetlights was uncertain, but I wasn't really seeing by the visible spectrum. My body was operating on memories that had imprinted operating codes on my nervous system so that my muscles and bones performed the necessary actions without recourse to conscious thought, as it had the day I had climbed the tree to find the spot where that boy, so long ago, had carved his initials coupled with Lola Cohan's.

In those days the area behind the Cohan stables and carriage houses had been separated from the alley by a high wooden fence, of the sort I fancied Tom Sawyer had conned his friends into whitewashing for him. It was still there. At least it hadn't been replaced by brick topped with broken glass or coils of razor wire. It had sometimes occurred to me to wonder why there was a fence back here when the front lawn of the estate was open to the street, but the ways of the rich are often mysterious.

Next to the locked gate I reached up and my fingertips found the two boards that were a few inches shorter than the others. The wood felt a little soft and I smelled mildew as I pulled myself up and scrambled over the fence. The ground on the other side was cushioned with moss and I made very little sound as I landed. For a minute I crouched there and listened and looked. There were no security guards with flashlights sweeping the grounds, no guard dogs patrolling purposefully. I straightened and began my approach to the house, moving cautiously.

This part of the estate had changed. It looked bare with the old carriage houses gone. There was a barn-sized building for the groundskeeping equipment, and a poolhouse by the small, kidney-shaped pool with its attached jacuzzi. The rain dimpled the sparkling surface of the water and there was a faint smell of chlorine in the air as I walked past it.

Here and there light streamed over the huge lawn from the windows of the mansion, but the rear was dark. The scene would have been perfect if there had been a single light in the cupola that crowned the place, surrounded by its wrought iron widow's walk. But my thoughts were on less Gothic things, such as burglar alarms. I wasn't exactly unskilled at breaking and entering, but these were people who could afford a top-of-the-line security system.

On the other hand, it was possible that, in their small-town arrogance, they had never bothered to install one. Who, after all, would dare to molest the Cohans? So I walked up four brick steps to a back door. It was of thick wood, its hardware probably dating from the turn of the century. In the middle of the door was one of the old-fashioned doorbells that you rang by turning a key in its center, for the benefit of underlings making deliveries in the rear. Above the bell were six panes of glass. Through them I could just make out a short, narrow hallway. At least two rooms opened off of it, and a stairway led up to the left. There were pegs for coats and hats, now bare.

Cautiously, I twisted the doorknob. Locked. It wasn't going to be that easy. I ran a fingernail down the edge of the door and found a noticeable gap between the door and the jamb. Hoping that the locks here were as obsolete as the ones in Edna's house, I took out my library card. As I did, I had a brief, ridiculous flash of memory to the day my sixth-grade class had all trooped from St. Anne's to the old public library to get our first library cards. They had been of heavy paper back then, and the elderly librarian had held one up and told us solemnly that it was the key to knowledge. I wondered what she would have thought if she'd known the use to which I was putting my plastic card.

The search for knowledge took forms she probably never dreamed of.

I turned the knob by increments, slipping the card between door and jamb and wiggling it against the bolt, using the lock plate for leverage. The bolt began to give, then it snapped open and the knob twisted to the left abruptly. The noise seemed loud in the pervading quiet and I froze there, waiting for somebody to come and investigate. I gave it five full minutes, but there was no sign that anyone had heard.

Very slowly, I pushed the door open. It made only the faintest of squeaks as it swung inward and I stepped inside and closed it just as carefully. For another few minutes I just stood there, turning my head from side to side, straining to hear the faintest sounds, trying to penetrate the dimness with my eyes. After the soft, but insistent, hissing of the rain, the silence in the house was all but deathly. But as my eyes adjusted to the interior gloom, my ears began to pick up sounds that were nearly subliminal. From somewhere in the front of the house I heard voices, people talking. Once in a while a voice was raised a bit. Maybe they were arguing. From the stair that led up to the left, I could hear the ticking of a big grandfather clock, counting off the seconds of a deathwatch that may have gone on for more than a century.

I could tell I was near the kitchen from the pantry smell in the air; that mix of spices and cooking smells that even the most sophisticated venting system never eliminates. In Patrick Cohan's day the place must have reeked of corned beef and cabbage, but the current generation had more elegant tastes, to judge by the faint herbal tang.

I walked past the kitchen and the voices grew a tiny bit louder, but they were still indistinct. I was pretty sure that I wouldn't find what I needed in the relatively public, socializing rooms of the ground floor. I turned left and began to climb the stairs. The old house was solidly built and the stairs didn't creak beneath my feet. The ticking from the grandfather clock grew louder, then I was on a second-floor landing.

Here the walls were of dark wood, hung with portraits and edged with ornate molding. It smelled of old family money and power. I walked down the hallway and looked into open doors. There were bedrooms, both feminine and masculine. Then, in the southwest corner, I found an office. I was pretty sure that it had been James Cohan's office when I was a boy, so it was a good bet that it served Ansel in the same capacity now.

There was a massive, leather-topped desk in the middle of the office, with a plush, overstuffed Victorian chair behind it. An arched desk lamp with a green glass shade sat centered on its front edge. A telephone was the only other thing on it. I went in and closed the door behind me. The southern and western walls had windows. An open doorway gave access to a sitting room that featured more overstuffed furniture and a baby grand piano. I slid that door almost shut. I might have to make a fast exit through it and I wouldn't want to waste time or make unnecessary noise. Then I went to the windows and pulled down the shades. When that was done, I turned on the desk lamp.

By its light I made a circuit of the room, looking behind pictures. They were mostly photos of Ansel with various important people, including the last four Republican presidents. There was a stunning portrait of Lola, and an old family portrait with James Cohan beaming and Angelica looking stoic. Ansel and Lola appeared to be about fifteen and ten, respectively. It had been taken at the lake cottage. But there was no safe behind any of the pictures.

I went to the desk and sat in the plush chair. For a moment I wondered how it must feel to wield power from such a throne. I suspected that it felt very good, indeed. The top of the desk was bare, except for the lamp. I began to go through the drawers.

They were full of the sort of materials any business-oriented piece of furniture collects. The shallow middle drawer held a litter of pens and pencils, many of them defunct, along with the inevitable paper clips, staples, rubber bands, rubber stamps and stamp pads, and all the paper litter Ansel had been unable to find a suitable place for. It almost made me feel better toward him, knowing that he had the same cruddy middle drawer shared by just about every businessman and, for that matter, every desk cop.

There were two large drawers on each side. I pulled out the

top left hand drawer. It was full of files and I riffled them in a few seconds. Nothing there but Cohan Chemical materials. Same story with the bottom drawer on that side. I tried the top right drawer. More files, but these were political. There were dossiers on local judges, state politicians, state party chiefs, and so on. It looked as if Ansel took his political ambitions seriously. I could find no files on Ted Rapley or Lester Cabell. Reluctantly, I slid the drawer shut, knowing I wouldn't have time to give those files the attention they deserved. I slid the bottom drawer open. All it contained was a big, leather-bound photo album. I took it out and placed it in the center of the desk, then opened it.

The first pages held photos of men, alone, in pairs or in groups. Ansel was in some of the pictures. Some of the men were quite young, probably in their upper teens, but Ansel didn't seem to be a pedophile. A few of them were nude, but they didn't look like models posing for the impersonal lens. These were all men who had meant something to him, at some time or other. I was about to give up on the album when I hit the last two pictures.

One showed Ansel and Edna making love, undoubtedly taken during the same session with the automatic camera as the one I had seen earlier in the evening. In this one the two were pressed tightly together. Ansel's longish hair half-hid his features, but Edna's were exposed mercilessly; her head thrown back, long, black hair streaming over the edge of the mattress, her eyes squeezed tightly shut and her teeth bared in a convulsive, orgasmic rictus. For once, Sally Keane was utterly oblivious of the camera. I wondered how many years he had contemplated this picture while the woman herself had lived on the other side of the fence.

Then I turned the page and exposed the most stunning photograph I had ever seen.

Once again, the subject was a naked, dark-haired, young woman. But this photo was as far removed from skin mag soft porn as Michelangelo's *David* from a Priapic caricature sketched on a men's room wall.

The woman stood, her weight on one foot as she leaned in a

doorway between two rooms of an apartment. One arm hung relaxed between her body and the doorframe, a cigarette between the fingers of the elegant, long-fingered hand that dangled by her thigh. The other hand was splayed on her cocked hip, indenting the flesh and emphasizing the sinuous S-curve of her body, at once both awkward and graceful.

No trace of cosmetic, depilation or airbrushing compromised the pure animality of her body. Her legs were unshaven, covered to the upper thighs with a coarse, dark growth. Tufts of black hair showed beneath her armpits and her lavish pubic mat grew wildly tangled and untrimmed, rich with the mystery of fecundity. Her breasts were youthfully full but the nipples were flaccid, sunk into their wrinkled aureolae. A girlie photographer would have touched them with an ice cube to make them stand up.

The unsparing light exposed every crease, every freckle and mole on her exposed flesh as it exposed the peeling wallpaper, the cracked paint, the worn bindings on the shelved textbooks, bought second-hand at a student bookstore. It also brought out the fine-lined beauty of her angular face, framed by her short, square-cut hair. It was a face of startling intelligence, her eyes regarding the viewer with a coolness that matched the relaxed unself-consciousness of her pose.

In all the Sally Keane pictures I had pored over in the last few days, the tacky settings and second-rate photography had been rescued by her ability to take over the camera and transform herself into a work of art. Here I saw the opposite. The woman, beautiful as she was, was merely the subject. The picture was a masterpiece by a photographer who was also a great artist. And while the age of the model and her lovely body and dark hair created a certain similarity, this was not a picture of Sally Keane.

The woman in the picture was Angelica Cohan.

"Beautiful, is it not?"

The image had held me so rapt that I had lost all consciousness of my surroundings. The voice jerked my head around and there, in another doorway, the one leading to the piano room, stood Angelica herself, more than fifty years and an ocean of booze from the magnificent young creature in the photograph. She was even holding a lighted cigarette, although this time her other hand held a martini and her brittle, aged body could never assume the lanky, effortlessly relaxed pose of the picture.

"It's fabulous," I said, meaning it. I was putting together all sorts of things I had seen and heard and learned over the past few days. I thought of the framed photos I had seen downstairs. "Was it taken by Ansel Adams?"

She shook her head. "No, Adams did very few figure studies. It was taken by his contemporary and, in my opinion, the greatest photographer who ever lived, even greater than Adams. This was taken by Edward Weston." She said this as she walked across the office to stand beside me and gaze fondly down at the image of her younger self. She placed her feet carefully, one in front of the other, and although it was an effort for her to stay upright, there was nothing slurred or unsteady in her words.

"When I was in my senior year of college, Mr. Weston came to give a summer seminar and it was my great privilege to attend. He had just finished his famous series of nudes and sand dunes in Mexico. He was reaching the apogee of his work on the female form as a subject before going on to other things. He was kind enough to give my poor, amateur efforts serious personal attention and the day before he left, he asked me to pose for him. Of course I was thrilled and flattered and I assented at once." She smiled gently, her mind ranging back over the decades to a better time.

"As you can see, I was in my brief Bohemian period at the time. I was a serious artist and I would have nothing to do with bourgeois artificialities like shaved legs and stockings and styled hair. Well, I was very young. And, as it turned out, that was exactly the look that Mr. Adams wanted. Have you ever seen a work of such uncompromising honesty?"

I thought of some hideous crime-scene photos I'd seen, but those weren't exactly art. "Never," I admitted.

She nodded. "My roommate, who also considered herself a liberated artist, was shocked no end. She had no idea what nudity meant to an artist like Mr. Weston. Do you know what Edward Weston photographed when he wanted to convey eroticism? Do you think it was naked women? Hardly. He photographed bell peppers."

"Really?" I said, trying to picture it, wondering if it were some vagary of her pickled brain cells.

"Exactly. The Weston studies of bell peppers, ordinary still life subjects in the lens of any other photographer, are so voluptuous that one would hesitate to print them in any magazine that could be sold over the counter."

I wondered how many over-the-counter magazines she had looked into lately. "And just when," I asked her, "did your Ansel find this picture?"

"He was eleven or twelve years old." She took a drag on her cigarette and washed it down with a sip from her martini.

"Naturally, I had to keep it hidden. Not out of shame, of course. On the contrary, this photograph has been a source of great pride and satisfaction for me. Knowing that once, for just a few hours, I took part in the creation of a work of art, has helped me through some truly barren periods in my life." She paused and collected her thoughts.

"No, I had to hide it from James. He was a deeply, deeply vulgar man, just a common Paddy Irishman for all his money and political influence. As a model of Midwestern philistinism, he could never countenance the idea that such a picture existed. So I hid it in the bottom of a chest in the attic." She stubbed out the butt of her cigarette, fumbled in a pocket of her jacket and came up with another. A little more fumbling produced an old-fashioned Zippo that shot up three inches of flame. She lit her cigarette from the miniature torch and smiled wanly.

"Of course, small boys poke into all such hiding places. One summer I went up into the attic and found Ansel looking at it. He was playing with himself, but that is to be expected of a boy just reaching puberty. He was mortified when he saw me, but I assured him that I was not at all angry with him. I told him about Mr. Weston and how an artist differs from an ordinary photographer. I showed him an album of Weston's work and gave him some real insight into a world beyond Monticello and its little inhabitants."

Another drag, another sip. "Of necessity, I had to tell him he must not tell his father about this picture. It became our little secret."

I thought about that; about what it must have been like for Ansel at that age, already confused by sexual urges he knew were different from those of his male friends, then coming across this picture: not an ordinary girlie pic, but a stunning statement of raw, female sexuality, starring Mom. Then it became more than something to treasure in solitary, guilt-ridden fantasies, but a secret to share with his mother, shutting his father out.

"They were bad years, Mr. Treloar," Angelica went on. "There was no photography for me, no contact with creative, artistic people. James wouldn't have it. I was to be his hostess, to entertain his business and political associates, to appear in church every Sunday with my children properly groomed and turned out in their best clothes." A shiny tear ran down beside her nose and paused at the corner of her mouth. "Ansel was a great comfort to me during those years. He showed real artistic promise—we shared so many interests in common.

"James tried to break him, and Ansel rebelled as boys did in those days. He adopted the hoodlum persona so popular then. He associated with the town's riffraff, he got in trouble with the authorities for petty offenses, but he was not a bad boy. It was James who forced him into that absurd pose."

Yeah, poor little Ansel, I thought, remembering the weasel-faced punk of thirty-odd years ago, just getting started on his illustrious career. Forced into a pose? The mask that didn't fit was the one he was wearing now.

"And what else did James force Ansel to do?" I asked her.

At first she mistook my meaning. "Oh, those—those *proclivities* of his—how James overreacted! It needn't have become a permanent, oh, lifestyle, I suppose is the current expression. It was just a phase, the sort of thing confused adolescent boys so often go through. But James wouldn't have it. He humiliated and banished Ansel for fear that the boy's little escapades would somehow disgrace him. Really! As if the opinions of this narrow, cramped little town were of any importance."

She tore her eyes away from the Weston photo and looked at

me as if she really wanted me to understand. "But James sent him away, and he went to California and he met *that woman!*" She could pack a lot of venom into two brief words. She grunted a short, bitter little laugh. "You saw that other picture. At least, if nothing else, she showed Ansel that he could be normal and healthy that way." Her mind drifted back, drawn by her primal hate. "Of course, James called him back when he needed him."

This was better. "Tell me about that, Angelica."

Her face firmed up, her eyes sharpened and cleared. "Mr. Treloar, I must insist that you stop persecuting my son."

"I'm trying to get at the truth, Angelica. Two women have been murdered and I'm being framed for one of them, maybe for both."

"Two?" she said. "I thought it was just the Tutt woman."

Just the Tutt woman, no big deal. I fought my anger down. There were far worse people than Angelica in this house, and she was just about finished, anyway. Between the booze and the passing years, I gave her another year, maybe two.

"Last night around this time a woman named Ann Smyth was murdered near your lake cottage. She was Mel Skinner's woman. Mel is Jarvis Skinner's son and Jarvis and Ansel go back a long way."

She sighed. "For the life of me I cannot understand how Ansel ever got involved with that tribe of neolithic savages. It did seem to me carrying rebellion a bit far. Well, if the woman was being troublesome, I suppose what was done was necessary."

"Spoken like a true Cohan, Angelica," I said, out of patience. "Christ, Ansel was right in his element when he got together with the Skinners! It must have been like going home. You should have whelped him in Skinnertown, not at Holy Name or Polk County General."

"Ansel was born in a clinic in Columbus," she said, unruffled. She seemed to reserve all her anger for James and Edna. "I wasn't going to entrust myself to any of the rube doctors here."

"That will be quite enough, Treloar." Yet another voice from the doorway. This time it was Ansel. He was pointing a pistol at me; a slick little European automatic that went well with the new, improved Ansel. I kept my hands on the desk and looked him over. His grooming was impeccable and he was dressed in a dark suit and necktie even at this late hour.

"Something's missing," I said. "This house, that gun—I know: the whole scene fairly cries out for a smoking jacket. You have one, Ansel?"

He smiled a little indulgently. "There are few things more tedious than a cop with intellectual pretensions." He walked slowly into the room, keeping the gun trained on me. Angelica sipped at her martini moodily. He sat in a chair opposite me.

"Uh-huh. I've been putting the old intellect to work the last few days. I admit I sort of let it atrophy for a few years, but once it got working I surprised myself. I guess I have Edna to thank for that. She was a good woman, Ansel. Why did you kill her?"

His mask began to crack. "I didn't. Your deductive faculties must be failing you after all."

"Oh, I don't mean it was you who used the knife or the soldering iron, you don't have that kind of balls. But you were there and that makes you one of her killers."

"That wasn't Ansel's doing!" Angelica hissed. "It was his *friend* Ted Rapley!"

So there was another rival for Mommy's affection.

Ansel's head jerked around. The gun wavered for a second. "That's enough, Mother!" He jerked back around to me, his face gone tight and pale, the gun steady. I was going to need another outburst like that to get a chance at the gun. Of course, he was just as likely to shoot me, but you can't have everything.

"Come on, give me a break, Ansel, I have to know." My right hand went to my breast pocket and he made a warning gesture. "Oh, cut it out. You can see I don't have a gun in here." My fingers went into the pocket and came out with one of the two and a half by six slips of newspaper and a couple of the paper bands. "I want to know about this."

He looked puzzled. "What is it . . ." the light dawned. "Shit! You found it!" Young punk Ansel, coming back again.

"That's right. Now, let me see if I have this figured right—

you will indulge me, won't you?" I was banking on his reluctance to shoot me in front of his mother. More likely, though, he was waiting for his executioner to arrive.

"Go ahead. There's no rush."

"Back in '63, the old man kicked you out. You were at loose ends and you linked up with your old pool hall buddy Jarvis Skinner. You couldn't hang around Monticello, but Jarvis had a jailhouse friend out in L.A., Stanley Kincaid. You decided to go out and visit him, maybe get in on any jobs he had going. L.A. was Mecca to every small-town hood with a ducktail haircut in those days, even though the James Dean image was already getting passe. So you went to California. Am I right so far?"

"Grossly oversimplified, but basically accurate," he conceded, the mask settling back in place.

"So you went there and supported yourself with marginal jobs and the occasional petty theft, just like Stanley. Did a little surfing, I imagine."

"Actually, most of the time I worked as a lifeguard. I did surf a bit."

"But then one day you met Stanley's sister, the one who was supporting him half the time and bailing him out the other half. She was a photographer's model and the most beautiful thing you'd ever seen. She reminded you a bit of your mother. You didn't guess she was almost your mother's age, too. Did Stanley tell you?"

"It didn't matter," he said, shrugging.

"For a while there, you were actually happy with a woman, weren't you?"

Angelica made a noise of disgust and fired up another cigarette with her flamethrower.

"So what was it that interrupted your happy life of small-time larceny and romping with Edna—I guess you called her Lucy?"

"I called her Lucinda. It was her real name."

"Good for you. So did your father call or did he come out in person? It would have been too indiscreet for him to write you."

The phone on the desk rang. Ansel picked it up and listened

for a few seconds. "Come on up." Then he hung up. Then, to me: "Either you have more brains than I thought or that was a lucky guess. My father came out personally to make his plea. What tipped you?"

"It was one of several scenarios I was playing with. This tipped me." I tapped the slip of paper. "There was never any two and a half million, was there? Just a lot of newspaper bundled like bills."

"Actually, there was just over two hundred thousand."

"Your services came high."

"I wasn't alone." There was a sound of footsteps from the hall. He leaned forward and gently closed the album.

The door to the hall opened and Ted Rapley came in. Angelica glared poison at him. Lola was right behind him. Behind her was Lester Cabell.

"The gang's all here," I said. "Ansel and I have been having a nice talk. He's helping me fill in the blanks."

"Ansel always did like to talk too much," Cabell said.

"Cut the man some slack, Lester," I said. "He's had to keep this bottled up for years. It'll do him a world of good to get it off his chest."

"Talking like a smartass is unwise for a man in your position," Rapley warned. He took a chair. Lola and Cabell remained standing.

"What's my position, Ted? Are you here to cut a deal with me? Do I have something to gain by crawling?" I looked over at Lola. She didn't look happy and she didn't look pleased with herself, but her steel-marble eyes stayed right on mine. "*Et tu, Lola?*" I said, just about exhausting my store of Latin, except for a few hymns and Mass responses I never understood.

"You shouldn't have come back, Gabe," she told me.

"I didn't have anything better to do," I said. "I wouldn't have missed this for anything. So tell me, Ansel, how did your old man get Cohan Chemical into such a mess?"

Ansel leaned back in his chair, more confident with his friends close by. "As much as I hated the old bastard, I have to admit that it really wasn't his fault. It was the Democrats."

I had an urge to laugh out loud, but I managed to suppress it. "The Democrats?"

"Specifically, Lyndon Johnson. During the Kennedy administration, my father realized that there was going to be a big, long war in Southeast Asia. In our business, you know about these things long before the population at large. He began an ambitious expansion program in anticipation of some very lucrative government contracts. Unfortunately, the contracts were slow to materialize."

"How did the war fail you?"

"It was that bungler, Johnson!" he said, still mad about it. "He didn't want to admit that there was a war, to protect his presidential powers from Congress, so he tried to supply the forces out of inventory. By the time he was ready to face the facts and go to Congress for a real war budget, my father had gone catastrophically in the hole."

"So he faked a robbery to cover his shortfall and let the insurance company take it on the chin."

Ansel shrugged. "It's done more than you'd think. Of course, it wasn't as simple as all that."

"Of course not," I said. "There was the matter of the accountant, Raymond Purvis. Harmon Gilchrist told me he saw one of the robbers deliberately kill Raymond. Not Harmon, who was a witness, not the driver, just Raymond. I've spent a lot of years dealing with crooks, Ansel. There are two reasons to kill an accountant: he's skimming, or an investigation's coming down and you have to cover your ass." I turned to Angelica. "Sorry to speak of the Cohans as common crooks, Ma'am. It's just that that's what you are."

"James was such a fool," she said, "such a fool."

"Poor old Ray wasn't the only accountant in those years," Cabell said, smiling his smile that was half-sneer. "Those cooked books from '62 and '63 have Ed Treloar's name on them. Lots of big-time felonies in those pages: tax evasion, plundering the pension fund—old James was resorting to anything to keep the company afloat."

It came almost as a relief. Poor Dad. "So my father finally had enough and quit, was that it?"

Angelica was still with us. "Edward came here and he and James got into a frightful screaming match. It was right here in this office. Edward threatened to go to the authorities but James knew he would never have the backbone for such a thing. Edward was fully as culpable as anyone else. James just let him go and told him to keep his mouth shut."

"I'll bet it was the chemical substitutions that got to be too much for Ed," Cabell said. "You think that was it, Ansel?"

"It's history, Les." His face got tight and defensive. So even a Cohan could feel shame.

"But we're being honest with Gabe, aren't we?" Cabell said, grinning at him. "We owe him at least that much. See, Gabe, one of the ways old James was saving money was by shorting the government on some vital but expensive components of the explosives and propellants he was selling them. He knew that almost all of it would go into storage, mixed with products by other firms. It's military practice to use up the oldest ammo first, so the Cohan stuff would probably sit for years. Most ammo gets used up in training between the wars. Of course," he grinned again, "that war turned out to be a long one. There must've been some disappointed boys over there, but none of it ever got traced back to Cohan, so James must've been right."

I remembered my generation's war: what it meant when a grenade failed to explode, when guns fouled and jammed because of inferior powder, when the artillery dropped short rounds among our own soldiers because the propellants weren't as strong as they were supposed to be.

"Shut up, Les," Ansel said through gritted teeth.

"But, hey," Cabell went on, cheerfully, "there's probably a lot of North Vietnamese alive today because of James, so it all must balance out, karmically speaking."

"Spare us the homespun humor, Lester," Rapley said.

"Did James have my father killed?" I asked.

"Not that I ever heard," Ansel said. "My father was extremely jittery after the robbery, he may have worried about Ed blabbing, but I doubt that he was seriously concerned. Even if Ed knew what the robbery meant, it made him that much more culpable. I think he took care of the problem all by himself. Some people can't handle guilt."

"Edna told me that my conscience had robbed me of proportion," I said, looking at Lola. "All those years I believed, on some level, that I was responsible for it all, because I had my hands in your pants, that night out at the boathouse."

She looked honestly puzzled. "It was that big a deal for you? Did you think you were the only boy I took out to the boathouse back then? I was sixteen, I was practicing a lot."

"So you didn't panic? You'd just had enough of a workout for that evening?"

"You were far from the only kid who saw the inside of that boathouse," Cabell assured me. "I can vouch for that." He put an arm around her casually, possessively.

"Children, really!" Angelica muttered.

Rapley glanced at his watch, getting bored.

"So what happened, Ansel? What happened when you went back to L.A. and told Edna that you'd gotten her brother killed in your botched robbery?"

His eyes narrowed. "She . . . got a bit hysterical, as you might imagine. I thought she would calm down in time and see sense, but she didn't wait."

"He got drunk," Lester put in. "When he passed out she gathered up everything: the bags, the real money, the fake money, incriminating pictures, and she disappeared."

"I looked for her," Ansel said. "God, how I looked for her! All over California, Las Vegas, New York, anywhere models worked or there was some sort of show business to attract her. I went to her home town in Tennessee. Not a sign of her. For a while I checked in with the modeling agencies and the photographers she'd worked for, but they all said she'd just disappeared."

"She must have given you a few anxious years before your father said it was all right to come home. It never occurred to you that she'd come straight here and move in practically next door."

"I had no idea who she was," Cabell said. "I wasn't with

Ansel and Jarvis and Stan out in California. I was recruited locally, so to speak."

"So I figured. You were the one who killed Sheriff Fowles and Raymond Purvis. Harmon said it was the bigger of the two surviving robbers who shot Raymond."

"Actually, Ansel and I were both shooting at John Fowles, but I will take credit for Raymond."

"And you stayed behind to take care of Richard Percy."

"That coward turned yellow on us at the last minute!" Ansel said, getting a little wild. "It would have been perfect otherwise! I had it planned to the last detail, but he called in sick and Fowles went instead with that damned machinegun!"

"Didn't it make you a little suspicious, Lester?" I asked. "When Ansel told you there wasn't any cut for you after all?"

"He said some woman ran off with the money. To be honest, I thought it was sort of funny. James Cohan took care of me."

"Your cut was never very important was it?" I asked him. "What counted was that you had a lock on the Cohans for life."

"We all have the goods on each other," he said. "It makes for a sort of warm family feeling."

"That *evil* woman!" Angelica said, starting to unravel. "She blackmailed my son for all those years!"

"Was that it, Ansel?" I said. "Was it blackmail? Or was she just trying to keep you from being an even bigger rat than you are by nature?"

"I loved her, goddammit!" He shouted. "And she loved me! She never stopped loving me! She kept quiet about it for almost thirty years!"

"It must have been nice, those little, almost normal vacations you and Edna took, those forays into the heterosexual world." I kept my eyes on Rapley, watching his jaw tighten, the anger flitting across his face. "But all good things come to an end. She loved you, but she knew what you were, and she couldn't stand the thought of you going into politics. You couldn't do much harm here in Monticello, but you and your boyfriend Ted in positions of real power; that was just too much for her to contemplate.

"The day Lola brought me to your house you were on your way to a fundraiser where you were going to announce your intention to run for the Senate. That night I heard her crying. Did you tell her or did she catch it on the late news? Was it the next day that she told you she was going public with what she had on you?"

"I loved her," Ansel said, his eyes going a little glassy, "but I couldn't let her do that to us. If she'd just have given us the evidence, she wouldn't have been harmed."

"Sure," I said. "Lester and Ted would have let her go, knowing what she knew. You loved her, huh? Is that why you wouldn't let them touch her face?"

Ansel's mouth worked, but he couldn't say anything. Abruptly, Rapley got up.

"This is a waste of time. I have to go." He looked at Cabell. "Lester, you'll take care of things here?"

Cabell nodded. "I'll get whatever he has and clean up."

Rapley laid a hand on Ansel's shoulder and left it there for a few seconds. Hesitantly, Ansel reached across and laid his hand on top of Rapley's. Then Rapley was out the door.

"It wasn't hard to get me away that night," I said, looking at Lola.

"I did what I had to do, Gabe," she said. "For the family. I'm still a Cohan. I really didn't want it to end like this, believe me."

"The flashlight was a nice present," Cabell said. "Thanks."

"Did Mel tell Ann that you and Ansel were the other two men on the Cohan Chemical job? Was that what she wanted to sell me?"

"I honestly don't know," he said. "But I couldn't take the chance."

"I guess Mel's not going to make it home from the slammer."

"People there owe me favors." He shook his head, sighing. "I can't believe what a mess this has all turned into. If Edna'd just given us the goods, she could've spared herself and a lot of other people some grief. She was a strong woman, though. She took it for a long time. If Rapley hadn't gone crazy with that knife, I think she'd have cracked."

"She had her own sense of what was right," I told him. "In

her way, she was doing it for Ansel. And for poor, dead Stanley. And for me."

Ansel extended his arm and pointed the gun at my head. His hand was shaking. "Enough of this, Treloar! Where is it? You found it, now tell me where it is!" His voice was cracking.

Cabell turned to Lola. "Lola, honey, why don't you go on downstairs. This isn't going to be very pleasant."

Obediently, she started to leave, but she turned at the door. "I really am sorry about this, Gabe." Then she was gone.

Cabell said, "You'd better give me the gun, Ansel. You're really not very good at this sort of thing." Ansel hesitated, but after a few seconds he handed it over. He looked drained and old, closer to seventy than to fifty.

"Too bad, Gabe," Cabell said. "You just came home at the wrong time."

"Work on him," Ansel said, wearily. "Find out where he's stashed . . ."

"Not in this house!" Angelica snapped. She stuck another cigarette in her mouth and snapped her lighter on. While her attention was centered on getting the tip of her cigarette and the flame together, Cabell shot her through the forehead. The martini glass went flying in one direction and the lighter, still burning, in another as she slumped to the floor.

Ansel's head snapped around at the sound of the shot and he stared in disbelief as his mother fell. He tried to say something, but Lester shot him just above the bridge of the nose and his head snapped back. He settled in the chair, his arms relaxed along its armrests. He looked almost happy. Lester Cabell pointed the little automatic at me.

"They were getting entirely too unstable," he said. "They just had to go. Anyway, there's still Lola, if I should need a Cohan." Behind him the lighter had rolled beneath some curtains and it hadn't gone out. It was a promising development, as long as he didn't notice. "The Cohans are about finished anyway. But Ted Rapley's on his way up and I'm going with him. Nothing to tie him to all this, unless I decide otherwise. Nothing to tie me in either. Since I wasn't on the California end of that operation, Edna had nothing on me."

"I take it you held back on Rapley?" I asked, buying a little more time, knowing that schoolyard bullies have to gloat.

"He gave me the knife to dispose of. Well, Gabe, I'm sorry we can't part friends. You sure tied things up for me nicely. Under other circumstances, I'd offer you a job." He shook his head with mock-wonder. "It was really something, the way you came back to town with your crazy vendetta against the Cohans and you killed poor Ansel and his mother. It's a good thing I got you before you killed Lola and made a clean job of it."

"No, no, no, Lester," I said, wagging a finger, watching the flames lick up the curtain behind him. "It doesn't work if you use that gun. You have to shoot me with yours, then leave that one in my hand."

"Now that you mention it, I guess I should. Leave it to an L.A. cop to know all about drop guns. You sure are a helpful man, Gabe." He was reaching for his sidearm when he caught the glare or smelled the smoke. He turned a little to see what was going on behind him and I snatched up the heavy photo album and heaved it at him. From six feet away it hit the side of his face hard enough to stagger him back a couple of steps.

I dived for the side door and went through rolling. A shot chased me through and I heard it smack musically into the piano. From the sound, it was the little gun, not his .45. A panic shot. I scrambled across the floor, almost low-crawling like a grunt in an ambush. I could hear him thudding after me as I weaved behind furniture, desperately looking for a way out, for a way downstairs. I'd have dived through one of the windows and taken a chance on the fall, but they looked as solid as bank bars.

"What's happening?" It was Lola's voice.

"He got Ansel's gun and shot him. Shot your mother, too. Be careful, he's up here somewhere."

"How the hell did you let that happen?" Her voice went shrill.

"We'll talk about it later. Help me find him."

I couldn't see them, but I could see the bright glow coming

from the office. Goddamn Cohans: no burglar alarm, no sprinkler system, no smoke detectors. What an arrogant bunch.

"Here, take this," Lester said.

"How did you get it?"

"I wrestled it away from him, but he got through the door before I could shoot him." So now Lola had a gun. "You take that end of the hall, I'll start here, we'll work toward the middle a room at the time."

"My God, Les, the house is on fire!" Shrill, but no panic yet.

"The fire department'll be here in five minutes. We have to get him now! Get to it!" There was some shuffling and I made a dash toward the far end, going from room to room through the connecting doors. Better to take my chances with Lola than with Cabell.

Then I was in a room that didn't open onto another. It was a corner room and the only way out other than the way I came in was into the corridor. Lola came through that one while I was trying to decide which way to jump. She stared around wildly. I moved and she snapped off a shot, missing by several feet. She fumbled for a light switch and I remembered she was blind in dim light. I dashed back the way I'd come and she fired again, missing. Five shots gone from that pistol. How many did she have left? Two, at least, maybe three.

No sign of Cabell. Had he decided to run, or was he waiting out in the corridor? I saw another door across the hall. No sense stalling. I ran out and a bullet cracked by my head as I had the doorknob in my hand. I didn't even bother worrying about it being locked. The knob turned and I was in, slamming the door behind me, locking it frantically.

I was in a high, dim ballroom, musty and unused for many years, its chandeliers hanging forlornly, dreaming of Edwardian gentlemen in Chesterfields and elegant women in low-cut gowns. A heavy smell of smoke was quickly crowding out the musty smell. The dry, old wood of the house was going up like a torched wasp nest. I ran to the far end of the ballroom and eased the door open. Smoke came in and I could feel the heat. It opened onto a wider corridor or landing of some sort.

I heard a noise and looked back. Lola was coming in through a side door. She saw me and raised the pistol. I jumped through the door and slammed it behind me.

"Forget it, Treloar." It was Cabell. He was standing at the top of the big central stairway. "This is the only way off this floor. 'Bye, now." He should have shot the second I jumped out into the corridor, but he had to gloat. Then he started to dance: odd, jerky little steps that took him up against the wall, shimmying like a Holy Roller taken by the spirit, the pistol flying from his hand toward me. The fire was roaring now and I didn't really hear the shots, except maybe subliminally.

He stopped dancing and lurched forward, taking a header down the stairs even as I dove for the pistol, grabbed it rolling and came up with it pointed back down the hall. Lola stepped out and raised her own gun.

"I'm sorry, Gabe," she said. At least, that's the way I read her lips. She fired and something tugged at my belt on the left side. I had the forty-five leveled right between her lovely, whiteless gray eyes, safety off and my finger on the trigger.

And damned if I could do it. Not to Lola. I dropped the gun and made a dash for the stairs as she fired once more. Something burned across my shoulders and I ran down the steps. Mark Fowles was at the bottom, standing over Cabell's ragged body, holding the old Tommy gun propped on one hip. He was utterly unperturbed, a man at peace with himself.

"First thing I did when I was elected sheriff," he said as I joined him. "I bought a new clip for the Thompson."

I looked back up the stairs. "Lola's still up there."

"She can come down if she wants," he said. "I won't stop her." The smoke was getting dense and the upper floor was turning into solid glare. "Come on, Gabe. Let's go outside."

We went out past the portrait of Patrick Cohan and into the cool, clear air. Over the roar and crackle I could hear fire engines and ambulances screaming their way toward us. The neighbors were gathering from blocks around, coming onto the fringes of the huge lawn, gaping at the spectacle. Lew and Sharon came running over to join us.

"You hurt?" Mark asked.

I checked my waist. There was a gouge out of my belt and I'd have a bruise there, but that was all. My back stung a little, but the main damage was to my shirt.

"Nothing serious."

"Then let's go talk and talk fast. I've got a busy night ahead."

So we walked over to one of the huge, old trees and while the fire crews began their futile efforts to save the house, I told them everything. It amazed me, how quickly I could tell it all. It seemed like it took an eternity to live it. When I was through, the weariness hit me and I sat down, leaning against the rough bark of the tree, ignoring the pain in my back.

"My God!" Lew said, marveling. "My God! This is . . . it's utterly unbelievable. Mark, what are you going to do about Rapley?"

"I'll get him," he said, phlegmatically. "I'll find where Lester stashed the knife, then he's done. I don't imagine he'll wait for a trial. He'll suck on a gun barrel first. I have to go. Gabe, don't you go anyplace. You're not finished talking."

"Later," I said. "After I've had some sleep."

Lew was scribbling away on a pad. "Sharon, how does this sound as a headline? 'Monticello's House of Usher'?"

"Too sensational and too literary at the same time. But it's catchy."

"I'll never get a more sensational story than this," he said, all eagerness. "I'm going with it."

She shrugged. "Suit yourself." They wandered off to interview people and take pictures.

I sat at the base of the tree for a long time, watching the old place burn. My mind wandered around over the years, visiting old places, seeing old friends and loved ones, saying goodbye to them all. I looked at my parents' graves and gave them some sort of benediction or got theirs, I'm not sure which. I said goodbye to Murray, and he just laughed and said to join him for a beer sometime. Last of all, I saw Rose, young and beautiful the way she was before the cancer got her, wearing her favorite cheongsam, the little silver crucifix shining at her throat. She kissed me and gave me her blessing and went away.

It wasn't time to say goodbye to Edna yet.

The sky was turning gray in the east when the house was just smoldering cinders and the fire crews began to pack up. The trucks started driving off and the neighbors wandered back to their homes. They'd had a hell of a week.

Lola never came out.

After a while, Sharon came over and sat next to me, her face streaked with soot, her dress a wreck, her high-heeled shoes sticking out of her purse. She sighed and she looked over to me and smiled; a tired, easy smile.

"People do the goddamnedest things for love, don't they, Gabe?"

I smiled back at her and was surprised at how easy it was. "That'll make a good title for your book."

She tugged at me, getting up. "Come on, time to get you to bed." She hauled me to my feet and I needed the help. I was weak as a water-lily stem. "That's not an offer, I have too much to do today. Maybe later."

"Maybe later," I said, knowing there would be no later with Sharon. We were going in different directions.

With my arm across her surprisingly firm shoulders, we made our way back to the garage behind Edna's and up the stairs and into my tiny apartment. She got my shirt off and mopped the bullet burn across my back with a damp washcloth. Then she pushed me back on the bed, efficiently took my shoes, socks and pants off, pulled down the blinds and walked out without another word.

Sleep came to me peacefully and easily, because I knew that, for the first time in many, many years, I didn't have to fear the nightmares.

17

Two days later the coroner's office released Edna Tutt's body and we buried her. I'd spent most of the interim talking, talking, talking, mainly to state investigators. I wasn't accused of anything. Within twenty-four hours Mark Fowles turned up the knife in Lester Cabell's house. An hour later the state investigators were knocking on Rapley's door. The gun barrel was still warm in his mouth when they found him.

Mark was there for Edna's funeral. The garden ladies were there, and some other friends and acquaintances. Lew and Sharon were there. Sue Oldenburg sat in the back, wearing full mourning. I couldn't remember when I'd last seen a woman wearing a black veil. The outfit had probably been her mother's.

The minister gave a nice, but generic, eulogy about a woman who minded her own business and wanted only a life of peace and quiet, whose life was cut short by an act of senseless violence. People got up and said a few words about what a fine person Edna had been. Sue stood and tried for two full, agonizing minutes to say something, then she sat back down, sobbing. Finally, I got up. I did the usual fumbling and throat-clearing.

"I knew Edna Tutt for all of four days, and she was one of the most important people in my life. When I drove into my home town two weeks ago, after an absence of almost thirty years, I might as well have been dead. She grabbed me and gave my life back to me when she knew she was about to lose her own. I could never have imagined anyone could do that, but that's the kind of woman she was.

"Edna had one of the saddest, strangest lives I've ever encountered, but she lived that life the very best way she could. She wanted to harm nobody, even the people who had wronged her. For a while I thought she was a woman who loved too much and too easily, but now I don't think it's possible to do that. Certainly it wasn't possible for her.

"In a way I knew her most of my life, although we never met until hers was almost at an end. I miss Edna, and I know I'll always miss her." I sat back down and I let the tears run. They felt good.

The flowers at the graveside were live, potted ones that the garden ladies promised me they were going to plant there and tend. I helped carry the coffin and I tossed in the ritual handful of dirt and I turned away. I walked back to my Plymouth and Sue Oldenburg was waiting there.

"Thank you for avenging her," she said.

"She never wanted vengeance," I said. "You and I, we wanted it for her." I reached into the car and took a thick packet off the seat. It held the Sally Keane photos, all except for the one I'd promised Irving Schwartz and the one Edna had signed to me. "You should have these." I handed them to her.

Sue took the packet in her black-gloved hands, then she pushed her veil back, stood on tiptoe and kissed me on the cheek, just the way Edna had that night. Then she lowered her veil and walked off.

I made the usual awkward goodbyes, telling Mark and Lew and Sharon that I'd be back to visit sometime, knowing that I never would, and when the handshakes and shoulder-pats were over I got into the Plymouth and put it in gear.

The road from the cemetery took me back through the center of town and around the square with its Civil War soldier keeping eternal vigil over the peaceful little village. Then I was back on the road I had come down two weeks before, for my strange, unplanned homecoming.

I drove away from the town where I had been born twice.

ROBERTS   Roberts, John
          Maddox.

          A typical American
          town.